A Calling for Charlie Barnes

ABOUT THE AUTHOR

Joshua Ferris was born in Illinois in 1974. He is the author of four novels and one collection of short stories. His debut, *Then We Came to the End*, won the PEN/Hemingway award and was shortlisted for the National Book Award and his novel *To Rise Again at a Decent Hour* was nominated for the Booker Prize and won the Dylan Thomas Prize. He lives in upstate New York.

A Calling for Charlie Barnes

Joshua Ferris

VIKING
an imprint of
PENGUIN BOOKS

VIKING

UK | USA | Canada | Ireland | Australia
India | New Zealand | South Africa

Viking is part of the Penguin Random House group of companies
whose addresses can be found at global.penguinrandomhouse.com.

First published in the United States of America by Little, Brown and Company 2021
First published in Great Britain by Viking 2021
001

Printed and bound in Great Britain by Clays Ltd, Elcograf S.p.A.

The authorized representative in the EEA is Penguin Random House Ireland,
Morrison Chambers, 32 Nassau Street, Dublin D02 YH68

A CIP catalogue record for this book is available from the British Library

HARDBACK ISBN: 978–0–241–20286–9
TRADE PAPERBACK ISBN: 978–0–241–20287–6

This book is dedicated to

William Woodrow Kramm
drinker of martinis

&

Brendan Kennedy
more of a beer man

Models of honor
in a world full of men

I'd like to thank my brother, Brian, for standing by me when we were growing up and while I wrote this. I'm also grateful to my mother for believing in art and truth and for supporting the idea of the book; to my brilliant and talented older sister, Lori, for coming around to it; and to my younger sister, Maureen, whom I will always love.

—Jeannette Walls, from the
acknowledgments page of *The Glass Castle*

Farce, or
105 Rust Road

A Strictly Factual Account of the Day of His Diagnosis

1

Steady Boy woke, showered and spritzed, skipped breakfast for the time being, and headed in to work.

Oh, what a glorious morning! Maybe. The weather in the basement was unknown. The computer required waking. Made its little nibbling noises when stirred from its slumber, said its staticky hellos. The old office chair. The cold basement damp. Steady Boy had a desk calendar from 1991, a letter opener in the fashion of a gem-encrusted rapier, a ratty-ass Rolodex, and at his feet a rug. The rug, however, made moving around in the roller chair a living hell. So a sheet—listen to this. This is a true story. A sheet of stamped plastic specifically designed to facilitate the easy rolling of roller chairs in challenging terrain was purchased from Office Depot some years back by Steady Boy—

Steady Boy? No one had called him that in thirty, forty years. Back then, Charlie Barnes had found it hard to keep a job, either because the pay was bad, or the boss was a dick, or the work itself was a pain in the ass, and someone, an uncle, probably, dubbed him Steady Boy and the name stuck, the way "Tiny" will stick to a big fat man. Steady Boy's knocking off early again, Steady Boy's calling in sick...that sort of thing. The paying gig that another man considered manna from heaven was for Steady Boy an encroachment on private land. He valued his freedom. He enjoyed his sleep. He liked to read the funny pages at his leisure.

So much for all that. Steady Boy was Mr. Charles A. Barnes now, sixty-eight years old that morning, a small businessman and father of four, and likely to live forever.

2

Ah, but it was all pretense and fakery. He was a big fat fraud!

Shouldn't think like that, but it was true. Goddamn it was, certainly where his teeth were concerned. Other areas, too. His achievements, his...*framed certificates.* Big deal! He hadn't even finished college. Hang that up on your wall, Steady Boy. Failure number one, as far as he was concerned: no college degree. Failure number two: all the times he lied about having a college degree. Failure number three: ah, screw this. (Failure number three was his reluctance to look back for too long.) He was too proud and too pressed for time to be reviewing all his damn failures. We'd be here all year. Steady Boy didn't have a year. Steady Boy had cancer, that's what he had.

But hey, not just any cancer. The big kahuna of cancers: pancreatic. Heard about that one? Cancer of the pancreas is the piano that falls from the sky. You have time to glance up, maybe. Then, *splat*! Like a bug on the cosmic grille.

His achievements—ha! He'd spent half his life prepping the next big thing. It never panned out. Steady Boy did not, in fact, have a hard time holding down a job. He just never wanted to be a sucker, a schlub, or a midlevel this or that. Like anyone, he had hoped to make a killing, become a household name, live forever. Well, he would not, now. That was just a done deal.

We really need to stop calling him Steady Boy.

Good God, he thought first thing as he took a seat at his desk, the failures! All the marketing materials he still had somewhere, still shrink-wrapped. Bales of the stuff. Beautiful four-color trifold brochures in service to nothing now, nothing. His sunk costs alone could bury him alive. In pursuit of the American dream, Steady Boy had spent a small fortune on promotional ballpoints. He'd branded water bottles, key chains, stress balls. Bold Charlie Barnes would have branded his own ass with a red-hot poker to give his ideas a better shot in the marketplace. But what happened, every time? Nothing happened. Without so much as a whimper, they just withered and died.

3

What do you want from me, huh? What did you expect?

Those were some of the questions Steady Boy was asking that morning, after waking his computer and sitting awhile with the rapier-style letter opener, contemplatively cleaning his nails.

But of whom was he asking them? His children? Ex-wives?

Old colleagues, maybe. Like that bastard Larry Stoval.

He knew Larry from his time at Bear Stearns—that scrappy brokerage firm with the dog-eat-dog mind-set, now kaput. He and Larry Stoval were good buddies back then. This was years ago. Charlie worked the retail desk while Larry cleared dubious trades at the direct orders of Jimmy Cayne, Bear's CEO, doing God knows what damage to the moral universe... but what was it that kept Larry up at night? It wasn't boiler rooms and FTC fines. It was Charlie's affair with a nurse at First Baptist.

It was fall, 1992. The nurse's name was Barbara. Larry didn't like her. Didn't like the *idea* of her. Larry, the Oak Brook deacon, didn't give a damn about Wall Street thievery, but coveting thy neighbor's wife—now *that* Larry could not abide. Human hypocrisy of this magnitude was one reason Charlie always felt far from God. Little did Larry know that that guilt-ridden affair, which ended when Charlie left Evangeline and married the nurse, sent him, for the first and only time in his life, to a therapist's couch just to pull himself together. Honestly, he'd assumed the extramarital shame would go on eating him alive, like the guy who stole fire from the gods and had his liver picked clean by birds. But did Larry offer him any comfort? Take-home pay that put Larry Stoval in the halls of Valhalla, but he still couldn't afford a little compassion for his fellow fallen man. "Larry," Charlie had said, making himself vulnerable to his good old friend, "I'm in real trouble here," and what'd the guy do? Treated him like a fucking pariah. He set down the letter opener, picked up the phone, and dialed.

"Wells Fargo. Larry Stoval's office."

"So," Charlie said, "Larry works for Wells now, does he?"

Charlie was in the roller chair, on top of the slip mat that lay on top of the rug, the cordless at his ear. It had been over fifteen years since he had last spoken to Larry Stoval.

"He sure does," the woman said.

"He was at Washington Mutual before Wells," Charlie said, "and UBS before WaMu." When the woman said nothing, he added, "As you can tell, I like to keep an eye on his career."

"I can see that," the woman said. "But unfortunately, Larry hasn't quite made it into the office this morning. Can I leave a message for you?"

"Sure," he said. "This is Charlie Barnes calling. I'm an old colleague from Bear Stearns. Can you tell Larry that I have pancreatic cancer, please?"

The receptionist went silent.

"That's Charlie Barnes," he said. "Old colleague. Pancreatic cancer. Thank you."

He hung up.

4

The events currently being narrated unfolded in the fall of 2008, at the start (hard as it was to believe at the time) of an era of hope and change. There was a sudden massive liquidity freeze, the banks were crumbling, the feds were scrambling, the Great Recession was on its way. It was a golden era, believe it or not, yet things were bad. People were losing their homes, their livelihoods, their nest eggs. Government bailouts followed the corporate bleeding. The asylum, meanwhile—by which Charlie meant banking institutions, state governments, the White House—had been overtaken some time back by the inmates themselves, a slate of elected officials and their functionaries that was, to a man, entirely fucking corrupt.

The reckoning at Bear Stearns had come six months earlier, in March. If you don't remember Bear, all the better. But make no mistake, this is a true story: Bear Stearns was once an estimable American institution and Jimmy Cayne its hotshot CEO. Then the fifth-largest investment bank on Wall Street went belly-up after a single bad quarter. Hard to believe. But was it, really? They were a bunch of swinging dicks getting filthy rich off risky bets and boiler rooms. Wasn't it just a matter of time?

Jimmy Cayne—oh boy! For Charlie Barnes, that man was the face of every greedy deal now coming back to haunt the country. He knew him firsthand—had met him once, anyway. Little guy, not much to look at, but charismatic in a bulldog way. He had swanned through the Chicago office chomping down on one of his famous cigars on a day in '92—and it was beholding this plump, rotten, smug Jimmy Cayne in the flesh that, in part, prompted Charlie to quit Bear Stearns and go out on his own the following year, specializing in retirees.

Now, fifteen years later, the million-dollar ideas had compounded all around him, and stacks of paper climbed his desk. He reached for the monkey's-paw back scratcher he kept inside a coffee cup (claw and container branded for separate concerns, but blaring the same toll-free number) and worked it between his shoulder blades, then along the pink purlieus of his salt-and-pepper beard. At a moment he was dying of cancer, could he get in touch with Cayne, as he had just done Stoval? Odds were not good. But then Charlie darted the monkey's paw back into the coffee cup with a clatter and turned his attention to the desktop computer. After a moment's search, there was a listing for Jimmy Cayne, complete with phone number and a Manhattan address, all for a twenty-dollar fee. It was like having sudden access to J. Pierpont Morgan. Steady Boy didn't have twenty dollars just hanging around, but he did have an ax to grind and not much else going on besides.

"Good morning," he said when the caller picked up. "I'm looking for Jimmy Cayne."

"Who?"

"Jimmy Cayne? James Cayne? Former CEO of now-defunct Bear Stearns? Is he available?"

"I'm afraid you have the wrong number," the man said.

"Hold on," he said. "I just paid twenty bucks for this number. Are you sure?"

"There's no one here by that name."

"I'm looking for Jimmy Cayne," he said. "I'm looking to give him a piece of my mind."

"There's no one here by the name of Cayne."

"How dare he sell subprime mortgages to any stiff with a pulse? How dare he leverage the hell out of Bear and leave the taxpayer holding the bag? You tell him Charlie Barnes thinks he's a rat fucking bastard—"

The man hung up.

Probably hadn't cared for all the profanity. Who could blame him? Guy's going about the ordinary course of a morning, picks up the phone and gets cursed at. But you know who that caller—he wasn't the caller; technically, *Charlie* was the caller; still, Charlie thought of him as the caller—who that caller really wouldn't have cared for, in that case? Jimmy fucking Cayne, that's who! Every word out of that man's mouth was a curse. He called the man back.

"Sorry to bother you again."

"What do you want?"

"Please allow me to apologize. You answer the phone and the other guy goes off. That's not fair. But you see," he said, and paused. "You see, I have pancreatic cancer." He paused again, swiveling a little, idly smoothing back with a fingertip the desk calendar's frayed edge. "I don't know how much you know about that particular type of cancer."

He fell silent to allow the man time to reply.

"Let me give you some idea, then," he said. "You die. They diagnose you, and a few months later, or a few weeks later, that's it. You die."

Still nothing from the man.

"Guess it's fair to say I'm angry. I'm still pretty young, relatively speaking."

"How old are you?" the man asked.

"I'm sixty-eight."

There was a long pause.

"That's not exactly young," the man said.

"No, I suppose not. But consider this," he added. "There is no silver lining with pancreatic cancer. It combines the agony of ordinary cancer with the fear and suddenness of a heart attack."

The man made no reply.

"Fact of the matter is, I've spent my entire life pursuing the

American dream, only to find out here at the eleventh hour that it was nothing but a scam. The books were cooked. And now I'm dying. I've wasted my life."

Unbelievably, the man still had nothing to offer him.

"Are you sure there's no Jimmy Cayne there?"

"Positive."

"I'll let you go, then," he said. "I'm sure you have better things to do. And I don't have much time myself. Sorry again for the cursing."

"Good luck to you," the man said.

"Thank you," he said, then hung up.

5

Turns out they weren't such different men, really, Charlie Barnes and Jimmy Cayne. Cayne was from Evanston, outside Chicago. Charlie was born near Chicago himself. Cayne played bridge. Charlie played bridge. Both men were rather vain of their bridge games. Neither Cayne nor Charlie had graduated from college. Cayne got his start in sales—photocopiers, then scrap iron. Charlie, too, had a career in sales, beginning (like Cy Lewis, another Bear CEO) on the sales floor of a shoe store. In Charlie's case, the store was Jonart's off East Main in the town of Danville, Illinois, where he was born in 1940. Jerry will tell you the store was Mosser's on Vermilion. It was not Mosser's, Mosser's came two years after Jonart's. At Jonart's, and later at Mosser's, Steady Boy distinguished himself. He was a hell of a shoe man. Had a feel for people and a nice soft touch. Happily fell to all fours just to squeeze an instep. His way with laces could wow the casual onlooker, and he even knew how to make the ladies with hammertoe happy.

Eventually, Jimmy Cayne and Charlie Barnes entered the world of high finance, both as retail brokers—Cayne in '69, Charlie in '85. By the time Bush was "elected," Cayne, W.'s biggest booster, was earning fifteen million dollars a year as the CEO of Bear Stearns. Charlie's haul as the top dog of his own concern that year was roughly thirty-four thousand dollars and change. Five years later, it was flat, while Cayne's had more than doubled. The big difference seemed to be that Cayne wasn't specializing exclusively in retirees.

For here is where Charlie Barnes and Jimmy Cayne diverged radically. Charlie wasn't willing to sell out his country just to make a buck. When he could take no more of Bear's dirty tricks, he quit. He saw how old-timers were getting fucked, quite frankly, by the conflicts of interest at all these churn-and-earn brokerage shops like Bear, where a perfectly good portfolio would be raided every six months for the sake of its commissions. Charlie's idea was to eschew commissions altogether in exchange for an annual fee, which would cover everything from the initial consultation and financial plan to all subsequent trades and transactions, year after year, thereby guaranteeing an honest broker. Fiduciary duty, it was called. The year Charles turned fifty-three, he was entirely dedicated and doing noble work on behalf of the little guy, putting the era of Steady Boy permanently to bed. He called his company the Third Age Association, or TTAA. Fifteen years later, it remained his going concern. It paid him peanuts and brought him nothing but grief.

For he currently had under management a mere eleven mil. Sounds like a lot, maybe, but in the world of high finance, goddamn chump change. He had cobbled that money together from the cup holders and change purses of his aging clientele, and managing it barely rose to a pastime most days. He woke, moved a little money around, fielded a few phone calls, and then broke for lunch.

Missed his true calling, maybe—who knows? Squandered too much time early on scrambling for purchase (as, behind his desk, he ruminatively resumes cleaning his nails with the letter opener), then hit fifty and panicked. Life was a delicate balance. If only he could have taken a breather in, say, '67, really buckled down and completed his college degree, then he might have done something with his life. He played the dilettante instead. Just ask Jerry, his oldest son. Always giving him copies of religious books, Jerry—the Zen master—hoping to enlighten him. Jerry had his degree. Three of them, in fact. You might say Jerry was addicted to the acquiring of advanced degrees, as the light of pure reason led him out of the profane world where his father dwelled. Earning a keep—now that proved a bit harder for Steady Boy's son. Jerry was a chip off the old block where regular employment was concerned. He loved his truer truths, but the ones he found waiting for him in the corporate world, the eternal corruptions of the modern workplace—annoying coworkers, the profit motive—disgusted and besmirched him. He always quit in a huff. Then he ran out of cash and had to take new work, only to quit again, angrier than before. Now, at forty-nine, Jerry had been forced to accept a subpar coding job for a multinational headquartered in Brussels, Belgium. He hadn't been eager to go all the way to Belgium for a paycheck, but he had alienated every HR person in corporate America by then and was in dire need of money.

"Hello?"

"Good morning," Charlie said. "I'm looking for Jerry Barnes."

"May I ask who's calling?"

Charlie had been expecting a formal and lilting European to answer the phone when he called the number Jerry gave him, but he got this guy instead—another American hire, he presumed.

"This is Charles Barnes calling. I'm Jerry's father."

"Oh, right," the guy said. "Right. No, Jerry is, uh . . . Jerry just stepped away. From his desk. For like a minute. For lunch. Can I take a message?"

"A little late for lunch, isn't it? What time is it there?"

As Charlie raised a starched wing under basement rafters to consult his wristwatch, a vintage Rolex, the only authentic piece in his stable of fakes, the man on the other end made no reply.

"Never mind. Have Jerry call me, will you? Tell him I have news. Tell Jerry that his father has pancreatic cancer."

"Pancreatic?"

"Oh," he said to the man. "Sounds like you know a thing or two."

The man went quiet.

"Personally, I knew very little until just recently. Turns out it's the most aggressive of all the cancers. Hard to detect. Spreads quickly. Five percent survival rate. I should have all the details later today."

The man again said nothing in reply.

"It's arguably the worst way anyone can die, with the exception of being hacked to death, I suppose. Tell Jerry he might want to fly home. Up to him."

"I'll give him the message," the man said.

"Thank you," he said. "I have to go now. I don't have much time."

He hung up.

If Jerry had doubted that Charlie would ever "get real," if the Zen master suspected that Steady Boy would never touch some fundament of the True, which he himself was always passing back and forth between his Buddha's hands, here was the Angel of Death in his pancreatic disguise to prove him wrong. Charlie would not elude the long nightmare that was motherfucking reality this time around.

6

But he couldn't die just yet. He had to get out of that house first.

How he hated 105 Rust Road! He had arrived there in '93, an eventful year in Steady Boy's life. He was through with Bear, had fallen in love with Barbara, finally managed to serve Evangeline divorce papers, and launched TTAA. That house was intended to be a temporary station in which to summon up the blood once more, make a killing, have his second act. Then, with Jimmy Cayne–like money, he would leave behind the low ceilings of 105 Rust Road, its bad carpeting and cramped bedrooms, to name just three of its odious features, and buy for his dearly beloved the house of her dreams.

But TTAA hadn't panned out, and now his temporary station was turning fifteen years old. He knew he was lucky to have it just as the banks were foreclosing on so many others. But would he die there? Would he really go to his grave right there in the house on Rust Road?

Not if this new idea of his was as good as he believed it to be. He needed only: a name, a tagline, a logo, a trademark, a color palette, a marketing plan, an angel investor or two . . . so much to do! Then he recalled that he could strike one of those line items from the list, as the perfect name had come to him (during the previous night's tossing and turning) all in a flash: Chippin' In.

"I'd like to send a Word doc your way," he said in the next phone call he made that morning, intended to get all good things rolling. "An idea still in its planning stages, so go easy on me, but give me your gut, too, if you don't mind. Do you mind?"

"I don't mind," Rudy said.

His kid brother, two years his junior. Rudy lived in Tucson, Arizona, but Steady Boy could still see him clearly: skeptical brow furrowed like a hound dog's, flaring nostrils one cup size too large for the slender stem of his nose. Charlie didn't want to burden him with the bad news. If Rudy, their mother's favorite, knew Charlie was sick or dying, it would quickly derail the conversation, for his brother was a quack who ran an online venue for vitamin supplements and miracle cures. Charlie didn't need some dubious regimen. He needed honest feedback.

"Sending now," he said. "Call you later."

He hung up.

7

He stepped away for a quick bite, walked up the stairs to the kitchen. That's right: fifteen years after leaving Bear, he was still headquartered between a clothing rack full of winter coats and a Whirlpool dryer—the only honest boiler room in the brokerage business. Honesty tossed you down the basement stairs, and no amount of whimpering would persuade the gatekeeper to let you up again, to feel the sun, breathe fresh air and take a much-needed piss on the green green grass. An honest man was a damn dog in this world, made to heel and told to stay put, while the dishonest man got filthy stinking rich and stuck the country with the tab.

He went outside to retrieve the morning paper. As he emerged from under the portico, the bright day bushwhacked him. The warmth percolated, pricking him. Steady Boy paused, lifted his face to the sun. He felt a little drunk. He was present, in heat like that, at the launch of Apollo 11. He felt the same heat ten years later, on a rare vacation, under a Florida palm. He ran naked in summer as a little boy. He shucked corn during an Illinois drought. He watched his pebbly footprints evaporate behind him on the poolside concrete. He rode in a canoe under a canopy of trees as a trickle of sunlight danced over the water, as elsewhere in memory it did over old barnyards and forest floors. A thundering, brain-clearing sneeze, exquisite in every way, followed in the next instant, and he opened his eyes and carried on in the shuddering aftermath to the curb and the *Chicago Tribune*.

On his way back up the drive, he was filled with rage again, briefly, as he read the headline through the blue plastic sleeve.

It was a terrible time to be dying, what with the world in the crapper. He took it personally. For what did any of it matter, what was the point of life, if you couldn't sense, however dimly, that we were making progress? Almost instantly, he recalled his son. No, not Jerry—Jerry's younger brother, the boy called Jake. Of all his children, Jake represented Charlie's own private hope and change, with his intelligence, his eloquence, his handsome—

Wasn't picking up.

Having regained the portico, a concrete slab one step up from the lawn, Charlie turned to survey the neighborhood while Jake's voice-mail greeting played in his ear. Ordinarily a suburban blight—there were tarred cracks all down the asphalt and cheap chain-link fencing around not always the best yards and crabgrass burned to a crisp and rusted grates to catch the rainbow runoff—Rust Road looked almost beautiful that morning, tranquil, even, as birdsong and blue sky made him grateful to be out of the basement. He left a message for his son, then speed-dialed his daughter—let's call her Marcy—who lived, let's say, in Deer Park, Texas. She was a good person, this Marcy, though she was also quick to anger and reluctant to medicate. You just never knew which Marcy you were going to get: the sweet, docile Marcy who exhibited the decency of all the best daughters, or the standard-issue Karen who did not give a fuck and delighted in tormenting a one-armed kid by holding him down and dangling saliva over his face in a faraway Florida of the distant past.

"Kinder Morgan, Bethany speaking."

"Good morning, Bethany, Charlie Barnes calling. I'm looking for Marcy Mahony."

"Could it be Marcy Barnes you want?"

Marcy, who worked as an operations manager for an energy company, had divorced so often herself that Steady Boy could hardly be expected to keep straight what surname she was going by on any given day.

"That's the one," he said. "Didn't know she had returned to her maiden name. Is she available?"

"I'm afraid Marcy's on-site today. May I take a message?"

"I guess you can, sure. This is her father calling. Can you tell Marcy that her father has pancreatic cancer, please? You might know something about pancreatic cancer, Bethany. I never like to presume."

There was a long pause.

"I don't know anything about it," she said.

"Well, I can tell you this: it's not good. People with pancreatic cancer go to their graves as if shot out of a cannon, okay? Hospital personnel can hardly collect a gurney quickly enough to send that particular patient off to hospice care before he keels over right there in the lobby of the hospital. You want to know what it's like?"

There was a long pause.

"I'm sorry, are you asking—"

"It's like priority mail," he said. "It gets you where you're going faster than the other methods, but you have to pay extra—in fear, I mean, and the surprise factor, and physical devastation. There's no time to make amends or settle your accounts. You just die."

"I will be sure to give Marcy this message right away," Bethany said.

"Thank you," he said. "Odds are she won't know much about

pancreatic cancer. Ask her to do a simple Google search. Two minutes should be more than enough."

"I will absolutely give her this message the minute she comes back into the office."

"But what I really need her to do is to fly into O'Hare. I'd happily pick her up, take her to lunch. Her stepmother will be of enormous help to me during this time, but there are one or two things I can't ask her stepmother to do. Her stepmother has to work. She's an ER nurse. She can't take off as easily as Marcy can. Ideally, Marcy would set aside this silly little beef she has with her stepmother, and then everyone could come together like family. The doctor will be calling me later today to give me the rundown. It's not going to be pretty. In the meantime, I'm hoping Marcy will look into making the necessary arrangements. I know there are no guarantees, but tell her that I'm really looking forward to seeing her in Chicago."

There was a long pause.

"Are you sure you wouldn't prefer to tell her all this yourself?" Bethany asked.

"I don't think so," he said. Upon further reflection, he added, "No, definitely not."

He hung up.

8

Sure, he'd married young. Nineteen years old—just ridiculous. The only way they could . . . you know. Although technically, little Jerry was already on his way. Just a real different time, back then. Totally different world. Yeah, they'd divorced. Of course they had. They were a bad match, still kids themselves when Jerry came along—a recipe for unhappiness all around. You know the score. No one could blame Jerry for holding a grudge.

Then, in 1970, he met the woman of his dreams, his life partner, his soul mate.

Just kidding: his second marriage, forged over whiskeys at 810 Tap, was a classic rebound and lasted all of six months. Her name was identical to his current wife's. She was the first of his two Barbaras, Barbara Lefurst.

It was the third time's the charm for Charlie Barnes.

A revision, forsooth! Each divorce a discarded draft, every remarriage a fresh page upon which to write a new story, this time with a happy ending. We will meet each of his ex-wives in due course. Right now, it is enough to convey the fact, the indisputable fact, that he was indeed married a total of five times, despite a tendency among certain people to revise that number downward, to reconfigure an epic cast so that a perfect shit show might be retold as a pretty little fairy tale. Never mind. The facts speak for themselves.

His third wife was, fatefully, named Charley—note, however, the minor yet tantalizing variant spelling, which effeminized his ho-hum handle to such wild sensual effect that it drove him crazy just thinking about it. They were Charlie & Charley of Danville, Illinois. Charley was a local beauty. She looked just like Ali MacGraw in *Love Story,* although her confidence and sass were more in keeping with the sitcom star of the day, that Mary Tyler Moore. He was madly in love. But then Charley Proffit of Peoria, Illinois, decided to start fucking someone new, so the third time wasn't the charm for Charlie Barnes after all. You had to marvel that he would marry a fourth time, let alone a fifth... but hope springeth eternal, and where hope is, change can't be far behind. His fifth marriage was alive and well, and not simply because timewise, pancreatic cancer will always move faster than divorce proceedings. With his earlier wives, he was a work in progress: a scoundrel to some, a salvage job to others, a real slow learner all around... but here he was with the nurse at First Baptist, in a successful union at last. The kids didn't care for her much, especially Marcy in a bad mood, but he couldn't worry about that. He had this one thing going for him, and he wouldn't fuck it up for the world.

"Hello, young man," she said.

Speak of the devil: it was Barbara calling from the hospital. He spoke to her via the wall-mounted landline in the kitchen. Forty-nine that May, she was three days older than his eldest son and three days younger than his fourth ex-wife, an awkward bit of coincidence better never to bring up in conversation. Barbara preferred no talk of Evangeline whatsoever—in fact, wished to blot out of existence all of Charlie's romantic history. It diluted the dream.

"Hello, young lady."

"And what are you up to this morning?"

"Oh, not much."

"Thinking about Jimmy Cayne again?"

Boy, did she have him pegged! He swiveled around with the cord in hand.

"Honey," he said. "I'm under the gun here. Do you really think I have time to be thinking about that rat fink bastard?"

She didn't immediately reply.

"But did you know," he said, "that to kick off his long weekends—get this. Oh, boy, this burns my ass. To kick off his long weekends, the almighty Jimmy Cayne would leave his office in midtown Manhattan on Thursday at noon—by helicopter, Barbara, at seventeen hundred bucks a pop—just so that he could play a round of golf in New Jersey before it got dark? Same man who then demanded a taxpayer bailout!"

He drifted off after that, into a bitter reverie about Jimmy Cayne.

"And there's plenty more where that came from," he added.

"I don't doubt it," she said.

Barbara was a workaholic with a single outside interest: her husband's well-being. She was eager to hear the latest from the doctor—and to get her hands on the raw data from Charlie's recent round of tests to do her own interpreting. She was quite clever, this Barbara Ledeux, despite however Marcy might feel about her. At the same time, it was a busy morning inside the emergency room. A tall man with a parrot on his shoulder had just appeared before the triage window, bleeding from the hand. "What have you heard from the doctor, Chuck?"

"Nothing yet," he said, fighting a dizzy spell brought on by his reverie. "Listen, young lady: some of us are out here trying to play fair, we're trying to play by the rules, and we're meeting with resistance because the damn game is fixed. I never knew it before, but the dice are loaded in favor of the rat bastards who lie, cheat, and steal. If you don't keep that in mind, you could attribute a lot of these disparities . . . in compensation, I mean, and media attention, that sort of thing . . . simply to personal failing."

"I think you're doing just fine," she said.

"Do you?"

"I do."

His first handful of wives would not have agreed. They would have wanted him to interrogate those personal failings a bit more. Matter of fact, they'd have gone so far as to insist that the game was not rigged and that Charlie's gripe was a convenience meant to obscure his preoccupation with other things, like his hard-ons, the sports page, trips to the mall, workday matinees, and afternoon naps. They saw his failings crystal clear while missing the bigger picture. Barbara saw the bigger picture.

"Love you," he said.

"Love you, too," she said. "Call me when you know more."

9

His lower back pain was a function of bad posture. His rare headache was always the result of too much beer. Otherwise, he was healthy. But he had smoked for years, which haunted him.

How he loved to smoke! Pulling the lever on the cigarette dispenser (he is back at 810 Tap, the man in midwinter all muttonchops and wool), retrieving the new pack amid neon and noise and packing it still tighter against his palm before tearing into it—first the ring of gold plastic, followed by the square of silver foil. He would then gently pry out the first of those intoxicating cylinders and pass it under his nose for a woodsy whiff of tobacco. It was all such a sensuous delight—and this long before he'd taken the first puff.

He kicked the habit with everyone else sometime during Carter's only term, when the evidence became irrefutable and overwhelming and after which no one ever smoked another cigarette again. Cancer was canceled! He put it completely out of mind. Years later, walking down the street, if he saw a pretty young lady puffing away, he would not hesitate to go straight up to her and caution her, hector her, chide her. For she had her whole damn life ahead of her, and all that youth, and all that beauty. God, how he loved beauty. He was in thrall to it. He lived and died by it. And there beauty was, blackening her lungs. It broke his heart.

Trouble was, he'd recently weighed himself. Since losing his teeth at the age of twenty-four, a mortal misfortune in its own right—his dentist, a Dr. Paul O'Rourke of Bethlehem Dental, had pulled twenty-two in one go, an absolute hell, before fitting him for a pair of dentures, whereupon he gained thirty pounds overnight because he could chew solid food again without pain—since then, Charlie never moved on the weight scale more than three pounds in either direction. It was not for a lack of effort. He zipped through double cheeseburgers. He inhaled racks of ribs. He ate like hell morning and night—and yet what followed the bloody civil war in his poor rotted mouth was four decades of good solid health. Then the last two weeks of July rolled around and he lost nine pounds. It was a decline unaccompanied by other symptoms, or even an apparent cause. Some portion of him simply vanished—was vanishing still.

"So what do you think?"

"About?"

"My new idea," he said, having discovered that he had returned to the kitchen landline and dialed his kid brother's number without really being aware of it, or knowing why. "My Chippin' In."

"Charlie," Rudy said. "It's only been half an hour since you sent me that doc."

Rudy made a pretty good nut selling water pills and horse powders to the internet's deluded desperate. In the past, when Charlie complained of some bane or ailment, Rudy would gift him with whatever vitamin supplements available on his website that he believed would cure the complaint, as well as extend Charlie's life expectancy—as if *that* were the goal. He could well remember once opening a box from Tucson and finding, among the ten or so bottles of obscure enzymes and hard-to-pronounce amino acids, one clearly marked FOR CANINE USE ONLY.

"Turns out, Rudy, I'm in a real hurry."

"Why the rush, Charlie?"

Should he come clean? He didn't think so. He didn't want pity points *just* because he was dying.

"Eager to get it off the ground, that's all."

"Chippin' In," Rudy said.

"That's right. Chippin' In."

In the silence that followed, the gloom pressed in on him from every direction, and with the landline at his ear he drifted out of the kitchen but could go only so far on account of the cord. The one thing he found enlivening the dull suburban sitting room into which he stepped was, in his opinion, the crossword puzzle on the coffee table, companionably filled out in his and Barbara's hand the weekend before and left unfinished, the stubby pencil abandoned in the paper's hollow. They had been stymied by 48 Across: "Experts at exports."

After clawing T-R-U-T-H into the light of day, they could take the clue no further, and their efforts fizzled; nevertheless, that puzzle represented two contented hours with his hardworking wife, who, that Sunday morning, had made her famous coffee cake. On the table next to the puzzle, between two cheap bookends, sat a small collection of novels, one written by his son, which Charlie had endeavored to finish more than once to no avail.

"Sorry, Charlie, you gotta give me a little more time here," Rudy replied. "I'm still working on my morning joe."

"Tell ya what," he said. "You call me when you're ready. I won't bother you again."

10

In the east-facing kitchen, where the sunlight at that hour fell in a single polygon of heat through the sliding-glass doors, he put things in order. He sealed off the natural light by closing the venetian blinds. Then he turned on the overhead light, encased in its stained-glass dome, to create a more mellow artificial morning. He collected the bowl followed by the spoon before crunching something underfoot—a bit of egg noodle, which cracked and scattered—as he retrieved the skim milk from the fridge. He made room for himself at the crowded kitchen table, where he sat eating his breakfast while nibbling away at columns of newsprint—the sports page to begin, followed (on Fridays) by the movie reviews.

It was impossible, however, for Steady Boy to resist the

conclusion that he was a big fat failure in life. He tried to stay focused on slicing and dicing, with his expert spoon, those deliriously addictive crunchy Os in their sweet cold milk, but he was slowly consumed by terror. His efforts had never been enough. When they were enough, they were wrongly directed. On those rare occasions when his every effort was perfectly on the mark, his timing sucked. When his timing was right, he lacked the funds. When the funds came through, he botched the execution. When the execution was seamless, the market failed to materialize. But no, there was always a market, it just wanted something different, something better, something unsoiled by his clumsy hands. All he touched turned to shit. He was born a nobody and that's how he would die.

He abandoned his breakfast and walked out of the house.

He was coming, he was going, he didn't know what the fuck he was doing. He was just out there, under the sun. He'd enjoyed it a minute ago, felt intoxicated by a sneeze. Now nowhere did the world seem drearier. Rust Road was a nasty little strip of crumbling blacktop, a diseased tongue, the bowels of the earth saying *ahhh*. All down the block, blacktop, and garbage toters, and rusting minivans, and telephone lines and the shadows of telephone lines. Each house, one selfsame suburban ranch after another, was invariably set too close to its neighbor. Planes dropping into O'Hare flew directly overhead, a thousand daily Boeings skimming the rooftops. One was descending even now. He could taste its exhaust. This was no one's idea of a final resting place. But he would die here. He would die in that house.

A neighbor loading up his minivan across the street turned at the peripheral agitation of an old man describing small circles in his driveway while muttering to himself. Charlie hadn't seen him at first. Now he felt like a jerk. He stopped circling on a dime and waved. Pretense and fakery. Nothing to see here, friend. No one losing his fucking mind in a mortal panic, ha ha. Now, knowing Steady Boy as well as I do, I know he will want to save face, but what action will he take to—

Ordinarily, in a work of fiction, one is free to move a character around at will, to swap the cat in the window for a dog at his feet, outfit him with a cardigan or (considering the heat) blink away the cardigan while dampening the pits of his button-down, force the feds to pull up and place him under arrest for securities fraud or (knowing his heart, his scrupulous heart) tweak the SWAT team into something more fantastical, like that trio of meticulously dressed sponsors of a million-dollar sweepstakes—the cameraman, the notary, and the nice lady in pearls—appearing out of the blue with an oversize check: Charlie rescued, Charlie redeemed. It is even ordinarily within my power to have hover with no advance warning, and capable of being observed by Charlie alone, a lenticular UFO over the skies of Schaumburg, beaming him up from Rust Road so that he might bow out of this mortal little game without playing by its rules, which was his private wish. But I promised the old man to tell it straight this time, to stick to the facts for once, to abide by the historical record, and to exercise the discipline imposed by real life (the "harsh truth," in Stendhal's phrase), which has always been so loathsome to us both.

Pivoting, he walked to the mailbox. He opened it. He peered inside. Finding the nothing he knew would be waiting, he closed it up again. In that way, he feigned for the neighbor a greater purpose for being outside than resisting an ugly fate at his kitchen table. Then he tramped back up the drive and into the house. True story.

11

His career as a working stiff began, for all intents and purposes, on a night in October of 1956, when a young lady named Sue Starter walked by him at a high school football game as he was picking his nose in the middle of a dreamy youth. Against all odds, she found him fetching enough in his buzz cut and bib overalls to make a demand. "Buy me a Coke," she said.

His reply was a dumb and startled look. "Who, me?"

"Whatsa matter?" she asked him. "Don't you got any money?"

Hell, no, he didn't have any money. He had a curfew and a birthday: the sum total of his worldly possessions in 1956, and an indication of his sweeping power. At the sound of Sue's voice, he woke from his boyhood as if stepping through an interdimensional shimmer dividing Before from After, dreamer from damned, and vowed there and then to get a job.

Before long, there were more demands just like it: buy me a milk shake, Charlie, buy me a cheeseburger, buy me those shoes in the window. Let's go to the dance, Charlie. Let's go to the movies. Let's go to the state fair.

Let's have a closer look at Sue. Appearance-wise, Jerry's mother was a dark dream with full lips and almond eyes; fashion-wise, she spared no expense but looked as conservative as all the rest; in terms of morals she was entirely conventional;

in personality a flirt; in outlook a skeptic; in disposition a bleak and dire depressive; in political mind-set more progressive than most; in matters of sex, boldly forward, then discreetly withholding; she was mercurial at parties and dances (a charmer one night, a mute the next); in love a total slave, but as an object of a man's desire, she was a merciless and cunning manipulator. If her kindness was subject to moods, she had her table manners down cold, and her telephone etiquette was impeccable. Charlie knew as much because within a week of their first encounter, he had called her residence to let her know that he was bundling and delivering the Danville *Commercial-News* for four bits a week plus tips. Would she like to go out on a date with him?

He would not last long as a paperboy—four months, by his current reckoning. At the time, it felt like an ice age: waking in the predawn in the heart of winter, sick to his stomach from lack of sleep, pedaling through the freezing dark and wanting to die long before bundling the first of those morning editions . . . he started looking for a new job almost immediately. By the time he graduated from high school, he'd worked at a poultry farm, a lumberyard, the Lauhoff grain mill on North Avenue, and the refractory plant in Tilton, a two-mile walk.

Never a calling, these jobs. Thrilling at first, with the promise of more pay and future potential, they soon grew dull and proved short-lived, premised as they were on a simple exchange: my time for your money. Not even good money, really: one cent a bushel, two bits an hour, three dollars a day. But what amounted to pocket change and gave him a taste of power ended up blinding Charlie for too long, false gold foreclosing on too much: a college education, a law school degree, partnership at a law firm (pictured as a crystal decanter on a mahogany bar cart), or perhaps some steady climb up the corporate ladder, a place in the academy or in the halls of power. More damnably still, pocket change prevented him from seeking *any* ticket out of that dead-end town, as he was convinced he wanted what tethered him to Danville: a wife and child at age nineteen. Happily he took jobs, quit jobs, got fired, walked into storage closets and meat lockers forgetting what he came for, his mind always on some more palpable dream.

Courtship, adults called it; it was "necking" to teenagers; among sophisticates, "lovemaking": to young Charlie, it was a barnyard urge, and it would determine entirely the first decade of his adult life. When he looked back on those lost years, he could only shake his head. Other boys managed to overcome it, moving with alacrity out of the barnyard into lecture halls, conference rooms, military bases, you name it, where instead of indulging it, you could tease out its marketing power or write treatises on its role in history, making real money in the process. Charlie kilned brick instead, hauled lumber, flipped burgers, made ballast, sluiced cow guts off tile walls, attached castings to chassis at the GM plant, coated fiberglass for Tee-Pac, sorted jellied candies on a conveyor belt, and drove a truck for Fred Amend out of Hoopeston before finally putting on a suit and tie to sell shoes for Mr. Jonart, all in the name of keeping his young wife as happy as fate would allow so that he might continue to get laid.

She was never all that happy. He was holding Jerry in his arms before work one morning, pointing out squirrels through the kitchen window, when she told him she hated her life. Hated him, and the baby, too. Jerry wasn't yet a year old. Then she confessed through tears that she was in love with someone else. Blew his fucking mind. Pretense and fakery. Was anything real? "I love Marshall," she kept saying. "I don't love you, I love Marshall." Who the fuck was Marshall? Marshall Giacone, who ran the ball for Westville the year they took state. Charlie didn't stand a chance. He was devastated, angry, confused. If "Buy me a Coke" had barged in to a boyhood dream, permanently waking him to some greater reality, "I'm in love with Marshall" inaugurated him into the living nightmare that adult life could be. Deception, shattered dreams, the heavy burdens of parenthood... and Charlie Barnes, at twenty, still secretly a boy himself.

"I'm in love with Marshall" should have spelled the end of his union with Sue Starter, but it dragged on another ten years—ten more years!

12

Ten minutes later, he dumped the bowl of cereal that had gone soggy during his time outside, poured a fresh bowl, his third, and took up the newspaper again, somehow managing, this time, to remain seated. He soon found himself absorbed in another round of reporting on subprime mortgages, collateralized debt obligations, and the collapse of the global economy... when the power went out. He looked up. The overhead light was dead, and the radio had ceased midsong.

He glanced at the microwave to his right, down the sunnier side of which a thirsty philodendron unfurled. The blank display confirmed it: the room was suspended, irrevocably it seemed, in a monochromatic lifelessness he didn't care for one bit. It felt like someone had come along and tossed a dustcloth over the entire room, including the human being at the center of it, as if to say now just imagine it like this for all eternity and you have your fate. He was begging the light to reignite, the music to burst forth again, the status quo to go on, and on, and on... when the phone, the wall-mounted landline he used to call Rudy, began to ring. It was that line his doctor would be calling to offer his update.

He didn't immediately answer.

Later, he would play back this hesitation—really, this revelation—and break it down into its component parts, slice the experience finer and finer while praying to God that it never recurred, but in real time, there was only the raw, unfortunate thought, which arrived in a flash: *I would rather go insane.* For the insane know something that Charlie intuited at the phone's first mighty roar. And what exactly was it that Charlie knew? I've asked myself that question many times, and though I've never taken prescription medication for a mental illness or spent time in a locked ward, if I were to hazard a guess, I'd say it comes down to this: engagement is optional. No one asks to be born, but once here, we elect to remain—or not. Suicide might seem to most like the epitome of crazy, but to a different subset it is sanity disguised. The freedom to disengage from everyday life never occurs to the well adjusted as they go about busily pursuing their fortunes, starting their families and completing their adventures in living color, but it is murmuring from the basement, whispering from the cell, screaming from the walls of the asylum all the while. Until the power blinked off and the phone began to ring, Charlie was in it, one among oblivious millions. He answered the door. He rotated his tires. He obeyed garbage night. But when the ringing phone required his further participation in life, for the first time he hung back, wondering: Why give it?

It reminds me (as it did him at the time) of something similar in the historical record, only of less consequence. The year was 1953. Charlie Boy to his mother, Chi-Chi to his little brother, Steady Boy was thirteen the year he fell in love with the game of basketball. The whole memory descended as the phone rang a second time, as if its horrible scream were also a most delicate summons. Intact again, sturdy, even, were his two rickety knees, his earliest hopes and dreams. The ball, a gift wrapped in soft leather, contained more marvels and mysteries than a spinning globe. One fun trick was to bounce it hard on the blacktop at just the right angle so as to send it through the hoop on its downward journey. It hardly mattered that he failed once to move out of the way in time and the ball came for him, pile-driving his nose into his brains and making his ears ring; even the game's treacheries were beguiling. That summer, he would stir at the break of dawn, and with one whole foot still in some dream recall the basketball. His eyes would ping open and he would reach out and begin dribbling at his bedside in the half dark regardless of who might still be sleeping. His mother, a constant confiscator of that ball, would sit up from a dead sleep and move her head birdlike, while the unhappy lump lying next to her—Charlie saw all this perfectly in his mind's eye fifty-five years later—prepared to answer the debt collector's rhythmic knock in a swiftly souring dream of his own. Into that bright dawn and new day, and into the long, luxurious afternoon that leafed its green hours in great abundance, Charlie *dribbled,* man. Frank Santacroce, the grocer's son, whose mother purchased for him a pristine white pair of Chuck Taylor All-Stars with "Sure Foot" suction soles and whose father built him a hoop behind the family store, might have shot the ball better, might have scored more points, but Charlie was the ball handler. A whisper, a whoosh, a rumor of a ghost, Charlie faked—and went by Frank every time. It was with the confidence earned from his one-on-one games against Frank that he entered the court during junior varsity tryouts his freshman year of high school believing no other dribbler at Danville High could beat him. The coach, one Stan Butkus, a World War II vet with a fused spine that prevented him from bending over, so that at least once every practice he would stiffly kick some errant ball to kingdom come as if out of sheer instinct, regarded Charlie that day as though he liked what he saw.

"Very good, son," he said with all the loose baller jive of an iron rod. "Now show me what you can do with your other hand."

"My other hand, sir?"

"Your left hand, son. Pass the ball between both hands."

Both hands... it had never occurred to Charlie to regard that as an option. Why give over to the left hand what the right did with such grace? "I could try it, sir, I guess," he said, and promptly had the ball stolen from him by some showboat who had no right to leap out like that. The whole clutch followed after, leaving him alone to notice, at midcourt, all the two-handed dribbling going on. Was that really how dribbling was done?

As it turned out, there were rules, customs, advanced

techniques, all very difficult to master. He did try. He fell in line, ran drills. Did all he could to overcome the awkwardness of two-handed dribbling until, exhibiting no great improvement, benched most games, and turning bitter toward the ball, he dropped out, gave it up, joined the dramatics club instead. It proved a better fit. And now, as the phone shrieked a third, extra-long time, demanding he talk to the doctor, whose requirements for further life were bound to be more exacting than Coach Butkus's sporting demands from half a century prior, he wanted to drop out with that same sigh of insufficiency and mournful wising up that tainted the end of his brief devotion to basketball. But drop out of life? There would be no dramatics club waiting in the wings, while suicide would only hasten what he hoped to forestall. Bowing out could only mean a break with reality, opening a trapdoor in the stage somewhere and laughing, laughing while falling down a chute, into a fiction.

He stood and answered the phone.

This was without a doubt what I admired most about Steady Boy in his decline: he did not quit. And look: we see how he flirted just now with madness, how little that appealed to him in the end, how he stood to participate still more in the game of life in spite of its promise to reveal its most demanding rigor yet. He would not bow out, go nuts. And yet, by the popular definition of that state of mind—doing the same thing over and over again and expecting a different result—Charlie had been effectively insane since about 1960, when he first began making cold calls, licking envelopes, registering trademarks, handing out business cards, drawing up marketing plans, and giving it his all according to his lights—yet never making any progress that he could discern. Let me tell you something about this man: he had heart.

"Dr. Skinaman?" he asked timidly upon answering the phone.

A woman's voice replied, "No."

He was instantly relieved. "Oh, thank God," he said. He didn't really have any desire to hear from the doctor who would be calling, or any doctor, ever, about his condition, the future, anything, and breathed easy again.

"I'm calling for Charles Barnes," said the voice.

"Speaking."

"This is Sophie Crowder, Charles. I'm Evelyn Crowder's daughter-in-law. I'm afraid I have some bad news," she said. "Evelyn passed away in the night."

A name, a mere name to you and me, but to Charlie, a client of twenty-three years and *the* representative figure of his change in fortune when at last he came north to Chicago and took a job with Dean Witter, Bear's precursor, and started realizing some of his potential in life. A short, sweet old lady without an ounce of investing acumen, Evelyn had appeared before the Dean Witter kiosk inside a Sears anchor store in the Oakbrook mall, where she removed one stiff green hundred-dollar bill after another—for a total of twenty-seven thousand dollars—from her ostrich-hide purse, inquiring if there might be some better way of keeping it safe. In the intervening years, he had grown Evelyn Crowder's twenty-seven thousand dollars to a wisely allocated one hundred and thirty grand.

"Oh, no," he said. "This is terrible. This is terrible."

"Charles?"

"This is terrible," he repeated. "What happened?"

"We believe it was a heart attack."

He squatted down with the phone at his ear. Had to seek a lower center of gravity at the dizzying news. Death. Poor Evelyn, poor human being. The tears were spontaneous and unexpected. He had loved her. Always an old lady, heavily rouged and scented, clueless and far too trusting, but entirely innocent, beautiful and lovable. Poor thing. Had to have been scared, late at night, dying alone. "Call me night or day," he tended to say upon ending a phone call with a client. Had she tried to call? "Charlie, I think I might be dying." Without knowing it, he took up a bit of the cracked egg noodle near at hand, close as he was to the floor, and worried it between his fingers as he tried to fix his mind on the elusive fact. It ends. It all ends. Unimaginable.

"This is a complete shock," he said. "I really loved your mother-in-law. She's been a loyal client of mine for years."

"It's a shock for us, too," she said. "Can I ask you to hold on a second, Charles?"

When she returned a minute later, she gave him the name of a funeral home and the date and time of the service before quickly getting off the phone. He collected himself and stood. His head was spinning.

13

As it happened, he would not make it to Evelyn Crowder's funeral. As more pressing concerns, private disasters moved in, Evelyn Crowder would slip from his mind. In the meantime, there was sadness, there was reflection . . . and there was panic.

Evelyn's money would likely go away now, dispersed among her heirs, and with it Charlie's custodial fees. And hers was not the only account he had lost of late. His clients were restless. Their holdings were down. Some were ill-advisedly pulling their assets and in the process destroying his business. He hated 105 Rust Road, but it did not follow that he wished to be evicted from its scuffed and tired walls. Even with pancreatic cancer, they weren't going to let him live! He would be homeless. He would come to nothing as he had always feared and die on the streets in disgrace. Sixty-eight years old . . . this goddamn life!

I have failed to mention that while Charlie was outside pacing during an earlier moment of panic, forced by the neighbor's gaze to feign a search of his mailbox, he expected to find in that silver tomb with the tight-fitting lid nothing at all, since he diligently collected the mail at the same time every day. And if initially I suggested that he did find nothing and walked back inside empty-handed, that was only to instill in the reader right now the same surprise Charlie experienced back then at finding, in fact, a single white, mildly weathered item deposited the night before by a neighbor who had received it by accident—the only time I intend to be playful in this otherwise true account. It was a payment-due notice from a Dallas collection agency addressed to Charles Barnes. He had torn into it, and it made him mad: a misbegotten charge for a trial period he never canceled, for a service he never used. He tossed it in the trash and planned to ignore it. But then news of Evelyn's death sent his fearful heart dominoing from one worry to the next, culminating now in his pulling the letter from the can, brushing off the cereal and the coffee grounds, picking up the phone he cradled only a minute earlier, and dialing the toll-free number—

"Credence Credit."

"You people have a lot of nerve," he began.

"Name, please."

Name, case number and a long wait later, he was finally transferred to his case manager, to whom he tried to explain why he didn't owe upwards of three hundred and forty dollars to Platinum Warranty, Inc., or its agents at Credence Credit Corp.

"Why don't you take a deep breath, sir?" the debt collector suggested.

"Don't you dare tell me to take a deep breath. You're not the one facing eviction and death here!"

"Eviction and death?"

"That's right, asshole—your three hundred bucks adds up. And I have pancreatic cancer! Know anything about that? Don't imagine you do. It starves you, then it wastes you, then it drowns you. Sound familiar? It sure should, because *you* are the pancreatic cancer of the capitalist system! You offer no warning, no appeal, no logic, no fairness, no mercy—just ultimatums and punishment! Do you think I have time for this? But here I am, forced to spend my precious few remaining—"

He was getting another call.

"Can I ask you to hold, please?"

"Sure."

He clicked over.

"Charles Barnes?"

"Yes."

"This is Nurse Keeler calling from Dr. Skinaman's office."

His heart instantly kicked, the dizzy spell returned.

"How are you this morning?"

"Fine," he said, in a voice far less confident than the one he had just deployed to curse out his case manager. "I guess."

"We have received your test results, and the doctor has had a chance to look them over."

"Okay."

"Your scans are clean. Your numbers look great! The doctor was very pleased."

There was a long pause.

"Beg your pardon?"

"No need for a follow-up."

"Hold on," he said. "What are you saying—that I don't have . . . pancreatic cancer?"

"You don't have cancer of any kind," the nurse said.

There was another long pause.

"You're clean as a whistle."

"But the weight loss," he said.

"The what?"

"The weight loss?"

"Oh," the nurse said. "Who knows? That could be anything."

He made good on his wife's request that he take down the raw numbers on the test results, which he did on the first thing at hand—a little white napkin.

14

It was the fucking internet! Barbara, who knew better, had told him to steer clear of that goddamn thing. Had he listened?

No! In the disquieting days following his appointment with Dr. Skinaman and his battery of tests, he'd lost all perspective and given way to fear. He went on that machine day and night, read every last user post and grim prognostication, and every symptom described him to a tee. Pancreatic cancer, *c'est moi*!

Boy, was he relieved. But he was also a little . . . well, embarrassed, now, for having told a few select people that he was as good as dead, basically, goddamn it. He thought he should probably call Jerry back, and Marcy, too, and maybe a few others, and tell them the good news. But the phone was already ringing.

"Hello?"

"You were saying, Mr. Barnes?"

It was his case manager from the collection agency. It appeared their connection had never been broken.

"You again," he said.

He liked it better when he had pancreatic cancer. Not really, of course. That was absurd. But he did enjoy the clarity it gave him. A deadly cancer like that will put things in perspective and everyone in their place. Now he had to go back to being just another everyday schlub paying down debts from a basement office. Who cared about that guy? In this world, a perfectly healthy man could either make ends meet, or fuck off and die.

"I'm going to have to call you back," he said.

He hung up.

One thing you have to keep in mind about Steady Boy. If my father was something of a joke, he was also a fucking colossus. There was no bringing him down, no killing him off. Recall the gods that dwelled upon Mount Olympus. They, too, could be easily mocked by the poets and their lives described in terms of farce, because they were immortal.

15

He had a seat at the kitchen table to gather his wits. So he would not die. He would live, forced by good health to continue to participate sanely in all of life's ways. Try again. Fail? That, too, probably, if history were any guide. It had been, he supposed, kind of nice to think it was all over with, briefly, his ongoing effort. Now he had a lot of time on his hands... a whole lotta time. What to do with it? Turn everything around, of course. Yes, success. There was always that. The second act. Getting the hell out of that basement office and buying the nurse at First Baptist, who deserved better, a new house, something befitting the high regard in which he held them both.

The power returned, and with it the kitchen light, the radio, the microwave display, now blinking, the hum of the refrigerator, and a palpably renewed sense of animation, of life, that was somehow greater than the sum of its parts... but Charlie himself didn't brighten. He had begged the power to come back on when it seemed to be staging a dress rehearsal for biting the big one. Now there was too much light shining down on the old dull things: the kitchen in need of renovating, the house he would never escape, the narrowness of a life that was incomplete at sixty-eight but that could not be changed or improved no matter the effort he made. He would die in that house. The phone began to ring again. It was his kid brother, Rudy.

"Just finished my joe, Charlie, and been reading over that document you sent me."

"Uh-huh."

"Your Chippin' In."

"Right," he said.

"You asked me to give you my gut."

"Go ahead," he said.

There was a long pause.

"What's wrong, Charlie? You sound low."

Dumb move, to hand that man a dream. If Charlie—who would live now, not die, and who needed a dream to live by—had to hear (even from a know-nothing peddler of dog pills like his brother) that his Chippin' In was bad, it was doomed, it would go to hell like his other ideas, he might really go nuts indeed, take matters into his own hands and make the quick death that was pancreatic cancer look like a protracted war by putting a gun to his head and blowing his fucking brains out. He couldn't risk that. So when his poor brother, put upon all morning, began to speak... Charlie quietly hung up on him.

How I might wish it were otherwise—that this man, whom I loved, possessed the strength of character to always hear the truth. But who doesn't turn away from the truth now and again? In any event, the facts as he dictated them to me plainly state that he poured himself a fourth bowl of cereal that morning and drank a fifth cup of coffee while ignoring the ringing phone. Then he drifted through the house he dreaded, feeling wiped. He thought a nap might dispel his dark mood, but when he looked at his watch, it was only ten fifteen.

16

Who was I to judge his sad case? Steady Boy's mother, Delwina, the naive girl with the ugly name, didn't have a clue how to raise a child. Her mother, a pious hypocrite, was no help to her, nor was the man who'd gotten her into trouble; he never once lent a hand. From the moment Charlie came home from the hospital, she was at a loss. The baby never slept. He cried night and day. And her breasts were open sores. She was just about to go stark raving mad when her fat Aunt Cessarine climbed the five stairs to the shanty porch and knocked at the front door.

In a moment, I will retell the story Chuck always urged on me of how his parents met and married. This other story, of how his Great-Aunt Cess nearly destroyed him, he told me only once, in passing, but it strikes me as the more interesting of the two, and the more revealing. She was an enormous woman—three hundred pounds, even allowing for the boutonniere. The majority of that weight resided in her elephantine hips, while her upper body remained as lithe as a little girl's. Taking a fresh pass through family photos, Chuck once joked to me that his great-aunt was all bird above, brontosaurus below. Eternally old, she was born around the time of the Civil War, hit middle age at the turn of the century, and was still alive in 1940, at which point she appeared on Delwina's porch possessed of an absolute authority. Her niece invited her in, and Cess lowered her immense carriage onto the divan.

"Do you always go to the child the minute he starts crying?" her interrogation began.

"I always try to, Aunt Cess. That very minute."

"Even when it's just a whimper?"

"Even when I'm asleep. I just bolt upright. He means the world to me."

"And do you pick the child up? Do you soothe him, comfort him?"

"I do try. I don't always know how. He's so unhappy sometimes it just breaks my heart. But I do go to him, I hold him, I kiss him, I do everything I can to make it better."

"Then you are ruining him," Cess declared.

She then presented his mother with a book called *Care for the New Baby,* which, as far as I can tell, probably determined Steady...Charles Barnes's fate more than any other single factor—genetic, environmental, you name it.

"What do you know about nervous spoilage?" Cess asked his mother.

Delwina admitted that she knew nothing at all about nervous spoilage.

"That's just as I supposed." Cess shook her head in dismay and added, "You are an ignorant girl."

For the next hour, she tutored Delwina on the mortal dangers of nervous spoilage. It was now scientifically proven: there should be no rushing to the baby's side, no picking the baby up with the intention of dispelling a nightmare, no unnecessary holding, pampering, or excessive admiration of the baby. According to *Care for the New Baby,* those were surefire ways to produce morally weak men.

"This is common knowledge, young lady. Get with the times, or that child will be lost."

"Thank you, Aunt Cess."

"Do not dally, girl," she demanded. "Your child's very soul hangs in the balance."

In over her head from day one, Delwina was saved by her aunt's visit and the book she left behind: at last, something to guide her. She began to read *Care for the New Baby* that very day, and though it was over four hundred pages long, and though she was exhausted and had no gift for study, she finished it within the month. It was nothing short of a revelation. She no longer picked Charlie up unnecessarily. She certainly did not hug or kiss him. She did not let his little hand curl over her index finger—the most wonderful sensation of her young life and a major cause of nervous spoilage. She was instructed to let him cry, and cry he did. Through a bad case of whooping cough, through the high fever that accompanied the measles, through rubella and a flu that almost killed him, he lay alone in his crib, crying for hours. Through the cold nights of his first full winter, when the wind sailed straight through the leaky Westville shanty, he cried. He cried to be cleaned, to be fed, to be held, to be soothed back to sleep. In keeping with the scientific evidence compiled in *Care for the New Baby,* she did not touch him to excess, or sing or coo when bathing him, or indulge in baby talk. When feeding him, she did not look him in the eye. As the toddler was learning to walk, she did not run to his aid when he fell. Resisting the temptation to weaken his moral character, she turned her back on him and carried on with whatever she was doing.

Later she would tell him how hard it had been. Tormented by his faintest whimpering, she was left brokenhearted, driven nearly insane by his open-throated bawling, and wasn't sure she would survive. Charlie's father woke at dawn, put on his boots and left for work, and was never any help at all. She was alone with Charlie throughout the long day and had to pinch and strike herself so as not to rush immediately to his aid and love him to pieces. Once, a neighbor, the wife of a sharecropper, long compelled by racist hate to mind her own business where white mothers were concerned, nevertheless climbed the shanty steps and knocked at the front door. Was the baby okay? Did the mother need help? Delwina might have simply said no, but she felt it necessary to explain herself. In the absence of Aunt Cess, however, whose conviction she lacked, the lessons imparted by *Care of the New Baby* slipped her mind entirely, and for a brief, terrible moment she could not recall the book's logic. She, too, wondered how on earth she could stand by and let a little baby cry. Only after the neighbor was gone did it all come back to her: she was instilling moral character in the child and guaranteeing his future success.

A year later, she was pregnant with Rudy. Consumed by morning sickness, she did not have the presence of mind to mark the last time Charlie held up his arms to her out of need or to ask when he began sucking apathetically on whatever was at hand—a thumb, a shoelace—or why he so often sat dead-eyed in the middle of the kitchen floor.

She threw a small baby shower for herself, which Cessarine attended. It was her first opportunity to thank her aunt for the baby book she had given her, as Cessarine had never again returned to the Westville shanty. Without her, Delwina would have done everything wrong. She would have ruined Charlie. She assured her aunt that she would be doing for the new baby everything she had done for Charlie to avoid the irreparable damage of nervous spoilage.

"That method is now out of date," Aunt Cess declared. "Now it is recommended that you simply hold them."

After that, Delwina smothered all her children with love.

17

He stood in the front room in house slippers, on plush carpeting, amid the persistent gloom. The venetian blinds remained shut against the bright day. Why? The cut-glass inlays in the front door didn't admit much light, either. Afraid. He was terribly afraid. Evelyn dead. His business doomed. And life, for him, a curdled dream with no end in sight. Under the morning's phone calls, silence reigned. Time flew by. He switched on the lamp, whose cone of light shone down on the TV tray, where he kept a tidy array of remote controls. He was seriously tempted to turn on the TV and resume watching *Popeye,* the Robert Altman movie, a copy of which he owned on VHS. It was a favorite of his. The recliner, with its brown piping, pillowy arms gone flat as shelves, and a small cowlick of crust on the seat that would not come out, could have belonged to no one but Charlie Barnes, who might have loved himself. Who did not love himself. Who thought himself an ass whose fate was worse than death: it was to live forever in the permanent fear of always dying.

"Experts at exports": T-R-U-T-H. The clue eluded him. He tossed the puzzle down on the coffee table and returned to the kitchen, where he took up the landline and called his mother. He had done so without exception every day since she had entered, at age eighty, a North Peoria nursing facility. She was not an easy interlocutor, however, mistaking him six days out of seven for the son she loved most.

"It's Charlie calling, Mom, not Rudy," he said.

"Well, thanks for calling anyway," she said. "But I'm not feeling too well this morning, son. It's all the joint pain. And I have... what do they call it? When you can't think straight. What do they call that, son?"

"Brain fog," he said.

"That's right, brain fog. And I can't see so well anymore."

"I know," he said. "Macular degeneration."

"That's right. Macular degeneration."

"And you have restless leg."

"That's right," she said. "The restless leg was bad last night."

The litany had resumed right away, unbroken from the day before. As soon as the conversation began, Charlie wanted off the phone and out of life. For it all seemed suddenly like one long, tired script, our blocks of speech assigned to us at the start of time. And though we might yearn for new adventures, happy ends, we lack the capacity to imagine even alternative lines.

"Hey, Mom," he said. "At least it's not pancreatic cancer."

But why bring that up? What was pancreatic cancer to her—or to him, for that matter?

"There are cures for cancer nowadays," she replied. "There are no cures for rheumatoid arthritis."

"Sounds to me, Mom, like you've never looked into the particulars of pancreatic cancer, so I have some news for you. There are no cures."

There was a long pause.

"You don't know how hard I had it when you kids were growing up," she said.

"What does that have to do with anything?"

"I'm just not sure it was worth it."

"Jeez, Mom, thanks. I'm sure it was some picnic for all the rest of us."

"You have never been grateful for all that I sacrificed."

"This again," he said. "Are you really the only person who suffers?"

"No one calls me. No one cares."

"I just called you, did I not?"

"I'm dying. Don't you understand that?"

"Well, guess what, Mom? So am I. I have pancreatic cancer."

Pretense and fakery. But he couldn't help himself. She was driving him nuts, and it just came out. Could she, for two seconds, think about anyone's plight other than her own? Well, he'd find out.

"Nonsense," she said. "You're as healthy as an ax."

"You mean 'ox,' I think."

"You've been dieting since you were twelve."

"That's Rudy, Mom. The vitamin man."

"I told you, no one dies from cancer anymore," she said. "They have cures."

"Pancreatic cancer isn't just any old cancer, Mom. It's a full-blown fucking nightmare."

"You know I don't care for that kind of language."

"Uh-huh. Well. You don't seem to be listening to me."

"And you don't seem to be listening to *me,*" she said. "They have come a long way with cancer."

"I have to go now," he said. "I don't have much time."

"Thanks for calling," she said.

18

His mother would soon lose her mind entirely to dementia. A peculiar variety, it must be said, with brief episodes of perfect clarity. Increasingly, however, she mistook him for Rudy, until at last he had to concede that he was no more in his mother's mind.

Then one day, about a year after the phone call documented above, it came to her: she had a firstborn. His name was Charlie. Never had she loved anything as she had once loved him. He was alive—had to be—somewhere in the suburbs of Chicago. She remembered as well a phone number that had not been in her possession for many years. It appeared out of nowhere as if lit in neon, flashing in the dark night for her alone. Eighty-eight that year and living in a different Peoria nursing facility, she dialed Charlie's number and let it ring. When the man answered, she asked to speak to her baby boy.

"Who, now?"

"Charlie Barnes," Delwina declared, distinctly and confidently.

"No one here by that name," the man said, then hung up.

But she did not have the wrong number, that much she knew. She dialed it again, and the same man answered.

"I told you, goddamn it!" he snapped at her before hanging up. "No one here by that name!"

But that was *his* number! She was as certain of that as she was of Charlie himself. Where have you gone to, Charlie? Where could you be? She felt quite lost in this world. Then she recalled a conversation in which Charlie might have suggested that he had cancer. Did that mean he might have . . . that he might be . . . without her knowing, or having remembered—

Suddenly, her mind went blank again, as if by an act of mercy, and the abyss of forgetfulness swallowed her up. She drifted off into a nap, and when she awoke she carried on as before, oblivious and invulnerable.

19

He remembered the shanty where he grew up as a place of packed-dirt floors, thin walls, no hot water, and an ice-box in place of a fridge. A delivery man came every morning with a solid block of ice, which he removed from his truck with a pair of giant metal tongs. He could still picture the man approaching the side of the shanty in summer, whistling under a hot sun. Hoping to spook him, Charlie ran to the kitchen and opened the inner hatch. But the iceman beat him to it every time. Having opened the outer hatch, he lay in wait for Charlie, hollering "Boo!" at him, and the boy—a skinny lad in a soiled tee, rings of dirt all down his neck—never failed to jump back. The iceman winked in at him. Then he offloaded the block of ice, shut the outer hatch, and, resuming his whistle, melted away into the morning.

Farce, or 105 Rust Road

He was, what—four? five?—when he first saw his mother laid out on that kitchen floor, her face contorted and wet with tears, a look of such hopeless agony that he, too, shed sympathetic tears alongside her. She didn't care for how tall she was, or how flat-chested, or how unloved. "Do you love me, Charlie?" she would ask him. "Do you think I'm pretty? Prettier than your Aunt Jewel? Prettier than your Aunt Ruby? Would you marry your mama if you could? She hurts, Charlie," she would say to him before breaking into a fresh round of tears. "Your mama hurts so bad." And he flung himself on her all over again, trying to squeeze the hurt right out of her.

The years went by, the hurt turned routine, and Charlie, canny by the time he was eight, learned to monetize their little exchange. She had taught him how when, laid out and low one freely sobbing afternoon, she repaid his moony looks with a penny from the coffee can where she kept her egg money, which he immediately took to Santacroce's Grocery. On the occasion of the next rough patch a few days later, when she was again collapsed on the kitchen floor, he helped get her on her feet again, but then varied the script at the end with a modest request.

"Do you love me, Charlie?"

"I love you, Mama."

"Do you think I'm prettier than your Aunt Jewel?"

"You're much prettier than her, Mama."

"Prettier than your Aunt Ruby?"

"Prettier than her, too."

"Oh, who loves me, Charlie? Who loves me?"

"I love you, Mama," he said. "Mama, may I have another penny?"

Soon it was all part of the farce, and firmly established the equation—*I flatter you, you pay me*—that he would confuse so often for love itself, as if love were a trade on an open market. It was one reason why "Buy me a Coke" would resonate so powerfully with him years later. Wasn't that how love worked? *I pay you, you flatter me . . . with your eyes, your* almond *eyes.*

The next time she bestowed a penny on him and he ran off to Santacroce's, she spied him coming home from the kitchen window. His cheeks bulged, and so did his pockets—and she knew she had a problem on her hands. She rushed down the steps and took him in back of the shanty, where she explained that they didn't have money to be spending on candy. If his father ever found out, he would thrash them both, and if his little brother saw, he would kick up a fuss and demand his own penny. She couldn't have that. So this exchange had to be their little secret. Did he understand? He understood perfectly and began to smuggle the Tootsie Rolls and Abba-Zabas and Turkish Taffies and Red Hots and Good & Plentys and Sugar Babies and Charleston Chews into his bedroom, secreting them under his pillow until everyone else had fallen off to sleep. Then he took them out and sucked on them in the moonlight as he had once sucked on his thumb and shoelaces in the middle of the kitchen floor.

So it came to pass that he fell asleep for many years with candy in his mouth, bathing his teeth for hours at a time in acids, sugars, syrups, and dyes, and when he woke from his dreams, no one ever thought to ask the boy to brush.

20

He would hate this. Every intimate detail deprives him of what he firmly believed a man needs most: the projection of a successful image. There is no accommodating the truth in the pursuit of the American dream. Are you kidding? The market does not want the truth. The market wants fantasy and distraction. It wants the sublime. Get out of here with your goddamn realism, you puncturing little prick! You would tell them about my falsies, and my failing out of college? Why not strip me naked on Main Street, USA, and flog me up and down the street, you fuck?

Charlie had not yet made it back down to his basement office when the kitchen landline began to ring again. The caller introduced himself as Bruce Crowder. "You were just on the phone with my wife," he said. Charlie had never met Bruce before but had, over the years, heard much about him. He was the apple of Evelyn Crowder's eye.

"Please accept my condolences, Bruce," he began. "Evelyn was like family to me."

"Uh-huh," Bruce said. "And when are we going to get that ten thousand dollars back, Charles?" Bruce asked.

There was a long pause.

"Beg your pardon?"

"The money my mother invested in your 'small business.'"

By "small business," Bruce meant the Third Age Association (TTAA). Like all companies, TTAA had required funding, and naturally Charlie asked Evelyn if she cared to invest in an exciting new endeavor. Fifteen years later, that investment had yet to see much of a capital return.

"Hello?"

"Would you like to talk about that now?" Charlie asked.

"Why else would I be calling?"

"Right. Well, she does get a dividend every year, Bruce."

"Does she," Bruce said.

"Yes, she does. Every year."

"And what was the dividend she earned last year on this 'investment' of hers?"

"Well, I'd have to check . . . if you'll just . . . if you hold on while I . . ."

Pretense and fakery. He was deliberately stalling. Not to deceive the man, not to con him, but because that dividend embarrassed him. He had meant to make Evelyn a millionaire.

"This year, Bruce, looks like we paid your mother"—as if reading from a document, though in fact he was gazing down at the kitchen counter, smoothing the warped linoleum as he had lately done one corner of his desk calendar—"forty dollars."

"Forty bucks!" Bruce cried. "On a ten-thousand-dollar investment?"

"Last year it was more."

"And the principal?"

"What about the principal?"

"How do I get it back?"

"I'm afraid it's not liquid at the moment, Bruce. It's bound up in a going concern."

"Your life, you mean."

"My business, yes."

"Listen to me, you son of a bitch," Bruce said. "You stole ten thousand dollars from my mother in her advancing years—"

"I beg your pardon, that is not—"

"And now she's dead."

Bruce hung up.

21

So it was not just the failure of the Third Age to make him a man of wealth and sway, not just the manifest disappointments of fee-based financial planning or his continued basement dwelling that placed poor Charlie Barnes behind the eight ball on the day he believed he would receive a diagnosis of pancreatic cancer, but also the shame of an active and ongoing debt acquired when he decided to leave Bear Stearns and strike out on his own.

There were start-up costs: rents and supplies, the need for a salary. And there was a marketing strategy essential to the grand design. He needed to speak directly to the people of regional Illinois, which required advertising dollars. Once they saw a better way of doing business, he would corner the midwestern market before expanding out to the coasts. It was that simple, and with a business plan in a three-ring binder, with new letterhead and business cards, and with an unbounded confidence in his product, he solicited men and women to get in with him on the ground floor, including his old boss from Dean Witter, Tom Kennedy; Frank Santacroce, a Danville pal; Evangeline's mother, Keiko; Jake's friend Chris's parents; and a few select clients with a long-term investment horizon, such as Evelyn Crowder.

He had no intention of screwing anybody. As one by one they presented him with a personal check, saying, in essence, "I trust you, Steady Boy, I believe in you, I'm investing this money in you personally," he didn't cash out and head to the Caribbean. He buckled down and completed the necessary paperwork. He headquartered at home to keep things lean. He bought the marketing materials and rented the billboards. He had the ballpoints branded in gold with a drop shadow: TTAA. He hoped that that abbreviation would become a household name along the lines of an HBO or an NCAA. TTAA was certainly nothing like some of the companies involved in the subprime mortgage mess he'd been reading about just that morning: Washington Mutual, Countrywide Financial. Alongside Bear Stearns, they had bilked and defrauded their way to multibillion-dollar valuations, while his honest operation hummed along to the sound of the Whirlpool spinner winding down in the basement. But hey, Bruce, guess which one remains a going concern in 2008: Bear Stearns or TTAA? And *I'm* the fraud?

The two hundred and twenty grand he raised in that initial round of funding went lightning quick—billboards are expensive—and now what did he have to show for it beyond one big debt and Bruce Crowder's disrespect? Boxes of outdated brochures, that's what, shrink-wrapped and gathering dust. The minute Bruce Crowder hung up, he dialed the number to Dr. Skinaman's office.

"Charlie Barnes calling," he said. "I'm a patient of Dr. Skinaman's. May I please speak to the doctor?"

"I'm afraid Dr. Skinaman is currently in with a patient. Would you like his nurse?"

"Do you know if the doctor has a financial adviser?"

"A financial adviser?"

"I run a company called the Third Age Association. We offer fee-based, conflict-free financial planning along with estate planning and tax services. I noticed that Dr. Skinaman and I had a good rapport, so I thought I would just call, you know, and see if he'd be willing to receive some free literature from the Third Age, in case he needs an adviser or is unhappy with his current one."

There was a long pause.

"I'm sorry, are you a patient of Dr. Skinaman's?"

"I am," he said. "But I'm also a financial adviser."

"And you would like to . . . ?"

"Send the doctor some free literature. Dr. Skinaman treated me very well. I would just like to repay the favor."

Outrageous puppet masters, incorrigible forces had his balls on a string, and he danced for them, he danced, and knew no shame. He would not go back to working for the Man in his declining years, as collection agencies and a dying clientele, falling markets and a failing business, would demand he do. He hung up with the doctor's office. Down in the basement again, the debasing basement, astronomical quantities of a once-stunning brochure, in boxes, in bales, confronted him in the corner. He removed one from the topmost brick, dusted it off, addressed it to the doctor with a personal note, and readied it to be taken to the mailbox with the rest of the day's mail.

22

His first stab at making a killing took place in '59 when, a year out of high school, he had an idea for a landscaping concern. Newly married and low on funds, he mowed the lawn and trimmed the hedgerows of the apartment complex called Dodge Flats on Vermilion, the first in a series of bad rooms he shared with Sue, in exchange for a discount on rent. He hated mowing the lawn. If he were correctly interpreting life, no one in his right mind would ever do it willingly, which was how he came to devise an alternative. He persuaded Rudy, a more promising Danville scholar, to make a proprietary weed killer using his chemistry set and a selection of poisons procured from Greeley Farm & Tractor. Together they created a knock-off of American Chemical's Weedone which Charlie christened "Endopalm-T." If it was not designed to crackle upon application or to release a visible miasma unscatterable even by a stiff wind, it did a damn fine job of eliminating every living thing it came into contact with. They expanded their experiment from a little test patch in one corner of Delwina's yard to her sister's crosstown residence, a stately Victorian with green, gorgeously conforming lawns, where their recently widowed Aunt Jewel sat grieving day and night. Without fully understanding what she was agreeing to, Jewel consented to their offer of free labor in exchange for allowing Charlie to advertise with a little sign from Speed Lang's Print Shop, complete with phone number, which he planted in the yard near the curb.

Endopalm-T worked wonderfully well. It turned the grass white overnight, and by the time the two boys returned the next morning, a wee bit twitchier than they were the day before, the tough stuff was so routed it needed only a light kick to crumble to dust. But then Jewel came stumbling out of the house calling the name of her dead husband.

"Leonard, is that you? I don't feel too good, Len."

She collapsed on the porch and was rushed by ambulance to the Minta Harrison Wing of Lake View Hospital, where she was treated for confusion and cardiac arrhythmia. She had to move out for a time. The Danville Fire Company paid Charlie a visit at the apartment he shared with Sue and the new baby. Endopalm-T was shelved forever, and he went back to mowing the lawn the despised way.

His next real stab was in '62, during the pinnacle of America's clown craze. A lover of children and a natural performer still capable, at twenty-two, of tapping firsthand into what made boys fall down with a belly laugh, and what made girls slap their cheeks and freeze, and what common spectacles could hold such primal foes as girls and boys rapt together for a full half hour, Charlie Barnes painted his face and put on clown shoes and became Jolly Cholly, available for hire at birthday parties and special events.

And he didn't do half bad. All his tricks were self-taught and his routine unscripted, but he brought an energy to every show that more than compensated for a lack of original genius. When it failed to launch him to national stardom, however, he grew a little bored. He had bigger dreams. Then one day, it hit him. He was driving down Vermilion Street in full regalia on his way to a gig when, one after the other, he encountered the Cadillac dealership, the Standard Oil filling station, and the Osco drugstore. Reflecting on the ingenuity of the American franchise, he determined that Danville's Jolly Cholly was all well and good, but a cadre of Chollies, a franchised fleet of clowns, an army of profiteering performers sweeping the nation, would mean, for him, a cut of the action on every backyard party in the land, and the Clown in Your Town™ was born.

He was working for GE at the time. Ronald Reagan was the host and occasional star of *General Electric Theater* and a spokesman for GE while Charlie, damn near as handsome, was busy assembling ballast for fluorescent lamps inside the plant on Fairchild. Using half a paycheck, he had Speed Lang print him up some more promotional materials, which he delivered by hand to libraries and veterans' halls in towns like Kankakee and Decatur: ARE YOU CREATIVE? DO YOU LIKE TO ENTERTAIN CHILDREN? HIRING OPPORTUNITY! Then he lay in bed at night, worrying about logistics. How to contract with potential clowns in Indiana and Ohio? How to expand out to the coasts? (He was always expanding out to the coasts.) Sue was irate over the expense, especially as his costs kept ballooning (which, he joked, he would take in hand and begin manipulating into wiener dogs and lions' manes), but he soon had interest from two guys in Chebanse and a third outside Morris. He found all three a little too weird for the sort of respectable outfit he hoped to run, but a fourth guy was perfect: a fellow shoe man, for Nunn Bush, he was a graduate of Northwestern Business College and a Springfield Jaycee. They agreed to meet halfway, at the I-72 HoJo, where Charlie bestowed seed money on him in return for a 40 percent cut. But he never heard from the man again, and when he drove clear down to Springfield to demand his money back, his address turned out to be a vacuum-cleaner dealership.

That seed money was also rent money. Sue stopped speaking

to him. He put the franchise on hold, but now, broke and behind on rent, his side gig as a clown became a crucial lifeline. After one particularly successful Sunday party in Westville, as he was packing up his supplies, he was approached by an evidently coulrophobic young man in a bolo tie. "Hello, good sir!" Jolly Cholly said. He was accustomed to people coming up to him after a show to request a booking. "What can I do you for?"

"Your tricks are stupid," the man said.

This undesirable, when he spoke, which he did with quiet menace, somehow managed to keep his cigarette smoke clinging to the cave of his mouth, so that he looked almost demonic. Charlie's smile behind the makeup faded quickly. "Beg your pardon?"

"I said your tricks are stupid, and your show is a pile a shit."

The man stared at him with stone-gray eyes. It looked like he might just haul off and punch him.

"You're a goddamn fraud," the man continued, taking a step forward, "and you stole these good people's money."

"I did no such thing," Charlie objected. "I gave them a good time."

"You gave them herpes," the man said as he poked Charlie in the testicles with the two fingers that clenched his cigarette. "You gave all these children herpes, too."

As the man walked away, Charlie felt it was unconscionable that someone could be so damn mean on such a pleasant afternoon. It made positively no sense in a civilized Christian nation. "Fucker," he mumbled, and flipped the guy the bird behind his back. But then some kids saw the gesture, and soon it was all a big mess.

It wasn't long before the poisonous seed the mean man planted in an impressionable mind took root and flowered. Maybe the reason he hadn't been launched into national stardom had something to do with a performance that was less than sublime. What easily tickled the hicks and farmers of Hoopeston and Westville was to the discerning viewer just a case of herpes. He quit clowning altogether. He ate four hundred dollars in sunk costs and retired his would-be franchise. They found a cheaper apartment, their fourth, this one with water bugs.

23

"What the fuck? Why would you leave a message like that at my work?"

His daughter, Marcy, returning his call. Marcy was the spitting image of her mother, Charley Proffit of Peoria, Illinois, and had her toughness, too. A man wanted his daughter to be able to defend herself in a world full of dickheads, but when she turned on him (he could well picture her contemptuous squint, the skeptical twist of her mouth), he relived in an instant all the scorn and vitriol of a mideighties divorce.

He had just fed the fish and was vacuuming the front room when she called. The pattern in the plush carpet was important to him. Straight lines, strict rows: small consolations for the room itself, which displeased him. The vacuum cleaner displeased him. The mind he tricked by making pleasing patterns in the carpet displeased him most of all, so easily soothed yet constantly clamoring. Well, what will it be: resigned contentment? Or permanent struggle? He unplugged the vacuum cleaner and wrangled the cord into place, its retraction button having broken some months ago. Vacuuming for whom? he wondered as the phone began to ring. That nice neat pattern for whom?

"Good to hear your voice, too," he replied.

"Is it true you have cancer?"

A damn fool thing not to call the kids back and immediately inform them that he wasn't dying.

"So you got my message," he said.

"Is it true you have cancer, Dad?"

Marcy was lucky to have Charlie, an American original, for a father, but she had her gripes, same as Jerry. Charlie adored her, of course—she was daddy's little girl—and longed for her good opinion, but that came and went, depending.

It seemed he was getting the irked daughter that day, the one with funny ideas about 9/11 and fluoride, the wackadoo loner who liked to keep people at bay.

"I was just about to call you with an update," he said.

"I'm not flying home, Pop. I will *not* fly home."

"Okay," he said. This changed things. "And why not?"

"She's jealous, she's vindictive, she's cold, she's calculating, she won't look me in the eye or say my name, she hates seeing me on her couch, she hates having me in her kitchen, she turns her back on me and segregates me at family functions, she freezes me out and denies my existence, but there's just no way I can open your eyes to any of these otherwise universally acknowledged facts."

"Universally acknowledged?" he scoffed. "By whom?"

Marcy paused confidently.

"The universe," she said.

Charlie was sorry. He knew he'd fucked up. But alongside his efforts to earn Marcy's forgiveness, he retained the right to perpetuate a dear hope into the present day: that his children might accommodate his current wife. Yes, Barbara was aloof. She disappeared too easily into her work and proved difficult to get to know. She lacked the hot-blooded passion so endemic to the Barnes clan, the Agincourt speeches and histrionic displays, and made no attempt to blend in. She preferred to read alone in a quiet room those biographies of plagues and hospitals so curious to the rest of us, or to tend to her summer garden at a green distance, or to spread across the bed the Sunday circulars and patiently clip the week's coupons, or to change the oil in her car on her day off (a habit peculiar even to Charlie)—solitary activities that hardly included him any more than they did his children. But by God she was his wife, and by some yin-yang magic (and a sexual chemistry he wisely did not try to explain to his children) they got along, and he wished his kids would respect that and treat her well and not like some part-time help whose shift was about to end.

"So your father tells you he has cancer," he said, "and not just any cancer, Marcy. Pancreatic cancer, which I assume you googled if you got my message. But you can't fly home to help because of some . . . I don't know what . . . little beef with Barbara?"

"It's not my beef, Dad. It's Barbara's beef."

"Barbara doesn't have a beef."

"She does, too, have a beef! A big fucking beef! I can't believe I'm using the word *beef*."

"Pancreatic cancer," Charlie said. "People who've been shot at point-blank range will sometimes survive longer than the patient with pancreatic cancer."

"Dad, listen. I'm just going to be honest with you here, okay?"

"I would hope you're always honest with me," he replied.

"I have a hard time believing you actually have pancreatic cancer."

There was a long pause.

"And why is that?"

"Do you remember the time you read the NyQuil bottle wrong?"

"That was an honest mistake."

"You weren't having a heart attack. You were just accidentally overdosing on a sleep aid. And you didn't have testicular cancer, either."

"That was a real scare, Marcy! Testicular cancer is a *real* scare."

"Or Parkinson's. Remember that shake? It went away. And bleeding gums isn't even a sign of leukemia."

"You know what, Marcy?" he cried before slamming the phone down. "Screw ya! Stay home."

24

So he'd had a scare or two in the past. Being alive was, as far as he could tell, an unrelieved nightmare of strange twinges and mysterious growths. The least a man might be allowed to do is share his fear with loved ones at a moment of uncertainty—but no, you get a reputation for being tender.

Unfortunately, however, he couldn't forget that Marcy's suspicions were well founded and that he didn't, in fact, actually have cancer.

He called the nurse at First Baptist.

"Hello, young man."

"Hello, young lady," he said. "I just got off the phone with Marcy. She refuses to fly home."

Busy at work and totally unaware of the day's phone calls, voice mails, pronouncements, and reversals, Barbara hadn't known that Marcy's flying home was even under discussion and did not immediately reply.

It must be said, we were a tight-knit group, with our inside jokes and movie quotes, our comic tales of abandonment. It was no great surprise that Barbara might feel like the odd one out. We got together in state parks, split the difference between cities. Sunday evenings, we talked on the phone. It was all the bad shit we'd been through, the custody battles and whatnot, the new schools, the secret drunks. Strangers shacking up together, sharing towels. It was enough to overcome the age gaps and competing paternities. We saw many things we shouldn't have. We carried around a lot of shame. But in the end, there was something bronze-aged about our clannish bond, evoking concepts like kin and barter and hearth, though we remained tight by entirely contemporary means: the text message and connecting flight, the online multiplayer shooter game. Without a little hazing of the newcomers, how could we know for sure they'd stick around? How could we confidently give our hearts to them? It might sound strange that after fifteen years Barbara was still on probation, but we did that to protect ourselves—and one another.

"I didn't realize she was flying home," Barbara said at last.

"She isn't. And she won't. But it would have been nice to know she was willing."

"What would she be flying home for?"

"What for? To help."

"Do we need help?"

"I could always use a little help," he said.

"Is this your way of telling me that you've heard from the doctor?"

There was a long pause. He badly needed to tell Barbara, of all people, about his clean bill of health from Dr. Skinaman's office. He kept nothing from Barbara, or as little as possible, anyway, having learned from marriages past that secrets and lies end badly. But the morning was full of phone calls and panic and a bout of vacuuming, and it just slipped his mind. Then Marcy flatly refused to come home, which eclipsed every other consideration, and now, unfortunately, he was forced to twist himself into knots.

"Not yet," he said, quickly adding, "but I'm sure I'm fine."

"That wasn't your opinion this morning."

"I tend to assume the worst, as you know. But I'm trying to be more... what is the word?"

"Positive?"

"Optimistic," he said, "which is even better. When I do hear from the doctor, likely any minute now, I'm sure he will give me a clean bill of health and we can put all this behind us. However, let's not forget: something *will* get me, Barbara. Sooner or later, something's coming for me, something big, and it will get me."

There was a considerable pause.

"Is that your idea of being optimistic?" she asked.

He drifted off momentarily, into a reverie about pancreatic cancer, testicular cancer, rare blood cancers, and other forms of cancer.

"You would welcome her home, wouldn't you?" he asked. "You would be eager to welcome her?"

"Welcome who?"

"Marcy," he said.

There was a long pause.

"Barbara? Would you welcome Marcy home?"

"I guess that depends," she said. "Why is she coming again?"

"She isn't. I'm saying, if we needed her to."

"But why would we? Shouldn't we wait to hear what the doctor has to say before we start making flight arrangements?"

"You're right," he said. "Of course we should." He might have left it at that. "But you wouldn't mind, would you?"

"Mind what?"

"If Marcy came home."

"Why would I mind?"

"All the kids think you hate them," he said.

"That's ridiculous, Charlie, and you know it."

"That's what I tell them!"

"I don't hate them."

"So just give her a call, will you?"

"Give her a call? What for?"

"To tell her that I might be sick. She doesn't believe that I might be sick. It's a little insulting, if you ask me."

"But you might not be sick."

"She doesn't have to know that."

"I'm confused."

"I want Marcy to *want* to come home, you see? Not that she needs to. She probably doesn't. The odds are against it. Besides, she can't. She has a job. She has a life. And no doubt I have a clean bill of health. Who needs her? But she could offer. She could say, you know, sure thing, Dad. What do you need, Dad? That's all I'm looking for here. Hey, I adore Marcy. I cherish my time with her. But whenever I encourage her to come home, she says you don't want her."

"So... you want me to tell her to come?"

"Tell her to come. She can't, she won't, she doesn't need to, I'm sure I'll be fine, I'm trying to be more optimistic."

"Okay," Barbara said. "I will give her a call."

25

He returned to the basement, to his desktop computer and the spring-breeze odors that battled the static cling.

"I want to reiterate just how sorry I was to learn this morning that your mother had passed away," the letter he composed at his desk to Bruce Crowder began. "Evelyn was one of my first clients when I started as a stockbroker, in 1985. We have been a heck of a team these twenty-three years. In that time, I have overseen a 400 percent return in her portfolio. (With the current economy in free fall, Mr. Crowder, your mother's holdings have taken a knock, which I regret. I put some of the blame on Bear Stearns and its CEO, Jimmy Cayne.) I always made sure that she was conservatively allocated and well diversified. I saw to it that her monthly distributions did not erode the principal she was intent on leaving her heirs. I advised her on mortgage rates and minor legal matters. I did her taxes every year free of charge.

"Mr. Crowder," he continued, "in January of 1993, I offered your mother the chance to be an angel investor in a new enterprise called the Third Age Association (TTAA), which was designed to revolutionize the whys and wherefores of the retirement experience in this country. Our intention was to stop the churn that infected retiree accounts in every big brokerage shop across the nation and to align the financial adviser's interests with the client's, placing fiduciary duty front and center, with the added vow that profit would never be our motive. Evelyn learned about this and chose, entirely of her own accord, to invest ten thousand dollars in TTAA. I believed that she had an opportunity for a return that would make the annual dividend from her beloved Alcoa and her beloved GE look like child's play. Well, it didn't work out exactly as I had hoped. You see, in May of that year, the SEC contacted me with some concerns—"

Days after he launched the Third Age, in May of '93, the SEC contacted him with some concerns. He was in breach of this and in breach of that—most vitally, his fiduciary duty under the Investment Advisers Act of 1940. Oh, the bitter irony, for it was in the name of fiduciary duty that he had created the Third Age in the first place, to counteract the Jimmy Caynes of the world and their indefinite churn. The SEC saw it differently: he could not act as a registered investment adviser working in the best interest of clients like Evelyn Crowder while also serving as the CEO of an independent for-profit entity meant to revolutionize the retirement experience. In other words, no investing other people's money while running an investment company of his own. It presented a clear conflict of interest. But investing other people's money *was* the fucking company! Didn't matter. He had to choose one or the other, and fighting the SEC on that score ate up what little capital he had remaining after buying the billboards and brochures.

"Couldn't you have mentioned this *before* I dropped a hundred grand on marketing?" he asked the regional SEC guy in a Loop conference room.

"I'm not your lawyer," the SEC guy shot back. "Do you even have a lawyer?"

He did. Some tool named Einsohn out of Aurora.

As he put the phone to his ear (back in his basement office) and dialed, a moment of blinding clarity, ordinarily so rare, came over him, and he saw the dash and the two dates between them, and the headstone, and the sky above, and the absence of laughter and life on his walk back to the car after saying a final goodbye to the previous fifteen years, for now he knew how they had been permanently laid to rest: he went broke, the SEC lost interest in him, and no one gave a damn anymore that some poor slob called himself the CEO of TTAA while managing eleven million.

"Hartwell and Einsohn."

"Good morning," he said. "Charlie Barnes calling for Aaron Einsohn."

There was a long pause.

"Mr. Barnes," the woman said. "Haven't we been over this?"

"He ruined my life."

He was placed on hold.

"This is Aaron Einsohn."

"You ruined my life, Aaron."

"Hello, Mr. Barnes."

"Remember when the SEC used to call me? It's been fifteen years now. They don't call anymore. They don't give a shit. No one gives a shit."

"Frankly, Mr. Barnes, I don't give a shit, either," Einsohn said.

"I had one shot and you blew it, goddamn it."

Einsohn had heard it before, and hung up.

26

Charlie's father was an orphan who came of age at the Vermilion County Poor Farm on the Catlin-Tilton Road. He was twenty-five the year he made love to Charlie's mother in the middle of a cornfield, two strangers meeting cute on a night the circus was in town. Delwina found Alden dashing, with his pale eyes and pencil-thin mustache. They abandoned the campgrounds and cut through the cornstalks like children playing at a game, only to end up naked and mudbound in a little clearing organized just like a sacred cross. When the deed was done, pious Delwina, flooded by images of lambs and leather Bibles, broke into tears. A series of images quickly crowded into Alden's own mind—of mobs gathering, brothers swinging bats, and the shadow of jail-house bars falling across a dirt floor. He tried to soothe her, but her ingrained Christian guilt proved too strong for his clumsy rhetoric, and he got to his feet.

"Well, guess what," he said. "I should be the one crying, because you're *ugly.*"

With that, he tucked in his shirt and stormed off, expecting never to see the girl again.

They came for him two months later at Junior's Pool Hall in the Hotel Grier-Lincoln, where, in exchange for a taste, he laid bets for a man out of Little Egypt. Delwina's father and uncle offered him no choice but to get inside the car. He was quite surprised, after watching miles of generic dirt road go by, to be delivered to a farmhouse where the woman he had called ugly because she was as tall as a man and as flat-chested as a boy was waiting for him on the porch in her best dress from Cramer & Norton's.

She was just beginning to show. The family belonged to the Church of the Nazarene, a severe congregation whose chapel was then located on the Indiana state line. The farmhouse, as many miles west of Danville as Danville was of the chapel, belonged to the church organist and her husband, a soybean farmer. All the congregation's wayward were married in the front parlor of that farmhouse, far from the parish glare. Alden realized he was presently expected to marry the tall one with the satin frill. The idea dizzied him. He chose to concentrate on his growling stomach, as it was almost noon and he'd had nothing to eat. When he and Delwina stepped inside the farmhouse, the most heavenly scent of Alden's young life greeted him. Despite the vows he was being forced to exchange as his young bride hovered on the brink of tears and her parents shot daggers at him from the wings, the sweet warmth of some tender loaf wafting out of the kitchen and filling the organist's unadorned living room served as a reminder that life on earth wasn't exclusively arbitrary and dumb. Ten minutes later, the two strangers were married without joy or fanfare in a ceremony solemnized by nothing—not a flashbulb, not a church bell, not even a kiss.

This was immediately compelling history for Charlie, for obvious reasons, and from time to time he would suggest to his son the writer what a great novel it would make in the right hands. This was one of the old man's more curious features: an antipathy toward novels as a general rule, and absolutely no taste for reading them, together with a tendency to find their shimmering starts almost everywhere in the course of ordinary life. When I asked him to explain why, exactly, this episode between his parents would make a good novel—he had, on this occasion, called me up out of the blue with the express purpose of urging me to write it, and by now no one can doubt what a genius this man had for placing the random phone call—he replied, "Because it's true." I never found that very persuasive. Why should I give a damn about a quorum of sepia-toned sadists who forced two innocents into holy matrimony and the biggest mistake of their lives, all in order to save face? But I did care deeply about the man who would emerge out of that swamp to become the source of love in me. I'd been making a study of *that* man all my life, and I can tell you: it was never the truth of his circumstances or the facts of his life or the history I'm peppering you with now that made him an object of fascination, but rather the fantastical mind-set and the many fictional selves he hoped to make real, without which life, for him, would not have been worth living.

But to return to his father. He was pleased to have the wedding ceremony behind him. Now he could sink his teeth into whatever delicious comestible they had made in celebration.

The preacher averted his eyes when Alden attempted to shake his hand; his bride hugged her fat aunt. The church organist excused herself from the proceedings. Alden watched her enter the kitchen and pull a piping-hot coffee cake from the oven. Then he watched as she departed for the farmhouse that stood directly across the country road, where a neighbor was convalescing from tuberculosis. It was, for Alden, a loaf of bitter ashes. Not a minute later, the newlyweds climbed into the car together, two strangers bound for a shared life in a Westville shack.

27

After the failure of the Clown in Your Town™, there were other strokes of genius, hook-a-duck schemes, napkin-doodled empires and fever dreams full of franchises, including one for-profit endeavor he called Dog Owners of America, Inc., which required a membership fee and was DOA indeed. He also tried his hand at art.

Over a lifetime of Sundays, Steady Boy came to love the funnies like nothing else. He was twenty-five when he invested in a drafting set and sat at the kitchen table a few hours every night after Jerry had gone to bed dreaming up narratives based on his life as a harried young husband and father. After a month of effort, he concluded that he had no eye for a line and no talent for story, which is why the comic strip *The Too Bad Busters* never came to be.

His disappointment gave way, however, to a bigger and

better idea. Was there not an unmet need in the marketplace for individuals like him, stymied artists who lacked the skill to draw but would eagerly pay to learn how? To test the theory, he placed an ad in the back of a popular boys' magazine: IS BRINGING THE WORLD TO LIFE YOUR DREAM? ARE YOU FINDING IT NEXT TO IMPOSSIBLE AND READY TO THROW IN THE TOWEL? LOOK NO FURTHER THAN THIS DEFINITIVE BOOKLET— *ILLUSTRATION ILLUMINATED!*

The first check arrived three days after the ad ran, proof positive that this was a viable and necessary product. He deposited that check and the others that soon followed in a savings account at the Palmer Bank opened for that purpose and vowed to spend none of that money until he had located an illustrator. But try as he might, he never found the right man. The closest he came was Howie Rylance, the courtroom sketch artist, who couldn't write a sentence in English to save his life, while the fine-art appraiser in town, a man named Glen Glamour, didn't appear to know anything about art. In the meantime, the checks kept arriving. He began returning them to sender straightaway and canceled the ad in the boys' magazine. The roughly two hundred dollars he did deposit in good faith as he tried to commission the how-to guide languished at the bank; when it became clear that he had defrauded a handful of individuals of $6.95 apiece, he could no longer find their names or return addresses. He and Sue were constantly moving in those years, and he must have misplaced or discarded them. That money sat there earning interest for another year while his guilt and shame ripened until finally he closed out the account and donated all the money to the March of Dimes.

All the while he worked his day job at Jonart's. Jonart's was followed by a stint at rival Mosser's ("See the Experts . . . on the Mall"), followed by stints in the sales department at Flo-Con Systems, Hyster, Inc., Autotron, Enhance Corp., Dante Global, and Twin Tree Associates. Goddamn, he did move from place to place back then.

By '67, he'd had enough of such demeaning hustles and their quarter-hour coffee breaks, strict dress codes and petty squabbles over commissions. He wanted something better for himself and applied to college. In the fall of that year he moved the whole family into married housing on the campus of Michigan State, in East Lansing, and began attending classes. They left after a semester and a half. While his carefree classmates were jaunting off to their tailgates and frat parties, he, a young father required to work a full-time job, was slaving at the East Lansing Sears, or helping Sue hold on to whatever shred of her sanity still remained by taking Jerry off her hands for a night. It was just too much. His dream of a college degree was one more opportunity cost of starting a family while still a child himself.

Or so he told people. Being honest with himself, he knew he hated the nightly reading and simply couldn't finish it. Home by ten from Sears, he'd crack open the books and by ten fifteen start bleeding tears of terminal boredom. There was simply no narcotic like a textbook. It set off a tidal wave of exhaustion, just an absolute tsunami overwhelming every blood cell and muscle fiber of his being, and seven hours later, he would wake on the floor of the living room with no memory of how he got there. It was like going on a bender. Sue would come into the room and stand over him as if he had no pants on and someone had tattooed ASSHOOLE across his brow. He could not recall even a single line from the page and a half of Western civ he'd managed to weed through before conking out. Then he'd make Jerry breakfast, having seen not one lick of him the day before, and get him off to school before heading to class, cramming in whatever he could on campus before the day's deadlines. There is the old fighting chance, and then there are the house odds, whereby one is guaranteed to lose by year's end what seems a modest gain on any given day. The house odds caught up to him by final exams. Eventually he wondered what the fuck he was doing playing the scholar when he could go straight to bed being a dropout.

And as difficult as that admission was to make, even to himself, it still didn't get at the half of it, the really shameful half. Something more alluring than sleep, only something of a pathological compulsion, could truly explain the . . . oh, Christ, the *burden,* the fucking back-borne monkey that pounded its fists and shrieked bloody murder in his ear day and night, making a complete fucking shambles of the facade of Scholar/Father/Full-time-Jobber. On nights he wasn't bleeding tears by ten fifteen, he was pulling his pecker out of his pants! He was giving it a yank before his brain exploded with the frustrations of (2) the adult learner and (3) the rebuffed spouse. And what was (1)? Number one was always the unspoken law of his existence, as constant as gravity and as strong as the tides: the irresistible, properly deranging, life-affirming, and yet also totally annihilating urge to fuck. Surrounded all day long by campus coeds, by married ladies seeking his assistance on the sales floor at work, by memories of bras on hangers, naked ankles under fitting-room doors, and the not infrequent plain-spoken propositions that certain desperate housewives made to him at checkout . . . altogether, man, he needed release, and no amount of institutional resistance in the form of deans, marble busts, flowering quads, big-ass globes, Greek notations on chalkboards, large lexicons lying open in hushed libraries, or the many ponderous halls of learning all within spitting distance was going to make that pecker stay put. But when, ten minutes later, he would return to his reading, he always felt so demoralized. You never read about Napoleon having to masturbate. Napoleon never paused laying waste to fucking Europe by turning to his men and declaring that he'd be back in just a minute, he forgot something in the tent. Was that Napoleon's true importance to Western civilization, to give young men like Charlie some idea of the peril of hand-jobbing your life away? What was wrong with him? He couldn't do a damn thing without masturbating first. He had to masturbate *even in married housing.* They were back in Danville by Easter.

28

He returned his attention to the letter he was writing to Bruce Crowder.

"I hope you will consider allowing me to continue managing what is now your mother's legacy," he concluded, with some daring, "which I would happily do at a discount from my normal fee. But either way, Mr. Crowder, I promise to return to you the ten thousand dollars your mother, Evelyn Crowder, invested in my company, the Third Age Association (TTAA), one month from today, on or before October 12, 2008. As I mentioned earlier on the phone, the investment is not liquid, but that is not your concern. Your mother would want me to honor your request, and I want to honor your mother. You have my word."

He sealed and stamped the letter and addressed it to Evelyn Crowder's house in Barrington, collected the solicitation for kindly Dr. Skinaman along with his rebuttal in writing to any claim Credence Credit Corp. had on him, and marched all three out to the mailbox. Midway there he became aware of all the outside world flooding his senses—asphalt, birdsong, heat—now firmly beyond Evelyn's reach. Poor Evelyn, poor old girl. Life alone avails. And he was alive. He would live, not die. He halted. Looked up. Peered around. From a Westville shanty to the Chicago suburbs in a single lifetime. Not too shabby for a college dropout. And there was still time, still time. He shivered.

But the birdsong and bounty were soon drowned out by the low steady hum of paranoia. There was an unmarked white van parked at the curb. It hadn't been there an hour earlier when, pursued by terror, he burst from the front door and fled the house. It looked FBI-ish, kidnappery, lone shooter–like. Probably just some repair guy. He collected the day's mail, put the flag up for tomorrow, and while tracking the van with his eyes headed back inside.

There was only one item of interest to him that day: an official piece of correspondence from Michigan State University. Standing in the front room, he vented the venetian blinds in order to have another look at the errant van while tearing into the envelope. His reasons for requesting a school transcript had not been all that clear to him a few weeks ago, when he thought he was dying. Now, unfolding the document, he discovered without surprise a long list of incompletes. There was, however, something unexpected in those marks he had received for classes he saw to the end:

Literature and the Individual: A–
Introductory Economics: B+
Elementary Chemistry: B–
Descriptive Astronomy: B–
Western Civilization I: B–
Fundamentals of Speech: A

He double-checked the name on the transcript. It was his, all right.

Upon returning his family to Danville in 1968, Steady Boy entered a time of infidelities, of hushed and hasty and never entirely satisfying assignations, sneaked gropings in darkened movie houses, and old-fashioned trysts with married housewives. Returning home from these transgressions, he would envision the most extravagant fantasies of fate's revenge: rollicking avalanches would bury the wayward husband and floods sweep him out to sea, though he lived in the heartland prairie, while a serene God ordered up heart attacks and head-on collisions. Though a longtime antagonist of organized religion, Charlie was as superstitious as the next guy and never wanted to cross the last remnants of God that still resided in his mind. But then something bad *did* happen: running dangerously late for an already suspicious Sue, he was energetically backing down a lover's absurdly long driveway when he felt an ominous thud. His lover screamed. Her dog limped off. It would have to be put down but couldn't be caught. At last he cornered the frightened animal, who bared his fangs. When Charlie finally made it back home, he was covered in raw red claw marks, which he tried passing off to his wife as an encounter with a bobcat on the Catlin-Tilton Road.

Did she believe him? Never. The end was nigh anyway. Sue woke Jerry from an innocent slumber one night and dragged him out of bed. The poor kid! I have heard this story many times. He was alarmed and confused. Never had he known a night so late or so dark. As they were leaving the house, something flew out of the shadows and struck him in the face, and his cries raised the neighborhood. "Bats!" he hollered, his thin and frightened voice ringing out in the dead of night. "Bats, Mama!"

"Those aren't bats, genius," his mother snapped. "Now get in the damn car!"

Every seventeen years without fail, a migration of cicadas from deep within the earth overran the city of Danville, covering every inch of town with their crunchy hulls: front yards and driveways, flagpoles and parking lots, bank steps and water towers. It was a midwestern plague and source of otherworldly wonder. Sue put Jerry in the car and then worked the windshield wipers, bulldozing hundreds of crackling carapaces over the side. A few remained pinched under the glass and went along for the ride, unsettling Jerry. They had red bug eyes and black-veined wings like something out of his science fiction comics.

Roselawn, Meadowlawn, Lawndale—nowhere are street names prettier than in Danville, Illinois. Sue backed the Buick down the drive at twenty miles an hour (Charlie was later informed by a nosy neighbor) and smashed the chrome fender against the pavement, shooting off sparks. Then she tore through town, heading east on Vermilion past the Palmer Bank, past the sodium-vapor lights still burning above the deserted American Legion baseball fields, past the giant glowing scoop of vanilla in its tilted cone advertising the Custard Cup, past the water tower and the golf club and out to the city limits and the start of farmhouses, silos, and combine harvesters. She drove everywhere that night looking for her philandering husband's Plymouth: to the Sportsman's Club on Lake Vermilion, to Cannon Alley and the pool hall, to the Sunken Gardens at Lincoln Park, and to the nature preserve at Kickapoo State Park. Throughout their search, she filled Jerry in on all the many reasons that he should never forgive his father for as long as he lived... while Jerry, dumbstruck and heartbroken at the sight of his mother's tears, tried in vain to contain his own.

At last they found him in the parking lot of the Nutty Nut Shoppes ("Across from the Copper Indian"), where Charlie sat smooching a floozy in the back seat of his Plymouth. When Sue lay on the horn, Steady Boy, whose nickname had taken on new meaning as a married man, broke off from the part-time gal and peered out the rear window. He could still recall the terror that filled his heart at the sight of his wife. He stepped out of the car, tie off and shirttails untucked, crunching the cicadas underfoot. Caught red-handed, he responded the only way he knew how.

"You started it, Sue! You fucked Marshall first!"

Blinded by the Buick's headlights, his eyes took a moment to adjust. Only then did he see that his wife was not alone. The top of his son's head and his big frightened eyes peeked out just above the dashboard. But there was nothing Charlie could do about that just then, because Sue had hit the gas and was coming straight at him. When, many years later, Jerry informed his father that he was convinced he was witnessing, at ten years old, the murder-suicide of the two people he loved most in the world, Charlie understood just how badly they had fucked him up.

Delighted by his school transcript, he set it aside; he was due out in the world. He transferred all calls to his cell phone and entered the garage. Sunlight flooded that dank, dark space as the rattling door slowly retracted. His twenty-year-old Saab was having engine troubles; they were expected at European Motors in an hour's time. Whitney shrieked at him as he turned the key. He liked to sing along to her *Bodyguard* sound track on the highway when no one else was listening. He was reminded of the sniper's van only upon backing down the drive. It was nothing, a service call, he would ignore it . . . and he might have, too, had Jerry himself not stumbled from the front seat and waved.

29

Now we meet him, his mystic son, the Zen master, full of news nobody wanted. We finally meet this Jerry—Charlie's firstborn, and a towering giant. I mean it: when I was growing up, Jerry was like a god to me. I get almost giddy whenever I'm back in his company. But first, a story.

One morning in the fall of 1975, newly remarried but still living in Danville, Mr. Charles Barnes, of 1622 North

Vermilion Street, turning thirty-five that November and working at Old Poor Farm, opened his front door wearing a red velvet robe and a matching pair of travel slippers. His ex-wives were all behind him: Sue had married her beloved Marshall, while his rebound bride, Barbara Lefurst, came and went in the blink of an eye; he looked upon her as one would a bad dream. Jerry was doing fine, living but a few blocks away with his honeymooning mother, which was only appropriate. A child that age belonged with his mom.

He was delighted by his own domestic arrangement: he and Charley lived with their newborn, Marcy, in a house they owned. He was leading one of those humble, happy lives of the sort he never imagined possible for a man with ambition: one of potlucks and bike rides, softball games in the late afternoon, a feast on Sunday, and sun tea always brewing on the back porch steps. It was not the morning frost that caused him to shiver when he opened the door but the sheer delight of a new day. He swooped down to collect the newspaper, and it was only upon straightening up again that he spotted the boy on the stairs. With all the eye-watering pain of a basketball pile-driving into his face, he knew at once that he'd miscalculated. No fifteen-year-old boy doing fine would be loitering on his father's porch at the break of dawn. He didn't wait to consult his new wife. He invited Jerry to come live with him there and then.

You can bow out of almost anything, and sure, there might be consequences, but dodge them or square up to them, accrue them with interest or pay them down over time, there is the immediate illusion of freedom. On the day Jerry Barnes climbed from his unmarked van outside the house on Rust Road, Charlie had bowed out of Jonart's Shoes and Lauhoff

Grain, out of GE Ballast and Farnsworth Poultry, and out of his gig as floor manager of ready-to-wear at the Danville Sears. He'd bowed out of two-handed dribbling, a career in the law, four marriages and the mortgages they bound him to, and the many other debts that could not or would not be paid. And just that morning, he had contemplated (or had imposed on him) the strange option of bowing out of reality itself by letting the phone ring and ring, thereby denying his further participation in life. But in the end, there was no bowing out of two things: physical death and fatherhood. Biological children and the Grim Reaper had in common what was shared by nothing else in the world: an unerring radar with which to find you when the time came.

If we were to look at Jerry through a child's eyes, we would not see the unkempt, shabbily dressed, slightly overweight man of middle age who climbed out of a killer's van with a copy of the Bhagavad Gita in hand, slamming the door with a rusted screech, but that young guitar player and pilot in training whose Ping-Pong skills, mastery of campfires and beautiful belly laugh knew no equal. The child, naturally inclined to exaggerate a pretty young man into a myth, meets with so many adult abetters who wish the child to see his big brother's competence and charm rather than those creeping tendencies only adults can discern that will in time force the myth back into a man. The worst thing that could have happened to Icarus was not, in fact, his fiery end but his decision at the last second to go by Greyhound, and to start a nice family in Cleveland.

"What's this?" Charlie asked him, in the middle of Rust Road.

"The Gita."

"Jerry," he said. "Shouldn't you be in Belgium?"

Jerry insisted, and finally Charlie took hold of the book, the fourth of its kind to be gifted him by the Zen master. Jerry promptly had a seat on the fading yellow paint of the curb. It was the sort of perch that would have been uncomfortable even for a child, but then Jerry did childish things. It was, for me, part of his charm.

Biographically speaking, Jerry had graduated from Danville High in 1978, received his BA with a double major in musicology and computer science in 1983, returned for his MBA from the Kellogg School of Management, Northwestern University, five years later, and five years after that pursued the only advanced degree that ever mattered to him, in Eastern thought, from the University of Virginia. Between these episodes of intense study, he worked for Fifth Third Bank, Sysco Corp., and Sears, Roebuck—not, like his father, on the sales floor but in the corporate office, managing payroll for the retail department. He was licensed to fly in 1986. Owned an apartment in Boystown, then a loft in Wicker Park, then a town house in Naperville. Married once, briefly, no children. Had a taste for Triumphs and Ducatis. Was the coolest, bar none. What happened?

Charlie joined him on the curb. "What are you doing here, son? Shouldn't you be in Belgium?"

"Came to give you the Gita. It won't cure cancer, but it renders death meaningless, which is something."

"Thank you," Charlie said, and briefly looked the book over as if he were curious, as if it were the first copy he had ever received.

Charlie's two sons were always hounding him to take their master classes. Privately, he called these "Literature 101" and

"Advanced Religion," and he had no interest in either one. The readings were dull, the lectures long and didactic, and one of them, "Advanced Religion," had been on offer since Jimmy Carter's only term, when Charlie was kicking nicotine in all its forms and not in the mood. He had disappointed his religion professor going on about five decades now, receiving failing marks year after year—and severe frowns whenever the subject of his soul came up in conversation. Fact of the matter was, he had tried more than once with the Gita—Jerry always called it the Gita—but never made it past the bit about . . . well, whatever that first bit was about . . . before falling into a deep and restful sleep.

"What I mean is, what are you doing *here,* in Chicago?"

"I told you. Read this, Pop. It's never too late to square up to reality."

"What's this about reality, Jerry? I was led to believe you were just having lunch in Belgium."

Jerry shrugged and looked off. He had on his old Jesus sandals, a pair of cutoff denims with tassels the color and consistency of rat tails, while his white T-shirt, that unbranded emblem of austerity and resistance, glowed horridly with pit stains. It had come as an enormous relief to his father when Jerry got the coding job. He would have health benefits again, and a retirement account of the kind he had blown through before declaring bankruptcy. But it was his father's understanding that to do the actual coding, *Jerry had to be in Belgium.*

"You were never employed in Belgium, were you?"

Jerry made no reply.

"You were never hired by a multinational."

"Do you have pancreatic cancer, Pop?"

"Why did you lie to me?"

"To get you off my back. Do you have cancer?"

"You told me you were living in Belgium just to get me off your back?"

The magnitude of the lie set in. Belgium!

"No one goes all the way to Belgium just to code, Pop. Now I hear you have cancer. I'm here because of the cancer."

"Have you been twenty miles away this entire time?"

"I have an apartment on Western Avenue. You don't have cancer, do you?"

Charlie frowned. "Western Avenue?"

"When you called this morning and said you had cancer, that was a lie, wasn't it?"

"It was not a lie. I was reading the internet wrong."

"How do you read the internet wrong?"

They were getting off to a bad start.

"Hey," Charlie said, "come inside." The sweat was beginning to tickle under his collar. "Let's get out of this goddamn heat." He tapped Jerry gamely on the leg. "Come on."

Jerry made no effort to move.

"What are we doing sitting on the goddamn curb, Jerry? Come on, come inside. Let's talk."

"Is she in there?"

"Who?" he asked. "Oh, you've got to be kidding me. You gotta be pulling my goddamn leg. You, too, Jerry?"

"I'm happy at the curb, thanks."

"No, she's not in there. Barbara is at work. Your stepmother works hard. Some people do, you know."

"I should be getting back anyway."

"Back where? Belgium?"

When his children spoke to their therapists and lovers about their most recent stepmother, the revulsion was hard to justify. You don't like your stepmother because she evinces no warmth, expresses no joy, feigns no happiness when you're around? But that doesn't make her a criminal. Perhaps she is only shy or insecure. They went ballistic at suggestions like these. Yet there was no proof of iniquity or sabotage, no evidence to point to, no support for their claims. It was even a little amusing how desperate they were among themselves to identify the source of a universal feeling: Barbara was not just cold or withholding, but evil. They found themselves drawn to German folklore in an effort to explain their aversion to the nurse at First Baptist: she would banish them to the forest, turn them into blackbirds, poison their suppers when they weren't looking if it meant having the king to herself. But in the end, their lovers and therapists tended to argue, their complaints about Barbara said as much if not more about the age-old grudges they held against their father.

"What could that woman possibly have done to make my children hate her?" Charlie asked.

"We don't hate her, Pop. We just know where we aren't welcome."

"Oh, bullshit."

"Call it a sixth sense, honed over the many years and your many wives. We can distinguish now between the real welcomers and the..." He couldn't think of the right word. "The Barbaras," he said.

"First of all, Barbara does welcome you, with open arms, whether you want to believe that or not. She just has a hard time expressing herself with words."

"It's not so much her words I have in mind as her facial

expressions," Jerry said. "Also her eye contact, general body language, and her actions."

"And second of all, I live here, too, you know. And I hope you know by now that you are always welcome in my home."

Jerry glanced back. "Really, Pop—105 Rust Road?" he said.

"I don't claim it often," he said. "Why should I? It's a piece of shit. But it's all I've got, Jerry. And what's mine is yours, my boy. It's always been that way."

"You tell me it's mine, Pop. But it's been in the family for all of one marriage now—"

"Barbara and I have been together for fifteen years."

"—in a long line of them, so how do I know you won't just cross the street one day and start living over there? Besides, the woman who actually owns the house would not mind if I never set foot inside it again."

"Oh, hogwash. You want to stay out here? Fine. But don't blame that on Barbara."

"I don't blame it on Barbara. I blame it on the man who married her."

"Jesus Christ, Jerry. I don't understand. I don't understand any of this. What did I do to you? What did your mother and I do?"

"Shall we review, Pop? You might recall the night you and Mom tried to kill each other outside the Nutty Nut Shoppes."

"Sue came at *me.* I wasn't the one in control of the gas pedal."

"No, but you were in control of your pecker."

"I wouldn't be so sure," he said. "Not in those years."

"You couldn't keep your dick in your pants for two nights

running? I can still see those freaky cicadas. Jesus, the world is a fucking nightmare."

"Your mother started it, Jerry. She was sleeping with Marshall. What was I, a fool? Of course I slept around. But she started it."

Blocks of speech assigned at birth. He was no better at life than his mother, and full of the same self-pity.

"Look," he said. "Let's not rehash this. I feel terrible about how it all shook out. I wish I could go back and make it right, but there's little I can do about it forty years later."

"You could apologize."

"I've apologized a million times!"

"No, you've referenced Marshall a million times. You've blamed Mom a million times. You have not apologized."

"Okay, look," he said. "I'm sorry. Look at me, Jerry. I'm sorry."

There was a long pause while Jerry looked at him under the noonday sun on the curb of Rust Road.

"Are you going to tell me why you lied about having pancreatic cancer?"

"I told you, it wasn't a lie. It was a scare."

"Like that time you overdosed on NyQuil and thought you were having a heart attack?"

"Yes," Charlie said. "Like that."

There was another long pause. They might have stood up then, gone inside, started over. Who doesn't long for new adventures, happy ends? But the harsh truth takes us inexorably in one direction and tells a different story.

Jerry asked him, "Has it taught you anything, this scare of yours?"

"What do you have in mind?"

"That making a killing is totally unimportant, besides being a disaster for this planet, and that no right-thinking person should give a damn about who has the better hood ornament?"

"The better hood ornament? What the hell's that supposed to mean?"

Jerry began counting off on his fingers a list of toxic entities. "Bear Stearns. IndyMac. Fannie Mae. Lehman Brothers is in trouble. So is Merrill Lynch. AIG. Goldman Sachs. Even General fucking Motors. It's Armageddon, Pop. The great meltdown. We are at a historic juncture. Hegel is finished. Milton Friedman is finished. George fucking Bush and his cronies are finished. History itself may be at an end. Now, is there anything *you* would like to say to the American public?"

"Hold on," he said. "You think *I'm* the problem?"

"Have you not played your part?"

"Doing what, Jerry—eliminating churn? Investing a few old ladies in the Dow Jones and barely making rent with the fees I charge? You got a lot of nerve," he said. "Played my part . . . from where, Jerry, the fucking basement?"

"You've wasted your life on a false prophet."

"What false prophet?"

"Jimmy Cayne," Jerry said. "Your hero."

"That man is not my hero."

"For many years he was. How does it go? WWJD: What would Jimmy do?"

Charlie stood and looked down on his son.

"You can be a real prick, you know that?"

Jerry stumbled to his feet. "And you can be a real fraud," he said.

"Thanks for the book, son. I'll be sure to put it with the many others."

Jerry started for his van. "Good luck with your fake cancer, you fraud."

"And good luck to you in Belgium," Charlie said as he reached his car. "Do they teach over there how the apple doesn't fall far from the tree?"

"I'll be seeing you, Pop."

"Stop by anytime."

He set off in one direction and Jerry in the other.

Let the record show that Charlie was, in fact, a good father. Maybe not every single day, and not always to Jerry. It might be said of Jerry that, as a child, he drew the shorter stick. But Steady Boy was just a kid himself when Jerry came along. By the time he was thirty-four, when he had Marcy, he was a different man—he *was* a man, that is, and capable of learning from past mistakes. I just can't let Jerry's singular account go uncontested. A man grows up, he matures—how long do we hold his youthful mistakes against him?

Consider, for instance, how Charlie took Jerry in the minute he saw him sitting on the porch steps outside the house on Vermilion—took him in, no questions asked. He loved Jerry. If something was making the boy uneasy at his mother's house, he would put an immediate end to it. He threw the doors open wide. He gave Jerry his own room. A year went by. Jerry was a pimply-faced sixteen-year-old just discovering marijuana when he came up from the basement one day and failed to close the door behind him. Marcy happened by a minute later, not quite two yet, lurching off walls inside her walker. Charlie saw her come along out of the corner of his eye. He was at the kitchen table having a bowl of cereal. Then he saw one of the wheels of the walker slip from the smooth floor and catch in the doorway, on the threshold of the abyss. He knew he had maybe three seconds. He flew from the table but did not make it in time. That Marcy survived that fall was something of a miracle. She was diagnosed with a concussion at Lake View Hospital and kept for observation overnight. What did Charlie say to the boy at the first opportunity? Hey, he said, accidents happen. Don't beat yourself up. He knew he didn't need to pile on. Jerry felt terrible enough. These rumors that somehow Charlie loved his second family more than his first and that he favored his children from that union more than he did Jerry are just completely unfounded and not supported by the facts.

Now, I know what you're thinking. Jake Barnes has played his hand. He sides with Charlie and can't be trusted. He's unreliable. Yeah, right. Like reliability exists anywhere anymore, like that's still a thing.

For Love of Proffit

30

He made it to European Motors in record time. Finding himself with a moment to spare, he paid a visit to Nordstrom Rack, the discount clothing store. He could not stop replaying the conversation with Jerry in his mind, and nothing shed stress for Steady Boy quite like deals, steals, and lucky finds. For the next twenty minutes, he was the picture of concentration as he plucked potential purchases off the spinning racks, regarding each one skeptically while doing his best to put Jerry out of mind. While he shops, let us turn our attention to the Doolander.

Premised on that ancient folk toy the gee-haw whammy diddle, the Doolander's antecedents also included the Day-Glo Dragonfly and the hand-powered whirligig. Here is how it came to be: Happy Necker, real name Julius, was manning the grill at Kickapoo State Park on a warm day in September shortly after Nixon's second inauguration. Known for his good cheer and for co-owning the Cadillac dealership in town, Happy was one of Charlie's oldest pals and in his element behind a grill: a maestro with a spatula taking requests. The day was blue, the leaves just starting their death spiral into beauty. Happy's wife, a caseworker for Public Aid named Wyla, sat with Charlie's second wife, Barbara Lefurst, on a patchwork of picnic blankets, taking sips of that seventies special, Riunite Lambrusco. At that time, men in America dressed up like cubist paintings: Happy was wearing an atrocious combination of plaid and argyle, while Charlie, sporting a respectable beard, wore a light cardigan and smoked a briarwood pipe, the picture of a professor, but from the waist down he was a pro-baller as seen on TV, with pale knees and tube socks. He had stepped in dog shit earlier that day and, as if in a bad dream, spent the rest of the afternoon dragging his foot across the grass, trying to rid himself of a haunting stench that might have been all in his head.

A stray dog sauntered onto that scene, the culprit, perhaps, of Charlie's misfortune. Something about its appearance among them gave Happy an idea. Spontaneous, witty, always seizing on the creative urge, Happy had a certain genius for what might be called the unlikely inevitable. Despite being in the company of friends, many of whom were in the dark about his male pattern baldness, Happy set down his spatula and peeled off his toupee while calling for the dog's attention. What happened next was between Happy and the dog, a lark, a light little gesture incidental to being shared, and yet every picnicker seemed to turn at the moment Happy tossed his hairpiece as he might have a Frisbee while exhorting the mutt to fetch.

The toupee had no right to behave in the manner that it did. It had no aerodynamic lift. And there was no wind. A lump of latex and fur, it deserved to drop in the heavy air like a wet rag. On the contrary, it soared. Like something piloted by John Glenn, it glided over acorns and buckeyes, past picnic tables and elm trees. The rapt audience fortunate enough to catch this maiden flight held its collective breath, eyes wide in every head, before all at once turning to one another and collapsing in tears of laughter. For the dog had caught it! Heeding Happy's command, the stray mutt leaped into action, launched itself with a twist, and came down with the toupee, which it tore into as if snapping the neck of a squirrel. It was all so perfectly unlikely and utterly hilarious. Happy, standing erect and grinning wide, clapped both hands to his newly bald head and, turning to his friends, said the most remarkable thing Charlie had heard in all his time on earth. He said, "Looks like I'm a free man!" Having lived in mortal fright of losing his hair since he and Charlie were freshmen at Danville High, Happy, at thirty-five, was liberated at last. He would never again wear a hairpiece of any kind. It was as if Charlie had had the sudden resolve to remove his dentures and, winding them up like a pair of novelty choppers, set them down on the plaid blanket and let them chatter their way past the potato salad, a carefree spirit at home in the world. He just couldn't imagine it.

Nor could he shake the image of that flying toupee. The ticklish absurdity of such a thing taking flight and its proven ability to make people laugh whispered in his ear of monetary potential. Like the Hula Hoop before it, the Slinky, the Frisbee, the Pet Rock and the pogo stick, he could see it selling from sea to shining sea. But it was first and foremost a testament to joy, an ode to the ridiculous that put beauty before the bottom line and fun before riches and fame. The Original Doolander was his bid to satisfy an itch (as persistent in him as masturbation ever was) to be the man with the common touch—the cause of envy in other men and the object of their love.

He came up with the name before securing a patent, then borrowed six hundred bucks from Happy to hire an engineer.

"I would like your God's honest opinion of the toy I have in mind," he wrote that man in their opening correspondence, "if you think it's catchy and/or feasible, or just a waste of time and money."

The developer's reply was enthusiastic. He believed that the Original Doolander, the World's First Flying Haircut™, was interesting, probably ingenious, and almost certainly guaranteed to be a smash hit. With the prototype in hand, Charlie set out to entice financial backers. He organized meetings with bankers, made cold calls to financiers, wrote letters to Walt Disney and Spud Melin. He took the prototype around to local toy stores, looking for an angle, an opening of any kind. He hired an illustrator to reconstruct in a light seventies sketch the scene of the Doolander's first launch (ultimately executed by way of a rack-and-pinion device) and other wholesome images, promoting family fun in a Doolander "fact sheet" and brochure.

Still, too many people failed to get it.

"Why a toupee?"

"How does it work again?"

"Is there really a need for this in the marketplace?"

During his bout of stress shopping at Nordstrom, he discovered with great pleasure a pair of Brunello Cucinelli corduroys in fire-engine red, discounted to sixteen dollars on account of changing fashions and some irregular stitching. It was a real nice find, and he purchased them before walking out to his ailing Saab. I could not tell you where he was in that infernal suburban sprawl. Elk Grove Village? Evanston? I don't have the same superhuman grasp of suburban geography, with its parkways, toll plazas, and frontage roads—just ask Jerry about my sense of direction—as I do the little island called Key West, from the salt ponds to Fort Zachary Taylor. But Charlie, with his sixth sense, zipped out of the Nordstrom parking lot and aimed his car at European Motors like a heat-seeking missile. We pick up with him there, third from the end in a row of black vinyl seats, next to one patched with electrical tape, its yellow stuffing still pushing through. The time was one o'clock, the town Morton Grove. The difficult morning was behind him. He sat with his legs crossed, quietly reading the paper in a touring cap and floral button-down.

So much has been made of this man's many failures—entrepreneurial, matrimonial—that now, as he enters the wide and hectic world, an overdue compliment must be paid: he could really wear a hat. Most guys can't. Your best friend from high school, for instance, just looks like he's lost his bongos, while the rest are bald guys ashamed (contra Happy Necker) of having gone bald. Hat wearing among the masculine sex in the modern day is generally a bad idea... until it's brought off in spectacular fashion by one who, by dint of age, or bearing, or natural-born gift, can meet the hat halfway. Steady Boy put on a Kangol cap and immediately assumed the air of a journeyman guitarist. He donned a bowler and became Fred Astaire. Even the tartan tam-o'-shanter, whose sole purpose on earth is to turn men into fools, rendered him an ancient Scottish chieftain.

Typically at times like these, when he was hostage to car troubles, procrastinating Charlie Barnes, struck by a pang of conscience, had the urge to buckle down and take care of business... but, being out, saw no choice but to read the paper. Having lost its crisp antemeridian integrity, it required frequent shaking out and propping up, which he did with all the commotion of a man making a campfire. The others waiting with him, dignified cabbage heads sitting in anonymous silence, had resigned themselves to their mutual fate. It was companionable in its way, even reassuring: one had only to sit back and relax while the mechanics pursued their repair work... the howling was nowhere but in his own head.

Like Jerry, who so loved, despite his lies, to touch the true and contact the real, Charlie required a daily dose of straight talk, but he found it not as Jerry did, in religious texts, but in the *Chicago Tribune.* It steadied him. It soothed him. With it, he clucked, stomped, kept score, sorted good from evil, denounced old foes, encountered items of unexpected humor, and brought to bear on the world's nightmare all the reason and perspicacity of an old god. How many times have I stolen a glance at the old man in his recliner absorbed in his nightly ritual, the mouth slack, the mind rapt, the focus so complete he might have been at that very moment on the sidelines of some civil war, or in the stands of the UN, or personally casting a tie-breaking vote in the Senate? Of course, being actually totally powerless, he could do nothing, change nothing... but of late, there was at least hope and change. Send the clowns packing, he silently urged his countrymen between news items as he turned the page, and make way for the Black guy. Let the Black guy with the funny name show them how to conduct themselves with class. Let the Black guy with the whip-smart wife restore some goddamn decency to this great nation after the fiasco that was the last eight years. Charlie was not Black, but Frank Santacroce was—his best friend from Danville, another Black guy with a funny name—and Charlie loved Frank. He believed in Obama. He would have voted for Obama even if he *wasn't* Black.

And fifteen short minutes after he began reading, he felt better, for he had taken chaos in hand. Then he turned the page, politics gave way to economics, and he concluded (not for the first time) that there was no solution, none, and that this life was an absurd farce inside of which we were trapped with no way out.

"Seems another chapter of greed"—thinking twice, he qualified with *unbridled*—"of unbridled greed has been written," his letter to the editor of the *Chicago Tribune* began, as his eyes veered off the page and gradually lost their focus in the waiting room of the auto shop, "and once again, it is the little guy left holding the bag." He committed each word to memory, intending to transcribe and electronically submit this pithy, poison-laced missive the minute he got home, though they were no more likely to run it than any of the previous hundred he had composed. "I've been trying for decades to make an honest living in the world of finance, and it's only now, after reading your September 12 article 'Dubious Lending Practices Spurred Housing Crisis,' that I must conclude that my efforts were doomed from the start. Many people are losing their homes. I'm one of the lucky ones. But I'm also sixty-eight years old. What do I do with my life now that I have lost my faith in finance, in capitalism, in the American dream, and have nothing with which to replace them? I am at a loss as to how to... how to..."

How to what, Charlie?

How to carry on. The dream is dead, the life is over. And what was the point again? So that I might scam rather than be scammed? But that was not how I hoped to live my life. And now, in the wake of a massive, historic, global scam, I'm taking a clear-eyed sober look at all the pretty fictions I've lived my life in pursuit of, finally revealed for what they are. I took them for real. I took them for fair. I took them for possible. Indeed, I believed them to be always just right around the corner.

Let the record show how close he came that day, in 2008, to denouncing, long before the time of hope and change gave way to an era of demagoguery and despair, the degenerating machinery of his country as well as the animating force of his life: the inalienable right to score big, join the ranks of the filthy rich, and screw the rest. This was just one of many reasons he got so mad when Jerry reminded him of how much he had, admittedly, once upon a time, admired that goddamn Jimmy Cayne.

The howling was interrupted by his cell phone. It was Marcy calling from Deer Park.

"Oh, Daddy," she said. "I'm so sorry I was mean to you earlier. It was so dumb."

Gone was the contentious jerk and gleeful punisher who made life hell for dissenters and outsiders—he knew it at once. She had been replaced by her mellower counterpart, who valued perspectives other than her own and endeavored to see the big picture. This was the Marcy we knew and loved, her sharp transition part and parcel of her bipolar lunacy. He had it again, his daughter's goodwill. Her high regard? It was possible. All would be lost if his baby girl did not look up to him, at least a little. He lived for that. If she criticized him, as Jerry did, if she scorned him, he would lose heart.

"I love you, Daddy," she said, "more than anyone. Don't you know that?"

He removed the phone from his ear. The emotions of the day, its current of beauty, the urge to live, the fight still in him, yet the resignation, too, the weariness and frustration of keeping dissolution at bay, the news of Evelyn, the war with Jerry, the pointless self-pitying phone calls...but Marcy loved him. She said so. It was enough. He put the phone back to his ear.

"Oh, honey," he said. "How much better I feel now. Thank you."

"Do you forgive me?"

"Of course I forgive you, sweetheart. Do you forgive me?"

"But you did nothing wrong, Daddy. I had no right to doubt you, and no reason to, either. A few past scares should never be held against anyone. The good Lord knows I've had one or two of my own. It was just so dumb. And of course I'll fly home, Daddy. Of course I'll help you."

Her devotion as a little girl, her large and trusting eyes, and how she reached for his hand. It was enough.

"Thank you, honey. That's so wonderful to hear. And so generous of you, too. However—"

He was cut off.

"So I've just gone ahead and done it, Daddy. I'm flying in tomorrow at nine a.m."

"Hold on," he said. "Flying in where?"

"Chicago," she said. "I'm only sorry I didn't do it sooner."

There was a long pause.

"You bought a ticket and everything?"

"Don't ask me what it cost, okay, Daddy? They really gouge you when you fly next day."

"Jeez," he said. "You paid extra?"

"It's just money," she said.

"I'm touched," he said. "But I have to be honest, Marcy. I really wasn't expecting you to come through. Just how expensive was the ticket?"

"It was massive, Daddy. And I had to quit my job."

"You had to *what?*"

"That had nothing to do with you," she said. "It was a long time coming. My boss is an ass. I've been fed up forever. This was just the last straw. I even tried explaining to him about pancreatic cancer, how awful it is—"

"Did you read up on pancreatic cancer?"

"Of course I did, Daddy. You asked me to."

"I wasn't sure you would take the time."

"Of course I took the time. Why wouldn't I take the time?"

"I don't know," he said. "That was kind of you, anyway."

"It's awful," she said. "It's just an awful disease."

"It is awful."

"It moves really fast," she said. "So I was like, 'Look, here are the facts, this is my father, I have to go,' and he was like, 'Not so fast,' so I was like, 'Well, then, go screw yourself. I quit.'"

"You quit your job just to come see me?"

"Well, no," she said. "I quit because I'm fed up, my boss is an ass, and to come see you."

"I'm really very touched," he said.

"Hold on a second, Dad. Someone's calling me on the other line." She paused. "Wow, that's weird," she said. "That's Jerry calling. Jerry never calls me. Isn't that weird?"

"Jerry's calling you?"

"I should go. I should see what he wants."

"No, don't go, Marcy. Don't talk to Jerry right now. Talk to me."

"But I have to go anyway, Dad. I still have to clean out my desk and get ready for tomorrow."

"Let him call back, sweetheart. Let Jerry call you back tomorrow, or next week."

"I'll send you an email with all my flight information and I'll see you tomorrow. Oh, and Daddy?"

"Don't talk to Jerry, Marcy."

"You're going to beat it. I just know you are."

She hung up.

31

He pocketed his cell phone and walked over to the plate-glass window where, for a calm moment, he watched the mechanics at their work. He knew nothing about cars. How to turn a key, how to pop the trunk—that was about it. Now he marveled at how these bantering, hammering, cheery men knew by heart how to diagnose and repair big machines. They were playing their humble part, participating . . . he used to look down his nose at guys like this. Coming of age in a heartland full of gearheads and drag racers, he wanted no part of life in a garage. He wanted an office with a desk and a Rolodex and a gold nameplate. Now he wondered if the simple satisfaction of making an engine run smoothly again might be worth all the money and status imaginable. What had he been grasping for all these years when a wrench was within reach the whole time? He was on the brink of an even greater revelation about real value in the world when his cell phone began to ring.

"Well, well, well."

It was his kid brother, Rudy.

"Calls frantically all morning long . . . by the afternoon, you can't find hide nor hair of him."

"Sorry, Rudy," he said. "Busy day here."

"Chippin' In," Rudy said. "You want my gut, or what?"

He'd been ignoring his brother's calls since hanging up on him. Now he knew it was time to face the music, as he would live and not die—might just live forever. Chippin' In had to stand up to scrutiny if he hoped to make it a reality . . . and who better to tear it to pieces (as your potential investor might) than Rudy Barnes, peddler of dog pills and skeptic of practically everything else?

"You think you can kill me, Rudy?" he said. "Nothing can kill me, man. Go on, give it your best shot."

"Who's trying to kill you, Charlie?" he asked. "Charlie, you feeling okay?"

"Give it to me, Rudy. Come on."

There was a long pause.

"I love it, Charlie."

"You love it?" he said. "My Chippin' In?"

"It has enormous promise."

He couldn't believe it. Rudy never liked his ideas. He was a tough critic. But there was a reason his vitamin empire employed over two hundred and twenty people and had recently gone public, making its founder a millionaire, and why he continued to serve VitaSource as its CEO and sat on the boards of Whole Foods and PepsiCo: Rudy knew a good idea when he saw one.

"Hold on," he said. "Rudy, have you spoken to Mom today?"

"To Mom?"

"Lives in Peoria? Suffers from restless leg?"

"Is there a reason you think I might have spoken to Mom?"

But why spoil the moment? The man's encouragement was so rare. And disillusionment was so dreary. Here was a dream to live by. Was Rudy's polite deceit really something he should probe and puncture, just to be free of illusion?

"You know what?" he said. "Never mind. Forget I asked. Glad you liked it."

"Charlie," Rudy said. "Are you sick?"

"Sick? No. Why do you ask?"

"Are you sure?"

There was a long pause.

"If I was, Rudy, would that change your opinion of Chippin' In?"

"No."

"Are you sure?"

"I'm sure."

There was another long pause.

"Then no," he said, "I'm not sick. I had a scare recently, which I might have mentioned to Mom, but that's over with now, and I'm feeling better than ever."

"That's good news," Rudy said. "That's very good."

"Any second thoughts, then, before we wrap this up? Snide qualifiers? Totally undermining last-minute reversals?"

"I mean it, Charlie," Rudy said. "Go forth and conquer. It's a great idea."

32

Suspended, suddenly, in a mental bubble of well-being, Steady Boy tried returning to his paper, but he had too much to do now and could no longer sit still. There was the logo, the trademark, the color palette, the marketing plan, and the angel investors.

"Pierre!" he cried, knocking twice on the plate-glass window overlooking the garage and beckoning into the office the owner and head mechanic of European Motors.

Pierre Rabineau was a pale-blond, pear-shaped Frenchman of sixty or so, possessed of a notable limp and a walrus mustache, who had been working on Charlie's Saab for the past fifteen years. Together, they treated the old car like their delicate and ailing ward, two solicitous guardians of the Scandinavian machine on behalf of a god who loves antiques. Rabineau swung the door open and limped into the waiting room, cleaning his fingers with an inky rag. In that single gesture, there were implied other rags, other garages, and piles of manuals, and the history of engines, and dreams of heirlooms rescued from junkyards, and the Alsatian *père* who held Rabineau's hand while heroes zipped by in prototypes on a Paris-to-Brest road race and the zinc bars served cold lager.

"Pierre, I'm afraid I have to leave."

"But your car, it is not fixed."

"How much longer?"

Still moving the grease around his fingers and rag, the Frenchman replied, vaguely but with a sense of magnitude, "You have an engine problem."

"Right," he said.

He didn't care at all for what he was about to do next—and neither do I.

It is an admirable impulse to want a man near and dear to the heart to do the right thing, and equally admirable to want to spare him censure for doing the wrong thing. I still recall being eight years old and vaguely sensing that other men might not regard Charlie Barnes with the same admiration I did, as when he ran for public office and placed fourth out of four, or got lectured at by a man in the hardware store, or declined a fistfight in the YMCA parking lot, and on each of these occasions I was sad for him and angry for us both. I wanted to knock his detractors out cold. Likewise, now, I hate to think that you might be losing patience with him because he is failing his best self, or makes a poor ideal for mankind, or simply isn't worth your time and attention. I owe this man my life. I owe him everything. But I owe you the truth: he lied to Rabineau. He admitted as much to me personally. Am I at liberty to workshop away all that was unpalatable about my father, white-out his mistakes, in an effort to make merely likable a man I loved?

"Let me ask you a question, Pierre," he said. "How much do you know about pancreatic cancer?"

Pierre Rabineau, who lost an aunt in Cassis to pancreatic

cancer, expressed outrage at cancer in general before issuing a small, silent gesture with his blackened finger. He led Steady Boy through the garage and out back where, with a flourish, he presented a white Porsche parked in high contrast against a red brick wall: a loaner, if he wanted it.

"This thing? For me?"

"Take it. Drive it. Enjoy."

In his defense, Charlie didn't expect his lie to result in a loaner like this. He just wanted his Saab back. But if this fine car were really on offer . . . Rabineau opened the door for him. Guiltily but gingerly, he climbed in. Then Rabineau shot his inky digit into the air once more.

"I forget the key."

While Rabineau returned to the front office, Charlie surveyed the beautiful analog dashboard, the steering wheel coiled as tight as a Luger and, just past the space-age contouring of the windshield, the Porsche chevron, a pricey blaze at the edge of the hood. Feeling lucky and full of good will, he took out his phone and called Marcy in Deer Park.

"Kinder Morgan, Bethany speaking."

"Good afternoon, Bethany. Charlie Barnes calling for my daughter Marcy. We spoke earlier. I know she's quit, but I was hoping I might still catch her—or, rather, that I could leave a message with you and that you might catch her."

"Would you prefer her direct line?"

"Well, no," he said. "No, I think it would be better if you just told Marcy that, as it turns out, I don't have pancreatic cancer after all. I have a clean bill of health, which, if we think about it, is actually cause for celebration. But just because I don't *need* Marcy to fly in doesn't mean I don't want her to. I would love to see Marcy. We don't get together nearly often enough. So would you please tell her that I plan on picking her up at O'Hare tomorrow no differently than I would have if I *was* dying of cancer and taking her to lunch? Great benefit here being I'm not dying. I'll even be able to eat a meal with her. What else? No, I think that about covers it."

There was a long pause.

"She's standing right here," Bethany said. "Would you like to speak to her directly?"

Before he could reply, Marcy had taken the phone from Bethany. "What could you possibly have to say to me right now that would justify the lies you've told today?" she asked him.

Fierce, harsh, unforgiving: gone, again, was any hint of sympathy, any sweetly calling him Daddy. He could tell the change from her tone of voice. It was all accusation and blame, as her mother's had been. These Jekyll-and-Hyde types—they turn on you in an instant.

"I gather you talked to Jerry," he said. "Well, good news: I don't have pancreatic cancer."

Rabineau reappeared with the key to the Porsche, and Charlie quickly changed his expression to that of one recently diagnosed with pancreatic cancer.

"What comes over you?" she asked. "What prompts something like this?"

"I was reading the internet wrong."

"Do you know what Mom used to say about you, Dad?"

"Your mom used to say a lot of things about me, Marcy."

"She said she married a con man."

Rabineau handed him the key, which he accepted with a sobriety befitting the occasion.

"And I would stick up for you. I would stick up for you and stick up for you. But that's what you are, Dad. You're a con man, and you're a fraud."

"Oh, come on, Marcy. Don't say that!"

Bruce Crowder would have agreed. So would Jerry. But he had improved Bruce's mother's holdings by 400 percent. And Einsohn had screwed him. But he was probably doomed from the start: his mother, his teeth. Now his son felt free to lie to him, while Larry Stoval, a good friend from long ago, couldn't be bothered to call him back. But Rudy liked his Chippin' In. And he had Barbara. Charlie looked up at Rabineau, frowned on account of his illness, and turned the engine over. Its roar was pure romance.

"You should try telling the truth for once in your life," Marcy said.

She hung up.

33

He had tried telling the truth once, in what was probably his finest hour. He believed, by coming clean, he would end the pretense and fakery and be real at last—at least before the woman he loved. He had no idea he was doomed.

That woman was Marcy's mother.

At the time they met, Steady Boy was working at Old Poor Farm, a relic of the sixties and a real do-gooder's delight.

The physical structure was an unlikely brick manor on seventy acres of farmland, entirely reminiscent of a sanitarium. An incongruity among the distant red barns and silos, the main building sat front and center along the Catlin-Tilton Road, showcasing a dozen Doric columns and flanked by east and west wings. From proper poor farm during the Great Depression to private nursing home throughout the forties and fifties, the building had returned to the county's possession by 1960, when it began housing every last state agency and charitable organization in Vermilion County. Welfare was on the ground floor, as was Public Aid, Head Start, the Job Corps—any number of state-funded acts of kindness that, in the era of Jimmy Cayne, just sound utterly fantastical. Union chapters, Catholic charities, prevention leagues, agencies for affordable housing and economic opportunity, consumer protections, land conservancy, clean water . . . please pardon Charlie Barnes as he drifts off, on his drive to First Baptist in a borrowed Porsche, into a reverie about Lyndon Johnson.

Old Poor Farm, then, was not just a physical address but also a local designation for the helping hand. In 1973, the year Charlie and Charley met, the political concept known as *inevitable need* had not yet undergone its public-relations decay into *tax burden* by canny operators on the right. When it did, around the time of Reagan's triumph, the state's helping hand closed up its fingers—and became a fist. Old Poor Farm dissolved as a concept and died out as a destination vital to the public welfare. But before that could happen, all sorts of folks found their purpose out on the Catlin-Tilton Road: social workers, educators, feminists, EST adherents, bleeding hearts in bell-bottom jeans, self-described bull dykes prone to organizing softball tournaments, early adopters of carob bars and the five-mile jog, and other assorted Corn Belt misfits drawing a government salary in the name of a better world. Charlie served as the executive director of the Vermilion County chapter of Big Brothers Big Sisters, the mentorship program.

Now, you might be saying to yourself, the executive director of a mentorship program . . . this *is* Steady Boy we're talking about, right? The onetime clown, would-be franchiser, inventor of the Doolander and Endopalm-T, and the commissioned salesman working all the angles at Jonart's and Sears—when, and how, had he so pivoted that, by 1973, he was out of the corporate game and earning a living doing social work?

No doubt it would be easier to maintain the illusion that he hungered after profit all his days, a wannabe Warren Buffett cluttering the margins of the American marketplace with his schemes and knockoffs. But there was always this side to my father, the do-gooder side. It was the Doolander versus the do-gooder, his heart divided between the chamber of commerce and the March of Dimes. It was there from the beginning. While a bid for fame and fortune, the Clown in Your Town™ had its roots in his affection for children. He hoped to help his paying customers at Jonart's as much as he would later enjoy their commissions. When he founded TTAA, he was bringing together these two sides of himself, the black-hatted hope to make a killing alongside the white-shoe promise of fairness and probity. It should surprise no one that he gave himself over for a time to the kind of work that was Charley Proffit's only calling in life.

But Charlie & Charley did not meet at Old Poor Farm. They met at Red Mask.

A Calling for Charlie Barnes

A Danville institution and art lover's delight, the Red Mask Players was an amateur troupe founded in 1936. The theater itself, a former Presbyterian church, was an old brick structure with an ivy-covered turret that suggested a medieval fairy tale unfolding inside. Its modest lobby was carpeted in plush red, its walls draped in folds of red velvet. One bobbed through it all dreamily as if on a princess's pincushion. Dust as ancient as a Greek chorus swirled in the spotlights, and the musty odor of antique costumes hung in the air backstage. Charlie could still reconstruct on his retinas, forty years later, the sharp negative of the makeup mirror lights, the hot blinding lights of the main stage, and those gentle pools of blue light backstage that cut the sacred darkness on nervy opening nights. The thick clotting smell of pancake makeup and the toxic catch of wig glue in the dressing rooms were, back then, all he required to become drunk with excitement. But it was his ears that best recalled the delicate magic of Red Mask: the whispers of jitters backstage, the sudden shushes, the rude crashes, the soft murmur from the house before curtain, the roar of shared impressions during intermission, and the muted laughter behind the stage doors while outside the wash of oblivious traffic continued in a steady rain—there was simply nothing to compare to it even now. The dramatics club he exchanged for basketball had delivered Charlie to Red Mask, and only upon standing on its stage did he feel himself equal to life. He took bit parts after high school, had his first star turn in a production of *Blithe Spirit,* and pretty much ran the place after that, directing, producing, even doing a little light choreography.

Charley Proffit was active and engaged everywhere she went,

a fresh peach riding along on a bike or standing on the pitcher's mound at Douglas Park. A leader of young ladies in dugout chants, she would march along the first-base line rattling the chain link to rouse the fans to their feet.

"I don't know but I been told!"

"I don't know but I been told."

"You're down by one and your pitching's gone cold."

"You're down by one and your pitching's gone cold."

"Two, four, six, eight. Who Is Coming to Home Plate? NAN-CY! NAN-CY!"

Then the capper, which she alone knew: that snatch of Steam's popular refrain from 1969, ubiquitous twenty years later in every stadium and arena:

"Nah-nah-nah-nah . . . hey hey hey . . . goodbye!"

She was a romantic, always running late. She loved fifties pop songs, the sock hop and soda fountain, and the movies of Doris Day. The work she did, however, less to earn a living than to serve her God, was poised at the opposite end from the romantic on the spectrum of life: she investigated child abuse and neglect for the state of Illinois. It was a rare temperament that could do that job; she dressed sensibly, in slacks and flats. Charley Proffit did not know David Lynch, who was just then beginning to film his surreal masterpiece, *Eraserhead,* in Philadelphia, but she and Lynch had much in common—or so Chuck would observe to me in passing years later, after a screening of *Mulholland Drive*. That is, only a film by Lynch might hope to contain Charley's contradictions, her Technicolor personality and its sudden switch. (A tendency later pathologized in Marcy.) I have mentioned her resemblance to Mary Tyler Moore; unmask the Moore facade and what resided underneath, in Lynchian revelation, was no freak, criminal, or alien being, but the sworn enemy of those things, and something more terrible still: a born Puritan. All lightness in one scene, all song, all open-window carefree car ride and laughter, at her mineral core she was less forgiving than the judges at Salem and more fire and brimstone than Jonathan Edwards. Charley Proffit could rescue children from unimaginable circumstances *and* hold on to her sanity during her off-hours only by means of this bifurcated soul, but it did not make for easy domesticity. Her first two attempts at marriage swiftly ended in disaster. She was twenty-five years old.

Charlie was thirty-two that night. It was open tryouts, mid-February, 6:30 p.m. Stalking the house seats, already looking pained, he rolled still tighter an old script in his two hands while scrutinizing those auditioning for him. His charisma as a director was of the negative variety: by assuming the role of agony itself, he enlisted in his discontent those who longed for his praise and would work doubly hard to realize their native talents if it were on behalf of Charlie Barnes. Fortunately, he always had one ace in the hole, and that was Alfreda Sneed. He found Freya doing laps in the Danville talent pool while everyone else was either dog-paddling or drowning outright. He had directed her in the previous year's production of *No Sex Please, We're British* opposite a serviceable Glen Glamour, the fine-art appraiser. That star turn earned her her first Katy, "Danville's Oscar." She went on to portray a steamy Blanche opposite his own manly Stanley in summer rep's well-received *Streetcar,* for which they both took home statuettes. He was just then considering how wonderful Freya would be as Maria von Trapp when Charley Proffit appeared. Despite the dim light, he did a double take, and his heart fell out of its socket. He'd never beheld beauty until that night. With her short chestnut bob and stardust freckles, a simple gold cross at her neck, it was as if she had arrived fresh from the very same convent from which Maria herself departs at the start of the Rodgers and Hammerstein musical.

Alfreda, in the middle of her audition, paused. The pause turned to a full stop as her distracted director began to rummage through the shadows, ignoring her. What was he doing? The unfathomable: showing a newbie where the sign-in sheet was. A minute later, Charlie returned down the aisle. "I'm sorry, Freya. Please continue," he said, wondering suddenly if Ms. Sneed might not be more suited for Mother Superior this time around.

"And where are you from, Charley?" he asked when the newbie took the stage for her audition.

"I'm from Peoria," Charley said.

"Ah, Peoria!" he cried, as he gazed off into the middle distance. "The fields of Peoria."

He had said it with such grandeur she wasn't sure what it meant. The fields of Peoria... was that something famous, something she should know about? She laughed just in case. Charlie, meanwhile, proceeded to slap himself mentally. *The fields of Peoria, Chuck?*

After auditions, he invited her to join him at 810 Tap, where they discovered they had four failed marriages between them. And that they had Old Poor Farm in common. He worked in the east wing for Big Brothers, she in the west wing for the Department of Children and Family Services. She stopped by his office the next day.

"So it's true! You do work here."

"Did you take me for a liar?"

She gave that some consideration. "I took you for a performer," she said, and they laughed.

"Come in, come in," he urged.

She was pretty even under the bureaucratic light that plagued Old Poor Farm. Bearded Steady Boy, a landlocked sea captain, was dressed that day in a black blazer with gold buttons and pristine white trousers. As executive director, he spent his time pairing at-risk kids with members of the community, organizing charitable events, and walking in parades. Charley, by contrast, went into homes where hell was unfolding, found children chained to U pipes by parents attempting to potty train, took Polaroids of their black eyes and filthy bedrooms, their louse bites, and documented all this in her loop-de-loop script inside official case files. She carried five or six such files everywhere she went, including, that day, into Charlie's office, where one slipped from her grasp. Forensic Polaroids fanned out across the floor. He bent down to help collect them—and was taken aback. It was a disorienting thirty seconds: there she was, youth and beauty itself, and there *that* was, snapshots of pure evil—bruises, open sores. Jesus Christ, what had they *done* to that child? He looked over at the young lady responsible for confronting such violence. He'd fallen in love the day before. Now he was in awe. If he didn't believe in God, he did believe in those who did His work. She thanked him, and they stood.

"I'm just about to commence a case in Fair Oaks," she said. "Care to tag along?"

She drove a green Pinto. He lit a cigarette without asking

if he could smoke. No one answered at the row house in Fair Oaks. She was leaving behind a business card when the door opened and a man appeared. He quickly retreated back into the darkness. Charley called after him. When he failed to reply, she stepped inside. "Hey, you sure—" Steady Boy began. Personally he wanted the hell out of there and was ready to plead executive-director duties back at Old Poor Farm. But in the end he, too, entered. The stench hit him like a fist. Charley Proffit tried the lights—no luck. They made do with what leaked in through the distant windows. They reencountered the man in no time. In his forties, he was sitting on the toilet, fully dressed, reading a comic book. He was mentally handicapped and couldn't explain himself. In the kitchen, the refrigerator hung open. Some sauce or gravy had hit every shelf on its way down. The warm milk carton looked ready to explode. A foul juice leaked from trash bags piled in a corner. On the countertop, brazen roaches fed on cubes of what looked like stew meat. They did not scurry away even as she clapped her hands over them. Charlie's mind went briefly to the shanty in Westville where he grew up. So hell gets worse. Now he knew how.

A woman lay unconscious under the kitchen table, nude pantyhose rolled down to her ankles. Somehow Charley Proffit knew she was drunk, not dead. She proceeded to the bedroom. He was in over his head, but he'd gone too far to back out. The room was dark, the curtain drawn. He stood in the doorway—and knew they were not alone. It was an uncanny feeling. Charley walked to the window and opened the blind. The crepitations were coming from a bassinet in the far corner. He was happy to let her have the first look.

The executive director had never seen a child failing to

thrive before. The dirty light and the birth defect combined with a distended belly and a visible rib cage to make the listless thing laboring to breathe appear less than human, but the dark swirl of down on top of his head was unmistakable—and how Charlie knew he was looking at a newborn baby. Without that, he might have known, but he might not have wanted it to live. Upon noticing the dark down, he would have done anything for him.

"Do we pick him up, Charley?"

"Do not pick him up, you're likely to tear the skin. This baby needs... listen to me," she said. "I need you to look at me. I have to be sure you register what I'm about to tell you."

"I'm registering."

"Find a phone. Do not stop until you do. Call 911. Have police and an ambulance come to 1639 Fairchild. What is that address?"

"Sixteen thirty-nine Fairchild," he said.

What a first date! In point of fact, it was their second: only the night before, they were sitting in 810 Tap getting to know each other. I bring that rendezvous up once again in connection with the woman passed out on the kitchen floor, the birth mother with the taste for drink. Soon, Charlie would recall how he knew her: she was a regular barfly at that Danville watering hole, with its stuffed pheasants and fish lining the wood-paneled walls; indeed, if memory serves, and why should it, but here it must, as it often will, despite its being a *Barnes* memory, that very woman was sitting at the far end of the bar when Charlie and Charley entered for a drink after leaving Red Mask at the conclusion of auditions. That would mean, then, while the new mother was tying one on, downing boilermakers at a mean clip, and the two romantic hopefuls were nursing their gin and tonics in a booth in back, that baby was slowly starving to death in the Fair Oaks row house at 1639 Fairchild, where all three of them would convene the following day—an irony never lost on Marcy, who found this bit of family lore darkly amusing, illustrative of the compromise that would inevitably follow any attempt by her hapless parents to repair the world.

But for all her cynicism, Marcy can't deny that an innocent life was saved that day, and during a pretty singular second date. Boy, did they have a story to tell at mixers and fondue nights! They had saved a baby. Nothing half so momentous had marked earlier courtships, and it made this one feel like kismet. What was next for this crusading couple? The child, whose medical fate they carefully tracked, was transferred to the university hospital in Champaign-Urbana, where he slowly recovered and began to thrive despite severe malnutrition and a foreshortened limb—a "flipper arm." He was released from the hospital and placed in foster care. Charlie gave Charley the lead in the play. They were engaged to be married by the time she went off book.

The spring production of *The Sound of Music* at the Red Mask theater was a rousing success. The director received a standing ovation, the star two dozen roses. The cast party, a drunken sing-along on shag carpeting, was full of bawdry and torch songs. Striking the set a day later, their tears turned nostalgic. The following weekend, they drove to Peoria to marry, which they did in the backyard of the house in High Point that belonged to her aunt and uncle. The wedding bower overlooked a majestic view of the forest preserve.

"Look, Charley," he said to his bride during their reception, gesturing out at the beautiful green valley stretching below them and the river that ran through it. "The fields of Peoria."

They honeymooned in Chicago at the Drake Hotel. She bought him a wedding gift of a red velvet robe and a matching pair of travel slippers. They returned to Danville and began their life together. They had just signed the mortgage for the house on Vermilion Street when he suggested a road trip.

"A road trip?"

"Let's take a look at California," he said.

"Take a look at it?"

"Sure," he said. "Hollywood. Why not?"

"Chuck, have you lost your mind? We have jobs. We can't just up and leave for California."

"We'll tell them something."

"Tell them something? You mean . . . lie?"

"I mean we'll give them a good excuse. Look, Charles"—he loved to call her Charles—"we won't be gone long. A month or two at most."

"A month!"

"Three weeks, then. Come on, don't worry. Our jobs will be waiting for us when we get back."

They stayed with his cousin Noreen in a rented bungalow off La Brea. Charley would wake in the night with morning sickness, crawl to the bathroom and hug the porcelain, and wonder what in hell she was doing newly married, abruptly pregnant, and emptying her stomach into another woman's toilet in the state of California. Her new husband, meanwhile, was going on auditions. Over a hundred in twelve days, according to his own estimate thirty-five years later. Navigating blind with the Thomas Guide, scrounging under the seats for gas money, Steady Boy was trying to make it in Hollywood. Blame "Danville's Oscar," wig glue, the standing ovations. He believed he owed it to himself.

Things soured quickly with his cousin. Noreen liked to drink and entertain men, and Charley, who was chronically ill her first trimester, longed for silence and rest. The two women quarreled. After another long day of demoralizing cattle calls, Charlie arrived home to all-out war. Untethered and unhappy, his new wife finally demanded they cut the trip short.

Oh, well. Can you blame a man for trying? But here's the thing: on the drive home, blame himself he did. Stupid, stupid, *stupid* Steady Boy! It was the same old shit, the very same pie-in-the-sky nonsense that had gotten him into such trouble with his first two wives. How many pipe dreams needed to burst before he reconciled himself to a fate that—oh, hell, didn't even look half bad: a beauty on his arm, a new family on its way, a home on Vermilion Street all his own, and renown within the local community as a man who knew how to stage a good show? Why must there be more, huh? Looking for more had been, so far, just a guaranteed way of losing it all.

"I just realized something," he said, as they hit evening traffic outside Denver on the drive home. "It should have been you."

They hadn't spoken for two hundred miles. "Me what?"

"On those auditions," he said. "Of the two of us, Charles, you're the star. Not me. If someone had a shot, it was you."

"But I don't give a damn about that stuff, Charlie," she said. "There are children suffering out there."

To his great relief, their jobs were indeed waiting for them on their return, as he had promised, and now, to himself, he resolved never to pull a stunt like that ever again. What a damned dumb thing to do! Looking back—like a man on death row given a last-minute reprieve—he was overjoyed to be home, to be married, the recent past dead and buried, and forgiven another unaccountable...*swerve,* temporarily saved from his own worst self.

But howsoever correctly he judged Charley to have more talent, it was equally true that he was a poor judge of his own. Some time after their return, he got a call from his cousin. Newly sober because newly pregnant, Noreen was contrite and hoped to make amends. She gave him the phone messages that, for the last seven days of their twelve-day visit, she had withheld from him out of spite: one from this talent scout and another from that. Eight in all. The parts had been cast, the projects finished or set aside. He was months too late.

"You came in with an army cap," one casting director recalled when, one by one, Charlie returned those eight messages. "I remember you well—I liked your smile. Why don't you come in and read for me this Thursday? I have something that might be perfect for you."

"But I'm in Danville," Charlie said, bottle-feeding the new baby.

"Where's that?"

"Illinois."

"Oh," the woman said. "What are you doing all the way out there?"

Almost immediately, they had a hard time getting by on two state salaries. The economy wasn't so great in 1974; there were fuel shortages and sudden price hikes. The house on Vermilion came with a stiff monthly mortgage. It was fifty years old and in need of repair. His Newport kept breaking down, which was a happier fate than the engine fire that put her Pinto out of commission on the corner of Logan and Clay. They survived with only one car for the rest of the year—until the following April, in fact, when they got a little back in taxes, just in time for the roof to cave in. He hated living paycheck to paycheck, hated the chipped tableware they put out for guests, the threadbare towels on the bathroom hooks, the mismatched bed linens, the secondhand furniture, the stains in the carpets in every room...

And yet, what was the cause of this unaccountable happiness?

From the beginning, there was a quality to their lovemaking that resisted the old associations and terms. It *had* been a barnyard urge. So what, exactly, was... this? Among his kin, those country bumpkins, and as a young boy running around tin shacks, and later, as a man among men on sales floors, he came to know the crudest, vilest expressions for what a man did to a woman. Often enough in those few words and phrases, the woman did not so much as even factor in: some penetrating violence was aimed at a void and the man was pleasured—that was the sum of the sex act and how the world taught Charlie to regard it. With Charley Proffit, he began to think for himself: that sort of talk was not just ugly but inaccurate, as disrespectful as it was dead wrong. He had no words for what he and Charley did. By some physical process rooted, he supposed, in the same old body as he'd always had, its senses, receptors, instincts, the pulse quickening as before, the identical perspiring skin and dilating pupils, the endorphins coursing through selfsame veins, he locked eyes with her and entered a trance unlike any before it, entraining their heartbeats, rhythms, blood flow, their animal bodies becoming one...and pure transcendent devotion took hold. It was predicated on stuff outside the bedroom: her work with kids, her conviction, how she stalked a first-base line. It was a martyring, unmanning, dispossessing devotion. All that folktale and matinee-movie stuff he confused for entertainment turned out to be true to life, for this was as close as he'd come to a hero's tale and storybook romance, even as the house came crumbling down around their garden.

Three matching camel humps grading to a gentle stop made the backyard of the house on Vermilion ideal for sledding in the winter months, but in the summer it proved a real pain in the ass to mow. Self-propelled mowers were a luxury then, while dirt-cheap Endopalm-T had been retired long ago. The mower he could afford—a rusted shell over three spinning blades—was always threatening to shear his toes clean off. He was out there one Saturday afternoon, the sun was beating down, the insects were going from bad to worse, he was lightheaded, and every minute or two he had to kill the engine to wipe the sweat off his spectacles—compounding annoyances that might have led him to conclude that he was living a chump's life. But then came the revelation: he didn't mind. There would be a cigarette to reward him when he was done, and a cold glass of sun tea, and cornbread with dinner. He had a wife he admired, and a bathtub without water bugs, a newborn he might still do right by, and another on its way. They took in a foster kid to do all they could to help repair the world, as Charley required, and still others for a night or two while a domestic dispute simmered down or some lone caregiver had sobered up. There were always little Jimmys and Bernadettes, Graylins and Heidis coming and going, kids gone permanently mute or howling from morning to night. But he did his best to locate what was lovable about each one, even the lost causes, and to focus his attention on that until they were gone again. Altogether, these things did not make him a man to reckon with, not a rich or powerful man, but a happy man. Now, *that* was unexpected. When he was married to Jerry's mom, he mowed the lawn only to gain the upper hand in the marketplace that was their marriage. *I mowed for you, now you owe*... that sort of thing. But he wasn't married to Sue anymore. He was married to Charley. They were Charlie & Charley. The old equations no longer applied. *I flatter you, you pay me* was all wrong before the revelations of true love. He mowed to mow now, to acquit a duty without stinting or dodging or asking for something in return. He washed the dishes. He made the bed. He did the laundry. He folded the towels, and upon putting them away again did not worry that he was wasting his time, would die broke, unachieved, a fat nobody... the old equations no longer applied.

To disarm; to perceive, if dimly, a perspective different from your own; to credit that perspective with testimony even when it went against you, even when you couldn't see it yourself; to yield to another's narrative; to own up to your share of obstruction, self-destruction, casual cruelty; to see yourself clearly, as another might, in the context of your blind and busy life, your ambitions, your defenses; to accept, however innocently and belatedly, your culpability in the degradations of the moment, the petty fights, the squandered nights; to mature, to dawn to facts, to move beyond denial, and to move past pride, and to be a man, finally, and not a reflexive bully...all that, too, he was trying on for the first time with his third wife, during that sweet short window when he was his best self.

Move in the direction of love and life gets harder. He had known that much from the time he was sixteen, when he got a job so as to buy a girl a Coke. From dreamy youth to a paperboy pedaling in the predawn overnight. It was in the same spirit that he now decided he must quit Old Poor Farm and go to work at Waukegan Title. He had, God knows, bigger dreams than being regional salesman of the month and taking third in local golf tournaments. But Old Poor Farm didn't pay well, and his wife, the true devotee to the social cause, deserved to pursue her calling without worrying about the car breaking down or the heat getting turned off in winter. And it wasn't all that different from what he'd been doing for years: moving around when it meant more money or he was offered some perk the old gig didn't have.

Now, Charley Proffit didn't know any of that: Charley Proffit was in the dark about Steady Boy's professional past. She had married him for two reasons: his beard, which suggested he might make a good father figure, and his commitment to Old Poor Farm. He came in from mowing, removed his grass-stained tennis shoes, peeled off his tube socks and sweatband, and found his wife at the kitchen table doing paperwork while the baby napped and the foster kid watched TV.

"Hey," he said, "listen, I'm thinking about taking a job with Archie Baker at Waukegan Title."

A suggestion so strange he might have been proposing

another road trip to California. In the three years since that little swerve, her new husband had done much to live up to her expectations. He went to work. He cared for the baby. Now a familiar dread crept back into the pit of her stomach. How could someone who would quit Old Poor Farm to sell title insurance be wise or moral? He was everything she took him for, right: the crusader in God's army with the consistency of a Gregory Peck?

"Are you nuts? Why would you quit Old Poor Farm?"

"It's getting harder and harder to make ends meet."

"God will provide, if we do right."

"Do you really believe that?"

"Heart and soul," she said. "Don't you? What is Waukegan Title? And who is Archie Baker?"

He would have to back up. He would need to explain a few things if he hoped to be understood.

"I don't think I have a life calling the way you do," he confessed. "Social work, I mean. It's not in my blood the way it is yours."

"Since when?"

"Since... forever. What do you mean?"

"I mean this is news to me."

"To be honest, I kind of lucked into the job at Big Brothers."

"Lucked into it?"

"You know Happy Necker, who owns the dealership? Well, Happy has this cousin..."

He went on to explain all about Happy Necker's cousin. Before the cousin got him the gig at Big Brothers, he worked a gig at Gemco, and before that, a gig at Hyster.

"A gig?"

"You know, a job, a full-time job."

"What is Hyster?"

"Forklift assembly," he said.

"Forklift assembly? You assembled forklifts?"

"Not me. The guys in back."

"The guys in back," she said. "Chuck, what the hell are you talking about?"

"Look, I moved around, Charley. Didn't want to just settle. Figured if I kept looking, sooner or later I'd find the perfect thing."

"Old Poor Farm," she said, "is the perfect thing."

"I don't make that much at Old Poor Farm."

"What you make is not what matters. What matters is what you do."

"You see, I've just never thought like that."

"This is all news to me," she said. "How many jobs have you had?"

"Total? Jeez," he said. "Dunno. Never counted."

"Ten?"

He gave it some thought. "Forty, maybe?"

Her eyes bugged out. "Forty?"

"Thirty, forty, somewhere in there."

She was dumbstruck. "How is that even possible?"

She had had one job since graduating from college.

"I guess that's another thing," he said. "I never really got my college degree."

"I thought you went to Michigan State."

"I did *go* there," he said.

"But you didn't graduate?"

The sweat coming on now was of a different variety from

the one he'd worked up while mowing the lawn, and he was feeling a little sick to his stomach. Maybe he should start fudging things a bit, or back away entirely from this ballooning disaster. But he was sick of fudging. He'd been cutting corners his whole life. He had to come clean and be real or risk never deserving such happiness.

"I attended Michigan State for a semester and a half," he said.

She was very confused now. "A semester?"

"And a half."

"Did you study social work, at least?"

"I was a prelaw major."

He could tell by her expression that his attempt to get real was having the perverse effect of making him less substantial with every word, as if he were resolving into a total stranger, and she asked him outright, "Who are you?"

"Who am I? It's me, Charles. Same as before."

If "Buy me a Coke" had inaugurated him into working life and "But I love Marshall" into adult betrayal, each one stripping away an earlier illusion to arrive at some greater degree of reality, "Who are you?" led him to understand that he himself served as the measure of what was real in other people, those who depended on him to be who he claimed to be, a devoted social worker and a man with a college degree. He'd fucked up here, more than he realized. But the error did not reside in the disclosure. The disclosure was just a bookkeeping matter. The error rested in the life, the incongruent life.

"But who is that?"

"The man you married, Charles, come on! Same guy as before."

"But I didn't marry someone with thirty or forty jobs.

I married someone with a career in social work . . . a *life* in social work."

"That was a rough estimate. Could be twenty-five."

"Twenty-five!" she cried. "What the *fuck* is Waukegan Title?"

"It's what pays better! It's what would cover the mortgage and let you keep your job."

"Keep my job? Chuck, I don't *have* a job. I have a sacred commitment to God. And until about ten minutes ago, I thought you shared that commitment with me."

Which of these romantic nuts was more out to lunch? That they found each other, that they fell in love, that they joined together, however briefly, in holy matrimony—was that a miracle or a travesty? The one had never told the truth but was trying to come clean, trying to get real, while the other married only divine immortals and then quickly moved on when they fell to earth.

"What else have you been keeping from me?" she asked.

Move in the direction of love and your life gets harder. He told her about Endopalm-T and the Clown in Your Town™, his faithlessness with his first wife, the paramour's dog he backed over and the blood he blamed on a bobcat. Then he took a deep breath and told her what he'd never told anyone, lover, friend, child, no one. These were very exacting rules, all of which he alone imposed—yet he would not bow out.

"I had my teeth pulled when I was in my twenties," he said. "I wear dentures."

There was a long pause.

"I kind of guessed that," she said.

"You did?"

"I don't care about that."

"You don't?"

"But forty jobs? And no degree?"

She excused herself, left the kitchen table to step inside the bathroom. He could not comprehend how things had gotten so far out of his control. He only meant to share the good news that he had the offer of a better-paying job. Now his marriage suddenly felt precarious, all so that he could be "understood." What a crock. His first bid at honesty was for the other party the confessions of a pathological liar, while what he hoped to be the minting of hard truth and a fresh start turned out to be more like a coin toss: heads I forgive you, tails it's too much. He still didn't know how it would land. Yes, even the plainspoken truth was a matter of perspective. She opened the bathroom door and came forward, halted, stood backlit in the door frame holding her enormous belly with both hands.

"I think my contractions have started," she said.

They gathered the baby and the foster child and drove to Lake View Hospital. Their second child was on the way.

34

It was not Lake View but First Baptist where, several lifetimes later, he arrived in the late afternoon inside a luxury loaner, courtesy of his mechanic. He entered the ER by way of Imaging's well-insulated corridor. He was carrying flowers. His wife's delight at his sudden appearance was tempered by the trouble she was encountering from a lacquered ring of red onion. She had just forked it into her mouth as part of a side salad when Charlie appeared, but then it wouldn't be wrangled any further. She tried clipping it with her front teeth, but the satiny thing remained intact, and when she tried to fish it out with finger and thumb, it slipped from her grasp while Charlie stood by giggling, until at last she pinched it hard and fast and tossed it in the trash.

"Ugh!" she cried, then brightened. "Hello, young man!"

"For you," he said, and presented the lovely flowers. "And look at this, honey!" He held up the pants he found at Nordstrom Rack. "Brunello Cucinellis—for sixteen smackers!"

"You went shopping?"

"I had such a terrible morning," he began. "Got some just terrible news about a client of mine—"

"Charlie!" she cried impatiently. "Did you hear from the doctor?"

"Oh, right!" He smiled. "Guess who has a clean bill of health?"

She came around the nurse's station in her boxy scrubs and leaped into his arms. How good it was to hold her! He had learned his lesson. He had to be a better man for Barbara, a stronger man, invincible even. She loved his suits, his beard, his aftershave, his methodical thinking, his care with a client, his understanding of taxes and interest rates. Danville was behind him; Steady Boy was behind him; as of that morning, pancreatic cancer was behind him. He had his Chippin' In, an idea that even Rudy approved of, and a new pair of pants by Brunello Cucinelli. And he had her. It was enough. He lifted her off her toes and turned her in tight little arcs... when finally they broke off, she had tears in her eyes. She loved him.

He was her silver fox, a good man devoted to helping retirees, and handsome in a hat.

"Did they give you those numbers I wanted?" she asked.

He patted himself down. "Where are they?" he wondered aloud.

Finally he pulled from his back pocket a limp paper napkin. She received it with a laugh at how unceremonious a document it was—"It was the first thing at hand!"—and opened it. The surface was torn here and there by the sharp nib of the pen with which he'd taken down the raw data that only a doctor could make heads or tails of: CA 19-9 levels, amylase readings, his CEA numbers . . . how did his wife know what any of that meant? She asked him to confirm some of his digits.

"Forty? You sure?"

"I believe so."

She frowned. "Have a seat," she said.

"What for?"

"Have a seat, Charlie."

She departed, still looking down at the napkin, still frowning. He did as he was told and had a seat. But he knew. Before she returned, before he saw the man striding alongside her, the graybeard in the lab coat—he was the head of hem-onc at First Baptist—holding in his tan hand the wavering white napkin, he knew: she had frowned.

"And they didn't ask for a follow-up?" the doctor asked.

They were flanking him. It was happening too fast.

"Charlie?"

"Huh?"

He wasn't listening. People floated by him like extras in a dream. He believed he had a clean bill of health, returned to work, took his car in, went shopping. What would he have done with that time had he known? What would he have done with his life? Sixty-eight years old and he was still at a loss. He had known he was dying. There was the weight loss, which was undeniable, as was a change in his bowels. He had gone on pretending anyway. Pretense and fakery. Even now he was only a little wiser, for he knew only that he had passed another day like a dancing bear.

The bill had come due for all the bowing out he'd done. He'd cut corners, disappeared down trapdoors whenever it suited him, and spared himself hassles like an early start time, a dick boss, and the "fundamentals" of two-handed dribbling . . . but there was no bowing out of this. Steady Boy sensed he was in for more hard work than he ever could have fathomed as a younger man, the rules more exacting, the punishment more severe, and at the same time knew the end had come, the dream had died, he would never make a killing, found an empire, or prove his worth. He had been on a wheel—a wheel, no more—and now that wheel was winding down so that he could step off into his grave.

He would not have cared to live out his life as if in a farce, but it was in a farce he was forced to live. There his quarrel with the world began, and there his quarrel with the world ended.

"Why didn't they require a follow-up, Charlie?" Barbara was asking. "Did they give you a good reason, any reason?"

"I don't know," he said. "How should I know?"

It was at that instant that the power went out again, as it had that morning on Rust Road. Again there was no light, no sound, no song, no color, no texture to whatever struck his optic nerve, no dimensionality across the whole of his optic field, no hum or animation in the immediate surround, no life anywhere. Yet when he looked up at the wall-mounted television provided by the hospital, expecting to find it blank, he saw that it continued broadcasting uninterrupted, flickering with images and alive (for all he knew) with sound, and he was forced to admit that the power had not gone out after all. It was all in his head, and this was how life would be from now on.

He turned in agony to face his wife. "I'm someone's plaything," he said.

"Charlie," she said. "We're going to get to the bottom of this."

"I can't die, Barbara."

"No one's dying yet," she said.

"I can't fucking die!" he cried. "Not now! Not yet!"

35

One common side effect of a diagnosis of pancreatic adenocarcinoma, that tower sniper of cancers, is a case of old-fashioned whiplash, as the stunned patient, presented with equivocal and even contradictory indications, turns away from certain doom toward total and intoxicating Dostoyevskian reprieve and back again in a few short days, sometimes within the hour. Such is the fate of one suspected of carrying a time bomb inside him, tucked between the small bowel and the stomach, the faint ticking of which can hardly be discerned until the final second or two before detonation. You have to keep in mind—doctors see different things. There are competing metrics. The same fact set might generate two or more opposing interpretations or narratives. Charlie Barnes, who had the benefit of being married to a medical professional, was in some ways worse off for it, as he became the subject under scrutiny of yet one more of the experts this particular cancer delighted in thwarting. One case in the medical literature notable for the extravagance of its cruel reversals took place at Johns Hopkins in 2003, when a patient from Abu Dhabi received seven diagnoses in two weeks, was finally confirmed in his acute pancreatitis, and died of metastatic pancreatic cancer ten days later. Another apocryphal account Karen found on the internet put GreenMonster49's number of reprieves at no fewer than twelve before they opened him up and found pancreatic adenocarcinoma with widespread arterial invasion. Scanning technology, while awesome, remained crude, bringing certain metaphors to mind, like the bulldozer that was sent to study orchids. It simply wasn't subtle enough, and Charlie's diagnosis changed no fewer than four times. By the following Wednesday, however, pancreatic cancer was all but confirmed, and the next thing he knew they were admitting him; prepping him; handing him the gown; helping him climb up on the gurney; and presently he was being pushed down the corridor in the direction of the operating room. One minute given a clean bill of health; the next, laid out flat and watching the panels of fluorescent light above him tick down like steps in a duel. Might they have made some additional mistake? But no, they were pushing him through the double doors and parking him under the bright—

"Name, please."

Name, date of birth, and a short wait later, a man came and

hovered over him. Without knowing how, he knew the man to be his case manager at Credence Credit Corp., and that he would be doubling that day as his anesthesiologist.

"Can you confirm for me what procedure we're doing today, Charles?"

"No procedure!" he cried. "Let me out of here!"

But when he tried to launch himself off the gurney, he found his hands bound to the metal railings.

"What is this? What's happening?"

"Ready to die? It won't take but a second."

The case manager morphed into Aaron Einsohn, the shyster out of Aurora, who was about to cut out his heart when Charlie woke with a start. The room was dark. His heart was racing. The bleating he had confused for an alarm was his cell phone ringing on the nightstand. It was 2:37 a.m.

"You're a goner, old man," the caller said.

"What?"

"No one survives pancreatic cancer."

He sat up. "Einsohn?"

"I hope you die, you dick."

The phone went dead.

The facts, momentarily obscured by sleep, came flooding back. He had been diagnosed with pancreatic cancer earlier that day.

Barbara rolled over in bed. "Who was it, Charlie?"

He had made so many desperate calls the day of his diagnosis, that number could have belonged to anyone.

36

Things did not go as planned for Charlie after he resigned from Big Brothers in 1977. He thought little of Archie Baker, the owner of Waukegan Title, who ignored his recommendations for expansion and franchising. Steady Boy saw millions in untapped markets where Archie saw only risk. Still, Charlie hit a personal best there. He worked for Archie a full five years before the younger man had enough and gave him the ax.

Charley Proffit of Peoria, Illinois, had never been married to a man who had been fired before. She started fucking Glen Glamour, the fine-art appraiser and Charlie's number one rival at Red Mask. The affair didn't conform to the morals she professed or her Christian bona fides, but if it's consistency you're after, you'll have to read about a different family. No one was more surprised by her behavior than she was. Steady Boy scheduled a vasectomy and filed for divorce. Or was it the other way around? Then he laid seven three-piece suits across the spare tire in the trunk of his Newport and pointed the car north, toward Chicago. Danville had always been a bitter loaf of ashes. He needed a fresh start.

He was still within city limits when he had a bright idea and pulled into the Palmer Bank. He withdrew by pneumatic tube a large sum from their joint account, convincing himself that she deserved it, and now sucking on the free lollipop that came with his cash resumed his travels. But by the time he hit Hoopeston, he had second thoughts: from whom was he taking that money if not his children? He turned the car around. He pulled into the driveway of the house on Vermilion and banged on the front door. Glen Glamour answered his knock in a red velvet house robe and a pair of travel slippers.

"Hello, Charlie. Here to see Charley?"

"You can go to hell, Glen."

"Sure, let me get her for you."

For eight mind-boggling months in 1983, Glen, a home-fitness fanatic and total turd, was for Charley Proffit the be-all and end-all of romantic possibility. He hollered up to his fiancée that she had an old friend at the door before turning back to his vanquished foe and smiling. It was during this time that my father realized Glen was wearing his robe.

"Why, you son of a bitch..."

"What seems to be the problem here?" Charley said upon coming to the door.

"He's in my robe, Charley!"

Glen Glamour peered down at himself. "Oh, is this yours, Chuck?"

"It's not enough that he has my wife. He gets to have my robe, too?"

"Give him his robe back, Glen."

"Sorry, Chuck, I had no idea."

When Glen slipped off his rival's robe, he was revealed to be fully attired in pin-striped suit and tie. He had spied Charlie pulling into the driveway from the second-floor bathroom and tossed that robe over his work clothes before rushing downstairs to answer the door. Charlie took the robe with one hand while thrusting at her the two hundred dollars he had removed from the Palmer Bank with the other.

"What is this?" she demanded.

"Early child support," he said. "Now let me say goodbye to the kids."

"You've already said goodbye to them a hundred times. What is this money?"

"Goddamn it, I want to see the kids!"

"Oh, the *drama,*" she said.

This episode was every bit as broadly comic, the adults as close to cartoons of themselves, as I am depicting—and as I witnessed firsthand from the middle of the staircase overlooking the entrance hall. The rivalry was frightening, and Charley Proffit's cruel indifference toward Charlie unfathomable. I ran down to him in the doorway and threw my arm around him.

"Now, you call me night or day," he said to me. "Your mom's got my number and she knows to let you call whenever you want. And I'll be back to see you every single weekend, hear me? Every weekend, no exceptions. Saturday morning, you expect me, got that? And we'll spend the whole day together just like before. You just forget about Chicago. That's just some place I sleep. My home is right here." He made a fist of his hand and patted my heart. "And no stupid divorce can change that."

That Saturday morning, I did as he told me to do. I woke up at some ridiculously early hour and announced my intention to look out the window for him until I saw the big Newport pull into the driveway. My mother hated this plan. She interrupted it by insisting I eat breakfast, which I had to do at the kitchen table, far from the front window, and again when she demanded I make my bed and tidy my room, and a third time when I was forced to brush my teeth. I did these things half-assedly, testing her patience, and she made me do them over again until I had done them to her satisfaction. Then, reluctantly, I was allowed to return to the front window. He had not offered a specific time for his arrival, so I just had to stay focused on the street and on the cars passing by from both directions until one was the Newport. My mother came a fourth time into the room.

"I want you to go out and play, Jake," she said. "Get some sunshine. It's a nice day outside."

"I don't want to go out and play."

"You're just wasting your time in here. He's not coming. Go outside."

"I'm not wasting my time."

By then, she had discovered that the two hundred bucks he had thrust in her face was not in fact early child support but money taken from their joint account. If she didn't understand why he had withdrawn that money only to turn around and give it right back to her, she needed no more proof that I was banking on the wrong man. I defied her, on the verge of tears, determined not to budge again from my little narrow view of Vermilion Street. I heard each car approach, the faint whirr of tire tread in the distance getting stronger until all at once the whole thing was upon me and swiftly passing by again, that same whirr winding down, fading, gone.

"You're wasting your time!" she shouted. "Go out and play!"

I would not go out and play. I would not leave my place. Time crawled by. Was it an hour later, a full day, a whole year, by the time I had memorized every hole in the window screen and every dead fly on the windowsill?

Now, guess how this ends. Just take a guess.

He showed. There was never a Saturday he *didn't* show. Every weekend, *every single weekend,* it was back to Danville for Charlie Barnes, back to the backwater where his past lived on, where his failure thrived, where the whole sordid mess of his early manhood began. He made the three-hour drive south through Podunk towns, past endless rows of corn, in good weather and bad, to repeat to me time and again in word and in deed: you have not been abandoned. I need you as much as you need me. You have me for life. He was broke as hell, so we spent those Saturdays doing karate kicks in a parking lot or playing games of war on a picnic table in Douglas Park. On the rare occasion he did have money, he would take us roller-skating or to the movies. It was at the roller rink in '84 that Marcy fell and broke her arm, and so on occasion, he took us to the hospital. A lot of the time, we just went to the YMCA and shot hoops. Stan Butkus, the Danville coach with the fused spine, had nothing on Charlie Barnes. To me he was Kareem Abdul-Jabbar, with that same killer hook shot and bright smile. Down on his luck, thrice divorced, driving a Detroit special ten years past its prime, by some miracle, and barring some breakdown, he would always make it back to me. For that alone, although it is a far cry from everything, I've never met a more dependable man than this so-called Steady Boy.

37

If this history of Charlie Barnes has its breaks in chronology and the occasional gaping hole—if, that is, it seems an individually curated, perhaps even highly selective account of the man, and not the straight dope, as it were—well, I wouldn't know how to write it any other way. I couldn't possibly hope to highlight what the man himself would have highlighted or, for that matter, present the arguments he might have presented against what I have chosen to highlight. Imagine that: for every life, not one history but as many as there are people who observed and participated in that life; hundreds, if not thousands, of accounts for just one of the billions of human beings who have lived and died, a staggering proliferation of competing narratives that, no matter how close, can never be reconciled. This explains why my account of Charlie's life, presented here as a strictly factual one, as indeed it is, would not comport with Marcy's, as she might choose to highlight a slightly different fact set, obscure or dismiss what I have chosen to emphasize, and add that portion vital to her that is unknown or unimportant to me. I bring this up only to suggest that I do not have a lock on the truth, provided there is such a thing, and that, in fact, when we consider the necessarily curated nature of any narrated life, its omissions as well as its trending hashtags, if you will, we are forced to conclude that every history, including our own first-person accounts, is a fiction of a sort. Or, as Wallace Stevens put it much more succinctly, "The false and true are one."

He called me, of course, but I was a hard man to locate. Was I in New York or LA? In range or over the Atlantic? I had a flat in Pigneto at the time, but Italy is a confusion of phone carriers, and good luck getting reception in Pigneto. He stood a greater chance of reaching me in Bali, but I was done with Bali. I was falling in love, publishing a book. I was not nearly as married as I am now, with kids and a mortgage and all that.

At that time I would occasionally hole up rent-free in Lars's studio—the one in Johannesburg. The one in Oslo was always too cold. But I was not in Johannesburg or Oslo. I was under contract and in talks with producers, having a grand old time. I was writing stories on trains, filing assignments when I got back to the hotel. In the Cotswolds, a heaven of hedgerows and switchbacks, McEwan owns an estate where he and Annalena will have me, when the grandchildren aren't expected, for as long as I like. There one drinks deep into the night and wakes in Arcadia. But I wasn't in the Cotswolds, either.

When someone did manage to finally get hold of me, it wasn't the man himself but Marcy.

"Listen, I don't know why I'm telling you this, you do what you want, but Charlie's going to call you any minute now and tell you—"

I was getting another call.

"Can you hold on a second, Marcy?"

I clicked over.

"Jake?" he said.

He began crying almost immediately. I clicked back to Marcy.

"He has cancer," I said, completely stunned.

"That's what I was trying to tell you," she said. "He does not have cancer."

I listened as she explained herself, then I clicked back to Charlie.

"Chuck?" I said. "Are you sure you have cancer?"

He gave me the details of his weeklong odyssey, the competing interpretations and the definitive diagnosis, the name of his new doctor and the immediate plan for the days ahead, but not without breaking down again. By the time I clicked back to Marcy, he was doing more than shedding tears. He was heaving with outright terror.

"I really think, Marcy, that he might have cancer."

"He's a liar."

"Liars get cancer."

"Do what you need to do, Jake," she said. "It's none of my business. Like I say, I'm not even sure why I'm calling, knowing that fraud will always have a friend in Jake Barnes."

"Do you have to call him a fraud?"

"What do you suggest I call him?"

"Your father?"

"Call him whatever you want—he doesn't have cancer."

"Okay, hold on."

I clicked over. He was sobbing like a child. I clicked back.

"I really, really, really think he might—"

She hung up. I flew home.

38

For a time, Charley Proffit of Peoria, Illinois, encouraged her children to think of Glen Glamour as their dad. We even called him Dad for a time. That was a weird little interval. Then she kicked Glen out and started dating a different guy, this one a motorcycle owner, which was cool, and though I loved him he failed to reach the live-in stage, to say nothing of exchanging vows with her in holy matrimony. Then came along the guy I will call, in an effort to protect his identity, as is customary in true accounts, Dickie Dickerdick. Dickie was a detective for the Danville PD lately hired by the state of Florida to help conduct the War on Drugs. I didn't care for Dickie and almost didn't get in the van. I wanted Charlie. But Charlie was busy trying to land on his feet in Chicago. He was unavailable. So what did I propose, exactly—submitting voluntarily to foster care while dreaming of a scholarship to Schlarman Academy? I got in the van. I went to Florida. I joined the Boy Scouts and learned to fish.

What's interesting to me about Key West is how, from Miami, it's a straight shot west down US 1. You never need to turn right or left—a simple little bridge connects one island to the next... yet in my mind, it's all forking path, each creeping sky-blue mile another point of no return. It's impossible to say at this late date what Dickie Dickerdick and Charley Proffit hoped to find waiting for them there. It probably wasn't instant disillusionment and an eventual divorce, but something more like this:

After a short, happy zip down to Florida, the new family pulled up to paradise at mile marker 23: Cudjoe Key, an island of mangrove and slash pine, still untamed in '85. Monte's Fish Market and a Tom Thumb convenience store were all that was on offer. The house itself was elevated on stilts, a fantastical feature for flatlanders like us, rising like a real-life castle twenty feet in the air to protect against tidal surges. There was a private beach out back, with sand the consistency of brown sugar, a pair of cabana boys, and a nice new sound system.

Standing in the front yard, two men in dark suits and sunglasses—Secret Service. One raised his wrist as we approached, alerting those on the inside to our arrival.

"Oh, my *God,* Dickie," Charley exclaimed as she got out of the car. "It's the most gorgeous house I've ever seen!" She hadn't looked that happy in a long time, if ever. "But how can we afford it?"

"Easy, darlin'," Dickie replied. "We're the good guys."

Two porpoises presently appeared on a glass ocean doing tandem jumps in front of the setting sun. I became instant best friends with a cool guy who walked out of the water with his surfboard, swinging his long wet hair around and around in order to attract my attention. Yep, we were in Florida, all right, and I was never lonely there. The cool guy and I, and the two porpoises, too, taking tiny steps on their tail fins, joined Dickie and Charley on a front lawn full of flamingos and palm trees. We gazed up at the house as who should emerge but Ronald Reagan himself, there to welcome us all to Florida and to wish Dickie good luck in the War on Drugs. After personally tossing down the house keys, he gave us one of his wet-eyed Gipper smiles while a hologram of Jesus Christ began to flicker beside him, beamed directly down from a break in the clouds, and we all put our hands over our hearts and pledged allegiance to the flag before shooting our guns in the air.

And that was that. We got along great. Glen Glamour was erased, Charlie Barnes forgotten. We needed no one but Dickie from that time forward. He was every bit the savior that Charley Proffit, desperate to reverse a historic run of broken marriages, hoped he'd be when they tied the knot after only three months. He was never confused or tormented by the sudden presence of so many stepchildren, he never stormed about after drinking too much, and he always managed his finances. We have family reunions to this day where we will step off the plane and just sort of merge, if you will, like an amoeba, because being a "blended family" doesn't cut it; we must be *one*.

After our move to the Keys, I saw Steady Boy only on Christmases and summer vacations. When it came time to part again, unticketed Charlie would take a pre-9/11 stroll through security with us so that we could spend our last remaining minutes together. We huddled at the gate in abject misery, a boy and his best friend disconsolate at the prospect of another long separation. Our tears fell to the bolted-down chairs, a tiny ashtray at the end of each arm. I lived for my time with that man. Before boarding began, always ten rows at a time, inevitably sweeping me up in some early round, we would repeat like a mantra the date when we'd next see each other, fixing all our hope on that, all our happiness, our whole calendar year, which was the only way we might survive the hell of a fresh parting.

Now, with or without pancreatic cancer, he promised to pick me up at O'Hare like old times. I knew the routine. He would pull up to the curb outside Arrivals and wait for me, playing a game of cat and mouse all the while with some weary Chicago transit cop. If they caught him idling, they'd force him to circle, and he hated circling. There was only one thing he hated more than circling, and that was paying for airport parking.

The child of divorce and the parent without primary custody know these interstitial places well: the curb, the corridor, the terminal parking lot. It is there where you embrace, you shed tears, you thank God for reuniting you—or curse God for tearing you asunder once more. All the while, the elevator dings, the custodian sweeps up, the traffic cop urges you to get a move on. That day, however, we weren't menaced by anyone. I came out with one bag, dropped it, and threw my arm around him. I hardly recognized him, he'd lost so much weight.

"You came."

"Of course. You called. That's how it works."

"Tell that to the others," he said.

"You look good, Chuck."

"And you're a liar."

"All right—you look like hell."

"That's more like it. But you, my boy... you've never been handsomer."

We had hold of each other throughout this absurd and happy exchange, and now we buttoned it up with a final embrace. There was his aftershave again, his bony shoulder blades. He tossed my bag in the trunk while I admired the Porsche.

"Sweet ride," I said. "Sudden windfall?"

"It's just a loaner," he said. "But I'll tell you what, Jake. I know exactly what to do with it."

"I bet you do."

"I gotta get it back to my mechanic. But there's just so much going on..."

We got in and he showed me the key to the Porsche—itself an antique beauty. Before turning the engine over, he prepared me for its pleasing roar. He pulled out of Arrivals with a nice little torque, punched it into second, raced around a slowpoke in the right lane, and next I knew it was all open road. His touring cap suddenly flew up as if caught in a twister and tumbled away in the mirrors, and when we turned to each other, we howled with dumb delight. He didn't invite the loss, but he found a way to enjoy it. Then he did what he always did when I was new again and he was happy to see me: he reached over with a smile and touched the hair on my head. He was sure he would be dead by Monday.

39

That was when he was scheduled for a procedure called the Whipple. If the name suggests a carnival ride—"Step right up, boys and girls, and take a whirl on the Whipple!"—it was in fact a last-ditch attempt to save his life by removing the diseased pancreas, small intestine, gallbladder, and bile duct before sewing him back up and seeing if it held. A massive medieval ordeal, and the side effects were terrifying, like coming to late at night and finding three men in ski masks standing over your bed: you don't know what you're in for, you just know you have to submit. He was scared.

Difficult as it was to admit, I knew he wanted Marcy there with him more than anyone. It ate away at him that she remained in Texas, caring not if he lived or died. I don't think Chuck had any idea just how badly Charley Proffit—it will be easier to distinguish them if, from time to time, I call him Chuck—had run him down during Marcy's formative years, drilling into impressionable Marcy that her biological father was a phony and a deadbeat, and how much better she might do to consider Dickie Dickerdick her real dad from then on. That will always take its toll. I for one owe Charley Proffit a great deal, but she poured a lot of poison in that girl's ear. Chuck wanted Marcy to love him like she had at nine years old, but she was twenty-five years removed from being daddy's little girl and still nursing a grudge that properly belonged to her mother. Only I could see any of this clearly.

So I really had no choice in the matter. On the Friday before his surgery, I flew down to Houston, rented a car, and took the Pasadena Freeway out to Deer Park.

She was surprised to discover I was in town. She told me it was a busy time. I understood; I'd given her no warning. She said she'd call me after she got off work and maybe we could get a drink.

"But I thought you quit work," I said.

She didn't really answer me. I checked in at my hotel, and once inside the room went through the proofs my editor had sent me for a book that would publish in May. I got so absorbed in the task that I looked up at some point, momentarily unable to recall where I was or what I was doing there. A generic room, a nowhere view... was I on assignment? Private travel? In the States or abroad? The phone rang. Marcy's voice immediately returned me to... where was it? Deer Park, Texas. Good God—Deer Park, Texas!

We met at a sports bar and took a table in back.

"Been a while," I said.

"Has it?"

"Six years."

"That long?"

Marcy still awed and frightened me. She hated me a little, I think—though nothing like she hated Dickie. She and I would bike up and down the sun-beaten streets of Cudjoe Key together hour after hour, bored out of our minds, but we couldn't go back to the house because Dickie had banished us for committing some infraction against his bachelor furniture. He wasn't a bachelor anymore, but he sure wished his couch and love seat to be treated as the furniture of a bachelor, the sofa cushions always aligned just so and the pillows plumped up. Marcy took more offense at this than I did and despised Dickie for it. "He's supposed to be a cop, but he's just the cop of his stupid fucking furniture," she said to me behind the Tom Thumb convenience store after I'd stolen, at her urging, two packs of gum and some beef jerky. No one questioned me. I don't think Marcy had any clue what life could be like, although I agreed that Dickie was no Charlie Barnes.

Marcy and I rarely discussed our time in Florida. Too remote, too strange an experiment to bring up in casual conversation—and too unhappy. Charley Proffit, chasing romantic redemption, was led by one last lyre to the water's edge, where we all might have drowned. Maybe Marcy did. I couldn't say. I did know she was angry, that a lot of her anger was still unprocessed, and that she seemed to reserve most of it not for her mother and stepfather but for Steady Boy, who had let her down. Had he been a more dependable Danville son and Old Poor Farm employee, our little Florida interlude might never have come to pass.

Dickie worked historic narcotics, those drug deals so monumental as to reorganize street life, penetrate the heartland, kick-start the prison-industrial complex, and acquire names: the Santiago Run, the Ramirez Load. These were subsequently talked about the way people talk about moon landings and no-hitters. Dickie, the dime-bag *Dragnet* of rural Illinois, had somehow been tasked with dismantling these living myths back into their component parts—names of players, time of night—and handing down indictments, letting it be known that not even history was beyond the reach of American justice. He was almost immediately in over his head.

But Charley Proffit was happy. Unlike Chuck, Dickie was no dreamer. He was a man of action. He led interrogations. He tithed to his church. He earned a salary the moral way: not through schemes and handshakes but surveilling and policing. Like Charley herself, he was a world improver and not likely to quit the improvement trade for a few dollars more at Waukegan Title. This was all part of God's plan and what made a good man. Charley Proffit found it so refreshing, she confused it for the second coming itself.

We would get off track if I followed for much longer the endless island afternoons and the occasion that broke the spell: Dickie's son's molestation of Marcy over the summer of her eighth-grade year and Dickie's refusal to do anything about it. I don't mean to suggest he did absolutely nothing. When Marcy came to her mother with news of what happened, it was the middle of October some four months later, and Dickie immediately booked a flight. He returned to Danville to have a talk with the young man, whose name was... I suppose I could completely obscure his identity as I've done with his father and save myself a lot of grief, but I'm inclined to call him by his real first name, to serve up the only justice he's ever likely to face, and so Justin it is. Justin Dickerdick was a disaffected little punk who is now, everyone will thrill to learn, a Florida state trooper. Just as I spent some of my summer vacation with Charlie, so Justin spent some of his summer in Florida, and apparently that summer, while the adults were at work...well, it took place in their bedroom, on their waterbed. Dickie set off for Danville vowing to use all his penetrating policeman's cunning to get to the bottom of things. Fifteen and terrified, Justin swore up and down that Marcy was a willing and eager participant in all that occurred in the house on Cudjoe Key, and Dickie sided with Justin.

It was just that easy. He did not press the matter. He wanted to believe that his boy was innocent—and that he was came as a great relief to Dickie. (It goes without saying this would be the standard of law and order for the next twenty years for at least some portion of the state of Florida, as the lawman leaned on his hunches and wants more than he did facts and proof. Another fiction writer, perhaps?) Dickie needed to believe that Justin was a normal, healthy heterosexual young man and that Marcy, a troubled kid, was a secret tramp—a figure he recognized from the Bible, deserving of forgiveness, but a hungry little whore all the same, as most women were for Dickie, just as in his mind Black men were always pimps or dealers.

There is much to be said about America's future troubles residing right here in this episode from '87 involving Dickie Dickerdick and his son: the denial, the impunity, the scorning of fact and testimony, the cycle of shaming and enabling, the outstanding crimes that go unredressed, and the legacy of abuse that would require an actual second coming by a better man than Dickie to begin to heal the hurt suffered by women like my sister. Charley Proffit fared little better. The child abuse investigator's child had been abused. In her home. While under her protection. There is no understating the devastation this delivered up to someone who, until then, considered herself invincible. She wanted to kill Dickie's son. She wanted to kill Dickie, too, but the minor especially. One can't, however, go around killing minors.

When a child was in Charley Proffit's care, that child was ipso facto protected, immune from the world's hell. Justin put an end to that illusion. Charley could do no more to protect a child than your average Joe could, and in fact, when it came to her own children, whose safety was axiomatic, she might have been at a disadvantage compared to the average Joe, who knows instinctively that hell can happen anywhere, to anyone. Justin revealed her righteous and virtuous life to be a lie. She failed as a mother and she failed at her calling, which here were one and the same. She certainly failed as a judge of men's character and as a romantic who sought to be made whole by one. She failed at life as surely as Steady Boy had—and might not have failed had she just stayed with him. This was a bitter pill. She was ripped apart and had no one but herself to sort it all out. She consulted lawyers, took Marcy to see experts. She couldn't stand the sight of Dickie and stayed away from the house. I was alone with him there more and more. I tried keeping myself busy. There was school. And I found work in the kitchen of a place called the Eatery—I was tall for fourteen. Dickie put in for a transfer to Pensacola. But this strictly factual account of the life of Charlie Barnes has strayed off course for too long. I'd like to think they were doing me a favor when they abandoned me to my own devices. With protectors like these, who needs predators?

"What are you doing in Texas, Jake?" Marcy asked me at the sports bar in Deer Park.

"Your dad has cancer," I said. "Thought I'd pay you a visit, ask if you might come home."

"And where is home, Jake?"

"Schaumburg," I said. "105 Rust Road."

"Schaumburg," she said. "I had no idea."

To me, yes, it was a no-brainer: home was where he put his remote controls on a TV tray and where a hot shower atomized his cologne and the steam sent it rushing down the hallway into every room.

"Is 105 Rust Road really home for the great Jake Barnes?" she continued.

"'The great Jake Barnes'?"

"I hear you wrote a novel," she said. "You and Charlie make a good team."

"I don't know what that means."

"You both enjoy telling stories. That's all it means."

There was a long pause.

"Let's say I'm prepared to believe that he actually does have cancer this time. He didn't know it when he lied to me."

"He was confused," I said. "And then he was cornered. He didn't know how to come clean—not to you. He's desperate to have you think well of him."

"You find it so easy to let him slide," she said, "and I find that so maddening. He makes bad decisions and tells lies, but to Jake Barnes, he can do no wrong. You look at him like he's some kind of myth, like he's...I don't know what. Part Fred MacMurray, part Hugh Hefner. He wears the best suits, the best colognes—as if that's enough! For the rest of us, Jake, it's just not enough."

It was true that Charlie wore the best suits, double-breasted beauties from the eighties with wide lapels made of tweed or wool and lined in silk. He had retired many of them as their cuts aged and fell out of fashion. Besides, men were no longer expected to suit up as they once did, and he had retreated into khakis. But back in the day, Steady Boy was one sharp dresser.

"Do you remember that one suit with the..."

I began to describe the particular suit I had in mind. Marcy cut me off.

"We are not strolling down memory lane in a bad-suit parade."

The waitress came by and took our order. I make it a point not to drink alcohol and asked for a club soda. Marcy ordered a vodka martini and the waitress departed.

"Come home, Marcy," I said. "He needs you."

"He made a fool of me, Jake. I'm not coming home."

"It's an incredibly difficult surgery. Anything could happen."

"I won't reward him for accidentally not lying."

"So come see the punishment he's about to endure."

"He'll be fine. You know that. He gets away with everything."

"Come home."

"I won't."

"It would mean the world to him."

"Why do you care so much? Oh, God," she said. "Don't start crying."

She waited for the moment to pass.

"Look, Jake," she said. "It's touching that you love him."

"Just come home!"

"I'm not coming home, ya freak!"

We both had raised our voices. But that was not what

embarrassed Marcy. She looked back at me almost right away.

"Oh," she said. "Sorry, Jake."

At the Houston airport the next morning, I purchased a ticket for the identical flight into O'Hare that I would be taking in an hour's time, only for the following day and in Marcy's name. Then I emailed it to her with one final impassioned plea that she change her mind. I told her how rigorous the Whipple procedure was. I reminded her that there were no guarantees. Even if he did make it out of surgery, his recovery was far from assured.

She did not confirm receipt, nor did she redeem it.

40

I flew back to Chicago in time for Chuck's surgery. The night before that anxious occasion, I invited Jerry to join me for dinner at the Morton's in Rosemont.

I arrived early. The maître d' showed me to a plump red banquette, the adult equivalent of a bouncy castle. I felt like a respected gangster. I ordered a martini—not to drink so much as to supplement the decor, blend in better. Waiters came and went. Silver sconces lit the gelatin prints hanging on the walls. Someone had been eager to make this suburban chain steak house look like Frank Sinatra's living room.

Jerry had no intention of joining Barbara and me the next day in the waiting room of Rush Memorial. As with Marcy, I thought this shortsighted, a little vindictive, and very dumb. We are here, you idiots, to forgive one another. But I didn't often try to correct Jerry when he was prepared to make a mistake. Who was I before that man's resolve? A nothing, a hanger-on. Of all the ways to be wounded. I sent back the serrated knife on my cloth napkin. I had no genius for sawing.

From the beginning of time, Jerry was more of a story told to me than a man in the flesh. Jerry is going to college. Jerry is on the road with his band. Jerry studies a book called the Bhagavad Gita. That kind of story. Eventually, Jerry acquired the breadth and status of a myth. Jerry has taken a vow of silence. Jerry is learning to fly airplanes. Jerry is moving to Spain.

Now it occurs to me, and I say it reluctantly, that Jerry was a disappointment. I held him in high regard, he intoxicated me, I felt divinely favored to be associated with him, he was a towering giant... but he was also an extravagant liar entering middle age aggrieved and on the verge of homelessness.

I did not see this latest, vagabond version the same way his father did, as a sad falling off from the IT manager for a regional bank who funded his 401(k) and took the train to work. No, this latest iteration or phase of Jerry Barnes, a man of iterations and phases, was in fact the full flowering of what made him absolutely extraordinary. His pauperization had been entirely his own doing, one sign of the principled conviction that guided his life. He could not be bought. His soiled T-shirt, his recycled denims, his diving into Dumpsters, his dispossession of money and a mortgage and a good credit score were all ennobling responses to the same concerns Charlie had for his country. Only Jerry was not content to read the paper and work out his rage and heartbreak in quiet contemplation. He was a prototype of the sort of activist that would take root in America a few years hence, first in Zuccotti Park, then around the world, occupying the financial districts of New York, São Paulo, Hong Kong, and London and culminating in a global movement that continues to protest inequality to this day.

If I had a bone to pick with this engaged and agile patriot and preacher of sorts, my admirable older brother, it was the unrelenting persistence of the bone he picked with Charlie. For such an enlightened man, he sure did choose to live in the past. As I anxiously awaited him, turning my gaze continually to the front door, so eager to greet him, to be enfolded in his big bear hug, which always smelled faintly of peppermint and leather and marijuana smoke, nevertheless I reaffirmed my belief that he was way too hard on Charlie. He was even something of an ingrate, cavalier with his inheritance. He and Marcy both enjoyed warring with their father, and with themselves. It was a stupid war against tendency, habit, received trait, the hand-me-down expression hard to reckon with in the mirror. In Jerry's case, his lifestyle, principled though it was, was also an attempt to overthrow everything that reminded him of Charlie—an attempt, in essence, to enact the inversion of the plot of the New Testament, which, to take things one step further, I believed captured the dynamic between a lot of troubled fathers and sons: the young man nails the old god, his father, to the cross in an effort to redeem the world.

I had every intention of beseeching him with an unabashedly emotional appeal. I loved him. I loved Charlie, too. And I believed that just beneath the stupid grievances, there was a great deal of love between the two of them. I would ask him to put aside those grievances just for the time being and to join us tomorrow in the hospital waiting room, to lend the old man some moral support while butchers in surgical scrubs cut him to pieces and then stitched him back up, from ass to elbow.

But stare at the entrance all I might, Jerry never showed.

The old man was waiting up for me when I made it back to 105 Rust Road.

"Come on," he said. "Take a ride with me."

"Where to?"

"Fill up on gas."

Learn these two lessons well, kids, if ever you wish to become a suburban father: all lights must be turned off whenever you leave the house, and always keep your gas tank full, even if it requires a late-night outing. This latter rule applied not just to those cars Chuck owned but to loaners, too, apparently. We climbed inside Rabineau's Porsche and followed Rust Road around the bend to Shore Drive and out to Roselle, where the strip malls, drive-throughs, and gas stations of Schaumburg, Illinois, flourished in pallid light even as it approached midnight.

"I want to talk to you about the wedding," he said.

"What wedding?"

"The one I've mentioned to you a couple of times in the past," he said. "The one between my parents."

"Oh," I said. "That wedding."

"If you ever decide that it's something you want to write about, I hope you know you have my permission."

"Thank you," I said.

I got the impression that, for whatever reason, this was part of his idea of putting his affairs in order before going into surgery the next day.

"I would just ask one thing. It happened. So you should tell it with that in mind. No need to fancy it up. They were forced to exchange vows. They got nothing sweet to eat afterwards. Let the facts speak for themselves. Historically, Jake, no one in my family has been very good at telling the truth. If you asked my mother right now how she met my father, she would make no mention of a cornfield. She would manage to rise above the dementia to let you know in no uncertain terms that they met on Sunday morning in the pews of the Church of the Nazarene."

I saw the gas station he liked in the near distance. He put his signal on before downshifting.

"What if, one day, I wrote about you?" I asked him. "Would the same rules apply?"

There was a long pause while he considered his answer. Shadows passed over his face as he took the turn into the station.

"I think it should be a factual account," he said. "Why not? Somebody needs to correct the record!" He laughed as we slowed to a stop. "Yes, if you decided one day that you wanted to write about me, Jake, you'd do me an honor if you just told the truth."

He put the car in gear and killed the engine, pulled the hand brake.

"But that's not what I really wanted to talk to you about," he said.

We weren't out in the night to top off a gas tank. We were there so that we could talk privately, away from Barbara.

"I was really hoping Marcy could do this for me, Jake, but it doesn't look like Marcy's coming home, does it?"

"It does not," I said.

"So I'm going to tell you something I don't like admitting to anyone. It embarrasses me. It embarrasses me a hell of a lot. But I need something done, damn it, and Marcy's not coming."

He paused to gather his strength.

"Fact of the matter is, son, I had all my teeth pulled when I was twenty-four, and now I wear dentures."

Did he really think I didn't know that?

"But they're not going to let me wear them when I go into surgery tomorrow."

"How come?"

"Damned if I know. But if I complain about it much louder, they might just decide to leave a little cancer behind before closing me up again. Never bitch to a waiter right before he delivers your soup, if you know what I mean."

I liked that, and laughed.

"So that means I need somebody to find them when it's over and put them back in my mouth. Can you do that for me? I don't want Barbara seeing me without my teeth."

"Barbara doesn't know you wear dentures?"

"Why would she?"

"You guys have been together for, like, fifteen years."

"Barbara and I do not delve," he said. "We do not plumb the depths of each other's souls. I've tried that, it doesn't work. Better to leave certain things alone. It's good to maintain a little mystery in a marriage. It might just be the secret to our success."

"But would you really call that a success?"

"Hey, Jake," he said. "You gonna do this for me, or what?"

—

We woke at five the next morning.

I dressed and went downstairs, where from the sofa I signaled my readiness to walk out the door. No one wants to make a man late for life-saving surgery.

"Experts at exports." T-R-U-T-H.

Barbara was the next person to come down. I dropped the crossword puzzle when she appeared, not in her customary scrubs but done up for the occasion, as if a silk blouse might banish ill luck. We had greeted each other the day before—warmly, I suppose, though I had no illusions that she really wanted me there. I presently joined her in the kitchen, where, it must be said, she did ask me if I wanted a cup of coffee. Whoa, what's next? I wondered. A welcome-home banner and a wet kiss? I graciously accepted her kind offer, and we fell back into silence. She washed a dish, wiped down the countertop, straightened the napkins in their holder, hung a hand towel from the oven door, removed the milk from the fridge... in these minor tasks at that laconic hour, I thought I caught a glimpse of how she was when we weren't around and bringing our prejudices to bear, and it seemed to me that she had a very different take on 105 Rust Road from Marcy's or Jerry's or even Charlie's. It was not the site of a permanent battle or a temporary station to be upgraded at the first opportunity. For her it was home. Where she woke, made coffee, tidied up. Where she confronted misfortune, too, and in her quiet way. In fifteen years, I had never seen her or that house. I'd seen only a thousand compromises.

Ten minutes later, we were out the door and driving on the highway. From my place in the back seat, I watched him work the gearshift (his hand as familiar now for its liver spots as for an old memory of how big they once seemed next to my own) and recalled how he taught me, at twelve, to shift gears from the passenger seat of the Saab. I would reach over with my right hand, shadowing the angle of the shoulder belt as it plunged toward the buckle, and take hold of that shuddering stick skirted in soft leather as I awaited his command. "Okay, third gear's next... ready for third?" As he engaged the clutch, I did my best to unlock third gear, which contained within it all the mysteries of a manual transmission, without throwing it into second and revving the engine, or reverse and wrecking the whole machine—an adventure that began in tandem with him, his hand over mine, until I got the feel for it, after which we hardly exchanged a word as we tooled down the street at one with that car. There was joy in our conspiracy—a child shifting gears, why, that had to be against the law!—and conspiracy in our joy: father and son drove that car together. This sentimental memory brought with it not only the pleasure we made of running errands, not the smell of the old Saab alone, but also the long summer itself, the hot days, the full weekends, the relief at his physical presence, the renewal and delight, the apartments, babysitters, popular songs, trips to the amusement park and strolls through the mall, and all the late-night movies we watched. As dawn broke wide open in the blue sky above I-290, a pale proleptic moon hung off to our right, a little tear in the scrim, a trapdoor, a miracle, but out of reach for the likes of us, a marvel and nothing more. He took Barbara's hand after shifting into fifth, and they held on to each other in silence for the length of the ride.

He was admitted, prepped, and shaved, his identity confirmed and reconfirmed, and once up on the gurney swam in the hospital gown they gave him. The surgeon stopped by to say hello, a short, strapping man whose wiry build suggested strong nerves and eternal life. He had made it clear to the patient during the consultation that what he was looking for upon opening him up was stage II-B cancer; anything more would imply that the tumor had spread to the major arteries, and he would be forced to simply close him up again. In a fit of good humor that I understood was intended to disguise his mortal fright, my father said to him what he had been planning to say since the morning the witticism had occurred to him, unbidden in the middle of a shower.

"II-B or not II-B," he said. "That is the question, eh, Doc?"

The surgeon smiled and patted his shoulder.

Barbara followed the man out, presumably to ask one last question or to receive a final bit of reassurance. In the silence that followed there was the unmistakable drone of pure terror. He wanted out of there. He tried smiling.

"I've been false, Jake," he said at last.

"False?"

"I need to face facts," he said. He was talking more to himself than anything. "Make some changes in my life. Get real with myself. I was real once. I could be real again. Listen to me, son. Listen to me: if I get out of here—"

"You will, Chuck. You will get out."

"If I live—"

"But you *will.*"

"Then I make a solemn vow to you right here and now. I will be a better man."

The orderly came for him ten minutes later.

While Under

41

Hitchhiking into Key West . . . the blimp over Cudjoe called *Fat Albert* keeping one eye on Cuba, the other on Cartagena, Dickie Dickerdick had been inside it . . . Monte's Fish Market, Mangrove Mama's, the antique biplane at the Sugarloaf Lodge . . . cars parked down by the mangroves on Big Coppitt, mostly fishermen, the occasional masturbator . . . the military dead zone just after Rockland Key where the naval station sits, my nose fried to a crisp . . . Cubans fishing along the pedestrian paths, five, ten rods lined up in a row, the pink of the red snapper drowning in a dry bucket . . . "Free beer . . . tomorrow" painted on the face of the Stock Island bar . . . Mercedes and her husband, Paul, they owned the Eatery . . . sweeping the sand from the flagstones for $3.35 an hour just before the morning rush, returning South Beach to itself as the beachcombers slowly stirred . . . pausing to watch the waves hit the breaker, you could see all the way to Cuba on a clear day . . . running down Duval for café con leches, one for Paul, one for Hazel, one for Billy Ray . . . Mercedes demonstrating how to properly scour a cobbler dish after it comes off the buffet . . . the line cook saying to me, "Do you know what jailbait is, boy?" . . . fruit smoothies, fried plantains, conch chowder—all exotic to the kid who grew up going to state fairs and corn festivals . . . the crackhead, a former publisher of the *Key West Citizen,* whose morning ritual began at the Eatery and whose hand shook lifting the coffee cup to his lips . . . the Poles, Cubans, Bahamians, and hippies who showed up at South Beach around ten and did not leave it again until cocktail hour . . . don't be confused by "South Beach," a small clutch of sand on lower Duval next to the Atlantic Shores motel and a crumbling pier—worlds away from its Miami counterpart . . . cracking eggs for the next morning's buffet into five-gallon buckets with Mohawk Dave, the breakfast cook, he later died of an overdose . . . busing tables with Blind Richard, he died in a boating accident . . . Hazel smoothing out her dollar tips at the end of a shift, she died of ovarian cancer . . . receiving the week's deliveries, boxes of produce, sacks of potatoes, and carrying each item into the walk-in or dry storage . . . learning from Charlie (different Charlie, hockey player from Ottawa) how to thicken a gravy using cornstarch, he was stabbed to death in Bahama Village . . . watching O'Neil clear the mounds of seaweed from South Beach with his backhoe, he died of a self-inflicted gunshot wound . . . sharing a rum and Coke, my first, with Snake in his empty one-bedroom on Flagler, hard to say what happened to that guy . . . the three Polish brothers, not a word of English between them, manning the kitchen for Paul at night, as hardworking as they were mute and pale . . . the dough hooks spinning in the Hobart, mesmerizing... a stink that attached to me after a shift, a Dumpster stink and grease coating... Ms. Kaltran asking how things were at home, she disappeared off Big Pine in '89... Principal Menendez, with his million-dollar smile and gold herringbone chain... the Spanish instructor Hernandez, made to roam from classroom to classroom with a wheeled cart full of props and slides... our mascot, the hammerhead shark, a full-size gray one outside the main entrance, made of welded metal, the least waterborne thing on earth... doing my homework at the McDonald's on Roosevelt, or in the bright stands at Bayview Park... sleeping rough on occasion, between stilts, or on Smathers Beach... the names of bars painted directly on the stucco facades, doorless doorways leading into the adult darkness... Captain Tony's, the Hog's Breath, the Full Moon Saloon... feeding quarters into video games in the open-air arcade on Duval, getting propositioned, offered booze, weed, ten dollars to suck a dick... coconut trees and banana leaves... weaving dinner plates and top hats out of palm leaves as the Jamaicans taught me to do, selling one to a tourist in a Cubs cap... putting him securely in the past, as I had Danville, Charley Proffit, the house on Vermilion—why?... recoiling from the unremitting press in Key West of adult content, sex toys in the windows, phalluses marching in the Fantasy Fest parade... yet also going through puberty, sneaking peeks down tourists' shirts, they hated wearing bras on the island, on their honeymoons... crashing on Ella's couch, she had a son who was killed in Vietnam, until her roommate, the Eatery line cook who queried me about jailbait, woke me with his hard-on... AIDS everywhere, in the ranks of the waitstaff, hospitality workers, Conch Train conductors, moped repairmen, the tourists themselves... watching Billy Ray die of AIDS... watching Billy Ray, the queen of wit, who weighed all of a hundred pounds, put his lips on the spout of the orange-juice dispenser and blow giant bubbles into the thick liquid to disperse the accumulated pulp, then opening the spout to watch the juice flow freely again before returning it to the buffet and its "thirsty bitches"... watching hundreds of the unsuspecting from Kansas and New Jersey fill their little juice glasses... Mallory Square and the man who walked on broken glass, the man who walked across hot coals... the capsized boat with the garbage-bag tarps at the end of Houseboat Row, gone now with the video stores and the salt ponds... sneaking into Sloppy Joe's to take a leak, in the middle of chaos, on the edge of losing it... being called to the principal's office, believing I'd been caught, this would all finally end, they would send me north or put me away, but being told instead that I had won a countywide writing contest and would be treated to a canoe trip through the salt ponds with Jimmy Buffett, a musician of some kind... meeting Jimmy Buffett... Jimmy had a puppy, he ordered us a pizza, he had hired a Jamaican to do all the paddling... the moped I bought for seventy-five dollars from Hazel's fat boyfriend, a man with zinc on his nose... trying to throttle, brake and steer one-handed, difficult to do with so low a center of gravity... but needing to get from South Beach up Flagler over to Roosevelt into Whitehead bight to sluice the boats returning from their charters for two lousy bucks a pop... leaving Cudjoe for the last time... looking for trouble, starting to find it... smoking cigarettes, shoplifting... learning from Mohawk Dave how to cook and inhale... thinking I didn't need Charlie, thinking I didn't need anyone... being detained outside the Eckerd drugstore with a greeting card down my pants, a greeting card, while in my wallet there was over a hundred dollars in cash... the arresting officer saying, "Well, son... is there anyone you can call?"

It is hard to know now why I did not turn to him long before I was detained. I suppose Marcy was not the only one in whose ear Charley Proffit poured her poison. I suppose that I, too, knew all about crass, disappointing Charlie Barnes. Besides, who was I? A nobody. And he was in Chicago now in a whole new life. Did he even remember me?

But would it be worth a shot, I wondered, now that I was in custody? I didn't dare reach out to him before that, I didn't dare give him the option to decline, I didn't dare and I didn't dare... until, one day, I did.

We were reunited the year I turned fifteen. It was a brief and magical time. He couldn't believe that, as happened with Jerry in 1975, he'd assumed once again that all was right with the world because a boy was with his mother. He had no idea I was living on the street, sleeping on the beach, hanging out with drunks and the half dead while Charley Proffit and Dickie Dickerdick pursued their divorce... and I spared him 90 percent of it. He took me in, no questions asked, and we agreed to put the rest behind us.

My stepmother welcomed me with open arms. Evangeline was childless and happy to keep house. A native of Romeoville and the eldest of three daughters, she took great care to put her face on daily before an illuminated makeup mirror. She loved dried flowers and sachets of potpourri. She drove a Chrysler LeBaron and owned a blue-eyed Siberian husky named Stevie Nicks. All this was a far cry from Duval Street. She encouraged me to watch television with her in the living room, which she had nicely decorated with doilies and throw pillows. Evangeline's idea of heaven on earth was to curl up on the sofa with a lap blanket and a wine cooler and a new episode of *Knots Landing,* which was just fine by me. I don't recall now what she did for a living, but it had nothing to do with historic narcotics or child abuse. It was a leave-it-at-work kind of job, and she left it, happy to come home to me and our soap operas. We lived in Downers Grove, in a little cottage on Benton Avenue. She made us sloppy joes for dinner, bought me CDs from the Sam Goody and Fruit Roll-Ups from the Jewel-Osco. Downtown Downers had a discount theater called the Tivoli with a neon marquee out front. There, in 1989, for three bucks apiece, the whole family—the whole family!—saw the strangest double feature in the history of Hollywood: *Weekend at Bernie's* followed by *Do the Right Thing.* The old man was in heaven, went back for a refill of his tub of buttered popcorn. He had gained weight and gotten older, but he was still so much like a teenager himself. We played a lot of Ping-Pong in the basement and joined a pool league at a place called Muddler's, on Clybourn. It was at Muddler's, where I learned to shoot one-handed with a bridge, that Charlie first told me about Junior's in Danville and his father's time running a hustle for a stake horse in Little Egypt. His father died later that year, in Danville. I remember the funeral. I remember the tears streaming down my Uncle Rudy's face. I had been under the impression that no one cared for Alden Barnes, a deadbeat and a loner, but there was Rudy, shaken to the core, and Charlie right beside him. You can't lose a father and not be affected in some profound and unexpected way.

I considered myself the luckiest person on earth to be in the care of Charlie Barnes. An alternative fate was all too easy to imagine: landing in some central Florida penitentiary, or learning to suck cock for ten bucks a shot, or using the wrong needle on a whim. Instead, I was learning trigonometry at Downers Grove North, picking my zits and drooling through study hall. I had been rescued. I had to repeat the tenth grade, but at least I was alive. And this beautiful spell lasted three full years, until Charlie began his affair with the nurse at First Baptist.

Evangeline and I were in the basement one night watching *Knots Landing* when the phone rang. He said to offer her some excuse and to meet him at the McDonald's near the highway. When I pulled up beside him twenty minutes later, he rolled down the window and smiled under a beige Kangol cap. Still a year from starting his own outfit and leaving Bear Stearns forever, he was driving a high-end Lexus leased for a small fortune. We exchanged a few words. Then we rolled up our windows and I followed him into the night.

The geography of Chicagoland confounded me. We entered the highway and passed tollbooths and cloverleafs, corkscrewing irreparably into townships unknown. Our final leg consisted of a series of intensely local turns that left me bewildered. That Charlie *did* know where we were, that he went there by feel, that he pulled up before a second home, lesser in every way to the first, as if he belonged there, paid the bills there, parked in its driveway to announce the end of a night, astonished me, and that we approached the front door and went through it unimpeded and without knocking astonished me further still. The loyal stepson of another woman, I was being initiated into the house on Rust Road.

Was it fair of the old man? Was it right? He was too punch-drunk to think straight. To some extent, the discomfort I felt at his betrayal of sweet, domestic Evangeline was tempered by the flattering fact that he had not forgotten me. His new romance was incomplete or unreal until I, Jake Barnes, had stood witness to it. Once I set foot inside, once I beheld his new amour, he could say that he had united his two families, his past with his future, his delight with his duty. Nothing feels more natural or morally sound as having all your family under one roof.

"Come on in," Charlie said to me before crying out, "Honey! We're home!"

Honey? Home? There was chaos everywhere in this new home of his: library books climbing the staircase, unfolded laundry on the couch, dog toys littering the carpet, at least two competing televisions with volumes on high. He would eventually impose order on 105 Rust Road, but he didn't technically live there just yet and made no claim on its conditions. He still flickered uncertainly between a knight in shining armor and one more jerk who would come and go, and no one, not even he, could say for certain which way it would ultimately break. A dog skittered, its nails clacking, as it rounded the bend and came at me.

"Yort!" cried Charlie. "Jake, meet Yort."

"Yort?"

"Get down, Yort!"

"What kind of name is—"

Yort, a comically protracted dachshund-Doberman mix, had pounced. His nails were like a spiked mace, and he used my legs as scratching posts.

"Yort is harmless," my dad said, "but a pain in the ass. Just brush him off you, like this."

He demonstrated, Yort repounced, and a pattern was established, together with a new circle of hell. The pouncing persisted, it seemed, all night long, until my veins had been opened. But it was the act of brushing Yort off that stayed most vivid in my mind. He was free to take liberties with the pets.

"Shoes on or off?" I asked him.

"Whatever you prefer, son. I want you to feel at home here."

"But is there a custom?"

"Better take them off," he whispered.

I knew much more in that moment than "shoes on or off." I knew there were customs, indeed, and that they were whispered.

More information came fast and furious. Barbara had a son, a future private in the United States Army. He materialized out of nowhere, six years old at the time, and charged me like a bull.

"Charlie's here! Charlie's here!" this little guy sang out, naked but for a pair of camo undies. He stopped on a dime in front of me. "Saddam Hussein!" he cried, and with that, hauled off and whaled me in the nuts. I doubled over. He screamed away like a banshee. My father clapped after him in fury.

"Troy!" he cried. "Troy, come back here this instant and apologize! Sorry about that, Jake," he said. "He's a work in progress. Here, let me take your coat."

So disorienting, for me, were those first few minutes—from our free and easy entry to our pulling out chairs for ourselves at the kitchen table as if we had been dining there as a family for years—that I imagined it had to be a skipped reel of some kind, a waking dream, a hallucination. Where were we? And why would we swap the cottage in Downers Grove for this low-rent study in mayhem? Perhaps he's lost his mind, I thought, and the real man of that house, alarmed by our voices, will soon rush downstairs locked and loaded and force the two wandering maniacs out the door. But no one came threatening, and as the night wore on I noticed all the many quotidian ways Charlie's presence had been woven into the domestic tapestry all around us. His hats on the coatrack. His shoes on the welcome mat. His newspaper on the arm of the recliner. On the kitchen table, mail with his name on it. In the fridge, his favorite brand of beer.

"What the hell?" I whispered.

"What?"

"Where are we?"

"Jake," he said, "I can't hide it anymore, son . . . I'm in love."

"But what about Evangeline?"

Not unlike the sharp-taloned Yort, my father pounced. "Shhh!"

"What?" I said.

"Not that name! Not here."

"Evangeline?"

"It's tearing me up, what I'm doing to her." He was whispering again. "But I haven't felt this alive since I fell in love with"—he lowered his voice still further—"Charley Proffit!"

It must be said that, at the start of the affair, anyway, the house on Rust Road delighted him. It was where his new beloved lived, and he never wanted to leave.

Well, okay, I thought. I was open to change and always happy to meet new people. But the longer I sat there, the worse I began to feel, as if I were the one cheating on Evangeline. She had taken me in no less than he had. And I was not exactly gung-ho about starting all over here, in another house, adjusting mentally to the new accommodations, sleeping in whatever bed I was given, sharing breakfast with strangers, all that, but still expected to express gratitude, feign harmony, perform that old trick called family feeling. I was goddamn sick of starting over and had no appetite for a new crew when that delivering angel Evangeline was waiting for us with soap operas and snacks back in benign and orderly Downers Grove. I loved the old man and appreciated his enfolding me in this new charade, but he'd gone and ruined a good thing, and briefly I understood the complaint made so often against him: he was selfish and shortsighted. Jerry thought so. Marcy did, too. All his ex-wives. This was it: my first experience of the old man following his worst instincts. It made me mad.

"Evangeline," I said.

"Shhh, Jake!"

"Evangeline!"

"This is not the time or place!"

"Are we just erasing her from the record?"

"Absolutely not! No, only right now—"

"Right now, she's sitting at home watching TV, waiting for you to walk through the door."

"I know . . . I feel terrible!"

We heard footsteps on the stairs.

"Evangeline," I said.

"Please don't, Jake."

"Evangeline!"

"Stop it, Jake! That's it. No more."

"Evangeline!" I whispered, more fiercely than before.

That name remained on the tip of my tongue for years inside the house on Rust Road. *Evangeline.* The bearer of that name was a revenant capable of unleashing total ruin, of reminding them of the ruin *they* had unleashed—and I had the power to conjure her. I had the power to conjure them all—*Sue Starter, Barbara Lefurst, Charley Proffit*—to trace the bread crumbs of history back to earlier cottages, more legitimate queens. I was serving not as a witness to a new romance but as an accomplice to a broken vow, to a whole slew of broken vows, and when Barbara and I finally locked eyes, shook hands, said hello, we knew this as he did not. I was the institutional memory in a house of forgetting, and for that reason alone, Barbara would never accept me.

Curvy in scrubs, her hair cut short, Barbara was no local beauty à la Charley Proffit. But at thirty-four she was something of a honeypot for a man getting up there in age—he was over fifty by then—who had never thrilled to Evangeline's bony frame. After she shook my hand, all her calculated mirth dropped off her face as in a mudslide and failed to return for the remainder of the evening.

"Does he want a Dr Pepper?" she asked, rubbing her nose without looking at me. They were the first words I heard her speak, and they were directed at my father.

"Would you like a Dr Pepper, Jake?" Chuck asked me.

"Sure, I'll take a Dr Pepper."

"We only have diet," she said. "Is he okay with diet?"

"Diet okay, Jake?"

"Diet's fine," I said.

"Can he open it?"

"He can open a can, honey. He can even work a can opener. Can't you, Jake?"

"I can work a lawn mower."

"That's true," he said to Barbara. "He mows my lawn. I hate mowing the lawn."

"I don't mind it," I said. "I could mow your lawn," I offered.

"Chicken for dinner," she said. "Does he like chicken?"

"Great," my dad said. "Jake loves the bird."

My father got me a diet Dr Pepper and the two of us retreated to the living room. After a while, he thought he should ask Barbara if she needed help with dinner, and when he left for the kitchen, I was free to look around. Crocheted scenes of God and country hung in oval frames affixed to the wood paneling. There were a dozen VHS tapes and one dictionary, vaguely chewed, on an otherwise empty bookcase. Something else, too. I stood for a closer look: a blackened banana peel. I returned to the sofa. I later found half a hot dog lodged between two of its cushions. This, I thought darkly, was precisely what Dickie Dickerdick had been trying to avoid whenever he kicked Marcy and me off his bachelor furniture. I watched Troy, the future soldier, watch TV, which he did by gripping its side paneling and engaging with it as if it were sentient. Ten minutes later, his sister, Tory—fourteen, large and dark—appeared in that room fully naked. She was not yet accustomed to Charlie being there, let alone Charlie's children, and had no reason on earth to guess at my presence in that room. She was on her way to the basement to find some fresh clothes after a shower. She got one look at me, gasped, cupped her private parts and reversed in horror out of the room.

Yort, who had been chasing his tail for ten minutes, was now whining at the sliding glass door. A clever devil, he combed his elongated dog's body across the dangling venetian blinds to attract my attention. Then he turned with clacking nails and stared at me as the rattling noise from the blinds slowly died.

"Whaddya want, boy?" I asked him. "Or should I say 'girl'? Just what the fuck is a Yort anyway?"

Yort wagged his tail. I got up to see if I should let the dog out, but when I entered the kitchen, my father was gone. So was his new lady friend. They had retreated upstairs. I went back to the living room, resolved to finish my diet soda and ignore the dog completely. But a half hour later, I, too, had to pee, and my sympathies went out to the mutt, who was still whining and doing his trick with the blinds. I stood and opened the sliding glass door. Bursting—and beaming, too, I still believe to this day, beaming right at me like a freed prisoner—Yort, an indoor dog, went straight through the hedgerows and was never seen again.

Shortly after I returned to the couch, but well before everyone went out to search for the dog in the rain, live music made me start. I turned in alarm. An ancient old lady with a raspy voice was playing her heart out on the piano in the corner—I hadn't registered its presence until that moment. And when, exactly, had the human being materialized? She played a show tune to start, followed by an old standard. The little soldier swiveled his head without unhanding his television. "Grandma!" he cried. "Turn that down!" Grandma went on playing without a care.

My father returned from his time upstairs with Barbara. I gestured at the old lady. "Oh, right," he said. "Barbara's mother. Very musical." I revealed the hot dog between the sofa cushions. "Where's Yort?" he asked.

That desperately fleeing dog was a blessing in disguise for poor Barbara, who had reason to resent me without ever having to hear the name Evangeline. We didn't eat that night until ten.

42

By seven in the morning some fifteen years later, Barbara and I remained a pair of sorts, sitting together in the waiting room of Rush Memorial. Her son was in Afghanistan; her dog was still missing; her musical mother was dead.

Her husband was then undergoing a massive medical procedure. I read books during that time, did puzzles to distract myself, fielded a call about an appearance on Conan. At some point I looked over at her. Though inscrutable as ever, she had stuck by his side—and was solely responsible for questioning his test results and possibly saving his life. I recalled what Charlie had said to me the night before: "Barbara and I do not delve." Well, Barbara and I did not delve, either. In fact, what we did could hardly be called chatting. I preferred Evangeline, as Jerry preferred Sue Starter and Marcy preferred Charley Proffit, but Evangeline had remarried and moved to New Port Richey, Florida. It might be past time, I thought (now that the old man was undergoing lifesaving surgery), to ask what he saw in Barbara Ledeux. Who was she? And what made her special? I was just about to inquire when she looked up from her magazine.

"Just so we are clear," she said.

It was a rare instance of eye contact, very unsettling. She usually kept me in the periphery and preferred me in the third person.

"Should anything happen to him, moving forward, there will be no more talk about you know who."

"Who's that?"

"I think you know."

"I don't think I do."

Then it dawned on me: Evangeline. If he were to die, she did not want any mention of the wife that preceded her at his memorial service, in his obituary, in any remembrance whatsoever.

"The three of you—"

"Who?"

"You and your siblings," she said.

"There are four of us," I said.

"You tease him. You treat it like it's all just a big joke. Well, it's not a joke to me, and I don't find it funny."

"No one thinks of Evangeline as a joke," I said.

She looked directly at me again—twice in one day!

"I'm not talking about Evangeline."

"Who are you talking about?"

"The one you call by my own name. His 'second' wife."

"Barbara Lefurst?"

"There is no such person as Barbara Lefurst," she declared, "and you damn well know it."

"Beg your pardon?"

"There is no 'other' Barbara! That is a *fiction.*"

As in the cartoon in which the cat, primed for resentment, pulls from some hidden pocket a long, sharp pin in the presence of a balloon that, in the next frame, transforms into the revolving blue world, casting a shadow of doubt across the cat's brow even as the pin brightens, I was presented with a fiendish choice: drop it, or destroy the world.

"You've made her up to taunt me, the three of you."

"There are four of us," I said.

"You knew it would play on my vulnerabilities."

"As far as anyone knows, Barbara, you have no vulnerabilities."

That put an end to that.

His second wife a fiction! Had he failed to mention her? Had he selectively omitted, conveniently edited out, the original Barbara in conversation with the new one? He might have wanted to spare them both a little embarrassment, make his past a bit more palatable. Five *is* a large figure where wives are concerned. I wouldn't have put it past him. What's more, I wasn't sure I could blame him. We all need our little white lies. I would leave it to Jerry to stand on the street corner, stomping his rod of iron and crying, "Truth! Truth!"

"Okay," I said. "There was no Barbara Lefurst. I made her up. We all did. A little inside joke at the old man's expense. We didn't mean any harm by it—"

"I don't believe that for a second."

"But you won't hear me say another word about it for as long as I live."

There was a long pause.

"Thank you," she said.

She would have done us all in, I think: not just his second wife, the very real Barbara Lefurst, and the other wife she had been whitewashing for years, sweet Evangeline, but his first and third wives, too, and the children he bore, their pets and addresses and childhood interests, the afternoons in the park, the opening nights at Red Mask, the endearments, the snapshots, the road trips, the potlucks—everything that predated her and diminished the dream.

All we had to defend against this was memory. It was a sunset memory of bountiful, heartfelt Danville, Illinois, as much as it was of any one man. It was a memory of the house on Vermilion, the bunk beds, the foster kids, the man outside mowing the lawn. It was a memory of his headbands and wristbands and the hook shots he took on afternoons at the Y, and a memory of his Chrysler Newport, an old beater that Barbara never knew, but I did. What pleasure there was seeing him pull in again on another Saturday when he had kept his promise. Later, in transit, I would watch the road going by from within those shamrocks of rust in the floorboards at our feet. It was a memory of Kickapoo State Park and its picnic tables and our card games and of how, in one of those sweet surfeits of time, we sat around comparing the size of our hands. Finally, it was a memory of a rented motel room on New Year's Eve, an occasion he made special by buying a bottle of cider champagne and putting it on ice in the bathroom sink. We had every intention of popping the cork at the stroke of midnight, only we got caught up in a TV movie instead, a Jon Voight vehicle called *The Champ,* in which a father and son stick together through good times and bad, only to be separated by death in the end. Believe it or not, extensive academic study has determined in some scientific way that *The Champ* is the saddest movie ever made, provoking more tears from the unsuspecting than either *Bambi* or *Terms of Endearment.* It's not a tearjerker so much as a finely honed torture device. Well, we hardly needed the academy to confirm for us our feelings. "You're going to die!" I cried, clinging to him, and the only way he knew to redeem that holiday was to pop the cork early on our ice-cold cider.

I was a lifetime removed from these memories, and presently hostage to a dull mauve waiting room that drained the human soul of its magnificent contents and replaced them with seven generic watercolors and six rows of chairs. If you believe, as I do, in the mind's need to be out from under anxiety to approach even the borders of the past, to say nothing of its campfires and lakesides and sudden stunning views, inside that drab and sanitized room I should have shut down completely. I was under duress. A dear man's life was on the line, and my companion was Barbara. It was all the more surprising, then, that another, still more elemental memory came to me unbidden. I was in the bathtub. Steady Boy was at the mirror, shaving. Charley Proffit had been coming and going for ten minutes: swooping down on a used towel, pausing to comb her bob, climbing into a pair of slacks, popping back in to retrieve her hot tea. A red hair dryer, dangling down the wall by its tangled cord, came to rest an inch off the floor. Elsewhere, hand towels, tube socks, bikini underwear, softball jerseys, and a hundred other stiff and limp things from life in midaction hung from mismatching hooks and bars. The tub was lined with traction strips and was gritty from an old scouring agent. Just over the ledge sat a pink bath mat permanently branded by the tapering half of a hot iron. When I hung my arm over, issuing military instructions to those action figures holding down a remote base camp there, I soaked the floor, that rug, eventually their fresh socks. Presently, however, he was still shaving at the mirror when that foster parent extraordinaire, Charley Profitt of Peoria, Illinois, reappeared in her morning hurry, the frantic general to his ever-patient sapper, to issue another round of instructions: out! School in twenty minutes, and I still had to eat breakfast. I objected, conscientiously if not outright. Getting dressed, going to school—what were those things compared to the war of good and evil being waged in every corner of that tub? My Luke Skywalker, missing his left arm, which I tore from its socket with my teeth, was being swallowed up by the blind snout of the faucet. My G.I. Joe was done, swept up inside a lunar volcano, while green plastic soldiers paraded in formation across the slick ledge. Snoopy dangled over the lip in the hopes of being rescued by the Man of Steel. This ragtag team of playthings was all a jumble. I knew nothing of timelines or toy lines or the dictates of corporate branding. That's right: back then, I loved a blended family! These good and bad guys, supplemented by a silver bowl, a chipped mug, a plastic flute, and a powerfully squirting bottle of Pantene, as essential to bath time as the water itself, defied gravity, violated the laws of physics, and skirted death at my whim. Was that whimsy, that magic, at a time when Charlie was in such peril, the cause of the return of that particular memory?

Whatever the reason, there was simply no denying it: before the nurse at First Baptist, before Dickie Dickerdick and the Florida Keys, there was Charley and Charlie of Danville, Illinois. The one was a case worker at Old Poor Farm, the other an insurance salesman. They had a dog named Thumper. They had a boy named Jake. We had picnics at Kickapoo State

Park and went to church on Sundays. And just before she left the bathroom for good that morning, before he put on a fine suit and tie and disappeared down the drive on his way to the office, and before divorce blew our little family to smithereens, Charley put her finger to her lips to let me know we were conspiring, then reached out and pinched his butt. She goosed him, and always game, he jumped, he hooted, he shimmied, he marched up and down like a toy soldier.

I had one task that day at the hospital, and as time wound down I began to fixate on it. I had promised him that I would find his dentures and return them to his mouth when the operation was over. I got fidgety around five, ten full hours after the operation began. By seven, when there was still no sign of the surgical team, I began to pace.

"What is taking so long?" I asked.

Finally the nurse appeared. Surely that meant he was out at last and we would be taken straight to him. But I didn't have the damn things yet and tried to stall.

"If both of you will please just go back to your seats," the nurse said, "someone will be out to give you an update shortly."

"May I speak to you in private?"

"What for?" Barbara asked.

I turned to her. "I would like a word with the nurse, that's all."

"Are you looking for these?" she asked. From her purse, she pulled the blue container in which he kept his dental plates. She had them? But how? She rattled them in the air as I fell silent.

"Oh, don't be a fool," she said, and took up her seat again as the nurse had requested.

She knew, of course, and loved him all the same.

Fiction, or 906 Harmony Drive

Chippin' In

43

He came out of surgery gray, half dead. What was meant to heal him was, for me, the start of his dying. That man, that immortal, my father, a fairly standard midcentury model, Updikean in his defects and indulgences, besotted by the American dream and completely unkillable, with at least a dozen second acts already behind him, was gone. In place of the unique article was an imitation. He had not undergone some lifesaving surgery but an experimental whole-body transplant into somebody half his size. He writhed around, looked bothered by the light. He appeared to have an allergy to his own skin.

The morning after surgery, he came to feeling for his teeth. Finding them in place, he swooned again. Two days later, he could sit up. The doctor encouraged him to sip water, then to fast, then to sip again, to test the new seals on his old pipes. They took: no leaks, thank God. Days 4 and 5, he was urged to get out of bed. Slowly, he learned how to drag the IV pole down the hall and back; it later doubled in his dreams as an old-fashioned anatomy skeleton that graded, with dream speed, into the long and lanky figure of his mother. She was still alive, somehow—they had longevity, the Barneses—still wrestling with restless leg, and at last, he was her age: ancient, that is, and easy prey for self-pity.

Three tender trips to and from the commode to void urine were celebrated among the medical staff as passionately as any performed by a potty-training toddler. His daily walks were extended, his palate further expanded; on the tenth day, they told him to take a deep breath while they pulled the gastric drain from his abdominal wall. He was coming along like a model patient; was discharged; was monitored remotely until it was time to remove his staples, after which Barbara, taking time off work to see him through, applied aloe and vitamin E to the chapped ridges of his poor wound.

Her purse, a leather octopus, lay sprawled on a chair whenever I arrived at the hospital. Her black trench coat, which might come off in a moment of panic, would fall across the floor like a foreshortened shadow while she attended to some oversight, and the nurse on duty, suddenly superfluous, was left to pick it up and hang it from the door. I would nearly collide with her rounding the bend into his room as she was on her way out—not to grab a bite, as I had just done, or to catch up on her sleep, but to summon someone, to make a small adjustment to my father's care. And on that rare occasion when I entered and saw no sign of her, a second later the toilet would roar and out she would come drying her hands, dressed in the same scrubs she wore to work. Her famously cool disposition, the haughtiness that endeared her to absolutely no one, became, in a hospital setting and in service to him, a breathtaking display of devotion—and a special rebuke to my siblings, for whom the fifth in his line of wives was the worst of the bunch, and another reason to hate him.

"We've done her a disservice," I was saying to him by day 3 or 4, during one of his lucid spells. "She really loves you, Pop."

Tears came to his eyes. "Tell that to the others, will you?"

"I can try."

But they didn't care to hear it from me.

When it came time to wheel him out of the hospital and drive him home, it was Barbara who eased over the speed bumps and potholes, avoiding them altogether when possible, so that his delicate reconfigured center, an animal caught in a snare, would not jostle unnecessarily.

44

So he was home, so he would live . . . so what? The poor man had no appetite for food, for the newspaper, for telephone calls—and what was life without appetite? He subsisted on black coffee and protein shakes, mortally afraid of moving and tearing internally something he couldn't name but knew he needed. Regrets played on a loop. Depression, that still beast, came to roost. Depression laid its black eggs in him, which hatched, howled for food, and grew stronger on dark thoughts. It was not the cancer, but the reckoning, that came close to killing him.

To get up in the morning with a big gash in your side; to sweat through breakfast; to tremble; to feel tired and weak; to crawl from spot to spot; to endure—nothing more—and to go on enduring because it beats the alternative, is to confront the day with a lot of willpower. That was not my father.

He sat, did nothing, "healed," while time—as changing headlines, turning seasons—continued unabated. His surgeon, a lifesaver and a straightforwardly factual man, stated that the surgical team got clean margins and chemo was very good at taking care of the rest, but the patient had to eat or he would not live. The patient just shrugged. What was food to him?

Then one morning I set down before him a plate of eggs that I scrambled with whole milk and butter, and that did the trick. He scarfed it down. He wanted nothing but eggs after that, prepared just that way, three at a time, salted and piping hot. It was that perfect meal one goes chasing for years afterward, the rekindling of an appetite given up for dead, a rebirth...and for an entire month, he ate three meals a day of three eggs apiece and nothing more.

We watched more TV than you could possibly imagine, more even than when I was in high school and living with him and Evangeline in Downers Grove. Back then, we had a thirty-two-inch Sony Trinitron console set in solid oak, which he worked from his recliner by the luxury of remote control. I was sixteen when I bought a replica of that remote at a Radio Shack in the mall and synced it to the television. On nights I was bored, I would climb from my window and stand outside the house on Benton Avenue moving the volume subtly up and down. Sometimes I changed the channel. Steady Boy liked channel 7.

I liked channel 9. He would look up from his newspaper (he was never in front of the television without his newspaper) confounded by the sudden change. It seemed to have taken place entirely by some occult power. He reached for his remote on the TV tray and restored order before going back to his newspaper. I would let maybe a minute pass before changing it back to 9. He looked up, very solemn... I still have my regrets about this. I had not yet emerged from my punk-ass-bitch phase. What reason did I have to believe Charlie wouldn't abruptly change his mind and send me back to Florida—or to foster care? I just wasn't convinced that I deserved the fighting chance he was giving me. I was still smoking, too, and lifting the occasional greeting card. But back to him in that recliner, mouth gone slack in mystification: *What the hell is going on with my television?* He got to his feet and pulled the curtain back. Insecure Steady Boy was the first to believe that someone might be toying with him as he peered angrily out at the night. A veteran delinquent, I was well hidden, but silently shaking with laughter because I could still see him. On a different night, he simply stood up and started banging on the television, as if that ever works. Well, why shouldn't it? I correlated one of those bangs with a channel change, then another, then another and another, until he had every reason to believe that his Sony was obeying him in this crudest of manners, appeasing an angry god, and when at last it could be trusted that channel 7 would hold, he carefully withdrew, picking across the carpet backward and reaching out with a blind hand for his recliner, keeping his eyes glued to the screen until he was seated again, this time demurely, on the lip of the thing, as if fully occupying it might tempt fate. How carefully he sat there! I gave it a full two minutes before returning it to channel 9.

I can't tell you how often he would resort during this mind-boggling episode to that impotent hope of the layman: unplugging the TV from the wall socket and plugging it back in again. One night, he even dragged poor drowsy Evangeline out of bed just to have someone stand witness to his going mad. Of course, with the two of them in the middle of the room at the stroke of midnight holding their breath waiting for something to happen, I didn't do a thing. Remember that old Merrie Melodies cartoon about the frog with the golden voice who eventually drives his promoter insane because the beast will sing only for him? That TV went haywire only for Charlie Barnes. I found this amusing, as any teenager might, in the twilight of my not giving a shit, before I came to believe in that house and my place in it. Finally, he took the TV in to have it repaired, but they sent it right back for no charge because there was nothing wrong with it. My poor pop. In time, I stopped torturing him like this because I really did think he was going to lose his mind, and because I lost interest. He loved me.

In between interruptions, like his consultations and follow-ups, we must have watched close to twelve hundred hours of television over the course of his recovery from surgery and his two rounds of chemo. We watched, or rewatched, all of *Cheers.* We watched at least two-thirds of *Seinfeld* and half of *Friends.* Mindless, time-killing sitcoms helped keep him alive. There were also less familiar offerings: niche shows on the Syfy channel, Canadian whodunits, classic sitcoms he could remember loving back in the day, now so unwatchably bad that he questioned the judgment of his earlier self. If beloved old shows could crater, did that give the lie to today's amusement? Personally, I did not know what to make of the show *Lost,* which struck me as both aimless and tedious but uncanny, too, in the way life itself is uncanny, full of a grand, anachronistic, possibly scripted intent. We got through its six seasons in twelve days. He was conked out half the time, healing up, or dying a little more—maybe both, who could say?—so that each show, each season, each series we completed must have been for him a kaleidoscope of narrative more than any coherent story. When he began to snore, I'd pause the television and peer over at him. I owed him everything.

But he hurt me, too, during this time—inadvertently. Though it was nothing I didn't already know.

We had started watching *Downton Abbey,* more mindless fare. But every now and again that show went for the jugular, piercing the veil of a pretty little period drama to deliver pure dread.

The year is 1912. The heir apparent to Downton Abbey is a lawyer from Manchester called Matthew Crawley. As a newly minted aristocrat, Crawley finds himself chafing against the highbrow customs he's required to sustain. When Mr. Molesley, his proud valet, attempts to help him with his cufflinks, the thoroughly modern Crawley objects to such slavish interference. Surely, he remarks to the servant, you have better things to do.

Doing his British best to paper over his wounded pride, the servant replies, "This is my job, sir."

Crawley scoffs. He looks the man in the eye, in the mirror, and doubles down.

"Seems a very silly occupation for a grown man," he says matter-of-factly.

Matthew Crawley has done the unspeakable: he has destroyed the fiction that Mr. Molesley requires to go on believing that his life is a useful thing, that it's being spent with dignity and purpose.

Without so much as turning to me, Chuck remarked from his recliner:

"Sounds like what you do, Jake."

There was silence as I peered over at him. "Beg your pardon?"

"Writing novels," he said. "All that make-believe. That's a very silly occupation for a grown man, too."

It was not an attempt at humor, just a statement of fact. If it was uncharacteristically callow, I don't think he knew it. He went on watching. The scene changed. I must have turned back to the TV. Ten minutes later, he was asleep again.

I had believed that a silly occupation for a grown man was dressing in a clown suit and calling yourself Jolly Cholly, or manufacturing and marketing a flying toupee, but apparently these were sound pursuits compared to the concerted silliness of writing novels. I also believed I had his respect, but he had no more respect for my childish scribblings, comic sketches, and published titles than his ex-wives and children had for Steady Boy and his schemes.

He could treat real life as a fiction, wish away *this* and will *that* into existence, manipulate the truth and toy with people's feelings, leave off the old dead drafts and start over with a new cast of characters whenever the whim struck, trade an Evangeline in for a Barbara and swap Downers Grove for Schaumburg...he could put all the tactics of the writer's craft to good use in his *life,* but I was the silly one for making a career of it.

45

I did what I could for Barbara: tidied, shoveled the drive when it snowed. No great thanks was ever forthcoming. That was okay. I wasn't there for her. She may have been jealous that I had the luxury to act the hero, cooking for him and driving him to his doctor's appointments, when she was the nurse and natural caretaker between us, not to mention the man's wife. I walked on eggshells whenever she was home from work and even rented an apartment on Roselle Road to make myself scarce on weekends. I was rarely there, but I think it pleased her to know that I had a place to go, that I was a part-time valet like Mr. Molesley and not a permanent fixture. I turned down a residency in Menerbes, did the grocery shopping.

Six weeks after the Whipple, we took an involuntary hiatus from our television marathon. You might suspect, by that, an infection or sudden fever; it was not so straightforward. It was the middle of the day in Schaumburg, capital of TiVo, in the Kingdom of Netflix, and I was having a hard time keeping the political intrigue straight from the police procedural, the family drama distinct from the science fiction. We spent time in spacecraft and surveillance rooms, in precinct offices, law courts and strip clubs. Oh, the sound and fury of endless streaming! Yet every forty-four minutes or so, I would tune back in to the old man who was only ever half awake, and no matter where we'd just been—in Pakistan spoiling a plot, or rooting out a mole at the Pentagon, or solving the metaphysical puzzles of a sudden rapture—I was returned to the ongoing, essentially static, event-free drama unfolding on the recliner in a stuffy suburban living room, the cellular drama that will represent, for most Americans, the only one that threatens, that entangles, that destroys: the small, stupid drama of a person dying of cancer, the biggest and dullest drama on earth, which might have been called—if it weren't already the title of a TV show—the facts of life.

The power went out. The TV blinked off, the sound cut to silence. I was roused from a stupor and sat upright. I expected to look over and find Chuck snoring right through it, but he was awake; indeed, he had collapsed the footrest and was peering deeply into the room as if dazed, mesmerized. He turned to me and, with a curiosity I had seen no sign of since the surgery, asked if I was an alien.

"A what?"

"An alien?"

He pointed to the television. It was blank, but I got his meaning. All our news of extraterrestrial beings came from there.

"Not that I know of," I said.

It was a puzzling remark, not quite a joke. A moment later, I did what you do when the power goes out: drifted into the kitchen wondering dumbly whom I might call. When I wandered back into the living room, I found the front door open. Chuck was standing in the yard peering up at an overcast sky. It was a moody day on Rust Road, full of fog and bruised cloud. As I idly watched from the doorway, he walked to the curb where my rental was parked, opened the door and climbed in. By the time it dawned on me that he had my car keys and I might want to go after him, stop him, do something . . . he'd turned the engine over and was rounding the bend, out of sight.

At last, it made perfect sense. The temptation to blame himself had always been very strong. If a product didn't perform, the marketplace wasn't the problem. The marketplace was efficient. The fault belonged to the inventor and entrepreneur; it belonged to him. His ideas were off. *Is there a need for this in the marketplace? These nice people were looking for a good time and you gave them herpes. Do you even have a lawyer?* Voices, so many voices saying *No, not good, get lost*. How could a whole chorus of voices be wrong?

What a temptation!

He left the neighborhood of Rust Road and gained the expressway and a mile later pulled off to the shoulder near the interstate exchange. He let the car idle as he opened the door and stood looking out at the traffic converging at junctures east and west while commercial freight pounded past him and little sedans zipped by. He could feel his hair blow around in the currents. Very unlike him, to leave the house without a hat. To the north, the Woodfield Mall; to the east, the city skyline; to the south, stalled traffic glinting under the sun, inching along the highway; and to the west, a steady flow of it bifurcating and shamrocking into the four corners of the earth . . . and for the first time, he saw it all for what it really was.

He got off the highway at the mall exit and paid a visit to the Sears, Roebuck. No one called it that anymore. It was just "Sears" now, this anchor store among the last of its kind.

"Do you have the Doolander in stock?" he asked an employee who was making a display of pink antifreeze bottles.

"The what?"

"Endopalm-T?"

"Pardon?"

"Do you have Endopalm-T?"

"I don't know what that is," the employee said. "I can look it up for you in the system, if you'd like."

The system. He followed the man over to it, where he spelled out Endopalm-T, but the system had no match.

"Is there a different system?" he asked.

"Sir," the man said, pointing down at his feet, "you can't be in here without shoes on."

He got his start selling shoes—everyone knew that. But everyone also knew that Sears was by then a shadow of its former self. And they were worried about *him*? He left. He went next door to an office of H&R Block, the tax-prep chain, where he approached the woman sitting behind the front desk. She watched the sickly man approach, hair tousled, in plaid pajama pants and a Fighting Illini sweatshirt.

"Jimmy Cayne," he said.

"Come again?"

"Little guy, not"—he dropped his voice—"much to look at..."

He offered the woman a universal shrug: *What are you going to do?*

"What are you asking me?"

"I'm here to see Jimmy Cayne."

"There's nobody here by the name Jimmy," she said.

He nodded as if this, too, was entirely predictable.

"Little guy," he said.

"No little guy here," the woman said.

"The little games people play for big profits," he said, "headquarters, mansions, the 'brand names.' Tell him . . . I don't buy it anymore."

He was light an organ or two, but in his mind, where it mattered, it was America that had been hollowed out. He left the H&R Block for the Sherwin-Williams next door, where he drifted down the aisles collecting paint samples. The assistant manager approached him.

"May I help you?"

"I invented the spill-proof paint can," he said.

There was a long pause.

"Is that right?"

"In 1971. Worked all night on it. Opened up this can of paint, see, it spills everywhere. I think to myself gotta be a better way, gotta be . . . next thing you know, I'm doodling. Conceptualizing, you know. Run out to the garage. Bent this in place, bent that . . . voilà! Spill-proof paint can. Apply for a patten . . . Patton . . . sorry, pat *tent* . . . never heard back. Two years later, open a new can . . . there's my design. No recognition to this day. True story."

He waited for a reply, but the assistant manager was not human, either.

Was there one human being left in Schaumburg? Was there one honest, sympathetic, feeling person in all the suburbs? Not at the Sears, not at the tax store, and not here at the place that sold paint, either. And I'm sorry, he thought, it was that way throughout Chicagoland, the Land of Lincoln, the heartland,

and all the rest of America, too. It was stocked full of, crowded up with, overrun by... fakes, frauds, impostors.

He couldn't say for sure that every soul had been replaced, or even that he was still alive. A compromised world of fakes in which he felt ill all the time fit the description of purgatory pretty well. Either way, was it any great surprise that no product or idea of his had taken hold here? At last, it made perfect sense: his double-o's, triple downs, and what-have-yous, they were never going to gain traction much less *triumph* in a world overrun by extraterrestrial beings. He knew that the minute the power went out.

His side hurt where they had gone in weeks earlier and, in the guise of healing him, attempted to vacuum out his soul. Only they "missed a little," to use their parlance; they "failed to get it all." A little soul remained. It was all he needed to see far and wide what had really taken place in this world and all that was taking place still. Bankruptcy, disability, and homelessness now struck him as entirely advantageous to good fortune. The dispossessed, the disinherited, the ailing, those stuck in terminal holding patterns or arrested by their traumas and living as ghosts were, according to a terrific irony, the last of the living, while the overlords of wealth and good health were counterfeits. Martians? Mothmen? Humanoid flies? Hard to say. They could have been lizards zipped up in skin suits for all his command of the fine print.

It was no accident that, after the paint store, he found himself wandering the county hospital. The old were there, the infected, the immobile, the amputated, the sclerotic, and the deformed. They loitered around the dry fountain smoking their old-school cigarettes. They choked the hallways with wheelchairs and IV poles. They lay helpless and terrified in their deathbeds, real people with real problems, unlike those invulnerable aliens out there running the show. What a monumental task it would be to roust these sad sacks into a respectable resistance, but that was his final hope, the ailing and enlightened the last people on earth...

He had not had his scrambled eggs and was hungry when he departed the hospital. He took the rental around the drive-through. Ninety-nine billion served, the sign said. He had served no one. He had done nothing. When he got his food, he could not eat it. But at least he understood the disconnect between the sign and himself: what they served was alien grub, and what he required was real-person food. The flat gray patties, the nuclear cheese and the bright red-and-green goo on top all but crawled before his eyes. This was not a world for living in. He went around again to demand his money back, a favorite American pastime, but the prospect of attempting to explain all the suffering and outrage involved in "99 billion served" to one of the young and healthy drones at the window just frustrated and exhausted him.

He gained the highway again and followed the Tri-State to I-57 south. Once upon a time, he had done this particular drive every Saturday. Yes, it was back to Danville for Charlie Barnes, back to the good old days, back to high school football games and functioning bowels—and back to the can-do spirit of his youth, drained from him these many years (as if via gastric tube) by the big city and its suburbs. He navigated the drive by feel, leaving the highway for the back roads at Kankakee and taking a left at the first fork, a right at the next. It was a straight shot into Danville from there. Nothing ever seemed quite so nostalgic as the heartland cornfields he passed, the Podunk towns. But when he pulled into the driveway of the house on Vermilion, he was inside an unrecognizable rental car, not the old Newport. That was confusing. He tried to recall why he had come. He had lived in that house once. He was real there, young and in love. But time had rendered it unrecognizable, it was crumbling and in need of repair, and no boy ran out to greet him. By the time the owner emerged to investigate why a stranger was parked in his driveway, Charlie was racked with sobs.

"I'm looking for Old Poor Farm," he told the man upon powering down the window, his face wet with tears.

"Old what?"

"The poor farm? Out on the Catlin-Tilton Road?"

That was a real place once, realest place he'd ever known. People helping people, and heaven on earth just around the bend.

"Well," said the man, "if it's the Catlin-Tilton Road you're after..."

He followed the man's directions to the Walmart on the former site of Old Poor Farm. No trace of it remained: no more do-gooders in wool suits or pedestal desks holding jars of wheat germ. The social contract was over. Charley Proffit of Peoria, Illinois, had remarried and was living...where? And was she fake, too? He would have liked to know that at least one thing had been real once upon a—

He had to admit to himself something that only a real person could: time had passed; he had grown old and would die. He needed help. But there was no one around to help him. Even the seasons, with their suggestion of renewal—that crisp touch of fall, that old hint of spring—were gone. He was wandering down an aisle of the Walmart in the purgatorial half-light among the zombie hordes.

"I came up with the soccer ball," he told the cashier.

"You want the sports aisle."

"Not the soccer ball," he said, amused by his own mistake. "The *sno-cone*. You see, first I shaved some ice into a little cup, I did it for Jerry. Then I dabbed a little... what do you call it? I didn't call it a sno-cone. I called it poor man's ice cream. Marketing is everything. Timing, too."

The cashier looked to the bagger for help.

"I never had good timing."

The bagger said, "Mister, you buying something?"

He found, within reach, a display of candy bars. At last, real food. He took one Charleston Chew, one box of Good & Plenty, and two or three other old familiar items and placed them on the belt. Back in the rental car, he sucked on some Milk Duds in the handicapped spot. A pair of Danville police officers found him the next morning, 2:00 a.m., asleep in the front seat...

Barbara and I had been looking for him almost twenty-four hours by then.

"If you can't take care of him, why are you here?" she asked me. "Do I need to hire someone?"

"I didn't know he had my keys. And I didn't think he had the energy."

"First you let my dog out to die, now it's my husband."

"For the millionth time," I said. "I didn't know it was an inside dog."

"I should have just agreed to let Marcy come," she said. "Marcy is a disaster, but at least she's competent."

"Why is Marcy a disaster?"

"She's a spoiled brat. She sabotages everyone's happiness. She doesn't believe her father even deserves happiness. She's an asshole. Marcy is an asshole."

"Does Chuck know that's how you feel?"

"If Chuck were honest with himself, he would feel the same way. But that's his daughter. He can't afford to be honest."

"You've never liked her," I said.

"No, I never have."

"And me?" I asked.

She made no reply.

I was no fool. I didn't press her. It was her house, her husband. I was at her mercy. Marcy in Deer Park, Jerry on Western Avenue, Evangeline in New Port Richey . . . not much of a family to speak of without Steady Boy.

"No one thinks of you," she said, almost as an afterthought.

We were driving through the night. Dawn broke as we arrived at the hospital in Champaign-Urbana where he had been taken for medical evaluation and where I, too, had spent some time as a newborn. Barbara killed the ignition and was reaching for the door when I caught her arm.

"I screwed up," I said. "Give me another chance."

She paused before answering. "There are times when I honestly don't know who you are or why you're here," she said.

She got out of the car. She would later apologize.

He was transferred to First Baptist, where he was treated for psychosis with lithium and a second antipsychotic. It was less than ideal. He badly needed to seize that particular moment in time to start chemo, but he was too weak and weighed too little and was out of his mind anyway. It would have to wait. One of the doctors on his tumor board alerted Barbara to a case study from 1998 in which a patient who underwent a Whipple procedure became convinced some six weeks later that he was Bill Clinton. The trauma of that particular operation could produce a break with reality similar to the one experienced by soldiers on a battlefield.

With help from the medication, he had admirable recall of these events and detailed them for me with a bafflement that rivaled my own. There had been other occasions in which the power had gone out and he hadn't left the house to confirm a world overrun by extraterrestrials. What was different this time? It was, he thought, the result of an estrangement from all that he knew and loved on account of his compromised body. A world in which he had no appetite for a glass of cold milk, a tub of buttered popcorn, or a fresh sports page no longer made sense as the world.

46

There had been a brief window, between that first serving of scrambled eggs and his kind of losing his mind there, when he and I (between episodes of TV) resumed debating back and forth as we had been doing my entire life. The object of our debates had never mattered much. As inveterate gamblers never care about the nature of the contest upon which they lay down their money, as old addicts never mind what gets them high, chronic and incorrigible debaters like me and Chuck happily went at it over anything and everything: the pros and cons of a packet of salt, the performance of an orphaned ear-plug. It was our way of paying a compliment to the richness of the world and of each other's minds. We debated in private, on road trips and in restaurants, and we debated in mixed company until everyone else got drowned out and grew bored stiff. We didn't know when to quit: just as the birthday cake was coming out, as heads were bowing for prayer, as the final strains of the national anthem were sending shivers down the collective spine, on we went, eager to make one last point in a low murmuring aside, neither one willing to concede defeat. Was grunge the equal of opera? Could concentration camps take root here in America? Was a poet a salesman when he published his chapbook or by nature something more pure? Some of our debating was downright dull and gave even me a headache, but it was our sport, our bond, an expression of love and measure of our mutual respect.

Only now we debated how he might repair his relationship with his daughter.

"Does she really hate me?"

"I don't think she hates you, no. She's just angry."

"She won't call, Jake, she won't pay me a visit. She knows the cancer's real. I've apologized for the lie. What more can I do?"

Marcy had every right to be angry with Charlie. She'd been manipulated the day of his diagnosis, quit her job to fly to Chicago, had to learn from Jerry that her father had lied, and then had to maintain her resolve to make him pay a price for all this bad behavior even as he was put under and cut open and so vastly diminished that he was almost unrecognizable. I'd flown down to... where was it, again? Oh, yes, Deer Park, Texas. I'd flown to Texas to encourage her to join us in the waiting room on the day of his surgery, had even purchased an airline ticket for her to this end, but she could not be persuaded. She had made up her mind: her father was a con man, and nothing—not pancreatic cancer or the Whipple procedure or a daily dose of antipsychotics—was ever going to make him *get real.* It wasn't lost on me that when Charlie momentarily broke with reality, he conceived of himself as the genuine article in a world of fakes and impostors. It was never his aim to live life as a farce. His every harebrained scheme was intended to make him more real in the eyes of the world, and in his daughter's.

He had to shoulder responsibility for his trouble with Marcy, but there was also at play here a legacy of the past. As a younger, more impressionable person, Marcy had been heavily influenced by her mother's poor opinion of her father. A divorce didn't seem sufficient for Charley Proffit in her repudiation of her ex-husband. Falling in love with Charlie, marrying him, having his children—all that mortified her. She had been tricked by his full beard. When she found the man she was looking for in Dickie Dickerdick, she needed not merely to put Charlie in the past; she wanted to erase him from the historical record. To that end, she turned Dickie into Dad. "Ask your father," she'd say, in reference not to the man we'd grown up with from time immemorial, but to the virtual stranger who had driven us to Florida for a sun-kissed fresh start. "Let's give your father a call." "What would your dad say?" "Wait until your father gets home." Dickie wasn't our dad—and he was a far cry from fatherly—but he was very convenient as a shiny decoy in the systematic whitewashing of Charlie Barnes. Saying Charlie's name in earshot of Charley Proffit became almost as awkward and ultimately forbidden as the conjuring of Evangeline Barnes would be years later in the company of Barbara Ledeux. It was really impressive, the genius these people had for ghost stories.

I knew my task in Deer Park was a tall one, but no one else could afford to fly down there and plead his case in person, which was what he deserved. I rented a car and booked a room, then called her to let her know I'd arrived.

"Arrived where?" she asked.

"The hotel," I said. "The place I stayed last time."

"Hold on," she said. "You're back in Deer Park?"

"Yes, Deer Park."

"What the hell! Jake, you can't just keep popping up in Texas," she said. "Don't you know I live here for a reason?"

"What reason is that?"

"To be as far away from you people as possible."

"I was hoping we could get another drink," I said.

"You don't drink."

"Dinner, then."

"I've eaten."

"It's noon."

She agreed to meet at the sports bar where we'd met previously. I caught her up on his so-called recovery, his brief break with reality and how it forced the delay of urgently needed chemotherapy. I don't know that any of it did much good. Since his operation, she'd played things close to the vest. No flowers. No get-well cards. No texts or emails. No fruit baskets. No curiosity, it would seem, for how the old man was faring in the fight for his life. But that was Marcy, wasn't it? A mystery, a kind of split personality. You just never knew from day to day which one you were going to get. I made a final case for why he deserved a little mercy, then I went silent. She looked off. When she turned back, she had tears in her eyes.

"Is he dying?"

"He might be. I don't know."

"He's hurting?"

"He's very definitely hurting."

"Because of me?"

"Because he is who he is," I said, "and because he wishes to be someone better."

"Who doesn't?" she asked. "Except for maybe you, Jake."

"Oh, don't be so sure," I said. "I'm full of surprises."

"Why are you here?" she asked. "Have you really come all the way to Texas just to repair his relationship with me?"

"I owe him," I said.

"You could have called."

I nodded.

"If I were you, I wouldn't have come," she said. "I would have fled this family a long time ago and never looked back."

"I like you guys."

"You like *him*."

"I love him," I said.

She looked off again.

"Okay," she said. "Let me give it some thought."

It was about as much as I could hope for, and I flew back to Chicago the next day.

47

Christmas on Rust Road was a subdued affair: sugar cookies in tins and an artificial tree. Barbara's spinster sister, the mysteriously named Darge, came with her irrepressible nervous tic: the animatronic need to rotate her head sixty degrees to the right every ten seconds or so. She weighed ninety pounds and wore a Christmas sweater. Barbara's children—Troy Ledeux, on leave from the army, and Tory, a tire saleswoman for Pirelli—had developed in their adult years a curious sibling connection despite their difference in age. When in the comforts of home, their hair down and feet bare, my stepsiblings became preoccupied by their persistent little teases, hem pullings, back massages, high private squeals of laughter, impromptu wrestling matches that drove them out of the kitchen and into the living room, and finally those settled, languid moments when, as decaf brewed after the holiday dinner, the sister sat on the brother's lap and idly began petting the hair on his arm.

"Tory and Troy are awfully close," I whispered to Charlie in a private moment on Christmas Day. "What's that about?"

"I make no inquiries into that relationship, Jake."

"But you agree it's odd?"

"I don't even know what you're talking about," he said with a shit-eating grin.

His first post-Whipple Christmas, when his most ardent wish had been to celebrate in the company of loved ones the additional time he had been granted, was instead a thunderous rebuke to the life that had preceded the Whipple, because his children refused to participate. When Jerry, who lived all of twenty miles away, declined to stop by, he had to contend with the clearest evidence yet of a perfectly failed life. In fact I fix the date of the first steps he took to change that life to the day after Christmas, when, early in the morning, I returned to the house on Rust Road with bags of salt for deicing the driveway to find the television off and the old man in his recliner... reading a book.

"He's up already," I said, "and reading the Bhagavad Gita?"

He half shrugged as I resumed my place on the end of the sofa nearest him. I'd taken off my shoes before entering Barbara's house, of course, a rule I'd been following for fifteen years. "It renders death meaningless, apparently," he said.

"Hey, we should all be reading it."

"Jerry thinks so. This is his favorite thing."

"Oh," I said. "You don't say."

The mention of Jerry brought back his absence the day before, and Charlie looked downcast.

"I'm determined to make it through this time, Jake."

"To edify your soul, or to please Jerry?"

"I would like to please Jerry," he said. "But I'd better say the soul part, or he'll tell me I'm reading it all wrong."

"You can't read a book wrong anymore, Chuck. Not in the age of Amazon reviews."

"Tell me something, Jake," he said. "What's dharma?"

I have always consigned the desiderata of religious concepts, with their dry abstractions and dubious utilities, to a junk drawer of the mind, where inevitably they went to get all jumbled up and die of unholy neglect. I rummaged around now for *dharma* but came up empty-handed.

"Do you want the Buddhist's use of the term or the Hindu's?"

He looked uncertain.

"Joking," I said. "I don't actually know the difference. I run Literature 101, remember? Jerry's in charge of Advanced Religion."

"I'll tell you what I think it is," he said. "I think it means a calling in life, the one thing you were meant to do—you and you alone. Your duty, I guess. Almost a holy duty."

"For me," I said, "that would be taking care of you, Chuck."

"For you," he replied, correcting me, "it would be writing books. I've always admired that about you, Jake. Your determination. You've known you were a writer since you read Hemingway. How old were you when you first read Hemingway?"

"It was Dostoyevsky," I said, "and I was twelve."

"Twelve years old and reading Hemingway."

"It was Dostoyevsky."

"I never did anything like that. I don't do anything like it now. Sixty-nine years old, son, and not likely to live all that much longer—"

"Don't say that, Pops. Don't even think it."

"—and I still don't know what I want to be when I grow up. What is it, Jake? What's my duty? What's my dharma?"

Was he asking rhetorically?

"Financial planning," I said.

He dismissed that with a wave of the hand.

"What about Chippin' In?"

The look he returned was so curious—curiosity itself.

"What is that?" he asked.

"Chippin' In?"

His eyes had brightened.

"I know that, don't I? What is that?"

"You don't remember?"

"Tell me what that is. I know I know it."

He had no recollection! His dear idea, his million-dollar delight, had been rubbed out, effaced from the poor man's memory by his pancreatic ordeal. The only commercial concept ever endorsed by his stingy brother, Rudy, the hotshot—the bastard who, when his brother fell ill, couldn't be bothered to visit him over the holiday, despite my efforts to get him on the phone and plead with him. Charlie had clung to Chippin' In, prior to surgery, as his last best hope, only to wake Whippled and wiped clean.

But that, too, by God, yes, even that!—here his buoyant voice can't help but break through in memory—had its upside, for suddenly he found himself in one of those time-traveling, role-swapping, richly ironic scenarios that he and I knew so well from our hours of television viewing, in which he could have his own idea pitched to him by a cosmic surrogate. Would it warp the space-time continuum? Would it (more unlikely still) measure up? The minute I began to explain the concept, it came back to him, of course, but he insisted I revive every detail. When I finished doing so, I watched him closely for his reaction.

Suddenly, he sprang forward on his recliner, collapsing the footrest in a fit that made the whole thing ring, and seized upon my knee with a strong hand, just as he would have done in his days before the Whipple. "Not too shabby an idea, my boy!"

I loved him. The Gita, I remember, had fallen between the chair and the footrest before the latter came thundering down, and so was swallowed up.

—

On the first Monday of the new year, he clopped into the kitchen in suit and tie, his old perfumed and polished self. Our plan was to hit the banks.

In his day, a proper bank had pillars and vaults, and echoes ringing in the airy halls, and gentlemen bankers in three-piece suits whose Rolodexes would unlock at the sound of a good idea... but times had changed. The suburban branches of those Wall Street banks that we paid visits to that day, from Roselle Road to Route 53, to pitch Chippin' In, were as close to the halls of power as K was to the castle. We began with one bank in particular whose corporate parent, he believed, would be the quickest to see the synergies between his brainchild and their mission statement. But where he hoped to find venture capital, there were only padded armchairs and free peppermints and a branch manager busy converting an old lady's loose change into dollar bills, and we left that glass box with little more than brochures.

The mood of the financial markets in that winter of our Great Recession was grim. No one had any business asking anyone else for money unless that money was already theirs, and even then it wasn't a sure thing. I did take heart, however, as we went from bank to bank, at seeing a tie knotted at his neck again. Though pinning an old wattle in place, it restored his youthful vigor. He was jazzed again. He had purpose that morning. If he was also taking catnaps between our destinations, at least he was back out there, making an effort. Of course, he looked like hell warmed over. And by then he hated bankers. From their branches hung too many sour grapes. More revelations about Bear Stearns had come to light, Lehman had failed the previous September, and the mortgage mess was in full swing; his faith in a fair game was gone, and he took to calling the banks "the Five Families."

In practical terms, the day was a bust. The recent college grads manning the teller windows didn't know what to do with him, while their betters in the open plans had little to offer beyond a business card. Upon saying the words *Chippin' In,* he might as well have been standing there in loincloth and sandals with a cow on a leash. This was the glad-handing Charlie Barnes that Jerry most despised; he would have had no appetite for it. Dropping in unannounced on playacting bankers in glorified ATMs to discuss the funding of a goofy idea would have put the lie to more than the American dream; it would have stripped away the illusions necessary for maintaining life itself, and Jerry would have retreated behind a potted plant. Steady Boy's brash self-confidence when a good idea graced his pocket, despite the hundred others now tarnished and parked in some coffee can, clung to Jerry, as the father's iniquities are said to cling unto the third and fourth generations. Even I was a little embarrassed on Chuck's behalf. I loved him and wanted to help, but did he really believe he'd start inking contracts at the Schaumburg Citibank? What self-deceptions we require to get out of bed in the morning. The Clown in Your Town, the Original Doolander, TTAA, now Chippin' In... I was so moved by this pitiable string of failed campaigns that I parked and ran around my rental to the passenger-side door before he could even reach for the handle. I opened the door to the bank for him, too. I watched in dread as he pitched his idea to a teenager in suit and tie. And I walked defeated through the parking lot with him on our return to the car.

"What do I need these clowns for?" he asked from the passenger seat after I climbed in and shut the door. "They're a bunch of crooks anyway. I know this idea inside out. I don't need a damn bank. I just need to put it online. Let people look at it for themselves. If they take to it, great. Beats going hat in hand to a bunch of fucking schoolkids."

By March of the new year, his doctors determined that he was strong enough to start chemotherapy, four unfortunate months behind schedule. By then, the website for Chippin' In had gone live. Not particularly warm or attractive—in fact, profoundly ugly—and almost purely functional, it required daily upkeep and administration, which he outsourced to a company in India for a mere nineteen bucks a month. He shrugged.

"Not exactly a life's calling," he concluded.

48

It preoccupied him: everyone had a calling. It depressed him: he had not found his. It gave him hope: he might still do so before he died.

In the days leading up to his first round of chemo, he spoke to Barbara about it while I eavesdropped from the other room. She might have reasonably suggested that it was too late for him to find some calling in life, that he stop with the pipe dreams and focus on gaining his strength back, but she was quite solicitous of the old man and asked what a calling might look like for him. Was it spiritual in nature? Did it involve travel, or education, or activism? It was only then that he revealed he had three ideas in mind: divorce mediator (for which he already had the tagline: "A Fair Hand . . . *Always*"); a journalist of some kind, preferably on the opinion page; or a toy developer. Conceptor? He didn't know the exact term or career trajectory. "But," he said to Jerry the next day, "you get the idea."

"Why not a fourth?"

"Tell it to me," Charlie said. "I'm eager to hear it."

"General manager of the Chicago Cubs."

As condescending laughter rolled into Jerry's apartment from distant locker rooms, golf clubs, and corporate perches of the imagination, Charlie recoiled.

"If you're just going to laugh at me, Jerry, to hell with you."

We had arrived at his walk-up an hour earlier, a run-down hovel on Chicago's West Side, only to stand on the stoop for twenty minutes pressing the buzzer in vain. Jerry, asleep, or stoned, or coolly debating his desire to let us up, finally shot the bolt. I took one look at him, a big man in denim cutoffs and a soiled T-shirt, and thought, my God, even in winter!

"Cold out here, man. What took you so long?"

The timbre of annoyance in the old man's voice told me we might be headed for a bruiser.

"Buzzer's on the fritz," Jerry said. "Come on up."

The stairs were a minefield. "Watch that hole, boys," he said, and a hole it was, passing straight through a middle stair on the first flight and into a dark abyss. Had a bowling ball done that? But no, it looked gnawed. Sawed? Who knows? I stepped over it and saw the sign in my mind's eye: FAILED STAIRS, HALF OFF.

As we climbed, every turn and transition to a new odor told

of the distance Jerry had traveled from the one-time respectable suburban homeowner to the Dumpster-diving dropout with self-sabotaged credit. For Jerry, unemployment was the only principled stand in modern-day America, as the alternative was to work for rapists and thieves, which he would no longer do. His time was better spent diagnosing the power structures of neoliberalism via YouTube while reading deeply in his Eastern religion. The result was the radicalizing of a distinctly American monk: dropped out, plugged in, metaphysically enlightened but politically enraged. He was all tenderness one minute, all terror the next—a condition mitigated, when it wasn't made worse, by his marijuana intake.

Without offering me a reason, he had apologized for standing me up the night before the old man's surgery. I'd tried to get him to join us for Christmas, to no avail. I kept encouraging him to talk to me, to unburden himself to someone who loved him unconditionally, but he was almost fifty years old and fixed in his ways, and I don't think he gave a damn if I was in town or not. We reached the top landing and he invited us in.

Jerry had owned at various times such diverse keepsakes as a piece of the Berlin Wall, brass bells from a Kyoto monastery, and Jim Croce's acoustic guitar. He had owned birdcages and stone carvings of the Buddha, electric grills and full-length mirrors, matching furniture and a set of encyclopedias. Those days were over. With the exception of the kitchen table and a mattress in the corner, his apartment was bare.

I had driven Charlie over there that day so that he could discuss dharma with his professor in Advanced Religion. To what extent was that just a pretense to see Jerry and to dispel the awful memory of the last time they were together, when they went at each other like wolves? That would have been a sour note to end on, and was perhaps why Jerry, with a regret or two of his own, had let us in.

Presently, he said, "Why divorce mediator, Pop?"

Naturally, the old man just shrugged. "I have a lot of experience with divorce," he said.

"Look, I'm impressed you finally read the thing."

"To be honest, Jerry, I'm not *quite* finished with the Gita yet."

"But you're going about this all wrong. None of those things is your dharma."

"How do you know?"

"Because dharma isn't what you want to do, or what you'd like to do, or what you dream of doing... it's what you *must* do, Dad, without hope of personal gain. It's duty... not bliss, or excitement, or even contentment."

"Well, what is that, for me?"

"How should I know?"

"How the hell should I?"

"It's *your* dharma!"

"Oh, for chrissake."

They fell silent. Jerry rummaged around an ashtray for an old joint, lit it and inhaled. Such a profusion of pot smoke erupted from him a second later, it was like watching a steam engine leave the station. It put me in mind, for some reason, of *Anna Karenina,* and following that thought to its logical end, I concluded that Jerry combined the uncompromising Levin with the passionate Anna in a single soul—he was an idealist who would shake off propriety even if it meant suicide—but to the casual observer, he looked like nothing more than a drunken serf. Charlie gazed off, lost in his own little world. I sat mute and anxious. I saw the fight coming and wondered why on earth it was so hard for them to get along.

"Tell me something, Jerry," the old man finally said. "What is *your* dharma?"

"Mine?" he gasped, before releasing more pot smoke. "What's it look like?" he said. "To resist."

I suppose that was true in a way, but not, I thought, for the reasons Jerry believed. By organizing his life around Dumpster diving and YouTube and the withholding of rent from modern-day plantation owners, he was not resisting corporate America, the neoliberal crooks and the politicians who enabled their crimes. He was resisting Charlie Barnes. He was rejecting Charlie, sending back his insufficient love, his bungled attempts at parenting, and the disappointing example he set as a man in the world. It did not matter that, without a loving father inviting him to come live in the house on Vermilion Street one troubled morning in 1975, Jerry would have had no place to call home and no family to belong to. He was not especially grateful. His main concern was not becoming the old man. But a son's revolt against his father usually ends in parody, and in Jerry's case it had the perverse effect of delivering him more quickly to the fate he hoped to avoid. Jerry had bowed out of work, society, the hidebound world and all the exacting rules by which it operated, all in order to avoid the old man's fate. But bowing out was a Barnes special. He *was* Charlie Barnes, though he was blind to it.

"But I have news for you," he said to us both. "It's time I made a few changes."

We carry around ideas of people in our heads, fixed ideas

of their character and firm predictions of how they'll behave, what they'll say before the hour is up and the facial expressions they'll make that will unaccountably get under our skin. We tell stories about them that never vary, never improve, then confirm that our ideas are accurate every time we get reacquainted. I expected Jerry to do everything I predicted he would do that day: sit back, smoke pot, spoil for a fight. Above all, take exception to everything Chuck said. Brook no opposition, provide no comfort, give no ground. He'd be in no great hurry to leave for brunch, either, which was yet another reason we were there: to take him out to eat, be a goddamn family again, grateful that the old man was still around to break bread with. Well, sure enough, that came to pass: we would not sit for our meal until noon, by which time I was peckish and annoyed. But there was also this little revelation that he needed to make some changes. He confounded me that day, Jerry completely confounded me.

"Fact of the matter is, boys, old Jerry needs a job."

"A real job?" Charlie asked. "Or a job in Belgium?"

"A proper job," he said. He frowned, sat back, plucked at his T-shirt so that it fell more favorably over the belly. "What the hell have I been doing these past few years? What is the point of living like this?"

He gestured around at the hovel.

"What about the rapists and thieves?" Charlie asked.

"A man still has to make a living."

"Do you mean it this time? Or are you still pulling my leg?"

"Look around you, Pop. This is no way to live. So the world doesn't deserve me. The world doesn't deserve many of us. Is that a good excuse for becoming somebody else's problem?"

These extraordinary words stunned his audience of two. They were just so unexpected from such a hard and resolute man as Jerry. Was change really possible in one such as he? Perhaps we shouldn't have believed him. This was, after all, the same man capable of lying about living and working in Belgium. Regardless, tears welled up in the old man's eyes—big fat happy mothers that sprang to the surface out of nowhere. He was prone to emotional upheavals after his surgery, but it was a special relief to know that his son would have health insurance again. And all of Jerry's spiritual drive had curdled into complaint over the years and turned him into a big grouch. Well, here was some of that original spirit again.

"Where is this coming from, Jerry? This sudden reversal and . . . sudden insight?"

"Some of it comes from Jake."

"From me?" I said.

"Sure, you. Some of the things you said to me the other night at the bar—"

We had in fact managed to get together at last, after he stood me up three times running, and though I make it a point not to drink, we drank like brothers that night, as good brothers must from time to time, and had us a heart-to-heart.

"I heard you that night," he said now. "I heard you loud and clear."

I couldn't believe that whatever I said to him in a drunken stupor had really prompted him to make an attempt to turn his wayward life around. Did it ever work like that? More likely it was his living conditions: no working buzzer and no furnishings, and a hole in his stairs. It was diving into Dumpsters, the toll that was taking on his body. He was gaining weight, his asthma was getting worse. He dropped in to the ER as others do the post office. It was not having the insurance necessary to cover the cost of a trip to the ER. It was driving that van of his. No one in his right mind would get behind the wheel of that van. If it were me, I'd have found work just to be done with those ratty-ass denim cutoffs.

"And I have thirty days to make these changes," he said, "because in thirty days, I'll be homeless."

"Homeless?"

"Got the eviction notice yesterday."

There it was, the real cause for a return to the workplace: an eviction notice.

"Jerry, don't you know in a million years I could never let you go homeless?"

"I couldn't live in Barbara's house, Pop."

"But it's my house, too, son. It's your father's house, where you always have a place at the table."

"And a pillow to lay my head?"

"Damn right!"

"Sorry, Pop. Can't do it."

"You'd rather be out on the street?"

"In this weather, you bet."

"It's March!"

"Well, then, just imagine how nice summer will feel."

"Oh, Jerry, don't be an ass."

There was a long pause. Here it comes, I thought. The bruiser. They will come to blows and end in a single bloody heap.

But in a development more remarkable than his decision to get a job, Jerry did not escalate, or insist on having the last word. *He changed the subject.* I couldn't believe it. When it first dawned on me that it was taking place, I was nearly moved to tears. He might have simply been evading further discussion of living at 105 Rust Road, but he was also showing the old man respect. There he is, I thought, the deferential, expansive, sweet-natured Jerry I've always most admired. That particular individual has never made an appearance in these pages.

"It was wrong of me to lie about going to Belgium," he said. "I had no right to remake reality for you like that. I was writing you off, Pop, with that lie, washing my hands of you . . . and I never want to wash my hands of you. I need you. I owe you so much. I was worried I was going to lose you. Listen," he said. "I'm sorry we got into it like we did."

"No, I'm sorry, Jerry. Some of the things I said to you that day . . ."

"That was my doing, Pop. You didn't need me showing up with another damn copy of the Gita. You needed some compassion, and I had to taunt you about Jimmy Cayne."

"I deserved that," Charlie said.

"Anyway, I'm sorry I didn't visit more often when you were in the hospital. As Jake pointed out the other night, I can be full of dumb pride, and more than a little self-absorbed. I let all these stupid resentments from childhood hang over us. What's the point of that? Forgive me," he said. "Let's start over—what do you say?"

Charlie, who loved nothing more than a second chance, shot up and threw his arms around Jerry, who hardly had time to react. He returned his father's embrace while struggling to right himself. Finally on his feet, the chair tipped over. They hugged in the middle of that bare and happy room, that awful room.

When they finally broke off, both wiping away tears, my father said, "You won't have any problem finding something."

"I don't know, Pop. It's not like anyone's hiring at the moment."

"You're brilliant, Jerry. You have advanced degrees."

"I've been out of the workforce awhile now."

"This is America. People are always hiring somewhere."

We went to brunch. Before our coffee arrived, Charlie walked across the street to an ATM and withdrew what he could and came back and handed it to Jerry. He tried to take out more after our brunch was over, but his card was declined.

"Hold it," he said as we were dropping Jerry back at his apartment.

He removed the Rolex that I mentioned a long time ago, on page 13 or 14, the sole authentic item in a collection of fakes, which both Jerry and I associated with him from the start of time, and offered it to Jerry in the back seat. He was done thinking about his calling for the time being, that's for damn sure. Jerry thanked him but refused to accept it and got out of the car. On our return to Rust Road, the poor old man had to pull over. He put the car in Park on the highway shoulder and wept for his son and I could do nothing to comfort him.

One morning six weeks later, ruined, wrecked Charlie Barnes emerged from the house on Rust Road to retrieve the newspaper. The *Tribune* arrived at the end of the driveway tightly sheathed in a skin of blue plastic, a bitter contrast to the cells inside him that the chemotherapy drugs had reduced to so many bloated water balloons, thin sacs of poison on fire that, when popped, poured into his veins and pooled like toxic lakes throughout his body. With every heavy step, he felt like Dead Man Sloshing. Now he sloshed unhappily down the drive toward the aforementioned paper, which looked about ten miles distant and which he would not have the energy to read that day... and on his slog back, there was Jerry standing against the garage door in his cut-offs and T-shirt, a single duffel bag at his feet. It was reminiscent of that morning so long ago when the boy had run away from his mother's house into his father's arms—or onto his porch, anyway. He had been reluctant to knock on the door that morning, too, lest he wake Charley Proffit of Peoria, Illinois. Now it was Barbara Ledeux he might wake, which made him doubly reluctant. But Barbara hadn't kept Jerry away. He had lost his apartment. He had sold his van. He had swallowed his pride. He simply had nowhere else to go.

49

The reader can imagine how much Barbara enjoyed a second child showing up at her house, this one middle-aged, unemployed, and large. Jerry sang in the shower and snored like a bear. He was kind of hard to ignore. But she got no say in the matter, because anything more than a full welcome would have called into question Charlie's claim that the house on Rust Road was his house, too. She might have owned it, might have paid its monthly mortgage, might have raised her two kids there, quietly sipping her morning coffee as I had observed her doing on the day of his surgery, but it was a sacred stipulation of their marriage contract that his children had the same right to call it home as she did, and out of deference to him, and out of love, the evil stepmother held her tongue.

"I hope you know, I'm not drowning in debt," Jerry said to me in passing one morning on the stairs. "I have several thousands socked away."

"Is that true?"

"I'm just running a little experiment. Is it or is it not Charlie's home, too? Will she or will she not abide one of his own flesh-and-blood children? What if I bring home a lady friend? What if that lady friend charges by the hour? So many outstanding questions, Jake. I suppose only time will tell."

"You're joking, right?"

"Does it matter if I have money or not? I'm here. One way or the other, we're about to find out what she's made of."

"She will never kick you out," I said. "She loves him too much."

"Oh?" he said. "Have you started calling her Mom yet?"

I laughed. This light little ribbing, part of the casual exchange between two brothers as they passed each other on the stairs, was a breath of fresh air in that house of slumber and death. He retreated to Troy's old room like a surly teenager and I resumed cleaning the bathrooms and doing the laundry.

I might have returned to Rome once Jerry came to live in the house on Rust Road. Charlie didn't need two sons scrambling his eggs and driving him to his chemo sessions. But I stuck around. I liked the fact of the three of us under the same roof again, Father and Sons taking advantage of an unorthodox time to enjoy one another's company. I wouldn't have traded that for Rome or the Cotswolds or anywhere else in the world.

If this section of my tale begins to feel sentimental, workmanlike in its efforts to memorialize, that is because I strain to capture the competing agendas and mind-sets of that difficult time: Charlie slogging through chemo; Jerry humiliated and thrown back on his father and his fourth—fourth!—stepmother; Barbara desperate to be done with him (and me) and to return to her simple life in her simple home, going to work and doing crossword puzzles with her silver fox on Sundays and fooling herself that it could go on like that forever; and me. And me! What did I want? I called Marcy in Deer Park to give her the latest.

"The chemo's killing him," I said. "It's going after everything, right down to his eyebrows. It's the old story of the cure being worse than the disease."

I could not say how I knew, I just knew: the Marcy I got that day was not in the mood and didn't give a damn.

"What do you want from me, Jake?" she asked.

"Pay him a little visit," I said. "It would do him a lot of good. He needs reasons to go on right now."

"And why do I care if he goes on?"

"He's your dad."

"He doesn't have any money."

There was a long pause.

"What does that have to do with anything?"

"A good dad does all he can to leave behind a little something for his children after he dies, does he not?"

"Jesus, Marcy. The man's fighting for his life over here."

"What's that to you, Jake? What business is it of yours if I ever come home again? He hasn't earned this kind of slavish devotion from you, has he? A deluded old man, a man who dropped you—"

"He never dropped me."

"—a man who's been dishonest his whole life, desperate to be loved by everyone, but more than happy to let his dick call the shots."

"Not so much anymore," I said. "He can't do half the things he used to do as a younger man."

"So I should forgive him, I should fly home and cheer him on, because he can't fuck anymore?" There was a long pause. "What's really going on here, Jake?"

What was really going on was something I would no sooner share with her than Charlie would have shared his most delicate dream with his devouring younger brother. The energetic young father showing Jerry squirrels outside the window; a laundry-draped bathroom as in the house on Vermilion; jars of sun tea baking on the back porch stairs; softball games in Douglas Park; potlucks and backyard BBQs; Happy Necker manning a grill in argyle and plaid, picnic blankets, casks of cheap wine, a transistor radio playing AM standards from 1979; all the old friends, and all the old songs, and all the old feeling this family had before it went to shit . . . why couldn't we remake a little of all that right here on Rust Road?

"Why do you care so much? Why is this so important to you?"

I knew my answer wouldn't satisfy her.

"Because I love you guys."

"That's nice of you," she said. "You're a really nice guy, Jake. But I'm going to say this once, okay, and never again? Butt the fuck out."

50

The news that day was unbelievable. The one bank, the one estimable institution to have emerged unscathed from the subprime mortgage mess—Wells Fargo—caught red-handed creating fraudulent accounts. Well, Charlie thought, folding up his newspaper. The rat fink bastards were back at it again.

It was September of 2016. Almost eight years to the day had passed since his Whipple procedure, and three years since he was declared cancer-free.

He kicked the footrest to the floor. The living room, with its large square footage, stylish new furnishings and tall, tall ceiling, stared back at him (down at him, too, discerning the full return of his organic gray locks), though he hardly noticed, so lost in thought was he. It had been but a blink of the eye since Bear Stearns went down in flames. Lehman, too, went down. America itself damn near went down. Billions of dollars gone, millions of jobs shed—not to mention all the people who lost their homes. If there was one white hat in the whole damn stickup, it was Wells—but turns out they, too, knew how to screw the pooch.

He stood, and what he mistook for his imminent demise turned out to be just a minor backache. At the sun-drenched breakfast nook (a major selling feature of the new house) he sliced a grapefruit and sugared over the first of its open halves.

Then he set about extracting its pink meat from nature's neat honeycomb with a serrated spoon while delving deeper into the whys and wherefores of the fraud at Wells Fargo. Soon his mouth went slack, his sharp spoon sat stilled in midair, and all that moved were his pale blue eyes as they flitted across the page. Under terrific pressure to fill quotas, the bank had opened thousands of unauthorized accounts, charging millions in clandestine fees. There the story ended, his fever broke, and he sat back and shook his head in dismay.

With a jolt upright, he recalled that he knew somebody who worked at Wells: his old friend Larry Stoval. Larry had worked there back in '08, anyway, when Bear went kaput, a cold snap hit credit markets, and Charlie was diagnosed with pancreatic cancer. Taking up his mug of tea, he walked under the exposed oak rafters past the formal dining room and the wood-paneled library and descended the stairs to the basement office. There, waiting for him inside his old battered Rolodex next to the rapier-style letter opener—holdovers from the house on Rust Road—was the most current number he had on file for Larry Stoval. He returned up the stairs with both the number and the cordless so that he might place his phone call in the heavenly sunlight saturating the breakfast nook that so made his old bones shiver and thrive.

"Wells Fargo."

"Good morning," he said. "Charlie Barnes calling for Larry Stoval."

"I'm afraid Larry hasn't made it in this morning," the woman said. "May I take a message?"

"Old Larry," he said.

The woman made no reply.

"I was just reading about the scandal over there at Wells," he said, "when I was reminded of Larry. He and I worked at Bear Stearns together a hundred years ago. I don't know if you remember Bear. No reason you should. It was a ship full of rat bastards back in '08 and sure enough it sank, damn near taking the rest of us down with it. Anyway, Larry and I had worked for a guy named... guy named, uh... little guy, not much to look at... oh, good Lord," he said. "What was his name?"

Now, that was odd. He had thought about that guy day and night at one point in time, saying his name in praise or blame to anyone who would listen, and now he couldn't recall it to save his life. He could bring to mind what he looked like (not much), recall his affection for cigars and curse words, his ten-thousand-dollar golf games, and how he led Bear Stearns into receivership while demanding a ransom from the American people, but he was blanking on his damn name.

"Larry would remember," he said.

It sure did suck, seeing your mind go. But it wasn't just age. Charlie Barnes simply had no need to think so often of Jimmy Cayne anymore.

"Would you like to leave a message for Larry?" the woman asked.

"Last time I left a message for Larry," he said, "it was eight years ago and I never heard back."

There was no immediate reply.

"I called to let him know I had pancreatic cancer. I have no idea how familiar you might be with that kind of cancer, but it almost always spells a swift end. Well, I defied the odds. I've made it eight years. I have a new car now. I bought a new house. I even have a new job. But I should be dead."

"Well, how wonderful," the woman said. "You never know what life has in store, do you?"

"Unless it's death," he said.

There was a long pause.

"Right," she said. "Is... that the message you'd like me to leave for Larry today?"

In the lull that followed, he allowed himself to observe, with profitless abandon, the devastated grapefruit rind on the breakfast table, its cowlicked look when viewed at a distance, while up close it resembled one of those saturated landscapes in ruin after the water recedes, after the sun comes out and an eerie peace descends. He lost himself momentarily inside its fibrous and fascinating swales.

"Sir?"

"Sorry," he said. "Zoned out for a minute there."

"Would you like to leave a message for Larry?"

It was a real damn mess, the last time he left messages for Larry Stoval. A total of four, maybe five, each one contradicting the last, until it must have seemed to Larry a great farce. It was, too—those messages, and that day, and his life back then.

"Thank you, no," he said. "No message."

He hung up.

The house on Harmony Drive came up for sale just last year, in 2015. Built at the turn of the new century, it had five bedrooms and four baths, and at four thousand square feet was twice the size of the house on Rust Road. He and Barbara had been flirting with the luxury tower downtown called the Legacy at Millennium Park, with its doormanned extravagance and floor-to-ceiling views of Lake Michigan, but for some reason they drove to Oak Park one breezy Sunday in spring to have a look at 906 Harmony Drive.

Potential buyers were always struck by the solemnity of the high ceilings. Also unique were the eye-popping barnyard doors, sourced from Vermont, which opened onto the ground-floor library. Having mentally made the move downtown, they coolly appraised the rooms until Barbara walked into the kitchen and said, "Oh, Charlie, would you look . . . " and they both just knew. This was in fact every inch the paradise he dreamed of providing for her one day. Perhaps they weren't tower people, after all, but heart-and-soul suburbanites—make of that what you will—with an affection for lawns and neighbors. The breakfast nook, still lively with sunlight at noon, was set apart by delicate panes of glass with glazed mullions behind which the beautiful hedgerows bloomed. The real estate agent, a Dallas native in pearls and slacks, informed them that the empty lot next door was also for sale. They paid cash for that, planted bamboo for privacy at the landscaper's recommendation, and installed a pergola and birdbath. Charlie liked to take a glass of wine out there toward the end of the day. They parked what they still called Rabineau's Porsche, after the late mechanic, in the three-car garage. A mere thirty or so suburban miles from their former home, this new one combined the opulence of an Italian palazzo with the peace and quiet of a Zen garden.

But he just couldn't lose the landline. Despite all the modern amenities, the app-adjusted lighting and centrally cooled air, he remained attached to his relics: his landline, his cable box, his TV remotes, his recliner, his VHS player, his home-delivered newspaper, and his basement office. He also retained his desk calendar from 1991, his roller chair and his monkey-paw back scratcher, although he did manage to ditch the sheet of stamped plastic specifically designed to facilitate the easy rolling of roller chairs in challenging terrain.

Jerry was calling him.

"How's tricks, my boy?"

They fell to talking about a legal dilemma facing the company: an account creator out of Norway, having chipped in the equivalent of two hundred US dollars toward the infinity ring his girlfriend coveted but which the young man alone could not afford, had recently had his heart broken by the girl and withdrawn his money—minus the penalty forfeited to Chippin' In (per the user agreement) for withdrawal from an "unconsummated campaign." Now he was bringing legal action against the website with help from other "chippers" similarly penalized and, of course, a team of Delaware lawyers. Charlie was apprised of all this and then weighed his options.

"Let's give him his money back," he said.

"Too late for that, Pop. They've filed a class-action."

"So let's settle."

"And let the ambulance chasers win?"

"What if we—"

"Look, Pop, these guys don't have a leg to stand on," Jerry argued. "We're up front on the home page about fees and penalties. They have to agree to them again when they establish an account, and then every time they 'chip in.' We can't just let them wreak havoc with the revenue model. We run that model, we depend on it, we profit from it. Should we do away with the model and run a charity instead?"

"Okay," he said. "Put Einsohn on it."

"Einsohn," Jerry said, with a verbal roll of the eyes.

But Charlie, who always knew when he was in the wrong, had been in the wrong about Einsohn. He only had to come out from under his debts, real and psychic, to admit it freely. The failure of his dear TTAA was one of poor planning and misallocated resources, not bad legal advice from the man out in Aurora. Had he simply not rented quite so many billboards, had he not ordered so many brochures, TTAA might not have failed. When it did fail, he needed someone to blame. Charlie now had a little insight into the legal profession: you might hire a lawyer, but you always fire a fall guy. Now, in 2016, eight years older than he had any right to be, he would not blame Einsohn.

"We have our pick of litigators from here to Silicon Valley, and you like this two-bit Einsohn. I just don't get it."

"I gave Einsohn a hard time a hundred years ago for something that wasn't really his fault. I feel bad about that now and I'd like to make up for it. Do you see? Give it to Einsohn."

"Fine," he said. "I'll give it to Einsohn. And while we're at it, we've had other news. Facebook improved their offer."

"You buried the lede, Jerry."

"It's a better offer," he said. "As in a much better offer."

There was a long pause.

"We're talking a lot of damn money here, Pop."

It was such a curious thing, life, you simply couldn't predict it. The anticorporate proselytizer was now working night and day for a for-profit enterprise, while the born adherent and lifelong striver had his scruples and doubts, as anyone will after making a break with a cult. For damn near a lifetime, Charlie Barnes had proved easy enough to brainwash: his elders and betters had only to repeat the phrase *self-made man* enough times to convince him there was no other way to make it in America, and anything short of that was weak commie failure. The self-made man got no assists, enjoyed no preexisting network or infrastructure, took comfort in no collective, and owed no one an apology for his trampling and rough treatment. He simply sprang from the godhead with his native genius and oaken strength and immediately set forth clearing, herding, stamping, exploiting, acquiring, colonizing, and finally buying his way into office. These elders of his, these peddlers of fantasy, with their dear dead narratives, pretty much guaranteed that, until the day he got sick, he would not come into possession of a single original thought. It was all propaganda and petrified national myth. When sickness swept that away, when it left him vulnerable, when it freed up his mind to think for itself, an idea of his own came dimly into view... but he thought, that can't be right, can it? It was so obvious an idea, so modest in scope, essentially so dull, that he failed to see how it might be revolutionary. No, not Chippin' In. That idea came to him much earlier. (And, as the article in *Kiplinger's* pointed out, predated Kickstarter's April 2009 launch by one month while doing something distinct from it, namely, combining crowdfunding with gift registry.) It had made him a small fortune. It was no sweat off his back. No, he had in mind something else entirely: his calling, that tailor-made thing that was less revelation than resignation to who he was and always must be: Charles A. Barnes of Danville, Illinois, the man that was Steady Boy. His goddamn calling was a pain in the ass and cost him what remained of his strength, but that was the nature of bargains. If you're looking for a few good years, sell your soul to the devil. Want to save your soul? Give your life away.

"Answer's still no, Jerry," he said after giving it some thought. "I like us the way we are."

"Small and scrappy?"

"Unexploited," he said. "It was an idea I had once. Now it employs a few people. Shouldn't that be enough?"

"Don't you at least want to hear the number?"

His son, meanwhile—what a trajectory Jerry had had! The one-time commuter and company man turned Noam Chomsky acolyte... now contrite, and recommitted to the bottom line.

After coming to live with Charlie, he did what he could to reenter the workforce. He applied day and night. He expressed a willingness to relocate. He would have happily been lowballed. But his timing was bad. The economy had tanked. And he'd been out of the workforce by then for three full years. Prospective employers looked askance at him. His résumé had this glaring hole in it and he got very few callbacks. On the rare occasion he was invited to interview, he would bring up Krishnamurti or go on a mini rant about neoliberalism and blow it. Or HR would take a quick look at his Facebook posts. Or he would tell the truth about why he spent three years out of the workforce. Three became four, then four became five, six, and seven. *He lived at 105 Rust Road for four years.* This is why I would say Jerry was a lucky man. He needed Charlie at fifteen and he needed him at fifty, and both times Charlie was there for him. You can't buy that in life. You have to luck into it.

Then Chippin' In took off. Charlie was busy doing his own thing by that point and sought Jerry's help. Jerry seemed to slot right back into the filing cabinet and office chair. He had tried resistance, renunciation, life on the margins. Working just felt better. There was more to the morning. But for him to realize this, the gatekeepers—headhunters, HR reps—had to bar entry first. You want out of corporate America, pal? Fine, but be forewarned. We are a self-selecting group. You will not be welcomed back. And sure enough, they proceeded to deprive him not only of the paychecks and benefits necessary to survival but also of capitalism's foremost appeal: membership. When Jerry rejected *it*...no big deal. When it rejected Jerry, it *continued* to reject Jerry, indefinitely. The things he took for granted, like usefulness, personal fulfillment, collective purpose, went away, and he wondered, briefly, why not put a bullet in my head? I think Chippin' In saved Jerry Barnes's life. He was relieved to have been rescued, to be partaking of company pride again, to be part of a team, in the human fold once more. Now he ran a staff of twelve in a South Loop office.

"Sure, Jerry. For shits and giggles, give me the number."

Jerry told his father the number. Charlie went quiet.

"That is a large sum," the old man admitted.

"Does it change your mind?"

There was a long pause.

"It does not," he said. "Look, Jerry, do what you want with the company after I'm dead and gone. But truth of the matter is, son, I don't like Facebook. I sure as hell don't like what it's done to newspapers. I love my newspaper, Jerry. I still have it delivered. I read it under the pergola with a glass of wine."

"I know you do, Pop."

"And I think Facebook would like to do away with my newspaper and every other newspaper and bank the subscription fees. That can't be good for anybody. And who knows? They just might succeed. Well, in that case, they can't have my brainchild, too. Screw those wolves in sheep's clothing, Jerry.

They're not half the messiahs they think they are. Matter of fact, they might just be the devil itself."

"I didn't know you felt so strongly."

"They'll run their metrics, they'll squeeze the margins. They'll monetize everything. Fuck it, no way."

"All right, all right, I hear you."

"Screw venture capital, son, and screw Big Tech, too. When I'm dead, do what you want. But not until then."

"Not for many years, then, Pop," Jerry said.

51

Let us return briefly to 2009, just prior to Charlie's first round of chemo. He had a consultation with his oncologist, a Dr. Baruch Clement of First Baptist. Barbara was present, of course, and didn't hesitate to make her opinion known: she did not like the anticancer agent gemcitabine on its own. She urged Clement to be more aggressive. Of course, there was always a risk that a multiagent therapy would increase Charlie's toxicity and bring on neutropenia, a dangerously low count of a type of white blood cell crucial to fighting infection, but consistent blood tests revealed that he had near-normal bilirubin levels and a good performance status overall. It was her belief that either a GTX regimen or a gemcitabine with a platinum and a daily oral dose of Tarceva would give him the best chance of long-term survival. As she spoke, an all-consuming concern Charlie had for himself was momentarily overtaken by the growing awe he felt for his wife.

"How do you know all this stuff?" he asked.

Clement, too, looked impressed. "No kidding," he said. "When you're done helping this guy out, how about you come and be my nurse?"

As they resumed their technical talk, Charlie's awe turned back to dread. Every option they debated sounded, in the end, totally fucking terrible. Then he arrived at the chemo center, took a seat in one of the many luxurious leather recliners positioned around the room, and had the poisons they discussed that day pumped into him—and wondered if they hadn't been conspiring to murder him. He promptly hated life. Brain fog, of the kind his mother complained about, moved in and parked. Other lugubrious, agonizing morning-after side effects, which he dubbed his chemover, hit him methodically on the second day. His mouth broke out in open sores. By some miracle of misfortune, he managed both to lose his hair and retain just enough of it to go around with bedhead for three months running. A fanatic comber in a past life, he would no longer even glance in a mirror. As one does with mudslides, avalanches, and other breaches, I looked on in horror from a distance as his vanity gave way, then his hygiene, then deodorizing of any kind. He camped out on his recliner, where he made it known he would just as soon die—and where I believed him to be fast asleep when, on a Tuesday morning, he entered the living room from the direction of the dining room (an irregular entry point in that house) and stood facing me just to the left of the muted television. I had been half asleep, sprawled out on the sofa per usual.

"What is it, Chuck?" I asked, sitting up.

"I've had enough."

"Of?"

"Chemo," he said, and he raised a little pistol to his temple. I recall thinking, Lordy, that's one small gun, a saloon gal's gun, and unlikely to do anyone any harm. Sure enough, when he pulled the trigger, there was only the sudden sizzling *zap* of the television turning off, according to some metaphysical connection between the two. As shocked as anyone, he turned to behold the blank screen. His shoulders began to roll with sitcom laughter. Mine, too—or at least one of them did, and I opened my eyes and found Charlie standing over me, eager to wake me from my dream of suicide and sitcoms. It was not Tuesday morning but a late Friday afternoon.

"Look at this, Jake!"

I sat up in the front room in the house on Rust Road. In a daze I accepted the letter being thrust at me. It took a moment, but eventually I understood it was a transcript from Michigan State University.

"I thought you graduated from Michigan State," I said, running my eyes over so many incompletes.

"That's just a story I tell," he said. "But don't you see? That's the point. This is it, Jake!" he cried. "*This* is my calling!"

He had, by then, wisely dismissed the idea of becoming a divorce mediator or one of the other pie-in-the-sky professions he had landed on in conversation with Barbara. They were fine as individual choices go, but his general approach fit an old pattern: Steady Boy dreaming big again without reason, going for broke when he had no right to. He'd spent a lifetime lurching from thing to thing. This time had to be different.

Returning to school sounded right because it would require hard work and real sacrifice with no guarantee of personal gain, as Jerry and the Gita claimed a true calling demanded. He had to tell Barbara the good news and raced upstairs for his car keys.

He clomped down a minute later wearing the red corduroys by Brunello Cucinelli that he bought for a song on the day of his diagnosis. He'd been saving them for the right occasion.

"Hey, Chuck," I said. "There's something I need to tell you."

He was removing a hat from the hat rack when he turned to me.

"You asked me to find your teeth after surgery," I said, "but I couldn't do that."

"Why not?"

"Barbara had them. She's the one who put them back in your mouth."

"That wasn't you?"

"That was Barbara," I said.

"Barbara had them?"

I nodded. There was a long pause during which he stood very still, as if to steady himself amid such disorienting and devastating news. It did not make him happy.

I wish he could have owned it, I mean really *owned* it. Imagine him removing those fuckers on a whim for the comic shock or harmonizing with the harelips, walleyes, and stutters in a collective little song of sorrow. He could have done anything had he just owned it. I wanted that not for my sake, to confirm that he knew he was loved (accepted, embraced), but for his own, *to know that he loved himself*. There was the difference, in Shakespeare's formula, of man and man. Had Charlie the power to take out his teeth in a crowd, the power the crowd had over him would have vanished. The success that eluded him was always within his grasp but impossible to seize because of his stupid pride, the only justification for which was its own overcoming.

But wasn't I one to talk? I could hardly bear to imagine whom I came from or why I was left to die in the Fair Oaks housing project. My mother's taste for drink? My stupid birth defect? And while I attack Jerry's and Marcy's monumental scorn for their humble roots, regarding them as ingrates for wanting to put a little distance between them and Steady Boy, I go around pretending we share a common inheritance, when nothing could be further from the truth. I have seen my birth certificate. The stranger named as my father means nothing to me; I'd sooner call Dickie Dickerdick Dad. I, too, wanted to be a *self-made man* in my own humble way and was more than happy, as Charlie had been, to brush off reality and embrace the dream. My foster family, the Barnes clan, squanderers of riches they took for granted, didn't need me. They probably didn't want me. They might not have even *liked* me. Charlie Barnes was always bowing out because he didn't care to abide by the rules. I didn't care for the rules, either, but not because I wanted to bow out. I wanted to be let in.

"Thanks for letting me know," he said. "You're a good man, Jake Barnes."

Then he was off: opening the garage door, firing up the engine, and stealing away to First Baptist in a broken-down Saab. Or was it the Porsche that, these many months later, he still hadn't returned to Rabineau? Pesky little Porsche. Perhaps it was a third car altogether.

"It sounds perfect to me," Barbara declared the minute he announced his intentions in the cafeteria of First Baptist.

"It won't be easy, young lady."

"Nothing worthwhile ever is."

"We'll be pinched. We're pinched now. It'll only get worse."

"You *have* to do it, Charlie. It's more important than money or anything else. I'll pick up a shift here and there. We'll take out a few credit cards. We'll get by. And then you'll have your degree. Do you know what you'd like to study?"

He had learned his lesson: do not delve. He had done so in the past and it hadn't worked out. But move in the direction of love and life always gets harder. He was married to Barbara this time, not Charley Proffit. It was Barbara Ledeux who saw the big picture. He tapped his teeth.

"You know about these," he said.

She nodded.

"And you don't mind?"

"Of course I don't mind."

There was a long pause.

"You love me."

"Of course I love you, young man."

"I don't know why."

"You don't?"

"I don't."

She reached across the table and touched the brim of his touring cap. "Because you can wear a hat," she said.

He had identified his calling in life, had secured his wife's support and departed the hospital in good spirits. Those spirits began to dim even before he reached the highway. If completing the nightly reading had been hard as a young man of twenty-seven, how much more difficult would it be at sixty-nine, recently cut open, fried with chemo, and prone to fall asleep before the rigor of *Friends*? Then there were more practical considerations. Was there a college that would take him? A financial institution that would loan him money? By the time he arrived home, he was running a fever of a hundred and two.

In an event like that, the instructions were clear: any fever in an immune system compromised by chemo could be fatal. He had to return to First Baptist immediately. He spent the next forty-eight hours under observation by Dr. Clement, who did not hesitate to run a battery of tests.

While in the hospital, Chuck begged me to check out a bunch of books from the library so that he could begin his course of study. Ah, I thought, so this silly occupation of mine isn't so silly after all. Who else could curate for him a college reading list? I did so happily. He didn't think he had another moment to spare. I saw real panic in his eyes, the dread that awaits anyone who feels the clock running down on him. A day later, he hadn't touched a single one of my selection of classics. I walked in on him still having a go at the Gita, the book on his chest, the man fast asleep.

"Hey, Chuck," I whispered. "Hey . . . *Dad.*"

He sat up slowly and registered having fallen asleep.

"Oh, goddamn it," he said. "Who am I fooling? I'm no goddamn student!"

"Go easy on yourself," I said. "You're sick."

"No, it's more than that, Jake. I hate to read. What's the point of going back to school if I can't read anything but the goddamn newspaper?"

"Don't give up so easily, Chuck."

"No, it's not in me, son. Goddamn it, it's just not in me."

He was upset with himself, demoralized. He believed he had found it. And it did sound pretty good, at least on paper. But it was true: he couldn't stay awake. He gazed out the window in complete despair. "Hold on," he said.

"What is it?"

He got out of bed, went to the window. Then he did something more curious still: he turned in his hospital gown, sat directly on the floor and crossed his legs.

"What are you doing down there, Chuck? Is that... are you in a yoga pose?"

"Jake," he said. He gazed off. "It can't be about me this time."

"What's it got to be about?" I asked.

He loved her. No one could explain why. She lionized him all out of proportion. She understood that failure did not define him or curb his need to be loved. She called him her silver fox. She found it heroic that he railed against the likes of Jimmy Cayne and started a business that specialized in retirees. And when we looked up, she was standing in the doorway, a honeypot in scrubs and buzz cut.

"What on earth are you doing sitting on the floor?" she asked him. "And why are the two of you looking at me like that?"

52

Dr. Clement studied the numbers and scratched his head: Charlie's heme-8 was fine, as was his CBC. There had been no discernible drop in platelet count. He discharged him with a dose of Tylenol, which resolved the fever...only to have it return a week later, right on time and high as ever. The doctor threw up his hands.

"There is one possible answer," Barbara suggested.

"Please," the doctor said, "enlighten me."

"Someone's forgetting his prednisone."

Sure enough, the order for infused steroids to be administered simultaneously with the anticancer cocktail had gone missing two weeks running at the chemo center, an unaccountable clerical error. And it might have remained a mystery had it not been for a passing observation from the nurse at First Baptist.

"How did you know about that prednisone business?" he asked her on the drive home.

"Lucky guess."

"But how'd you know enough to guess?"

She was an ER nurse—"the nurse at First Baptist"—not a doctor. Her degree, from a dinky DuPage college no longer in existence, dated back thirty years, to 1981. In her graduation photo she wore starched whites and a nurse's cap as if mentored by Florence Nightingale.

"I am a nurse, Charlie."

"And most nurses," he said. "Would they have made that same guess?"

She just shrugged.

She had the next three days off work. She drove everyone from the living room, silenced the television, started the laundry and went through the mail, restoring the house to her liking. I returned to my rental, Jerry retreated to Troy's room, and Charlie battled malaise in the master bedroom. By the late afternoon, however, he was feeling well enough to accompany her to the bookstore, and on their way home, to no one's surprise more than his own, he suggested they stop for a pizza.

"Are you sure you're up for it?" she asked.

"Honey," he said, "what's it all been for if I can't do a slice of pizza?"

He would pay for it the next day, but it was also more fun than a couple of hours at a pizza joint in the suburbs had any right to be. He had a beer, then a glass of wine. She shared a few of the idiot things that had brought people into the ER of late, like the woman who sewed two fingers together with a hacked sewing machine and the teenager who swallowed a bouncy ball on a dare.

He had done some thinking by then. Her ability to interpret those numbers on that little white napkin... her opinion on "gemcitabine with a platinum"... his "near-normal bilirubin levels," words right out of her own mouth... solving the mystery of his fever: his wife knew more about the particulars of cancer than he ever would have suspected had he simply dropped dead of a heart attack. After the waitress brought them dessert, he said, "Can we go back to the prednisone thing?"

"What about it?"

"You knew more than the doctor. How did you know more than the doctor?"

"I read up."

"You 'read up'? Barbara, I don't even know what prednisone *is*. Even now! Honey," he said. "You could be a doctor."

She quickly dismissed that.

"No interest?"

There was a long pause.

"I wanted to be a doctor, but then I met Bob"—her first husband, a plumber in Gurnee—"we had the kids, and . . . well, like we had the time or money to send me to medical school."

"And what about now?"

She cocked her head across the remains of their crème brûlée.

"Like we have the time or money to send me to medical school."

On her final day off, he walked into the kitchen after a rough night's sleep to find her in reading glasses tackling the book she'd purchased only a few days earlier. She was responsible for holding down a full-time job, for keeping his spirits up and his doctors on their toes, and for running the house and paying the bills while he was out of commission. How did she also have time to read a book? Called *The Emperor of All Maladies,* it was subtitled: *A Biography of Cancer,* and it was one big mother . . . yet she was practically done with it. She turned another page. Hovering over her, he tapped the thick mound of pages already consumed.

"Astonishing," he said.

"What's astonishing?"

"You've had that book two days and you're almost done with it."

"It's a quick read."

"For you, maybe. For me, a climb up the Himalayas."

She smiled before resuming.

"Young lady?"

She looked up again. He had taken the seat across the table from her.

"It ain't gonna happen, my dear—my little dream of returning to school to get my degree."

"Why not?"

He told her of how little appetite he had for reading anything but the newspaper. "But you know who *does* like to read?" He pointed across the table at her. "I want you to go back to school for me."

"But I have my degree, young man."

"I mean medical school," he said.

At these words, she carefully closed up her book. She moved it aside and took off her reading glasses and folded them and brought her hands together. She made herself small, he thought, as if trying to disappear, and did not respond.

"You don't like the idea?"

"I'm forty-nine years old," she said.

"People go back to school at that age."

"We can't afford medical school."

"We'll take out a few credit cards," he said, quoting her. "You were prepared to do it for me. Why not for yourself?"

"That's not what I do, Charlie."

"Not what you do?"

"I don't..."

"What?"

"Dare," she said. "Dream."

He nodded.

"Okay," he said. "But I do. Look, is it a stretch? Probably. But is it completely irrational?"

"Probably," she said.

"Fine. Then tell me the great advantage to being fucking rational. Rational is the fact of death. Rational is chemo in response to cancer. Rational is sleeping all day long in the hopes of surviving until I've slept my life away. I am sick and tired of being rational. I want to dream again, Barbara. But I'm old. And I've failed too often. But you, young lady . . . you . . ."

He couldn't finish the thought.

A lifetime ago, when he was married to a local beauty dedicated to a life of social work, he took a job with Waukegan Title. His pride prevented him from admitting to Charley Proffit his reason for doing so: she pursued a calling in life as he knew he never would. He lacked her passion, her single-mindedness. The least he could do, he believed, was pull in a few extra bucks every month to better support her. God knows he wasn't doing it because Waukegan Title was his dream job. It lacked glamour. No one would adore him for it. He did it for her. But then he couldn't disclose that because he was the man, and the man was supposed to have the calling.

He had no such compunction anymore. He would have happily worked for Archie Baker, he would have shined Archie's shoes and washed Archie's car, then turned to every man in the joint to announce that he was doing it all for a woman, the amateur oncologist moonlighting as his wife.

"I want you to take the entrance exam for medical school," he said. "Will you do that for me?"

"How can we afford medical school, Charlie?"

"Well, I don't know," he admitted. "That I don't know."

"What would be the point?"

"Hope," he said. "And change. Something other than this goddamn dreary chemo and the constant talk of cancer."

"I don't know," she said.

He was the live wire, the pursuer of dreams; she was the steady, inscrutable one. But she could also read a thousand words a minute. She had a photographic memory for symptoms and procedures. She had learned Spanish simply by overhearing exchanges in the ER, and she required no more than four hours of sleep at night. What did she have to lose? he asked her. He urged her: What's one exam? They returned to the bookstore for an exam-prep book. Then she began waking before dawn to put in a few hours of study before her shift at the hospital, and when she came home at night she put in a few more hours.

She took the exam in June. She was at work when the results arrived in the mail. She forbade Charlie from opening them. She alone would know how badly she had failed. Then she would quietly deposit that letter in the garbage and put the whole mortifying episode behind her. And in fact, when she came home that night and tore open the letter and read the test results, she retreated from the room without a single word. But she didn't toss the letter. She left it on the table. When he picked it up and made sense of it, he climbed the stairs and found her lying on the bed in the dark, still dressed in her scrubs and staring up at the ceiling. He lay next to her without a word, wanting her to say whatever was on her mind, though his heart was full and beating fast.

"Why did you make me take that test?" she asked him. "Why, Charlie?"

"Honey," he said.

"How could we afford it?"

"I don't know yet," he said.

At last, she turned to him.

"I could do this," she said, going on record for the first time, because committing to anything before that letter arrived with its good news would have left her vulnerable, beholden to a pipe dream she would have left for dead had Charlie not drawn it out of her.

"Yes," he said. "I believe you could."

53

In a private moment of self-reflection, a man confronts the farce that he is. All his worst instincts, habits of mind, predictable appetites and easily parodied past actions crystallize in that moment into a punch line that prevails above all his refinements and respectability. He is a human exaggeration—if not to his associates or loved ones, then to himself. Then the moment passes. He ceases looking at himself in the mirror, turns on the tap and splashes water on his face. He returns to flesh and blood, to power incarnate, to possibility. He washes his hands of the past and leaves that temporary station where he was briefly nothing but a joke and walks out again, into the future.

He came out of the bathroom at the Starbucks on Golf Road where he and I had gone for an afternoon latte. He wanted to talk about what he might do, now that he was almost finished with chemo, to raise money so that Barbara could reduce her hours at the hospital and return to school. We sat at a table in the window puzzling it out. His money-management fees were way down; Chippin' In hadn't taken off; he didn't have many options. He started telling me about the Lamplighter Inn. The Lamplighter was the Danville supper club and entertainment venue located on Perrysville Road where, in 1961, he took a job washing dishes in back with the firm belief that—

"Within two years, I'd be the MC."

"The MC?"

"The crooner onstage, you know. In the bow tie. The one cracking wise."

I got an image of the Lamplighter Inn—round tables and cocktails, women in sequins and men in white dinner jackets, all the biggest shakes in a small town.

"From dishwasher to Dean Martin," I said.

"That's right, Jake. Dean Martin—why not? All they had to do was discover me."

"And did they?"

"What they discovered was how little interest I had in actually washing dishes, so they fired me."

We walked out of the Starbucks and into a bright summer's day. He was no closer to knowing what he was going to do. He only knew what he couldn't do. He couldn't dream big again, not even one last time, and go off half-cocked. He couldn't start something with the goal of franchising it. He couldn't come up with the tagline, print the brochure, hire an engineer, partner with the banks, or write letters to captains of industry pleading for capital funding. His days of expanding out to the coasts were over.

When we got inside the car, he looked tired and old. I put the car in Reverse; he reached out and touched my hand. "Pull back in," he said. I did as he asked. He unbuckled and said he'd be right back. He returned to the car a minute later with a job application. The manager of the Starbucks said that while they weren't hiring at the moment, she would keep his application on file and contact him if a position opened up. As we left the Starbucks, he asked me to drive him to Staples, the office supply store, where he purchased a file folder and a box of pens. Before departing, he asked the kid at the register for a job application. In the car again, he placed both the Starbucks application and the one for Staples in the file folder, then he asked me to drive him to the Sears in the Woodfield Mall. There he asked to speak to a manager; he told that woman his name and asked if they were hiring. He asked the same of managers at Nordstrom, JCPenney, Macy's, and Things Remembered. We left the Woodfield Mall and drove down Golf Road, then East Higgins, then Meacham and Algonquin, stopping at places like the Hyatt, the Dollar Tree, and the Hobby Lobby, collecting applications at each of them. Then we returned to the car and he carefully placed them in the file folder, filling them out later that night at the kitchen table in the house on Rust Road. He had an exacting hand, went slowly, and did not permit a mistake.

"What the hell's going on?" Jerry asked one morning when we met in the kitchen as the old man showered upstairs.

"What do you mean?"

"He's filling out applications for entry-level jobs," he said. "What's that all about?"

"He's feeling better," I said.

"Feeling better? He's out of his mind again."

It was hard for Jerry to wrap his head around it. There were certain points of pride from which he never imagined Steady Boy might retreat. Since he first put on a suit and tie, in 1963, it was suit-and-tie work for Charlie Barnes from then on, or work be damned. He traded in hourly pay for the yearly salary and would never go back. It would be shameful to go back. So what the hell was he doing applying at the Home Depot?

Charlie paid a visit to European Motors that day. His appearance had changed considerably for the worse in six months' time: the surgery and chemo had bent him and hollowed out his eyes so much so that Rabineau, the old mechanic, didn't recognize him at first. When at last it clicked, he was confused. For fifteen years, Charlie Barnes had arrived in his waiting room in jacket and tie, or button-down and slacks, or jazzy sweater and pressed trousers: the image of the American businessman. Now he was asking to sweep the garage floor?

"Sweep, scrub, be a gofer, whatever you need. I don't know too much about tools, though."

Rabineau shook his head. Times were hard and he wasn't hiring. Then something occurred to him and he shot up an inky digit.

"Can you balance the books?"

Steady Boy had long feared such an unglamorous fate. Not only would he fail to make a killing, but some fall from grace or bankruptcy would also send him back to the days of just scraping by on some job site or sales floor, and premonitions of the boredom together with the bad pay would turn him electric with dread. But then he saw how different it might be if he returned to the earliest days of his professional life of his own accord, yet on behalf of someone other than himself. With that simple shift in perspective, he had more equanimity busting his hump than he ever had as a younger man. It was not all that different from the moment he realized that he didn't mind mowing the lawn so long as it was on behalf of Charley Proffit. I remember thinking how unlikely it was that two weeks after his final chemo infusion, two short weeks after all that television, a mere two weeks after he was unable to make a sandwich for himself, he was waking at seven to shower and leaving the house by eight. Well, why not? The Whipple was a success. Chemo was over. His counts were holding steady. So while Barbara was applying to the Feinberg School of Medicine at Northwestern University, he was applying to Costco. While she applied to the University of Chicago, he submitted an application to Bed Bath & Beyond. And while he was speaking to a manager at Luna Flooring Gallery on Golf Road about an opening in their sales department, she was applying to the Stritch School of Medicine at Loyola University.

He worked at the Walmart on Roselle Road for a total of five days. He worked at the Target down the street for no more than two months. He stepped out of a Lowe's vest and into a Best Buy polo and exchanged a Panera visor for a Wendy's cap. He treated these franchises and chain outfits in the same fashion as they tended to treat people like him: as something to chew up and spit out. He leaped from $8.15 an hour at PetSmart to $9.65 an hour at Petco after working at PetSmart a single day. It was practically a full-time job just seizing opportunities like this one, dropping off his résumé with a dose of charm and asking for more money everywhere he went, from Applebee's to GameStop and from GameStop to Zales.

The money this patchwork of gigs and hustles provided (until Chippin' In took off) was just enough to pay the bills and stay current on the mortgage while also allowing Barbara to pull back at First Baptist. He took his half hour at noon and his fifteen at two thirty, clocking in and out. There were many shifts when he did not go that extra mile but merely offered up a warm body so that no one took off with the store. It was here his particular genius resided, for if anyone knew how to cut corners, fly under the radar, and play fast and loose with the demands of a dress code, it was that original son of Danville, Steady Boy Barnes. Working for the man was my father's calling.

Throughout this final career swerve, he never stopped working for Rabineau. He balanced the man's books, did his taxes, and made sense of his inventory, all while paying attention to the mechanics at their work. When he identified his first master-cylinder problem in a 1982 Porsche 911, the pleasure he carried home to Barbara was all the evidence she needed to know that he wasn't fibbing: he was out there busting his hump for his own sake, too. It brought him the greatest satisfaction to repair a preexisting thing. Some years later, Rabineau attended the housewarming party on Harmony Drive. The old mechanic didn't look well that day. There was no early detection in his case, no surgical option, no time to set things right. He just died. By then, Charlie had Chippin' In money. He bought European Motors and the Porsche that came with it.

54

I flew down one last time to Deer Park to try my best to convince Marcy that her father, one year after his initial diagnosis, had turned his life around and deserved her forgiveness. I had little hope of getting very far: she had told me repeatedly to butt out and fuck off, blocked my calls and texts, and refused to see me outright on two earlier occasions when, like some tool on a business trip, I'd flown in and out again without accomplishing much. This final time, I resorted to writing her a letter, which I made sure to post a week before my arrival, informing her of the exact day I would be in town and when she could expect me to be at the sports bar where she and I had previously met. The last thing I anticipated was to find her waiting for me in the lobby of the hotel where I tended to stay whenever in "The Park," or to watch her rise out of a rose-patterned wingback chair and come forward in order to put her arms around me. I dropped my bag and put my arm around her. When our embrace ended, she looked at me with her big hazel eyes full of stardust and thanked me for all I'd done for Daddy over the course of the year, the sacrifices I'd made, the love and loyalty I'd shown.

"Of course," I said.

"Thank you for never giving up on us, Jake. We can be a pretty crazy bunch, I know."

I was eager to sit down with her to explain all the many changes under way at the house on Rust Road, but I didn't manage to say much before she cut me off.

"Is Daddy really working at Best Buy?"

"And at the Menards in Hanover Park—but that's only part-time. If he gets between forty-eight and fifty-two hours of work every week between the two, then he thinks he should be able to cover the monthly expenses."

"And why is he doing this?"

"So that Barbara can go back to school and get her medical degree."

"He's doing it for Barbara?"

"I know you don't like her, Marcy, and it's true she's strange, a damned strange woman, but you should have seen her nurse him back to health when he got sick. I promised him I'd tell each of you how devoted she was to his care and how tenderly she treated him. Honestly, I think we've sold her short."

There was a long pause.

"Best Buy?" she said. "Jake, this isn't some kind of joke, is it?"

"You just have to see it with your own two eyes, Marcy. What do you say? I know he'd love to see you."

I couldn't believe it. She was actually giving it some thought.

"When do you leave?" she asked.

I worried that between parting that night and our plans to meet up again twelve hours later, changeable Marcy would reconsider her options, or suffer a manic episode, or recall her past delight at toying with me and simply not show, but there she was in the lobby the next morning at the appointed hour, ready to depart for Houston and O'Hare. It was curious to me how the chief complaint against Marcy was that she was constantly changing, while the chief complaint against Charlie was that he never changed. He was Steady Boy through and through. We wanted opposite things from the two of them: Marcy to iron out her inconsistencies, Charlie to surprise us with his sudden rectitude and dependability. Well, live long enough, it seems, and you might just get your wish at least once.

It isn't typical to land at O'Hare and drive straight to a big-box retailer, but that's what Marcy and I did that morning. We walked in through the automated doors and looked around for him under the industrial rafters, and when at last we spotted him in the distance under that deathly light, I witnessed her shock at the physical changes in him. That man so memorable for his muttonchops and curls, his strong push-off before a hook shot and his big bear hugs, and for the alacrity with which he fell to all fours to give an instep a squeeze, was for Marcy on that day the same man I saw emerge from the Whipple. It did more to move her than all my trips to Deer Park. I thought back on my years of envy, the dumb luck that gave her a dad and me a mere surrogate, always tenuous, and I realized that in fact it was tenuous for everyone always, the fortunate no less than the fostered, because in time the world makes orphans of us all.

"Look who it is," he said, as the tears hung in his eyes and the man opened his arms.

"Oh, Daddy," she said, and they embraced among the electronics.

"My dear heart, my dear, dear heart."

"I'm sorry I didn't come sooner, Daddy."

"You have made me so very, very happy."

And that was that. He took his thirty-minute break next door at the Starbucks, where he initiated a conversation with his daughter that continues to this day, as he approaches eighty-one. They didn't touch upon what happened when her mother made Dickie into "Dad," or what transpired the summer of her eighth-grade year. All that would come later. They talked instead about the cancer and the chemo, the enzymes he was forced to take with every meal, the diabetes he had to manage and the kidney stones he had to watch, and then he hung up. I mean, returned to work. At the Best Buy. Where he sold televisions for $8.85 an hour.

The following morning, Barbara was sitting at the kitchen table in the house on Rust Road in her reading glasses and scrubs poring over a textbook, while next to her, out of those dumb cutoffs at last and in khakis and a button-down, Jerry sat looking silently at job leads on an ancient laptop. The old man was there, too, reading the sports page and eating a grapefruit and two boiled eggs. He looked up from his paper when I entered and asked if I'd like some coffee. He poured me a cup. Jerry passed me the milk. I asked for a section of the paper. A companionable silence held for another ten minutes or so until Marcy rang the doorbell and everyone greeted her, including Barbara. It was possible to imagine that with a medical degree in hand one day, Charlie's brittle bride wouldn't be quite so insecure but would accept us, or them, at least, as unconditional objects of a father's love and decent enough people to have around. In the meantime, before she arrived, we ate, sipped, read, the four members of a very odd little family enjoying a bit of calm before the day's storm.

I had seen a little world go kablooey in Danville, another do the same in Key West, and a third in Downers Grove, and it seemed likely to happen a fourth time in the house on Rust Road. But it didn't. Charlie lucked out. Barbara returned to school. Jerry fell and was caught. Marcy came around. It was time for me to fly back to Rome. Barbara stopped me on my way out to my rental car on my return to the airport.

"You have been a great help to us, Jake," she said. "I didn't understand why you were here at first—"

"I wanted to be here," I said.

"Right, but why? Well, now I know. You love that man. You love him like I do. He couldn't have done this—*we* couldn't have done it—without you. You have a big heart, Jake, and you are a good son, and I love you like my own."

She'd never said so many words aloud to me ever, yet her eyes never wavered from mine. She pulled me in for a hug, and a year's worth of emptiness and terror and hope got jarred loose in me, and for what felt like a full day outside the house on Rust Road, I cried like a baby in that woman's arms.

55

He was long retired from the Best Buy and the other penny-ante gigs when, in 2016, he read the news about Wells Fargo and made one final attempt to get in touch with Larry Stoval. Then he spoke with Jerry about the future of Chippin' In, and then, believe it or not, he moved a little money around on behalf of those clients he retained from his days as CEO and sole employee of TTAA, to which he remained sentimentally attached. Then, with the newspaper in one hand and the cordless in the other, he climbed the basement stairs and collapsed in his recliner with every intention of taking a nap. In a few short weeks, he would turn another year older—on Election Day, in point of fact. He had had eight years of hope and change. Never had he had more hope. And in no other eight-year period of time had he undergone such change.

You believe in change, don't you? That a man need not be mired hopelessly in himself, confined to his appetites and checked by his limits, bound for the grave much as he came into the world, making promises he would never keep and fooling himself every step of the way?

When he woke from his nap an hour later, it was not where he remembered having nodded off, on the recliner in the front room, but under the ivy-laced pergola in his backyard. Sunlight played over his outstretched legs. He was preparing to return inside when the cordless began to ring. It was Dr. Clement, his oncologist at First Baptist.

"How about that wife of yours?" Clement remarked right out of the gate. "Our finest nurse, and now our newest resident!"

"She's so pleased to be back at First Baptist," Charlie assured him.

"We're lucky to have her. How she made it through medical school in such record time, I will never know."

"She's a quick study," he said. "But I don't imagine you're calling just to sing Barbara's praises."

"That's true," the doctor said. "Charlie, your test results have come in."

He had forgone regular testing in recent years, finding the wait for numbers every three months a morbid drumroll and a major fetter on his freedom, much as the full-time job had been before he found his calling. But in recent weeks there was no denying the persistence of his new cough or his need some days for supplemental oxygen. He had a little tank for that purpose, which he rolled around on two wheels but which didn't always fill his lungs as he might have wished, and which, on those days, he referred to as his moxygen tank, because it seemed to do little more than mock him.

"I'm afraid it's back, Charlie. It's in your liver, lungs, and spine."

He cleared his throat.

"I see," he said. "And my prognosis?"

"I'll be honest, Charlie, it's not great. But there are some experimental treatments out there and a clinical trial or two that might be worth looking into. It's a bit of a long shot, but hey, you've done an extraordinary job of beating the odds thus far. What do you say we make an appointment for some time next week, and you and Barbara and I sit down and discuss your options?"

"That sounds fine," he said.

After making that appointment with the nurse, he got off the phone and sat very still awhile, lost in thought. He knew he should call Barbara, and his children, too, and break the news. He had been so eager to do just that eight years earlier, before the doctor had even confirmed a diagnosis. How pathetic he was back then, he thought now, longing for an incontrovertible source of pity, like pancreatic cancer, to share with others, so that they might think upon him as tenderly as he did himself.

He deferred making those calls, set the cordless down, and went inside. He returned to the pergola with an old book his son had given him. He took up the chair again and resumed where he had left off in the book some years earlier, it must be said, not far from the end, though not quite there yet. The book had been swallowed up by his recliner and forgotten about just before his life got busy again. Now he read until he reached the end. Then he closed the book, knowing that his professor in Advanced Religion would be pleased. He had finished the Gita before dying.

Searching for Steady Boy

56

It was Charlie Barnes Appreciation Day, the first annual, which in subsequent years always fell on the Saturday closest to the anniversary of his diagnosis. A catered event with balloons and speeches, followed by cake, it took place on Harmony Drive in Oak Park. The inaugural theme: "Forgive Skinaman."

As he approached ninety, and especially round, golden one hundred, the event grew more elaborate and all-purpose, thriving in direct proportion to his decline, until by some gravitational pull all its own it detached itself from its humble origins and became the beloved local holiday it is today, between Harlem and North Oak Park Avenues on Lake Street, pink and gray the official CBAD colors.

57

I have no really vivid memories prior to coming to live with Charlie and Charley at the house on Vermilion Street, only vague ones of being lower to the ground and of moving around a lot. I recall a black-and-white selection of dead birds in a shoe box, swapping butthole odors with a much older delinquent named Kyle, and more than one humorless minder from Vermilion County foster care, all of whom might have been abandoned or abused in their time.

With Charlie and Charley began all things colorful: bedtime stories, nursery rhymes, rides on horsey's knee, snowy fields before sunsets, the crunch of deadfall underfoot, pumpkin goop on newspaper during our annual carvings, and other bright and surprising developments. Charlie, squatting, catches me coming down the slide. Puckering, he judges among many doughnuts. Calibrating, he corrects the rearview mirror. He dims the bedroom light and says good night.

They may have intended to adopt me, I don't know. I have two theories about that. One is that the divorce interfered, as it did with so much. And the second theory is that Charley Proffit, discovering on the eve of delivering her second child that the man she married was not as advertised, could not bring herself to commit to yet one more bond between them, legal or otherwise, and allowed the status quo to carry the day until Florida beckoned and it all dissolved. I know none of that for a fact. I only know that one day when Marcy was a baby, they chanced to recall another baby, this one left for dead in the Fair Oaks row house. They made inquiries and discovered that he was still living in foster care, still making the rounds, and they took me in. Then eight or nine years later, when our fresh start in Florida soured, they let me go again.

I must have observed enough that troubled me before the time I came to live in the house on Vermilion to always approach a new home with trepidation. This primal urge to flee only strengthened after the divorces and their sudden shocks to the sleeping arrangements, a serial misery that even an honorary member of the Barnes clan such as I was forced to endure over the years. The house on Vermilion Street, the house on Cudjoe Key, the balm of open Florida breezes, the cottage in the village of Downers Grove, the hot dog between the sofa cushions in the house on Rust Road . . . if Charlie wished to root his life in something worthwhile and meaningful before dying, I simply wished to root. But there was yet one more: the house on Harmony Drive.

On the first annual Charlie Barnes Appreciation Day, I pulled up to the curb. I peered out from my rental. I immediately wanted to return to the airport. I called Charlie for encouragement. He didn't answer.

That is to say, I loved my dad, his children, that family, but the new house changed the dynamic. It was kind of an estate. It was perched on a sort of hill. The driveway inclined up and around, encircling a magical little copse of birch trees, those peeling, leaning sticks that appear wintry in all seasons. The picture window reflected the blue sky in monochrome and reduced the plump three-dimensional clouds to UFO wafers. Someone, a party planner, perhaps—was it possible that the one-time nurse and basement stockbroker hired party planners now?—had lined the path along the drive with shepherd's crooks, those Bo-peep items from which red and blue Japanese lanterns glowed dimly in the daylight, guiding partygoers toward the house. I found all this intimidating, and I have not yet said just how fancy that house was. I recoil from such fine places when they are full of people I'm madly in love with. I loved the Barneses, all of them, almost, with the exception of one or two. I only ever wanted to be loved in return, treated like a son and brother. It was impossible. I was too anxious. Was I really welcome there? Was I wanted? What should my name be? Where did I belong? Who was I?

There was also that distaste, shared by my foster siblings, for reencountering the awkward and the alien in every new home—what for their sake might be called a stephome. There was too little warmth in stephomes, no feeling at ease there, no making yourself comfortable on the stepfurniture in the stepden, and never any peace of mind when taking a shower. Someone unknown might suddenly open the door by accident. A group of them might be standing right outside, overhearing your every disgusting noise. The steptoilet belonged to other butts, the shower curtain was poxed by the mold of a different clan, and the soap, a sliver of stepsoap reduced to the size of a guitar pick, invariably hosted a dark hair or two that everyone took for granted should be easy to overcome now that we were all one big happy family. The instant you walk into these foster homes and stephomes, you are expected to break bread with second cousins and their girlfriends, guys named Ron: people who come out of the woodwork and look pulled off a lineup. These weirdos and psychopaths get woven into your most intimate celebrations and the most vital days of the year. I would include among them all the Glamours, Dickerdicks, and Ledeuxs. I did not want to get out of that car.

But then I could, and did, because I recalled that Barbara and I had grown close, Barbara and I together had nursed him back to health. Barbara and I had hugged.

I was halfway up the drive in chinos and a sport jacket, a small gift in hand and all ready with a little speech, when she came out of the house dressed to the nines, affixing a final earring. She must have seen me from an upper-floor window and hurried down. She broke off from this difficult accessorizing long enough to firmly, brusquely point: away!

"Go back," she demanded.

"Back?"

She succeeded in pinning the earring in place just as she went past me. When I didn't follow, she turned and beckoned. Then she led me in fury down the circular drive.

58

The pages I emailed to Charlie Barnes a week earlier, the pages I ill-advisedly gave an elderly man about his youthful self before a festive occasion as a gesture of love and honor, were not yet labeled "Farce, or 105 Rust Road," as nothing about them was intended to be farcical. That is still the case. The words remain the same; only the name of that section has changed. However, it was then, and is now . . . a strictly factual account of the day of his diagnosis.

Was it brave of me, or just downright dumb, to give Chuck the first half of this book? It had taken me years to write, years and years, much longer than a work of make-believe might have, and included in it the true story of his parents' assignation in a cornfield and the crude wedding that followed. What is now labeled farce was (and is!) the true and accurate retelling of a single day in a confused man's life as he faces the prospect of a deadly disease, his dreams thwarted and his delusions intact, his contradictions thriving, his children mad at him and his debtors in hot pursuit—and zero resolution for any of it on the horizon.

Barbara took the liberty to climb uninvited into my rental, a cheap compact thing completely denuded of character, and slammed the door behind her before I even had the chance to walk around the rear and get in. That she knew which car was mine confirmed my suspicion that she'd been tracking my arrival. Now, the car filled with her perfume and rage, Barbara Ledeux fixed me with one of her rare hard stares from the far corner of her seat.

"Just who the fuck do you think you are?"

I was stunned, and didn't reply.

"Just when I was coming around to you, too."

"Have I done something wrong?"

"It's a shame, because you and I have something in common. You and I can see his children for who they really are. Hateful little bitches. You will never catch me saying that to him, and I will deny up and down ever saying it to you, but that is what they are. Hateful. Little. Bitches. If it wouldn't destroy Chuck, I'd want them dead. They serve no purpose and they bring no joy. But," she said, "this book of yours—"

"Hold on," I said. "What do you know about that?"

"—takes the cake."

There was a long pause.

"It's only half a book," I said. "It's unfinished, and I sent it to him, not you. Have you read it?"

"What is all this preposterous *shit* about a flying wig?"

It took me a moment to realize that she was referring to the Doolander, the novelty item Chuck hoped to commercialize after his friend Happy Necker peeled off his hairpiece at a picnic forty years earlier and used it to play fetch with a stray dog.

"So I take it you've read it."

"Is that just pure invention on your part?"

"I didn't make up the Doolander," I said. "He invented the Doolander in the 1970s."

I didn't know how else to respond. This was the same woman who had denied there was an earlier, different Barbara in his life—the result, I believed at the time, of his omitting that bride from his biography. He told a forgivable little fib meant to reduce by one his total number of past wives, and that one an especially uncomfortable precursor on account of a common name. Maybe the Doolander was another tender source of youthful folly for him, one he preferred to forget, and his wife was simply telling the only truth she knew.

"You don't seem to know the first thing about him, judging from what you wrote. You have a completely warped impression of him."

"*I* have the warped impression?"

"You turned him into a clown!"

"Well, Barbara, he *was* a clown, for a time there. A lot of other things, too. That's kinda the point. He's lived a full life. He has a complicated past. He's far from perfect. A man, he's just a man."

"He is *not* just a man. He is the *best* man."

"I agree!"

"And you've made him into a farce."

"There's not much I can do if the facts end up reading like a parody. Some people's lives just look like farces. That's who he was that day—by his own admission. There's nothing in there that isn't true."

"Nobody wants to hear it," she said. "But you have *written it down.* Why have you written it down?"

"Everything in there is based in fact," I said. "I got it straight from him. I just listened and took notes."

"Yet it's riddled with error and completely misses his essence."

That stung. Perhaps it was true. She knew the man. It was only fair to allow her to judge for herself. Yet I knew there were no errors and said as much.

"I beg your pardon," she said, "but he does not wear dentures."

There was a long pause. I recalled her rattling his dental plates in their plastic cup in the waiting room of Rush Memorial. *Don't be a fool,* she had said to me. She personally returned those plates to his mouth.

"You're denying *that?*"

"I'm sorry," she said, "but he does not have false teeth."

I knew that Barbara's capacity for denying reality was pretty robust. For years, her cool detachment toward me, her speaking about me in the third person while I looked on, her pointed and habitual lack of eye contact, and her glossing over my presence in the living room and at the dinner table helped edit me out, if you will, of the scene. She pretended I wasn't there, amended real life on a whim. But this was much bolder. This was a weird attack on the truth for reasons unknown. To save face? To defy me? I spoke slowly, clearly.

"His parents never told him to brush," I said, "so his teeth rotted. He was twenty-four years old and in extraordinary pain when he had them pulled. The dentist's name was O'Rourke. The bill came to three hundred and fifty 1964 dollars. I got all that from him."

"Which one of us is his wife?" she asked. "I think his wife would know if he wore false teeth."

"If he doesn't want me telling the world that he wears dentures because he is embarrassed—"

"He doesn't want you telling the world he wears dentures because he doesn't wear them."

"But you know that he does."

"I know no such thing."

Only then did it occur to me that there was no way Charlie had withheld the Doolander from her. The prototype still had pride of place on the bookshelf in his basement office, and forty years after the fact he'd not hesitate to sell the uninitiated on its pleasures. What's more, he'd learned what damage withholding does from his days with Charley Proffit. He was a wiser man. He had delved with Barbara. It was *she* who denied the Doolander, together with his other Barbara and now the dentures, because they were facts incompatible with her idea of Charlie, inconvenient and unpalatable facts—as his ex-wives were unpalatable, and his children.

She checked her earring in the mirror, then violently flipped the visor back into place before turning to me.

"You're no longer welcome at this party," she said.

"Are you speaking for him when you say that?"

"I have news for you. That's *my* house, and you're not welcome in it—not today, not ever."

She opened the door and stepped out. I did the same. She turned back when I called her name.

"I stuck up for you," I said. "No one else would. No one else likes you. No one can comprehend what a warm person like Charlie sees in you. Okay, you're gifted, you're disciplined, you're everything he's not, but at least he's capable of love and affection."

She turned without a word and carried on up the drive.

59

Ban me from a foster home? That was no great loss to me, lady! I would be damned if I entered that house.

But I would get an invitation. I would get a warm, welcoming, *engraved* invitation to join the man of the hour inside. *Because it was his house, too.* And I was his son. He loved me. It made no difference to him that I wasn't his flesh and blood. He would want me there no less than he would his real kids.

I called him. I called him again. No answer either time.

I suppose I was hoping just to ignore what really sucked about Barbara—like her third-personing, her lack of eye contact—as well as ignore my suspicion that behind that cool exterior, which made her such a gifted clinician, there worked an almost sociopathic mind with heaps and heaps of damnation and scorn for Marcy, for Jerry, and for me. I could ignore this terrible reality no longer, nor could I remain neutral in the vain hope of family happiness. German fairy tales had nothing on the Barnes family chronicle in the age of Barbara Ledeux. I sided with Marcy.

I tried Charlie again. On his cell phone. On his landline. Sent him a text. No answer. Naturally, I tried Marcy next.

Marcy was still living in Deer Park but had flown into O'Hare for the occasion. What a strange occasion! A red balloon slowly floated over the house on Harmony Drive and up, up, and away.

"Are you on your way to this party or what?"

"I'm already here," she said. "I'm inside the house."

"Well," I said. "Wait till you get a load of this."

Pacing the sidewalk, I told her everything, including Barbara's doozy about his dentures and her disinviting me. If there was one person primed to froth at these outrages, it was my fierce and reactionary older sister. When I had finished, I asked her to find Dad and put him on the phone or send him outside so that I could explain. I planned to remind him that he had requested I tell the truth if ever I chose to write about him. He wanted a factual account, which I had written. There was, I thought, a real long pause.

"Dad?" she finally said.

There was another long pause.

"Chuck," I said.

"Jake, did you really think it was going to go over well, all this bad stuff you wrote about Daddy?"

"What bad stuff?"

"In that book of yours."

"Hold on," I said. "How do you know about my book?"

"I've read it, Jake."

"You have? You read it?"

"Did you really need to be so..."

"You've read it, Barbara's read it... who else has read it?"

"... descriptive?"

There was a long pause.

"Descriptive?" I said.

"I don't think Daddy... Daddy didn't think so much about... or have as much... the whole sex thing, Jake. You've blown that way out of proportion. Haven't you?"

There was another long pause.

"I hardly scratched the surface," I said.

"Daddy had... a libido?"

"Your dad? Um, yeah, Marcy. A sizable one."

She didn't immediately reply.

"So he really liked to..."

"Yes, he really liked to."

"That much?"

"According to the man himself, yes."

There was another long delay.

"I wish I didn't know that," she said. "Jake?"

"Yes?"

"Did Daddy really drop out of Michigan State?"

What was going on here? Did these people not know the first thing about one another?

"It's a factual account, Marcy. I made nothing up."

"But it seems like you must have," she said. "What about this suggestion that he called you first?"

"Called me first?"

"On the day of his diagnosis. You claim that he called Jerry, who he believed was in Belgium. Then, on his way up the driveway after getting his newspaper, you write that he called you next and got your voice mail."

"You really did read it, Marcy. You really did."

"Would he do that, Jake? Or would he call me first?"

"Why does it matter who he called first?"

"Maybe he was simply going down his list of contacts," she said, "and because *j* appears before *m* alphabetically, he dialed you first. But in that case, he'd have called you before he called Jerry. And that's not really how Daddy works. You know what I think? I think he called *me* first, and then *maybe* he called you."

"I present his entire life story," I said. "I give you his history, his hopes and dreams, and a sense of his character, and you get all hung up on the sequential order of a few phone calls?"

"It's your claim that this is a factual account, Jake. Isn't that your claim?"

"That's my claim."

"Well, it's also your claim that Daddy called Jerry first. That part kinda makes sense. Jerry's the firstborn. Hi, Jerry. I have cancer, blah blah blah. Give me a call. But then you claim that he calls you next. How is it that you describe yourself? Oh, that's right: his personal hope and change."

There was a long pause.

"But why would he call his personal hope and change before he called me, his favorite child? I think we can both agree that I'm Daddy's favorite child. And what are you again, technically? Aside from being hope and change."

"Okay," I said. "I get the point."

"No, it's important to say it, I think. If it's really a factual account, Jake, you should come out and say it."

"I'm his son."

There was a long pause.

"His foster son."

"Who would he call first?"

"He would call you first."

"So you might want to fix that," she said, "in this true account of yours."

She hung up.

60

After Marcy refused to put him on the phone, I called him directly. There was no answer. I called him two times more. The difference between a foster kid and an orphan is this: a foster kid might have someone to call. Yet he wasn't picking up. Had I offended him with the truth? But he *wanted* the truth! I should not have told the truth. No one wants the truth, and no one should ever tell it.

I didn't know what to expect from the first annual Charlie Barnes Appreciation Day. Brats on a backyard deck? Dunk tanks? I snuck up the side to the backyard for a quick peek, despite being banished. The caterers were the farm-to-table kind, busy in their starched whites sautéing mushrooms and putting cold soup in shot glasses. In time these would be passed on silver trays. The yard was dominated by two white tents. There were linen tablecloths and tiki torches, and a DJ was setting up near the pool.

Charlie's guests began arriving. Little old ladies followed the Japanese lanterns up the driveway bearing gifts. A caterer greeted them and handed each newcomer a disposable camera from inside a wicker basket. A sudden peal of carburetor thunder concluded with a half dozen motorcyclists pulling to the curb and dethroning, men he must have known from Rabineau's garage. Another set of men, hired help in white jumpsuits, arrived in a branded minivan from the local bakery. They threw open the back doors and unloaded a large sheet cake as if it were a light little love seat. Taking in this vibrant start, I thought: *So much for brats on a back deck.*

Returning from the backyard, I skirted none other than J. Patrick Boyle, a pal of Charlie's from his clowning days. I confess to always feeling a little uneasy around J. Patrick—receiving his self-printed business cards, listening to his vaguely hostile projections of all the great things just around the bend for him in the "pyrotechnic arts." It was the same prediction he'd been making half his life, and always with one hand on the same unicycle seat. He was getting his act under way when I slipped past him unnoticed. For the next hour, I watched an uncertain crowd ask itself if the juggler in buttoned vest and bowler animating the driveway was a paid performer or a fellow guest. Not everyone could say for certain as late as the drive home.

Cars crowded bumper to bumper around the circular drive, then along both sides of Harmony Drive, before I noticed that Charlie had someone parking cars for him. A skinny young lad in black jacket and bow tie taking keys at the foot of the cul-de-sac. First a party planner, now a valet! I couldn't believe it: Steady Boy was a hirer of help and a friend to monied types. One pulled up just then in a vintage Mercedes convertible. The driver stepped out wearing a seersucker suit and carrying a silver trumpet—just the trick, when the time was right, to bray the gathered into a conga line. After the valet drove off with his car, he aimed his instrument at the sky and blew.

I was standing on the sidewalk in the unseasonable heat wondering what to do next, hoping my dad would return my calls, when a man and his wife appeared with a potted orchid so red, so other, it might have been cultivated in the tropics of Andromeda. On their way by, they casually inquired: "Is this the party for Charlie Barnes?" I told them to follow the lanterns. They had started for the house again when the man turned back.

"Are you his son?"

Was he a distant cousin? One of the doctors who had saved his life?

"The writer, am I right?"

"That's right."

Who was this guy? I knew everyone in his life by then. I could recognize anyone.

He stepped forward with an outstretched hand. "Bruce Crowder," he said.

It was Evelyn Crowder's son, the man who had demanded his mother's money back in September of 2008. He was nothing at all like I had imagined him, the aging alpha male peering squint-eyed at all that might be out to screw him. Nor was he some impersonal force backing Charlie into a corner on the day of his diagnosis. He was about fifty, I would say, with a little gray in his hair and the eyeglasses of a biology professor. He shook my hand warmly as his clear blue eyes sought a connection with mine. I liked him immediately. His wife, too, had a ready smile that put me at ease as we said hello. I turned back to Bruce. The soft-spoken man I mistook for a bully, the guy I assumed had been a big dick to a good man, had probably only been beset by grief on that day long ago.

"Boy, is your dad proud of you," he said. "He tells me you had a book on the *New York Times* bestseller list. Is that true?"

"A hundred years ago," I said, repeating one of the old man's favorite phrases.

"Are you working on anything at the moment?"

"An invitation to this party," I said.

Bruce laughed at this in a way that made me like him even more.

"That shouldn't be too hard to come by," he said. "I can't think of anyone who's prouder of his son than your father is of you."

"Now, tell me, Bruce. Is that true?"

"Absolutely," he said. "And there's no one I respect more than your father. He looked after my mother for twenty-three years before she died, and now he does the same for me. He doesn't need to manage other people's money anymore. He has enough to do just managing his own! He feels it's his duty, I guess. Your father's a loyal man."

"Tell me something else, Bruce. Did you ever get the ten thousand dollars he said he would return to you after your mom died?"

Bruce looked taken aback by the question, as why should I know anything about that?

"I did."

"All ten thousand? And within the time frame he promised it?"

"If not sooner," he said.

"So he's a man of his word."

"Your father? Absolutely."

Bruce said he hoped to see more of me on the inside, and he and his wife carried on to the house.

Had I been, as a writer, an idealist, a reformer, or just a heartless bastard, I might have told the really awful truth about Steady Boy, the naked stuff he shared only with me late at night, and only in a whisper. He disclosed these episodes and inclinations to reassure me that I was not alone in my disgustingness, that I did not need to be separated from the human fold. Oh, boy! *Then* you would have seen Barbara run me right off the curb and out of Oak Park forever. Truth as true as that debases, it alienates, ultimately it renders us all animals. I might have gone on about the relentless fucking; the unbridgeable gap between him and greatness; his stubborn mineral selfishness; the sick thoughts; the perverse urges. I held back. I made it honest, but respectable.

I won't spare myself the same way. You want abject? I was mentally at the curb even in the midst of them, pestering someone to pick up, another to pay attention, a third to invite me in. They threw a good party, but old Jake knew he could always be sent back with the rented chairs.

61

The nut-brown muscle car, now a bona fide classic, that Jerry arrived in, fully restored on his own dime after he landed on his feet courtesy of the old man, was a wild contrast to the unmarked white van he drove for years. It shifted my understanding of Jerry. That shift had, as its closest correlative in the material world, the clever little toy that had delighted my father as a boy whenever he dug it out of a Cracker Jack box, the 3-D lenticular portrait efficiently demonstrating (with a pivot of some twenty degrees) the kinetic potential of the subject at hand—the lion at rest now roaring, the slugger squared up now connecting with the ball—as well as the work of time: the glamour-puss aging into a spinster, the pirate degrading to a skull. The pitiless fate mankind was subject to in toys of this kind had, in Jerry, been reversed, and the rag-clad bum of recent memory, in denim cutoffs and stained T-shirt, replaced with the smiling, suntanned executive. It was a bit of beautiful magic.

He handed the keys to the valet and with flowers in hand began heading up the drive.

"Jerry!" I cried. "Come over here! Don't go in the house just yet, Jerry. Come talk to me first."

He reversed his tracks and joined me at the curb.

"What are you doing out here, Jake?"

"Want a quick word," I said. "Hop in the car."

"What for?"

"A quick word. Hop in."

I smiled at him after we shut our doors.

"Here we are," I said. "A couple of truth tellers. Feels good to be out here, doesn't it, away from all those phony steppeople?"

"I'm kind of eager to get inside, actually."

"Do me a favor, would you, when you get there? Find Dad for me and ask him to come out. I'll be right here, at the curb."

There was a long pause.

"Dad?" he said.

"Chuck," I said. "Charlie."

"What are you doing out here at the curb, Jake?"

"Barbara objected to something I did and now she's banished me from the house."

"Is it that book you wrote?"

There was another long pause.

"What do you know about that?"

"I'll be honest with you, Jake. I'm not sure how I feel about being one of your characters."

"Did you read it?"

He nodded.

"You read it?"

He nodded again.

"Barbara's read it," I said. "Marcy's read it. And now you've read it. Has the old man read it?"

"I don't know," he said. "What I do know is that it made me uncomfortable. I didn't like being one of your characters."

"You're not a 'character,' Jerry. You're you. You're Jerry."

"You know what I mean. I'm not crazy about being in it. It depicts a time and a place I'd rather forget. You might remember, Jake, not much was going my way back then. I'm not eager for a reminder—certainly not a *permanent* reminder. You're not going to publish that thing, are you?"

"I don't know," I said. "It's unfinished. But there's not much I can do about the past, Jerry, and how things were for you then. It's a factual account."

"Can't you take me out?"

"No, I can't take you out. For Christ's sake, Jerry, you're his firstborn son."

"But it's *his* story. Who cares about a firstborn?"

"It's not a novel," I said. "It's a factual account of the day of his diagnosis. I can't just make shit up in a factual account, Jerry. I'm obliged to mention the firstborn. And if that first-born happened to tell him he was in Belgium on the day of his diagnosis when in fact he was living on Western Avenue, I think that's pretty pertinent information. You were there that day, you played an important part."

He wasn't happy about that. "That was a terrible time for me, Jake. I was stuck in a rut, depressed, angry. I'm no longer that guy. Anyway, I'm a dynamic human being. There are many different sides to my personality. I play the guitar, I fly airplanes, I can code with the best. I was gainfully employed for many years running, Jake. Did you forget about that? And I don't know if you know this, but my spiritual insights are real. My Buddhism is real. Those aren't poses. But you hardly touch on any of that because you're so fixated on my goddamn Dumpster diving, which I did for like two years at most, and my goddamn denim cutoffs! I'm not a pair of cutoffs, Jake. There's a lot more to me than smoking pot and reading Krishnamurti. But in this book of yours—"

"Half book," I said. "It's unfinished."

"—Charlie Barnes isn't the only man living out a farce. I'm a fat joke, too! One-dimensional, unchangeable, grotesque, dishonest. I wear the same clothes day after day after day. I never do laundry. I never shower. I never put on a suit and tie. I never eat a fancy meal or make love to a woman. I'm hardly the human being I know exists out here in real life.

I don't want to cast aspersions on your execution here, Jake, but I'm never more than a caricature in this so-called true account of yours. And I get it, I get it: at that particular time, I *was* a caricature! I was little more than a ranting troll—for the left, of course, but still. Don't take me back to that time, Jake, please. Don't stick me in that time forever, the same static, strident, unhealthy motherfucker from here to eternity, ranting and raving against all of society's ills and his poor disappointing father. Leave me out. Otherwise, you do me an injustice. I need a longer time frame and a bigger stage for my soul. Cut me out, or—or—how about this, Jake? Make me the hero."

"The hero?"

"Sure, why not? You like me, don't you?"

"I love you," I said.

"And you know how dynamic I am. You even say it yourself somewhere: I'm like a myth. Jake, forget about Charlie. Write about me. I'll tell you everything you want to know."

"But this book is about Charlie, Jerry. It's a testament to Charlie and my love for him."

"Then do me the favor of leaving me out of it, Jake. Make me the hero or cut me loose, one or the other."

It suddenly occurred to me just how nice Jerry smelled. The bland rental had filled with the *fleurs* of a lush masculine springtime on account of his French cologne. He smelled *expensive*. He was out of those dumb denims we both hated and in a pair of tapering white chinos and leather loafers, which he wore *au courant* without socks. He'd slimmed down, too. I was duly impressed. And they say people can't change! On me at that moment, he tried a different tack.

"If you can't make shit up, Jake, and everything is true, then why are there so many inaccuracies?"

"I suppose you're about to tell me that he doesn't wear dentures," I said.

"Of course he wears dentures," he said. "There's no sense in denying that. I'm talking about that part where my mother and I go around Danville looking for him during the time of those cicadas. Do you remember that?"

"Sure, I remember it. I wrote it."

"Well, you have us driving east."

"Driving east?"

"On Vermilion Street. But Vermilion doesn't go east-west, Jake. Vermilion goes north-south. It's a north-south street, Vermilion. So why do you have us going east-west?"

"That's your objection?"

"Then you have us passing the Palmer Bank. The Palmer Bank wasn't on Vermilion. The Palmer was downtown, Jake. It was downtown! The Palmer Bank was downtown!"

There was a long pause.

"You might as well have us driving through Hoopeston!"

"Hoopeston," I said.

"That's right, Hoopeston. Or Brisco, or Flat Iron . . . Danville could be any one of those small towns for how cavalier you are with Vermilion Street."

"You want out of a true account because I get my directions wrong?"

"Jake, this is *north, south, east, and west* we're talking about here. You can't just have your way with north south east and west! Take me out. Or at the very least, obscure my identity. Isn't that something you writers usually do?"

"Would you like me to obscure your identity?"

"You use my real name, for crying out loud. I can't even plausibly deny knowing you people. What if we go public someday, Jake? Or everything goes into the shitter again and I'm out there looking for another job? HR learns I'm the guy in your book, I'm fucked. Let's say I'm out to dinner and my date discovers that I'm the dickhead in that famous book who lied to his dad about going to Belgium. Am I going on a second date? I don't think so. I'm never getting laid again. My name is plastered on practically every page!"

"What would you like to be called?" I asked him.

There was another long pause.

"I've always been partial to the name Jerry," he said.

"Okay," I said. "Jerry it is."

And I made him Jerry, just like I said I would.

"I'm sorry, Jake. That's still not good enough. I don't want to be in your book, period. Take me out. If you can't get the little things right, like which way Vermilion runs, how can anyone trust you with the big stuff?"

"So you can effectively hate the man for years, hold all these grudges against him, lie about living in Belgium, move back in with him when you go broke and get evicted... you get all these second chances, but I'm not allowed to make a little mistake about which direction the streets run?"

"Sure," he said. "I'm his son."

He stepped out, but before shutting the door and heading inside, he bent down for a final word.

"Just out of curiosity, Jake... what did you hope to do, redeem him?"

There was a long pause.

"Now *that* would be a work of fiction," he said.

He shut the door and walked up the drive in his leather loafers, with his pretty flowers.

62

I stepped out of my rental and resumed pacing. I tried my dad's cell again. Still no answer. A large discontinued Cadillac pulled alongside me. It was rusted along the edges and packed to the gills with old people. The driver, a hundred if he was a day, was spry enough to lean over the laps of his ancient polyester-clad passengers to holler out, "Are you the valet?" I pointed behind me. The man put the car in Reverse. As they retreated, I heard the voice of an old lady say, "So there *is* a valet." A second later, that same party was involved in a little fender bender with the actual valet, who was trying to parallel-park a Nissan in a neighborhood now crowded with cars.

Coming up the sidewalk a minute later was my uncle, Rudy, the vitamin peddler and life-extension fanatic. Rudy had made his fortune on the internet, and unfortunately the culture did not require that breed of man to dress well, if at all. Rudy had a habit of wearing high-on-the-thigh runner's shorts everywhere he went, showcasing the entirety of his long, ropy legs no less than if he were toweling off after a shower, while pairing that garment with a traditional white oxford shirt that hung below the skimpy shorts. Altogether this provocatively suggested that he might be wearing nothing at all below the waist.

This sort of thing made his nieces and nephews unaccountably depressed whenever we appeared in public with him. As I was not related to him by blood, I didn't mind it as much as, say, Marcy did, although it's true that Rudy was my least favorite Barnes. It was his opinion that my books were unreadable. According to Rudy, they were full of unlikable characters. Every one was either a dick, a cynic, a moral bankrupt, or a scumbag who gave the human race a bad name. Well, here you are, Rudy, a minor player in one of those books. How do you like the characters now?

He did not come solo. He was pushing down the paved mellow path Delwina Barnes in her ninety-fifth year, a cane crossed over the arms of her wheelchair and the old lady's arms crossed over the cane. Tall, white, and listing, she resembled a wheeled Tower of Pisa. I, like you, had assumed that Delwina was dead. She was not dead. Diabetic and demented, but not yet immobile, by God there she was, a monument to gerontology ready to party. I was attempting to slip inside my rental unseen when Rudy spotted me. He knocked hard on my passenger-side window, then a second time, which forced me to lower it.

"I don't sell dog pills," he said.

"Beg your pardon?"

"You have me selling dog pills in that book of yours. I don't sell dog pills."

Narcissism, justly lamented for doing so much damage, especially within the family unit, could also work miracles, as when a fundamentally apathetic collection of illiterates gets wind that they appear as characters in a book and transforms overnight into a bunch of rabbinical scholars. First Barbara, then Marcy, then Jerry, and now Rudy. Animals in the wild were more likely to read something I'd written prior to my turn toward the biographical, but now it appeared I'd never lack for readership.

"Is there *anyone* in this family who hasn't read my book?"

"I run a respectable online distribution center of high-end dietary supplements and herbal remedies. Everything I sell gets my personal seal of approval. I sure as shit don't peddle dog hormones, or whatever the hell."

"It's unfinished, by the way."

"What do I care if it's unfinished? A slander's a slander, son."

"I'm sure it's just a misunderstanding, Uncle Rudy, rather than an intentional slander."

"Do not call me your uncle," he said. "You know, from the moment Charlie told me that you might tell the story of how our parents met, I thought to myself we've got the wrong guy. My mother is a likable person. We are *all* likable people. This is a wonderful family. Ask anyone. But then you come along and give us your take on things, and there's only one word for it: unlikable. You don't really do likable, do you, Jake? You do quirky sometimes, you do dysfunctional, you do weird, diseased, mentally ill. You do ugly and unpleasant. You do varieties of the damned. We didn't stand a chance from the beginning. And now look. Sure enough, the decency is gone. The charm is gone. We are *completely* unlikable. It's a crying shame. But I'll tell you what, son. Change that shit about dog pills, or I'll see you in court."

As we were talking, the natural grade of the sidewalk set Grandma Del gently in motion. Rudy hurried over to the old lady, caught her before she really took off, and hauled her up the drive.

63

After that, I thought, fuck it. I'll go inside and find Charlie myself. For one of the accommodations he had made to his compromised life was to guarantee to his children that wherever he might find himself, the door would be open to them—and I was his child. Wasn't I his child?

I might have barged right in, too, and demanded an answer to that question, had it not been for a new surge of arrivals. Among them was that decorated veteran and member of an elite force, Barbara's son and my stepbrother, Troy Ledeux. Crisply buff, blindingly white, a buzz cut with military cap in hand, he seemed to want to mind his own business. But as he turned at the sidewalk to take the drive, his starched gleam, so bright and martial against the backdrop of a slumbering suburb, drew stares, and patriarchs broke off from their humble family units for the honor of shaking his hand. I stayed put. At six years old, after screaming "Saddam Hussein!" Troy whaled me in the nuts, and now they tingled at the sight of him.

Talking to his fans in the circular drive, he spotted me at the curb. He excused himself and walked over to have a word.

"Interesting book you've written," he said.

"You've read it, too?"

"But it made me curious," he said. "What about his time in the service?"

"Beg your pardon?"

"His two tours. You don't even mention them."

"His two tours?"

"From '63 to '65," he said. "He served two tours. Or so he's always told me."

There was a long pause. Steady Boy in Vietnam?

"He said this to you?"

"More than once."

"And he wasn't joking?"

"These were man-to-man talks," he said. "He was dead serious, every time. So it has to be one or the other. Is he a veteran, or a bald-faced liar and fraud?"

I didn't really know how to answer that. I did my best.

"He was present at the launch of Apollo 11," I said. "I know that much."

"Do you?" he asked. "Or is that just another story he likes to tell?"

With that, he turned and walked up the drive.

64

After watching from the curb as Troy entered the house, I had a simple epiphany that reframed my reality and aligned it more closely with the consensus view: in the stephouse on Harmony Drive, steppeople like Dr. Barbara Barnes and her Blue Star son were the real and substantial people, and I was the stepperson. I was even something grubbier: the foster kid with the stunted arm, related by blood to no one, a hanger-on from a nowhere town. I deserved to be kicked to the curb.

I think I loved Charlie because I, too, could feel terrible self-pity. If no one respected that about him, least of all Charlie himself, it gave me the secret feeling that he and I really were father and son, with more in common than he had with either Jerry or Marcy, both of whom could be so hard on him. Charlie spoke so little of his own father, and he was the more neglected and damaged of his mother's two sons. I think he could feel like an abandoned child himself, closer in spirit to the stray mutt than his well-nourished little brother. He saw himself in me. We had similarly squalid starts. And we had physical defects: my arm, his teeth. I loved him and he loved me.

Had I done something impertinent, then, by heeding his directive that should I ever write about him, I should write the truth? Real life makes for good novels because it's lived as a bunch of lies, and because fictions of one kind or another are the only things worth living for. That didn't mean that a man of great pride and ambition cared to be reduced to his carnal acts, misallocated resources, and impotent rage. He *was* a clown, in my retelling. And something worse than the real thing: the metaphorical clown that men become in the eyes of other men when their dreams flop and some dickhead with a bullhorn is there to broadcast it, disclosing all his insecurities and failures to the world. He must be furious with me, I thought. I'd betrayed him. What sort of surrogate son repays the man who made all the difference with public humiliation?

I tried him again, no answer.

What happened next was a lifesaver, even a kind of miracle after the passage of so much time. Sunk down in the discoloring gloom of my unbelonging, feeling as faint as the light flickering from those Japanese lanterns, I was sitting in the car when I noticed a man and his wife making a steady advance in my side mirror. They were proof of former times: it was my father's old friend Happy Necker, given name Julius, the bald, bounding, good-humored, unwitting inventor of (and early investor in) the Original Doolander. Beside him was his wife, the woman I had called Aunt Wyla as far back as I could recall. Trotting alongside them was a shaggy, black-matted mutt that had to be so old by then that it was its own sort of miracle. So much more real, more elemental was this Danville couple than those extras and specters arriving with them that I immediately hopped out of the car as if to cure myself completely of steppersonhood with the mutual warmth that would pass between us at first sight, such as:

"Uncle Happy?"

"Why—Jake Barnes!"

"So good to see you."

"And do you remember—"

"Of course—you were my Aunt Wyla."

"Indeed I was—and still am! Come over here, kid, and give me a hug."

And like that, enfolded in her arms again, reminded of picnics on warm blankets, wool hats in winter, and animal tracks in the snow—and of Lee Ann, their only child, my first crush. All the loot stolen from the galleon ship of my childhood when Charlie and Charley divorced might have been buried within these two old treasure chests whose sudden reappearance restored at once all that had been lost. I had missed them without knowing it, the way a middle-aged man observing a child at play will suddenly apprehend how much paradise has crumbled away since he was that age, and as we approached one another on the sidewalk, I put my hand out with only a smile to speak my thoughts. But the man said nothing, just frowned and shook his head in confusion as he slid past. The woman fell in line behind him. The dog marched on. Neighborhood strangers out for a stroll, they gawked up at the lively party in progress, turned at the corner, and disappeared.

Julius Necker died in Palm Springs in 1999. And if that dog had been the one I dumbly mistook it for, the mutt that caught Happy's toupee at Kickapoo State Park, in dog years it would have been two hundred and forty years old.

65

. . . when all at once, I recalled Karen. We were over an hour into the party by then. The flurry of traffic had died down and now it was just me and the valet kid idling around each other near the curb. I watched him pull a sandwich from his front pocket and consume it, except for the crusts, which he returned to his pocket. Ten minutes later, a barbershop quartet arrived on foot in matching silver vests and straw hats and marched up the drive. Strains of their harmonizing soon drifted out to us.

I didn't like asking Karen for favors, or putting myself at her marcy—mercy, I mean. I never wanted to be at Karen's mercy. I recently claimed that Rudy was my least favorite Barnes, but that was true only if you didn't take into account Marcy—I keep calling her Marcy. Forgive me. It gets confusing, even for me. There is Marcy, of course, my older sister, or foster sister, who lives in Deer Park, Texas, the one who—well, you know Marcy. Then there is Karen, our younger sister—that is, Marcy's full sister, Jerry's half sister, and the second of my foster sisters—

whom I haven't mentioned as much. Karen is the second and final child born to Charlie & Charley. How baroque the Barnes clan is when you really delve! I had hoped to smooth a lot of this out, spare the reader these blended-family confusions, the arch genealogies and branching family trees, by taking some of the customary liberties of a true account, like a memoir—in this instance, presenting two people as one and calling that hybrid creature "Marcy." In that spirit, I sometimes made Marcy a little meaner than she might have normally been, with a fouler mouth, having blended in a bit of Karen. For efficiency's sake, I was hoping to keep Karen out entirely, but then the old man wasn't picking up, Marcy refused to put him on the line, and Jerry was mad about Vermilion Street. Karen answered on the first ring.

"What's up, Flip?"

Karen called me Flip.

"Hey," I said, "can you find Dad for me and—"

"Dad," she said.

"Can you find Chuck for me and—"

"Hey, where am I in this book of yours?"

"Hold on," I said. "You're reading it, too, Karen—really? *You?*"

"I know, hard to believe, right? I don't usually read books. Good books, sure—but not stupid bullshit books like the kind you usually write."

"Thank you," I said. "That's very encouraging."

"I hear you're calling it a factual account. But it's the funniest thing, Jake. I can't seem to find myself in it anywhere."

"It's unfinished," I said. "And it was really only meant for Chuck."

"Jerry's in there. Marcy's in there. Even Darge Ledeux gets a little cameo. But Karen Barnes has gone completely missing."

"Not completely."

"I flicker in and out of this fucking thing like a hologram!" she cried. "You've effectively erased me from my own fucking life. What are you calling it, Jake? *The Son Also Lies?*"

"Do you have any idea how hard it is to write a book?" I asked her. "You have to make a million decisions, be absolutely ruthless. Inevitably, certain things end up on the cutting-room floor."

"An entire daughter?"

"If you don't like my account, you can always go write your own."

"Oh, sure—let me just whip up a book real fast. I don't know how to write a book, Flip. I didn't go to some stupid pointless writers workshop like you did."

I know it's a lot to throw at you, here at the eleventh hour—the fact of Karen. I know it's a lot to process. I probably should have involved her more from the very beginning. She could be abrasive, is all: vindictive, unyielding, and cruel. I'm pretty sure she hated me. She would have preferred a childhood that did not have me in it. For the record, any curse that issued from Marcy's mouth in this account very likely came from Karen's.

"If only I could write a book, Flip," she continued. "I'd tell the whole world what a creepy fucking kid you were—and what a furtive little thing you are now."

"Okay, what do you want, Karen? Want to be the hero like Jerry? Should I make you suffer from cancer, too? How about

I make you his only daughter? Better yet, his only *child!* Why don't I call it the Book of Karen?"

"No, none of that," she said. "But it would be nice if you said a thing or two about the time you punched me. Remember that, Flip? Sure, I held you down, but you *punched* me, hard as you could, with your one good arm, right when I wasn't looking. Who does that? Who coldcocks a little girl?"

"I don't remember that," I said.

"Oh, sure you don't," she said. "Listen, you wanna know what I think? I think you cut me out of this little book of yours because that's how you've always wanted it. You've never wanted to share Charlie Barnes with the rest of us any more than Barbara has. But I feel the need to remind you: I am the blood relative here. I'm an actual biological child. While you, my friend, you are a little leech with nowhere better to be."

"Please find Chuck for me and put him on the line."

"I was *with* you in that bathtub in the house on Vermilion Street, playing with those toys when she goosed him. I was *with* you on the front staircase when he showed up with two hundred dollars from the Palmer Bank. And I was *with* you on New Year's Eve when we watched *The Champ* and everybody cried and we drank sparkling cider. How could you leave me out of all that?"

"You were with us the night we watched *The Champ*?"

"I was seven years old. It was New Year's Eve. Where else would I have been?"

"I'm sorry, Karen. I honestly don't remember you being there that night."

"*I* am the reason he drove back to Danville every weekend," she said. "Not you. You were included, but only because you had to be. He came back *for me.* You just happened to be there."

"I don't believe that," I said.

"You think he would have made that drive for a foster kid? The very same kid he forgot about when you were living on the streets in Key West?"

"He didn't forget about me. He was broke. He was getting back on his feet in Chicago."

"Right. Keep telling yourself that."

"Besides, I ran away. He didn't forget about me."

"He sure as hell knew where Marcy was. He knew where I was. He didn't know where you were until you got arrested and he *had* to take you in."

"He didn't have to take me in. He wanted to take me in."

"Uh-huh," she said. "Because it just wouldn't be a family without Jake Barnes, would it, Flip? You know what? Give us a second, and we'll all join you down at the curb."

She hung up.

66

In one of my earlier books, a character quotes frequently from Ralph Waldo Emerson, but here I do so as myself: "It often appears in a family, as if all the qualities of the progenitors were potted in several jars,—some ruling quality in each son or daughter of the house,—and sometimes the unmixed temperament, the rank unmitigated elixir, the family vice, is drawn off in a separate individual, and the others are proportionally relieved."

Karen was our rank unmitigated elixir. She did more than hold me down. She spat on my face. She called me names. Thirty years later, she was still calling me names. Perhaps I did punch her once, when I was eleven—but only a glancing blow, and only after she had strangled my hamster. Now, as an adult, she shut me out of family games, excluded me from get-togethers. Everything had to be all about her. Her money-making schemes were like Charlie's, only intentionally criminal. Her inventions were debasing and cruel. She angled. She conspired. She lurked around bedrooms for jewelry and passwords. You could never trust her with your mail, you could never invite her to crash for the night. She brought ruin everywhere she went. If she dated a politician, he went to jail. If she was seeing a Russian, he ended up dead. She was hollow, too, a moral vacuum. She prayed and read the Bible and wore a cross at her neck, but it was all just another frightening tactic. She had the mentality of a born mobster, and my aversion to her was so profound, my hands trembled in her presence. They were trembling when she ended our call.

It may seem disingenuous at this late date, but part of me just hoped to spare the reader our Karen. And the other part of me—well, it's true, I guess, what she said. That part of me just wanted him all to myself.

I crashed the party after that. I had no choice. I was a wreck. He wasn't calling me back. He always called. He loved a phone call. There was nothing the man loved more. And to talk to him meant the world to me. It meant I had the ground beneath my feet. Without his voice on the other end I was in free fall. I had to take my chances, with or without an invitation, Barbara be damned. It seemed that my unfinished book had done what not even pancreatic cancer had managed to achieve: it had united the Ledeuxs and the Barneses. But I still had not heard a word from the man himself. I walked up the circular drive and around the house to the backyard.

As befitted that fine house, the yard was expansive, well-groomed, and tiered: a taste of manor life I hadn't seen since my time in the Cotswolds with the McEwans. Oh, who am I kidding? I don't hang out with the McEwans in the Cotswolds. But I have seen pictures of their place online, and this was not unlike that. The acre of backyard was more like a meadow brightly ringed by late-blooming gardens. Just beyond that began the local forest preserve, an ancient remnant of hickories, hop sedge, and fern populated by owls, muskrats, elk—yes, even elk—and many other becalming woodland creatures. This rustic reminder, forming the far border of the yard, could make you forget you were in the suburbs. The pool and bathhouse were off to my right, in what was once an empty lot. You might think it was evening. It wasn't. The water glittered gorgeously, like cut diamonds. The absolute centerpiece of this wonderland, however, was the cherrywood gazebo. Old men and new mothers chatted there, denim butts leaning against the banisters. Nearer the house itself, there was an ivy-laced pergola where dappled sunlight fell over still more of the gathered. They milled under the tents, too, and occupied the many little tables. Slices of cake had joined the passed hors d'oeuvres and flutes of champagne. I stood off to the side, taking it all in. I looked around for my dad. He was, by then, keen on pleated peach trousers, a collared shirt, white suede shoes, and a gold herringbone chain, plus the charcoal-heather cap for his head, but saw no sign of him. Someone walking by me was devouring a shish kebab with both hands; he fluttered three fingers in hello.

The many children in attendance had found one another by then and were running around in little packs. One kid was dressed as a ballerina, another in his tae kwon do uniform, a third as a princess in halter top and tiara, and as I watched them and their friends and enemies take sides, plop down on the grass, wrap their arms around one another and lift with all their might, leap from the tree swing and dart off in all directions, only to reassemble a minute later to gossip and conspire, I was reminded of how little I thought of their adult counterparts. Grown-ups comprise the ultimate secret society to which is automatically admitted every liar, cheat, and scumbag and yet to whom is owed, perversely, unaccountably, the respect and submission of every single child out there. Great souls in their childish guise are the temporary slaves of sadists and misers. And the only way they have of freeing themselves is to become grown-ups themselves, no doubt diminishing, dimming—damning—those souls in the process. I was sorry for what was about to hit those kids: the dawning of adulthood, that rude awakening into the longest-running hypocrisy in human affairs, and there was nothing I could do to soften the blow but urge them from afar to keep playing, play until you are no longer free.

I flung myself off the sidelines and into the crowd. I said hello to those I knew and introduced myself to those I didn't. I came first upon Barbara's sister Darge, still in her Christmas sweater, discharging her nervous tic and talking to Frank Santacroce, the grocer's son, Charlie's oldest pal in the world. In every crowd, there is always that one leftie who eagerly throws his hand out before he catches on, and I'm forced to take it and to shake it the only way I can, watching half amused as his mortification at my birth defect blooms. That crowd included old title insurance salesmen, desk traders and stockbrokers from his Dean Witter and Bear Stearns days, and fellow members of the Danville High dramatics club, all old now and enjoying a kind of reunion. The Jonarts were there, as were their rivals the Mossers: members of the dueling shoe dynasties of Danville, Illinois. I didn't expect to see Evangeline, and sadly I did not, but I did glimpse in the far distance Charlie's first wife, Sue Starter, together with her "new" husband, Marshall Giacone.

Noreen, Charlie's cousin from LA, came up to me to explain that one of the people who left a message for Charlie during his short-lived stint in Hollywood was Marion Dougherty, the casting agent who discovered Al Pacino and Warren Beatty. A woman carrying an ostrich-hide purse informed me that my dad looked great even in a bycoket. Some old Red Mask players had come up from Danville for the occasion. In homage to Charlie, they were dressed as popular types from the era of his reign, so that in among the contemporary guests you would suddenly find yourself face-to-face with the housewife in bell-bottom blue jeans, the wheelchair-bound war vet with shaggy hair, and the horndog pitcher for the Danville Keggers who, in pinstripes and sideburns, made beer spit fly from a pull-tab can.

Delwina Barnes poked me in the arm with her cane as I was making my way toward the house. She was on her feet and taller than I remembered.

"I will have you know, young man," she said, "that Charlie's father and I did *not* meet in a cornfield. We met in the pews of the Church of the Nazarene!"

I was eager to get away. Swiveling around to the first available person, I found myself standing before Stan Butkus, the Danville coach with the fused spine, and Dr. Paul O'Rourke, the Danville dentist who pulled out all of Charlie's teeth. There must have been two hundred years on earth between them. I didn't know either well enough to greet them by name, but I nodded and they nodded and I moved on again.

I made it to the big back deck, where a clown was making balloon animals for the kids. Long before it was my turn, he handed me a pink dachshund. I admired its taut twists and plump limbs. "Say, what's your name?" I asked him.

"Name's Jolly Cholly!" he cried, giving his red nose a honk. The kids loved it.

"No," I whispered, "your *real* name."

Out of the corner of his mouth, he told me it was Carl Wabanski, that he was the man out of Moline and that he did it all: the bunny out of the hat, the magic penny behind the ear. Then he slipped me a business card without anyone being the wiser. It read: CARL WABANSKI. THE CLOWN IN YOUR TOWN™, MOLINE, IL.

I stood on the deck a moment and took in that party, the whole resounding significance of the day. Off in the distance, near the giant oak, I caught two freckled schoolboys in shirtsleeves flying the Doolander—not the original model or the Moon-Lander Doolander from '79 but the catch-and-toss version with the Super-Stick Grip. They were having a grand old time. Someone nudged me on the arm: it was Sue Starter.

"Jake, I had the pleasure of reading that book you wrote.

I found a lot to admire. It's true, I was young once, and a ravishing beauty. But I can assure you that while Charlie was smooching floozies in the back seat of his Newport, Marshall and I were *not* carrying on."

"Oh, leave the boy alone, Mother," Marshall said. "It was forty-five years ago. Who cares?"

We conversed amiably enough until it came time for me to brave the stephouse. On my way in, I ran into Larry Stoval. "If we're being honest," he said to me, "I never liked him." He was leaving with my biological mother—who was drunk, of course. She was hanging all over the "deacon of Oak Brook." She didn't even say hello. As far as I knew, she was my only living relative.

Inside the house, the caterers were cleaning up in the kitchen. I went past them and down the hall. There were streamers in every room, abandoned slices of cake. I worried I was too late, he was too big, too popular, he wouldn't even recognize me. No wonder he wasn't picking up! *He was a long-term survivor of pancreatic cancer.* That alone warranted local news stories and viral fame. Add to that the sudden swank estate in Oak Park, the internet fortune, the doctor wife, and the natural charisma unleashed at last, now that he was free to no longer give a damn. He had named a day after himself.

I still hadn't seen any sign of him when I arrived at the front room that overlooked the street. I planted my knees on the olive-green love seat and peered out the picture window. After a while, a car went by, but it wasn't his. I could hear her voice from behind me, coming in loud and clear from a hundred years ago.

"He's never going to show."

"He is going to show."

"I was married to him, Jake. I should know."

"Well, he's my dad, so I should know even better than you."

"Suit yourself. But you're letting a perfectly good day go to waste."

I wondered where Karen was. I thought if I found Karen and we waited for him together, he would show that much faster, so I got off the love seat to look for her. But then it came to me. I knew where he was. Of course I did. It was a no-brainer.

I found the stairs to the basement in that stephouse, and sure enough he was down there having a little nap. It was his superpower and a natural wonder of the world, the impossible circumstances under which Steady Boy could drop off for twenty minutes and wake refreshed. I might have let him go on sleeping had it not been for the extraordinary number of guests in his house. I hovered over him, gently nudging.

"Hey, Pop," I said. "Dad."

He came to. He looked brittle, as one does after a nap: slits for eyes, and in the eyes, confusion. It took him a moment. He sat up, cleared his throat. Then he smiled.

"What a nap," he said. "Jake, what a nap. I love a good nap. Before the nap, life's hell on earth. After, by God, there's *nothing* you can't do."

"Don't you want to join your guests?"

"No, I do not," he said. "I want to be right where I am, doing what I'm doing."

"Are you mad at me?"

"Mad at you? Son, why would I be mad at you?"

"I tried calling," I said. "You didn't pick up. You *always* pick up."

"Hard to pick up when you're conked out!"

I nodded. I was relieved. I knew all this in my heart but it was nice to hear him say it.

I realized he was in the old recliner, which had been consigned to the basement—it didn't suit the fancy-house vibe. It was joined there by his roller chair and letter opener, his TV tray and its array of remotes, and his newspaper, ever near at hand. He had reconstructed the entirety of the house on Rust Road right here in the basement of the house on Harmony Drive.

"So you can take the man out of Rust Road," I said, "but you can't take Rust Road..."

I might have finished the formula, but I discovered in that instant the true cause of his deep and satisfying sleep: my half a book. It had snatched lucidity from him no less swiftly than a Western civ textbook had forty years earlier, or the Gita during his chemo days. What other Barneses had rapidly consumed, making a list of grievances along the way, was hard for him to get into, and the printout had fallen to the floor, where it fanned out in the direction of the TV. The few pages he did manage to finish were in a neat little stack on the arm of the recliner, facedown. I turned them over. He had made it to page 11.

"I'm awfully sorry, Jake," he said, acknowledging his failure. "I've been sneaking away all afternoon trying to crack it, but you know me. I get two pages in, literally the next thing I know I'm coming to and wondering what year it is. What year is it, son?"

I told him what year it was, where he was, and all that had happened. He seemed genuinely delighted.

"Now you don't have to read it," I said. "Which is probably all for the best. It's made a few people mad."

"How come?"

"I tell the truth. Sort of."

"Thank God for that, Jake!" he cried. "There's nothing I hate more than these goddamn unlikely scenarios you fancy writers are always springing on regular folks like me. By God, write about real things—or don't write at all! It's important to focus on what matters in life, am I right? It's important to be real! For instance," he said, and finding himself getting all worked up, he thundered down the footrest and sat up straight. "For instance! Why *not* a man in his basement who has hopes and dreams, and fears and debts, and regrets, and a car in need of repair, and a whole lot of other things? But no, we get long dream sequences, and improbable circumstances, and fantastical episodes, and just a lot of crap, if you ask me. No, you have to write the truth, Jake, no matter who it might piss off. I just have one request."

"What's that?"

"That name!" he cried. "That goddamn name I've hated since the beginning of time."

"Do you mean—"

"Don't say it, Jake! You know how much I hate it. Listen, I don't object to the facts. You've done a damn fine job. I did marry too young, I did divorce too often, and I told my share of lies, too. I made a hash of things, son. And I was embarrassed by my teeth. It's all true. But shouldn't that allow us to take a liberty or two? I'm just asking for a tweak here, Jake—and look, I have a ready-made alternative for you. Guy I used to work with at Sears called me this one day and I've never forgotten it. Friend of mine on the sales floor. I've probably told you this story a hundred times. But back then, you see, I had a real bad temper. Things didn't always go my way and I'd get mad. I'd go around frustrated. I'd just fly right off the handle. So one day this guy, he says to me, he says, 'Charlie, when people make you mad, I never seen anything like it.' He used to call me Steady Boy, like what you'd say to a great stallion that's about to rear up and let loose . . . 'Okay—*steady*, boy' . . . like that, like I was a real live wire. I didn't mind that one bit. Made me feel feared, respected, a man to reckon with—all that. I loved it! Nothing could stop Steady Boy. Steady Boy will go far. He comes out of the gate and makes himself known. The man called Steady Boy will never die. How could he? What do you say, Jake?" he asked me. "Do you like it as much as I do? Does Steady Boy work for you?"

The Facts

67

Then we came to the end of another dull and lurid book. Time to wrap things up, give thanks, move on. Important to move on. Fail to move on, you die. Wouldn't want that. Wouldn't want to linger or dwell. No living in the past, either. That's right, let it go. If the past is full of bitterness, the future is always bright. Right? How good does this feel? Eh? Feels pretty good, am I right?

I'm an amateur collector of authors' notes. I like this one, from Lilian Pagnani's Italian memoir, *Master:* "Names have been altered and characters combined. Some of the events described happened as related; others were expanded and changed." And this one, from a classic of true crime: "Certain episodes are imaginative re-creations and are not intended to portray actual events." And this one, from Lowry's three-volume history of the Spanish Civil War: "Vicious contention between uncompromising factions marked the civil war in Spain. Why should its histories be any different?" And here is Nietzsche, in what amounts to an author's note in the middle of *Beyond Good and Evil:* "What forces us at all to suppose that there is an essential opposition of 'true' and 'false'? . . . Why couldn't the world that concerns us—be a fiction?" And finally, here is CJ Allerd on her unauthorized biography of Elon Musk: "Everything I've written is 100 percent accurate and true . . . but then again, what is truth inside the simulation?"

Every story we tell ourselves is some version of make-believe.

In that spirit, then, my author's note:

Everything I've written here is 100 percent accurate and true. The experiences detailed are mine and mine alone. Names and other identifying characteristics have obviously been altered, and I have taken certain liberties with chronology. I should also add that I've changed the dialogue where I needed to; combined real people into composite characters as well as the magical inverse, ovipositing multiple characters from a single source—my soul—as if it were a clown car; embellished scenes for dramatic effect while eliding and omitting others; indulged in flights of fancy; willfully manipulated the truth; and let stand whole chapters fiercely refuted by members of my family.

Larry Stoval is a composite. There is the original article, a Bear Stearns desk trader from Oak Park, Illinois, who withdrew his affection from my dad in his moment of need and who, in 2016, quit Wells Fargo to become national cochairman of Donald Trump's presidential bid. A deacon at his local parish, he served as ambassador to Italy. Inside that Larry nestles, like a corrupt and incompetent Russian doll, Larry Kudlow, Bear's chief economist until 1994, who once took Charlie to lunch, and within *that* Larry, smaller but no less bankrupt, is Kudlow's successor at Bear, the wildly errant economist David Malpass, who was Trump's undersecretary of the treasury for international affairs. (I write from Rome, some weeks after the 2020 election.) Malpass barely overlapped with my father at Bear but made a *big* impression on him as a kind of junior Jimmy Cayne, one who didn't have a clue and didn't give a damn. The tiniest doll of them all, P. Hartford Hurtneg, a onetime Republican operative and Charlie's boss at Bear, was indicted in 2006 by the state of Illinois for an elaborate pay-to-play scheme. He currently works for a Chicago investment bank.

Dismantling the constructions necessary to this book's composition seems the least I can do to settle accounts with Chuck, whose request that I tell the truth if I ever wrote about him I was unable to honor in the end. The Ledeux twins, presented here with a sizable age gap between them, have in fact one older brother, Letrois Ledeux, who threatened to sue me for libel if I dared mention him, despite the caveats and qualifications that typically accompany books of this kind. Buddy, as he's referred to within the family, reviles his mother and wants no memorialization of his connection to her. I briefly considered respecting Buddy's threat, but his vehement silence tells a compelling story all its own, and lawyers for Little, Brown assure me that he doesn't have a legal leg to stand on. Hello from the outside, Letrois. Hope the medication is holding.

Jimmy Cayne is alive and well and updates his *Wikipedia* page regularly to reflect his tournament wins at bridge. My Uncle Rudy died of complications from COVID-19 in May of 2020. Two months later, on July 1, Delwina Barnes turned one hundred and two.

I have recovered from my panic attacks and no longer talk about suicide with that gentle giant Dr. Wolfson. A genius, a hero, a saint: he is the Freud of Deerfield, Illinois, who transformed my hysterical misery back into commonplace unhappiness. I had become disillusioned, which is no easier to overcome than grief. It *is* grief, in fact—not for the death of a loved one but for the death of a vibrant ideal. I believed that death would have something to teach me, that I would be enlightened by it rather than impoverished. "I grieve that grief can teach me nothing," Emerson wrote at the sudden death of his beloved son, Waldo, age five—a much harder loss, no doubt, than that of some old dad, but the remark sums up my own experience. When Charlie died, I grew no closer to the astral plane, gleaned no hint of the beyond. The dying breathe their last and stay dead, end of story—a hard lesson to learn about the broader truth while you're also trying to mourn a specific and immediate loss.

Facts are full of dreary compromises and dead ends. Stare at them long enough and you'll go insane. Charlie's solution to this was to tinker, with headlamp and toolbox, in the workshop of the American dream, and to emerge sometime later with a diamond-cut hope that might make him a killing and redeem his lost time. This wasn't easy to dismiss as child's play or a variety of magical thinking; it was the most a man could be. He hated fiction when it was confined to a book, but out here, in real life, his fictions got him out of bed most mornings, and to take them away was to dim life, remove its color, silence its invigorating and melancholy score. He couldn't do without them, much as his foster son couldn't have done without this one.

Progress is a myth I don't know how to live without.

It's been thoroughly repudiated in one realm after another—ideological, ecological, political, generational, material, moral: is there anyone who believes in it anymore? Nevertheless, I keep inventing ways of carrying on. I'm good at tricking the mind. I believe it's not just what I've been trained to do by reading and writing novels but also what humans intuitively do best. I fantasize about splitting open the round, ripe, real-life fictions that members of my family carry with them wherever they go and saying to them, "See? Look! I'm not the only one who still makes shit up! I just happen to get paid for it! I've professionalized the family curse!" They would deny I was family and take no more interest in my equivocations than they do my books.

Lots of writers today spend time in writers' workshop giving and receiving feedback as they pursue their craft and a master's degree, and I was no exception. I've had a variety of teachers over the years. I've been taught by new drunks and old cranks, sat at the table with verifiable greats, later attended galas with Nobel laureates. I've learned from the best and know all the midlisters and second-rates, too. But none of them, absolutely no one, has taught me more about the centrality of fiction in our everyday lives than my former foster stepmother Barbara Ledeux, the nurse at First Baptist.

68

We were meeting that morning in advance of the memorial service to prepare a personal touch for Charlie amid the cold pomp of death. The idea was mine, actually, but the family ran with it as a way to honor the old man with something more than words.

I had seen it done in good taste at the funeral of one who died too young, a man of middle age memorialized with a gallery of photographs affixed to poster boards and mounted on tripods, seven or eight panels lining the far wall of the outer parlor. Before entering that close and carpeted room where death reclined in a glossy cherrywood casket, his mourners could experience (or relive) the life now lost one snapshot at a time, a panoramic profusion that tricked the mind (by the third or fourth poster board) into perceiving wholeness, movement, resuscitation: much as a flipbook projects the pole vaulter into the air and over the bar, the illusion in this instance animated all the stages, ages, and awkward phases of a life in full, its growth spurts, bad fashions, changes in facial hair, kisses blown to anonymous lovers and goodbyes waved to friends unseen. The man flowered again in defiance of death's best efforts to flatten him down to a single sorrowful fact in the adjacent room. I believed we should do the same for Charlie Barnes.

I thought for sure Barbara would hate the idea, if only because it was mine, but she liked it best, and we were meeting that morning two hours before the funeral to curate that life for the benefit of his funeral guests.

Turns out the task was done by the time we arrived at the house on Rust Road.

I never entered that house without first removing my shoes as he had instructed me to do years earlier, when Yort the dog was still alive and Charlie was, too. Marcy, whom I picked up at the airport that morning, was in heels and didn't bother; also, she was not as familiar with the rules of that house as I was.

As I have mentioned, it was my dear hope to leave his least and last daughter out of this account, to eliminate Karen completely, but there's nothing like the demands of narrative to make endless sport of your intentions, and sure enough there she was, waiting for us in the cramped front room where Charlie read his newspaper and kept his remote controls. There was really no avoiding her: she lived next door in Arlington Heights. She was in the waiting room during his surgery; she came to the chemo appointments; she was everywhere.

Jerry was already present that day as well; his white van was parked at the curb. He was sitting in Charlie's recliner when Marcy and I walked in. I took a seat on the sofa; Marcy sat next to me. Karen stood, pacing... we were all just sort of waiting around for Barbara to come downstairs so that we could start assembling the collage.

"What's taking that bitch so long?" Karen asked.

Marcy, who adored her father but hated his foul mouth, as well as the one her younger sister had inherited, said, "Can we please try our best to—"

"To what?"

"Not call the widow a bitch?"

"Is the widow not a fucking bitch, Marcy?"

"And is that not beside the point on today of all days?"

Karen, rolling her eyes, drifted away, into the dining room.

Karen in black, Marcy in black, me in black suit and tie... Jerry alone was in street clothes, his denim cutoffs and soiled T-shirt. Perhaps he had plans to run home and change after our task was complete, but it remained an open question:

Would he respect the custom of getting dressed up for the dead? Or would he flout that, too? Some people never change.

He leaned forward and took up the crossword puzzle on the coffee table.

"Experts at exports," he said, reading one of the remaining clues out loud. "Could be 'trade commissions.' They have T-R-U-T-H, but it could be T-R-A-D-E. But then 96 Down couldn't be 'nuh-huh.' What do you think?" he asked no one in particular. "'Polite demurral.' 'Nuh-huh'?"

He looked up. Karen had drifted back in.

"Are you doing a fucking *crossword puzzle* right now?"

He set the puzzle down.

"Are you stoned?"

"Of course I'm stoned," he said. "I'm not coming over here sober."

"He's dead, Jerry."

"I know he's dead, Karen. Thank you."

"He's dead and you're stoned."

"What does his being dead have to do with my being stoned?"

She pointed at him and at Marcy. "Will you two come with me, please?"

They stood, and the three of them retreated together into the adjacent room, leaving me behind with Troy Ledeux. He was there, for some reason, on leave, I guess, and being as quiet as a church mouse in the far corner. It was a common Karen tactic to divide real people from the foster siblings and steppeople, and I was unhappy being left behind. Troy moved into Charlie's recliner and took up the crossword puzzle.

"Could be 'nodear,'" he said after a while.

"Nodear?"

"Ninety-six down," he said. "'Polite demurral.' 'No, dear.'"

I got up and joined the others in the dining room.

To my surprise, the photographs we were there to select, the images that would tell Charlie's life story from start to finish, had been gathered in advance of our arrival and affixed to the poster boards laid out on the dining-room table.

"...cannot fucking believe this," Karen was saying.

"What's going on?" I asked.

"I'm not seeing a lot of me," Marcy said, slowly circling the table, appraising the thing for a sense of the bigger picture. "And I'm not seeing a lot of you, Jerry."

"I don't see any of us," Jerry said.

As Karen called up to Barbara to demand she come down, I took a look for myself.

According to that display, Charles Barnes might have been delivered into the world fully formed as a fifty-two-year-old man, at the start of his affair with Barbara Ledeux. There were no pictures of baby Charles in his sailor's outfit from Cramer & Norton's. There were no shots of the boy with skinny limbs standing before the Westville shanty with his mother in black-and-white. None of the bow-tied soda-jerk Charlie from 1957 hanging with friends in the glee club. None of the clean-shaven new professional holding Jerry as a toddler. None of those dark carpeted interiors he haunted throughout the seventies, sprawling for naps on bad recliners in his groovy duds and muttonchops. None of him shirtless in cut-off jeans, basking in a kiddie pool with his foster son Jake in a backyard in Danville, Illinois. I don't want to suggest that his children were *completely* absent. We were present just enough that our essential absence might have been inconspicuous to the casual observer. But set aside for the moment the outrage of such an edit. What violence had been done to the man himself! The farmhand and corn shucker, the shoe salesman, the clown-for-hire, the social worker, the inventor of the Doolander, the silver fox and stockbroker, the man who brought dignity to the hat—of that man in his totality there was scant evidence. "Steady Boy" had been erased, "Chuck" wiped clean. The hustler, the baritone, the ladies' man—gone. I understood the need for abridgment. There was no room at a funeral where the widow would be weeping for a long detour into his prior marriages. But the man presented here had no flaw or limit, no origin story or parent, nothing mortal attaching to him, and no cause that came before Barbara. That man was a fiction. By contrast, those boards were filled from one edge to the next with pictures of Charlie and Barbara. Here the one and only couple stood before the Grand Canyon. Here they toasted each other on the deck of a cruise ship. Here they were at ball games and campgrounds and weddings. There were many pictures of Charlie and Troy, and of Charlie and Troy's sister Tory, and of Charlie and Tory and Tory's husband Ryan, and of Charlie and Tory and Ryan and their newborn... the list goes on. Extras and steppeople! It felt awful to see them, at the story's end, take front and center. She had excised—redacted—his real children, their lives, and his life, too, from history.

"Just goes to show you," I said, looking up.

Jerry peered across the table at me. "What's that, Jake?"

"The power you have when you control the narrative."

When Barbara finally made it down, it was with a face so grief-stricken, so cried out and puffed up, that my heart went out to her in spite of everything. She loved that man, and I loved him, too, and that was something. She paused to straighten a rug with her foot before cutting in for the kitchen.

"Barbara?" Karen said.

"Hold on," she said. "Let me get my Diet Coke."

We waited for Barbara to get her Diet Coke.

"Is there a problem here?" she said when, with her soda can and a handful of baby carrots, she deigned at last to enter the dining room.

"You fucking bitch," Karen said.

"Hold on, Karen," Marcy said.

"Out of my house!" Barbara demanded, and pointed a finger at the front door.

Marcy attempted to calm everyone down.

"Barbara, hold on. Karen, please. Barbara, let me ask you: Where are we in these pictures? Why are there no pictures of his children here?"

What she hoped Barbara might do, while her husband's body was still warm, was take a moment and look at that display through his children's eyes so that she might see how she had offended them. Perhaps it was just an oversight. She could make up for it by sending Troy to the store for more poster boards and by taking a stab at revision. She might not have meant to make any kind of statement.

"You're there," she said, pointing with a baby carrot. After a longer pause, she pointed again and said, "You're there." And after a lengthier search still, she said with satisfaction, "And you're there." Then she snapped the carrot in two with her teeth and said, "I don't see the problem."

There was a brief pause.

"You are a sick cunt," Karen said.

"I want you *out* of my house. All of you—now!"

"With fucking pleasure."

We followed Karen out—though it might be more accurate to say Barbara frog-marched us out. It was, he liked to say, our house, too, but that offer was provisional, as they always are with stephouses. He was dead, and our warm welcome was over. I carried my shoes out by hand. The four of us ended up at the curb, dazed and loitering outside the house on Rust Road. Karen turned her rage from Barbara to the next best thing.

"You're no better than she is," she said to me. "She takes us out, you put yourself in. You've been inserting yourself into our lives for how long now?"

"Karen," Marcy said.

"What are you even *doing* here?" she demanded of me.

The phone in my pocket began to ring—not my ringtone, not my phone. I pulled it out; it was Charlie's phone. He'd handed it to me just minutes before going into surgery. The head mechanic at European Motors was calling for Charlie Barnes. His Saab was repaired and ready for pickup. The Porsche needed to be returned.

He didn't die on the operating table. He died a few hours later, after Barbara and I (and Karen) had left the hospital. Some kind of complication that went straight up the corporate ladder to the heart. They called us back in, did all they could. He was dead by the time we arrived. That was four—no, five days ago.

He woke a final time—for his teeth. Barbara had the chance to restore them in post-op, first the bottom plate, then the top. That part is true, and later came to feel occult: his fake teeth so distressed him when they were out of his mouth, he could postpone death just long enough to get them back in place before he let go for good. He knew his ghost would not rest without them.

That puzzle would never be solved. He would never wear his Brunello Cucinellis. And Jerry's last words to him would always be "Good luck with your fake cancer, you fraud."

It couldn't end this way, with his children banished, the man misremembered, the family in tatters. Inconceivable that it could end this way. I looked around at the disintegrating stepfamily; at immovable Jerry in his dumb denims; at Marcy, who refused to accept one apology, held one grudge, taught him one lesson—and what happened? He died, and it couldn't be undone; at Rust Road with its crumbling blacktop and cheap fencing; at the house he never made it out of, the ranch-style asylum with its small rooms and sorrows, its endless sources of discontent for a man with dreams now dead; at his bride in the window who loathed and rejected us, who would rather edit us out than accept us, or attempt to love us; at the entire miserable compromise cut short, offered no second chance, when I believe he might have turned his life around. I honestly believe that he might have.

We still had the goddamn funeral ahead of us.

I began writing this book in 2009, in the thick of grief. A year later, I'd taken the facts as far as they would go—up to the day of his surgery. For the next ten years I banged my head bloody against a wall of truth, searching for a way out. There was none—unless I defied his request that I stick to the facts and got a little fancy, gave him the ending he deserved. If he was not the angel Barbara believed him to be, he was a better man than most people knew. Suddenly, the color came back to me, the music resumed. It was the end of grief. I could play again. He's right: it's a silly occupation for a grown man. I had bowed out of an impossible situation, but without losing my mind. Turns out, he was *my* calling. I had only one trouble: What right did I have to control the narrative any more than Barbara did?

I would give it to them. Jerry could be more than his cutoffs. Marcy could say a final goodbye and never regret staying put in Texas. Karen could make an appearance. And they could all three slam me for the fictions I lived for and the lies I loved to tell, and for the limits my narrative imposed on them, all the ways I got them wrong. Even the evil stepmother would get a fairy-tale ending. She was awful, just awful, but she had a good medical mind and would have made a fine doctor.

As for me, it is the fate of sons to become their fathers, and I am like mine, a dreamer and a liar, and more deluded than not. I am the son of Steady Boy, and this is my Doolander, half fact, half flying toupee. Go on, take a brochure. Give it a whirl. Watch it soar, if it can get off the ground; past acorns and oak trees and out to the coasts—this lark and coffin lid, this old hairpiece on a rack and pinion.